SOLACE

Belinda McKeon

SOLACE

PICADOR

First published 2011 by Scribner, a division of Simon and Schuster, Inc., New York

First published in Great Britain 2011 by Picador
an imprint of Pan Macmillan, a division of Macmillan Publishers Limited
Pan Macmillan, 20 New Wharf Road, London N1 9RR
Basingstoke and Oxford
Associated companies throughout the world
www.panmacmillan.com

ISBN 978-0-330-52984-6 HB
ISBN 978-0-330-53232-7 TPB

1 3 5 7 9 8 6 4 2

A CIP catalogue record for this book is available from
the British Library.

Typeset by SetSystems Ltd, Saffron Walden, Essex
Printed in the UK by CPI Mackays, Chatham, Kent ME5 8TD

Visit www.picador.com to read more about all our books
and to buy them. You will also find features, author interviews and
news of any author events, and you can sign up for e-newsletters
so that you're always first to hear about our new releases.

For Aengus

'... for all the men of the world could not help us till we have gone through our time...'

From 'The Fate of The Children of Lir', translated by Lady Gregory.

Prologue

It had been years since Tom's son had spent so long at home. He stayed almost the whole summer, working the farm every day and sleeping in his old room, with the child's crib at the foot of the bed. The child, Tom thought, seemed content in her new surroundings. He saw in her no signs of lonesomeness, no signs that she was pining for what she could no longer have. That she could not yet speak, that she could not name names and call for them, that she could not tell them what she had seen; for all of this, Tom was grateful, and he carried the child about with him often, her wordlessness resting between them like a veil.

In August the weather turned. The mornings came blue and sun-dazed, a haze wrinkling the sky over the fields. When the forecast promised it would stay that way for days to come, red bands of high pressure stoking the country from the south, Tom and Mark readied to save the hay. Mark knocked three meadows the first warm evening, and Tom followed after him with the turner, whipping up the long blades of grass, setting them down neat as potato drills. As Mark began to bale two mornings later, Tom took the child to the edge of the meadow and showed to her the way it was done: the lines of grass, the huge yellow bales lurching out of the red machine, and the shape of her father in the tractor cab, a hand on the steering-wheel, his head turned to watch the progress of the baler hitched behind.

'Wave at your daddy,' Tom said.

The child sighed in his arms and crushed her hands into her eyes. She was only half awake, and the sun's brightness was beating down on her. The sheepdog, the only thing certain to interest her and to set her pointing and smiling, was out of sight somewhere in the meadow. She had woken crying early that morning, early as she woke every morning, and, like all the other mornings, her father and her grandfather had been awake before her, watching the day as it came in over the bog.

As with all the other mornings, Tom had heard Mark moving around in the bedroom well before dawn; had heard the scuffling, the coughing, the opening and closing of the door across the landing, the slow tread down the stairs, the water drumming hard into the kettle, the feeble ravings of the radio. That morning when Tom joined him in the kitchen there had been more to talk about than usual, more things to plan, and although the timetable of a haymaking day was known to each of them so innately that there had been little need for them to speak at all, still Tom went with the chance while he had it. He mapped out all the parts of the day, the jobs to be done, the potential pitfalls and the safeguards to be laid in place. Mark answered him, and agreed with him, and talked along with him, and when at last the child awoke, crying from the bedroom above their heads as indignantly as though she had been tricked or struck, Tom thought he had seen flicker across Mark's face an instant of the same regret he felt himself at the breaking of their peace. But too much flickered across Mark's face these days for Tom to understand him. Too much went on with him, whether in silence or in the hiding-places behind talk, for Tom to keep pace with or pretend to know.

Now the tractor had stopped and Mark was standing,

leaning out of the cab. He would need more twine, he shouted. Tom would have to go to Keogh's to buy it. This was not something they had talked about that morning; this was not something that, together, they had foreseen. Tom cursed as he turned and crossed the yard to where his mud-streaked jeep was parked. The child squirmed. She wanted to be down on the concrete, where she saw her tricycle with the red plastic wheels, where she had left scattered, the previous evening, a bucketful of her wooden bricks. But Tom kept her firmly on his hip. In the jeep, he buckled her fast into the baby seat he had fixed into the passenger side.

*

'That's a beautiful child.'

The girl in Keogh's looked at the child the way every woman looked at her now. The same sad eyes, the head to one side, the same carefully held half-smile. The hand out to touch the child's curls, to stroke the soft face, to clasp the chubby fingers as though they been offered for a shake. Tom knew it well by now, the rush to sympathize in that overdone way of women; the tears quick to spring and quicker still to dry, to be replaced with a high laugh and a story about nothing.

'What's this her name is again?'

'Aoife.'

'Aoife.' The usual sad wince. 'Hello, Aoife. Are you having a good time with your granddaddy?'

Tom sat the child on the shop counter. She grabbed at a stand of chocolate bars, and he let her grab. He nodded to the girl. 'Would you be able to keep an eye on her for a few minutes while I go out the yard to your father?'

The laugh, high as a fountain, there it was. 'Oh, now. He's not my father. I'm a good bit older than any of the Keogh girls.' She shrugged, and Tom knew by the way she looked at him that he had pleased her. Down his elbows, shooting through his hands, he felt the burn of impatience. What did he care how old or how young she was? She was a girl: the arms out, the eyes wide – the blouse more buttoned up, he saw now, than either of the Keogh girls would likely have worn theirs – but it wasn't his concern to know such differences.

'We'll have a great time, Aoife and me,' she was saying, nearly singing, as he went out the door.

*

Tar was soft underfoot in Keogh's yard. One dog slept between the bars of an upturned cattle feeder. Another sat alert on a stack of fertilizer bags. Keogh, his everyday white shirt untucked as a concession to the weather, was standing in the shade of the supplies shed, a huge, barn-like structure full of the things he sold to the farmers of the area: the feedstuffs for cattle and sheep, the seeds and grain, the bales of twine and the drums of oil. Fencing posts of different lengths and shades stood against the back wall. Tyres and hubcaps and old engine parts, culled from worn-out tractors and jeeps, were piled and hung and pegged in corners.

He watched as Tom approached, not moving or speaking until a few feet separated them. Keogh was a rich man. The half-rusted carburettors and planks of timber had made him more money, over the years, than had the bags of grain and the gallons of petrol and the shop and the bar all put together, but of this he showed no sign. The white shirt was the same shirt the whole week long: grubby by Tuesday, filthy by Thursday. The van he drove was years old, a Transit like a tinker's, deeply dented along one side. The house over the shop had changed little in the thirty-five years since he had bought it: no extension, rarely a new paint job, the old net curtains in the window, and the wife inside cooking his breakfasts and his teas. Tom's wife Maura had said that Breda Keogh was driven half simple by her husband's meanness, that she had stopped asking for anything a long time ago, but that the daughters knew how to turn the pockets out on him, how to get their new clothes and their money for drinking and their two jelly-coloured cars. There were twin sons, too, as tight-fisted as Keogh himself, living in the house with him still and counting coins behind the bar, waiting for the day when they could split the place between them and watch it splintering to the ground. Keogh never mentioned them, never seemed to speak to them on the nights he ran the bar with them, never seemed to want for them in the yard or under the bonnet of a machine.

He was stepping away from the shed now, exhaling long and loudly as he frowned up at the sky. He stretched his hand out to Tom. 'Fierce fuckin' heat, Tom,' he said, as they shook. There was sweat sitting slick on his palm. He had what looked like axle oil smeared under one eye. He must have been up to a meadow with a part or a wheel already that morning. 'How's all up in Dorvaragh?'

'Have you twine left?' Tom asked.

Keogh laughed at the question. 'Have I twine, Tom? Plenty of twine. Too fuckin' much of the stuff. That's what I have.'

Tom moved past him into the shed. As his eyes adjusted to the gloom he saw another dog move between tractor tyres.

Keogh came up close behind him. 'Got in too much twine, Tom, and hardly a one about the place lookin' for it the summer. Sure they're all hirin' them contractors from up at Granard this weather. Sure them lads brings their own twine. Fuckers.'

'Give us a couple, so.'

'You're in a hurry, Tom?'

Keogh was looking for news. He was hungry for a complaint. Tom glanced at the rafters of the shed and shrugged out the beginning of a laugh. 'I'm under orders, Paddy.'

Keogh nodded. 'Ah, you have Mark at it above.'

'Aye,' said Tom. He did not turn.

'Very good, very good.' Keogh pulled a bale of twine from a pile. It thudded to the ground. Before the dust had settled, Keogh knocked a second bale.

'You're keepin' on at things anyway,' he said. 'Here, take a hoult of this one, you, and I'll bring the other.'

The gate out of the yard was still broken, its top hinge sagging low. As they passed through it, Tom glanced at Keogh over his shoulder. 'You never thought of getting that gate fixed.'

'I thought about it all right, Tom.'

Keogh pushed out a short laugh, as if by way of apology. It was a laugh almost like the girl's, a laugh high and fearful of how best to land. Hearing it, Tom felt something in his stomach turn. Not you, too, he wanted to say. Not you, too, still at this shit like the rest of them. It had been three months. He was not an invalid. Not a child. Keogh had always been the dirtiest of them all, always the first to notice, the quickest to remark, and now here he was like the rest of them, swerving his words off on to harmless ground. Keogh would have known full well why Tom had remarked on the gate; to gibe at Keogh's laziness, his tightness. Before, Keogh would have fought back with a dig about the farm or the cattle or, most likely, about Mark; with a question, all innocence, about how long Mark would be around this time, with a sigh about how short a stay that was, with a shake of the head about how badly Mark must be needed up in Dublin, for him to have to leave again so soon. There was no sincerity in such comments, but if he could hear them now he would draw succour from them, would lean into them and come up stronger, surer, stocked with grit enough to steer him through the day. Faced with this silence that was Keogh's kindness, he felt only light and bloodless, emptied of himself and of everything that fixed him to his standing. He needed something to shoulder against, something at which to pitch himself, muscled with the old fury, with the old contempt. But there was nothing. There was only this air struck with summer, and even that was a thing that seemed to set everyone around the place smiling like a fool.

'That's you ready to go now,' said Keogh, slamming shut the back door of the jeep after he had stowed the twine.

Tom stood with his back to the other man, his eyes fixed on the faded green wood of the shopfront, the stickers and notices pasted inside the window pane, the woman's bicycle against the sill. The briquette stand was empty. Through the window, he could see the girl holding the child, talking to an older woman who held another child, a boy. He knew the older woman, not to talk to, but to see. She and the boy held ice-cream cones. As Tom watched, both women glanced his way at the same time. From him they both looked down to the counter, from there to each other, and from there to the child on the shopgirl's hip. It was as familiar to him by now as the sight of his own eyes in the bathroom mirror, the look that he had caught on their faces: fear and thrill and greed and pure excitement; a glimpse right into the wreckage on the side of the road.

'Who's is the babby she has?' Keogh said. He was watching the same scene over Tom's shoulder. He snorted and prodded Tom in the arm. 'Jasus, if it's hers I surely missed that happening.'

'That's Mark's,' Tom said. 'I asked that lassie to hold on

to her for me for a minute.' Inside, the girl was coming around the counter. Tom put his hand up to signal to her not to bring the child out to him yet. She nodded, smiling, and took the child over to the other woman and child in a quick, light dance.

'I saw the child's seat 'ithin in the jeep, all right,' Keogh said quietly. 'Ah, she's a nice little one, isn't she.'

Tom said nothing.

'Lovely little one,' Keogh said.

In the shop, the two women were pushing the children up close to each other; they seemed to be encouraging them to kiss. The boy stared, sullen, at Aoife as his tongue kept a steady stroke on his cone. As the shopgirl moved closer to him, he slowly and carefully moved the ice-cream out of Aoife's reach, almost above his head, his gaze still dull on her face. Aoife, throwing her head back and twisting herself, caught sight of Tom. Her cry came as a long moan of protest; she flung one arm towards him and, screaming now, arched her back higher still. The boy stared. The women's faces crinkled with sorry-eyed smiles.

'Here.' Tom rummaged in his pocket and drew out the notes he knew to be there. He handed them to Keogh. 'Fifteen a bale, isn't it?'

'Spot on.' If it had been too little he would have been told. Nothing made it all right to give Keogh too little.

'Yous are great to be doing so well with her,' the girl said, as she came outside with the child. 'She's a real little pet.'

Aoife, sobbing now and sticky-faced with snot and tears, her yellow dress driven high over the fat plastic of her nappy, looked ready to thrash her way out of the shopgirl's arms. She pushed sharply into Tom as he took her.

'She's her granddaddy's girl,' Keogh said, and as he

reached out a hand to Aoife she howled and buried her face in Tom's chest. Keogh laughed. 'She knows well where she wants to be.'

'Good luck,' said Tom, and he walked away from them. As he settled Aoife in her seat she quietened and began to reach towards the radio knobs. When he had the key turned in the ignition he clicked through the stations for her, watching her eyes following his moving hand, her wet fingers reaching out for his. He stopped at a music station and backed the car out between the petrol pumps, keeping one eye on Keogh and the girl in the rear-view mirror. They were talking and nodding and shaking their heads. They were putting the whole world to rights. Beside him, the child shouted with happiness at the music so close to her hands.

*

The tractor was stopped on the crest of the hill when Tom turned into the lane for home. As he drew nearer, he could see that the cab was empty.

'What's your daddy at?' he said to the child.

She ignored him, her steady chatter all for herself, her attention now on the toy set of keys she gripped and shook with one fist. From her lips hung a heavy thread of drool. He reached over to wipe at it; she jerked her head away, her babble pooling into a squeal. But he got it, caught its glooping wetness on his cuff, wiped it into the thigh of his trousers as he turned in for the house. Aoife whined and banged the toy against the side of her seat. As Tom carried her in he gave her his keys to play with as well as her own.

Through the glass of the hall door he could see Mark sitting at the kitchen table, chewing, a thick-sliced sandwich in his hand. His eyes were on the child as Tom brought her into the room. The neighbour girl who had come that morning to mind her was on the couch, a magazine open on her lap.

'Well,' Mark said, through a mouthful of bread.

'Well.'

'You got the twine all right?'

'All yours,' Tom said to the neighbour girl, as he placed Aoife on the couch beside her. The girl looked at him with wide eyes.

'Well?' Mark said, staring at him, holding a mug in mid-air. There was a cut across his knuckles, Tom noticed. He must have skinned himself somehow.

'I got it, I got it, of course I got it,' Tom said, walking up to the table and putting his palm to the belly of the teapot. It was still warm. He poured a mug, heaped in two sugars and slopped milk in from the carton. He leaned against the sink to drink it down. It was sharp, almost bitter, and only warm. Mark must have been at the table a good twenty minutes. Regardless, Tom drained the mug. He had no desire to make another pot, and the girl was busy with Aoife. He laughed a short laugh, just loud enough for Mark to look at him, and gestured out towards the jeep. 'Keogh's a fierce fuckin' nuisance, all the same.'

Mark took another bite of his sandwich and chewed slowly. 'Why's that?' he said eventually, vaguely, the question hardly in his words at all. He pulled with finger and thumb at his earlobe. He'd had that ear pierced, Tom remembered; he'd worn a small silver ring in it through the pus and the swelling that came on after he'd had the hole made, and for days his mother had left the room every time he walked in. The ear would heal around it, Tom had warned him, but he would not listen; he kept on wearing the ring through the redness and the crusts. After a while, it had disappeared. The hole was no longer visible. Though maybe he was looking at the wrong ear.

'Ah,' he said, laying a hand down heavily on the edge of the sink. 'You know yourself. Full of questions. He's a bloody plague.'

Gathering his plate and his mug, Mark came to the sink. He said nothing as Tom stood aside, but ran the cold tap and bent to splash his face, rubbing the water up over the back of his neck. The skin there was brown as a saddle. The cut on his knuckle was matted with dust from the field. He pulled away from the sink, still gripping it, and exhaled hard.

'Don't bring Aoife off again without telling Miriam,' he said.

Tom stared. Mark was running cold water into a mug now, the same mug he had drunk his tea from, his eyes straight ahead on the window to the yard. His jaw was tight. He was letting the tap run on even though the mug was full, letting the water spill over on to his hand, his cut hand.

'Don't bring her away without telling me,' he said, and he shut off the tap.

Tom wanted to laugh. 'Sure you knew I had her,' he said. 'Sure you saw me taking her with me when I went to get the twine.' As he spoke he was admiring the sense that ran through his words, the straightness of what he was saying; he was basking in it, barely even ready for the possibility of a reply, when Mark lifted the mug a hand's height and landed it on the bottom of the sink with a bang. Water went everywhere. Out of the corner of his eye, Tom saw the girl rise from the couch with the child and move quickly into the next room.

'Miriam didn't see you taking her with you,' Mark said, swinging an arm towards where the girl had been. 'Miriam came running down the fields, crying that she'd put Aoife up in her cot this morning at eleven and that she'd gone up to check on her twenty minutes later and that she wasn't in the cot any more, and did I know where she was, or did you?' He drew breath. 'Because Miriam thought the two of us were out at the hay with the tractors, me and you, and that someone was after coming into the house while she was out with the washing, and that someone was after taking the fucking child.'

Now Tom's laugh came, and it came like something hocked up. 'For fuck's sake. You're not going to listen to that sort of giddy rubbish from her, are you? What does she think this is, the television?'

Mark faced him. 'What did you take her out of the cot for?' He turned the tap on again. 'Miriam puts her to bed and you go up there without telling anybody and you take her down again. She was meant to be sleeping. She was meant to be on her nap. What did you do that for? Ha?'

His lips were pulled back from his teeth with anger. His fists were clenched on the counter. This was how it was getting with him: further and further from reason every day. He wanted to argue over everything, he wanted to agree over nothing, he wanted to pick and bicker and drag everything out past its natural end. Or else he was silent, going out to the fields in the mornings almost without saying a word, never stopping to ask Tom what needed to be done, never listening to Tom's thoughts on how to do things – even that morning, Tom had to admit to himself now, he himself had done all of the talking, and all of the listening too. Mark would just sit there, waiting for the child to waken, and for the girl from over the road to arrive, and then as soon as the work outside was done he would be back in to the child, and then gone for the rest of the day, off in the car to Longford or Carrick or Cavan. What he did there he never said. At night was when they spoke, when the child was upstairs and they were in front of the television; at night Tom tried with him, tried the small things of the day on him, tried the weather, tried the neighbours, tried the jobs yet to be faced into that summer. Everything was simple. Everything was straightforward. But everything sent Mark further and further into himself. He never spoke about his mother. He never spoke about Joanne. Tom tried with him; he could, he supposed, have tried harder, but it was hard for him to know where to start talking about them himself. The best he could do was try to talk to him about the child, and even that much Mark seemed to resent.

'The child was awake,' Tom said. 'She was roaring. I went upstairs and brought her down with me, and there was no sign of anyone to look after her. So I took her out with me. And then she was happy enough. What did you expect me to do? Leave her in there, screaming down the walls?'

'But you knew Miriam was here with her. You knew Miriam had come down this morning to mind her.'

Tom shook his head. 'I saw no sign of anyone. The dishes were in the sink and the child's clothes were all over the floor and there was music on the radio there going full blast. Wasn't much sign of anyone doing any minding as far as I could see.'

'Jesus Christ.' In three long strides, Mark was at the back door. 'You're great, aren't you?'

'Sure, for Jesus' sake, the girl hardly thought someone had come in to take the child? For Christ's sake, you can't be blaming me because she let her mind run away with itself? Who in fuck's name is going to come in here and take the bloody child? Ha?'

'Watch your mouth.'

'Sammy Stewart? Jimmy Flynn, racing up the stairs and

13

snatching her off to live with him?' He snorted. 'Get a hold of yourself, would you? You're as big a havril as the little girl.'

'You should have let Miriam know you were taking her. You should have let me know you'd taken her up without Miriam knowing.'

'Well, I'm telling you now.'

Standing on the step into the back kitchen, Mark ground with his foot at the floor. 'Just leave her,' he said. 'Leave her be. She needs her routine. She needs things to be like normal.'

He walked off into the yard. From the next room, Tom could hear the girl talking to Aoife in a low voice, the child's woozy laughter, the sound of some complicated toy plucking high notes above neighbours' engines on the day's hot air.

PART ONE

Chapter One

Everything was plastic in the beer garden. Plastic chairs. Plastic tables. Plastic pint glasses. The barbecue food tasted plastic – as, Mark noticed, did the beer. It was his second pint, or his third; he couldn't remember. It didn't matter. It was a rare hot Saturday in a summer that was already halfway through, and there was no point in complaining.

The place was mobbed. Teenagers from the flats. Pillheads still going from the night before. The rugby fans, spilling in after the match. The weekend crowd: groups of couples gabbing at each other around big tables, and guys in short-sleeved shirts and bootcut jeans, and women with shopping bags flapping at their sides like huge broken wings.

Mark was here because he had not been able to force himself to be where he was meant to be, which was in his carrel in the college library, finishing the chapter that was due on his thesis supervisor's desk on Monday morning. He had a chapter title – 'Patronizing the Place' – and he knew he wanted to do something on Edgeworth and her relationship to the local people she wrote about, but that, and a clutch of increasingly frenzied notes, was pretty much all he had. This was to be his second chapter. His introduction he had written during the first months of the PhD, in a white heat of interest he could now hardly believe he had ever achieved, and his first chapter he had wrenched out painfully, piece-meal, over the course of the following two years. Even by then he had begun to wonder about the wisdom of the idea: a thesis on Maria Edgeworth, the nineteenth-century novelist who had lived most of her life in the manor just ten minutes away from his childhood home. Even by then he had questioned his ability to see the thing through. By now he was almost in despair about the thesis, prone to moments of wishing that Edgeworth had actually thrown herself out of the upstairs window on which she had perched, at the age of five, telling the maid who pulled her back in how very unhappy she was; there were days, now, when Mark thought he knew how she had felt.

He spent his time trudging through the books on education Edgeworth had written with her father, or trying to decipher her wiry, cross-hatched handwriting on yellowed pages in the National Library. Or looking for his theories in her fiction. Scouring the novels and the tales for proof of the argument he had once so firmly believed he could make. He could see, now, only naïveté in the conviction with which he had chosen Edgeworth as his subject, in his confidence that a local connection would somehow give his research some edge, some particular authority. Because what did it add, to know Edgeworthstown as a real town, as something more than a placename in a biography? So what if he had walked its main street – its only street – a thousand times, if, as a kid, he had parked his bike against the walls of the old coach house where she had once taught; if, as a teenager, he had gone knacker drinking in the graveyard where she and her family had their tomb? So he knew how the old house looked inside: what of it? It was no longer the old house in any case, had not been for decades; the Sisters of Mercy had long since gutted it and turned it into the hospital where Mark's mother had been a nurse before he and his sister were born, and once again when they were settled at school. They were no use to his thesis, Mark's memories of those evenings driving up to the manor with his father to collect his mother after her shift, waiting for her in the high-ceilinged hall. And anyway, he remembered little: the phlegmy splutters of the old people doddering in the shadows; the nuns, in their thick-soled shoes, moving noiselessly across the parquet floors. The sound of a cry, sometimes, that maybe was only someone caught up in a dream.

None of this, Mark had quickly discovered, was valuable at all. It was nothing better than local gossip, and it could not help him get to the core of his central argument, if he could even remember what his central argument was. 'Promising': that was how his supervisor, McCarthy, had described it at first; later, 'promising' was downgraded to 'interesting', and later still 'interesting' became 'tentative', and Mark was not eager to know what McCarthy's current assessment was. But he had to get him the chapter; without the chapter, he risked losing his funding, that complicated marriage of university, departmental and government money, which, put together, allowed him to live a little more comfortably than he suspected a graduate student in Anglo-Irish literature should. Getting it for another year depended on getting McCarthy's signature on the renewal form – which could only happen, McCarthy had warned Mark, if the second chapter arrived before McCarthy left for his annual month in West Cork. And as Mark watched his housemate, Mossy, return from the bar with yet another round, he knew the chances of securing McCarthy's autograph were fading fast.

Walking with Mossy was Niall Nagle. Mark had known him when they were undergrads in Trinity – he was the guy who was always sitting, yammering, on the desk of some female business student in the library – but he had barely seen him since, and he was surprised to see him now, and to hear that he and Mossy were deep in conversation about the rugby. Nagle must have just come from the match: he was wearing the polo shirt with a bank's name plastered across the chest – a chest that was looking, these days, almost as generous as those of the girls whose desks he had haunted in the Lecky. With a paunch to match. He was telling Mossy something about backs, how hard they had to work, how much brainpower had to go into every move. 'Contrary to popular impression,' he said, and took a swig from his bottle of Miller. He had always been like that in college: a vocabulary like a radio pundit. How did Mossy still know this guy? How had they stayed in touch? And since when did Mossy care anything for rugby? He had always, like Mark, been contentedly indifferent to sports. It might matter to him fiercely whenever Clare reached an All-Ireland final, but everything else he ignored. Mark, meanwhile, came from a county where the teams barely lasted a month into the season, so it was a rare Sunday that Micheál Ó Muircheartaigh's commentary – like a cattle auctioneer let loose in Croke Park – became part of the soundtrack. But now here was Mossy, talking about this match as intensely as though he had been in the dug-out in Lansdowne Road.

To Mark, it was a mystery. But then, so much about Mossy was, even after six years of sharing a place with him. The people in Mossy's life were a mixed bag, seduced and snuck and stolen from the many lives Mossy seemed, already, to have passed through. A year ago he had been writing a master's thesis on de Valera, quickly abandoned; a year before that he had been temping in a borrowed suit at the Stock Exchange on Anglesea Street; a few years before that, he had been backpacking in an Argentina where money was suddenly worth nothing. And now he was working in a self-proclaimed arthouse DVD store on George's Street, shelving cases and calling in late returns and coming home with subtitled films and stories of the customers he dealt with: the widows and widowers in need of something to get them through the day; the new couples trying to impress each other; the Indian guys looking for Ben Affleck films; the porn addicts, some of them showing up twice or three times in the same day; the foreigners, looking for relief from the English language; the junkies, looking for a hidden corner.

'I'm surprised to see you here on a day like this, Casey,' Nagle shouted from across the table. He was smirking, lighting himself a cigarette. 'Don't you have hay to make or something like that?' he said. 'Cows to milk, turf to stack, whatever it is you do down the sticks when the summer finally cops itself the fuck on?'

This was how Nagle had always addressed him back in Trinity; the same loud amusement at the idea of someone his own age, in his own college, choosing to spend so many of his weekends on a farm. There were rugby matches to go to. Rugby bars to cram into. Rugby birds to pursue. What was Mark doing, driving tractors and testing cattle and shovelling shit-caked straw out of sheds? Nagle never understood, but he never seemed to tire of asking, either.

'Not this weekend,' Mark said now, but he knew it would not be enough for Nagle.

'Jesus, Casey, even when it's lashing rain you seem to be down there fucking around at some animal or other. Sun's splitting the stones today, and yet here you are, up to your balls in beer. What, did you finally get them off your back? What, did your old lad die?'

Beside Nagle, Mossy shook his head in laughing disapproval. 'Nagle, you bollocks.'

Nagle affected a wide-eyed look, the only effect of which was to accentuate his jowls. 'What? It's a fair assumption.

Isn't it, Casey? I mean, Jesus, I'm basically not sure if I've ever seen you in the sunshine before.'

'Right, right,' Mark said, as drolly as he could.

'I mean, for a while there, back in college, I was starting to look for fangs on this guy,' Nagle said to Mossy. 'No joke.'

'You're some tool,' said Mossy, reaching for one of Nagle's cigarettes. Mark could see Nagle noting this move as he inhaled, deciding to let it go as he blew the smoke out in a formless cloud.

'You ready for another?' Mark nodded to Mossy's glass. It was only half empty, but he wanted to get away. He took a long gulp of his own pint as though to justify the question.

Mossy nodded. 'I'll go with you,' he said. 'I need smokes.'

'Fucking right you do, Flanagan,' Nagle said, snatching up his pack of Marlboro and turning his attention to the girls at the next table. 'Beautiful day, ladies,' he said, to the back of one sleekly ponytailed head.

'Arsehole,' said Mossy, as they entered the cool darkness of the inside bar. In here, the place looked as it would at this time on any day, in any month of the year, a hard-chaw bar on a hard-chaw street in inner-city Dublin, full of life-pocked locals, all scowls and silences and sagging midriffs, all watching – they all seemed to be watching – as Mark and Mossy came in through the back door. But glancing up, Mark saw what they were actually watching: highlights of the rugby match on a huge television high on the wall. On the screen, a player was panting and pawing at his gumshield.

'When did everyone in this country start giving such a shit about rugby?'

Mossy shrugged. 'Civilized times, man.'

The barman signalled to say he'd be over in a moment.

'I didn't realize you still knew Nagle,' Mark said to Mossy, with more accusation in his tone than he'd intended. He cleared his throat. 'What's he up to, these days?'

'Over in one of the big banks on Stephen's Green. Doing well for himself. Doing something suss with other people's money. The usual.'

'See much of him?'

'The odd time,' Mossy said. 'Think whoever brought him in here today did a legger on him. He came up to me there at the bar like I was a brother of his back from the dead. Pure relief to see someone he could talk to.'

Mark looked around the bar. 'Probably afraid one of this crowd would go at him with a dirty syringe.'

'No harm,' Mossy said. 'Though they'd have a job ramming it into that neck.'

The barman came to them, and Mark ordered the drinks. 'He's still as obsessed with my old lad's farm as he ever was.' He shook his head. 'Prick.'

'Yeah,' Mossy said. 'Though I have to say I was wondering the same thing myself.'

'Wondering what?'

'Well, y'know. This good weather. I mean, I was sure you'd be heading down home. I thought I'd be getting up to an empty house this morning.'

'I have work on,' Mark said, without looking at Mossy. 'This deadline for McCarthy.'

'Decent of them to leave you at it for a change.'

'Five missed calls since yesterday evening.'

'Fuck.' Mossy whistled.

'Yeah.'

'Ah, man, that's a hard old buzz. You didn't chat them at all, no?'

'Ah, yeah,' Mark shook his head. 'I mean, I talked to my

mother this morning. Told her the score. She understood. I said I'd be down Tuesday.'

'Good stuff.'

'Good stuff as long as this weather holds,' Mark said.

'Well,' Mossy said, with a wince, and then gestured apologetically over to the cigarette machine, as though it were an obligation he could not escape, as though he would much have preferred to stay at the bar with Mark, reassuring him about the weather, about his chapter, about parents and the things they expected their sons to do. But, then, Mossy's parents did not expect their son to do things. Mossy's parents were busy with their own lives, with the friends they had, with the trips they took, with the visits from their children that they sweetly encouraged but would never demand.

'I'll just get these,' Mossy said, and he was gone.

Mark settled closer in to the bar. The irritation he had felt at Nagle's goading had faded, but still he was not keen to return to the beer garden, and to be alone with Nagle, even for the length of time it would take for Mossy to return from buying his cigarettes. What he wanted, he realized, was for Mossy to go out there alone and start up a conversation with Nagle, a conversation about anything, and for Mark to return to find the two of them absorbed in that subject, and to come in on it, and take part in it, mindlessly, for the rest of the evening, until the beer started to really take hold, until it no longer mattered what anyone said, because nothing could get at you.

On the phone that morning, his mother had spoken in the vague, terse sentences that meant, he knew, that his father was in the room. His father had never been one to talk on the phone, but that did not mean he relinquished his determination to know – and, as though by a sort of hypnosis, to control – what was being said and what was being agreed to at the other end of the line. Mark had seen it countless times: his mother, standing at the kitchen counter where the phone was kept, trying to get the conversation over with, while his father sat nearby, his chin pushed into his knuckles, his eyes roving the floor as he followed and weighed and dismantled every word – the words he could hear and the words at which he could only guess. It was a harmless charade, really, comical half of the time, because half of the time his father got it all arseways: the imagined details, the assumed scenarios. He was bored, Mark knew; he craved news, craved some new narrative to add to his day, and if, eavesdropping on Mark's mother's phone calls, he couldn't glean that thing ready-made, he would invent it for himself.

And his father would long since have invented his own reasons for Mark's decision to stay in Dublin that weekend despite the unfolding, on the farm, of the exact science they both knew so well: this was the second day with clear skies and temperatures above the mid-twenties, the second day in what was forecast to be a five-day spell, and it was a July day, so the meadows would be at their readiest, the ground would be baked firm. It was the day to cut, and tomorrow was the day to bale, and the next day was the day to gather, and without Mark, none of this could be done quickly or easily. And yet Mark was staying away. And as the explanation for that fact, his father would either settle on something depressingly wrong – that it was something to do with a woman – or depressingly right: that he was up shit creek with his college work. Though his father would add to the actual problem an extra dimension of crisis: Mark, he would decide, was on the verge of losing not just his funding, but his place on the programme, his right to continue with his thesis, to walk through Front Arch and set foot on campus at all. He would be thrown out. He would be disgraced in the eyes of Dublin. And the eyes of Dublin would be nothing compared to the eyes of home.

Mark knew that his PhD work, and any mention of it, held a power over both his parents; a power that was often very convenient for him. In the face of what his father insisted on calling Mark's 'studies', they became as quiet and uneasy as though they had opened a solicitor's letter or answered the door to a guard. It was to them something alien, unfathomable, something utterly intimidating, a degree beyond a degree, an essay that would take years of their son's life, that would turn him, at the end of all, into something just as alien and unfathomable: a university lecturer, a writer of books without storylines, papers without news.

The fact of his mother's having nursed at the manor house had formed a thread of delighted connection between them, for a while. That first year of his thesis work, when he was still in love with the idea of writing about Edgeworth, his mother had talked to him about the old house every weekend he came home; she had taken him to see the place, arranged for the caretaker to show him the parts that had been least changed since the Edgeworths had sold it in the thirties. But there were hardly any such parts left, in truth. A surviving cornice, high in the men's ward, high over the hooped backs and the spittled mouths. A section of tiles in a little washroom off the maternity ward where, for years, the local women had screamed their babies into being. In the room that had once been the library, the high columns still remained, but nothing else bore any resemblance to the old drawings of the room; it was now where the patients watched television, gathered around the screen in their dressing-gowns.

Mark was disturbed by how thoroughly the traces of the

Edgeworths had been knocked out of the place. Edgeworth had written all her books there; she had collaborated with her father there on all their projects; she had helped, there, to raise and to educate her twenty-one siblings; she had learned, there, to get along with each of her father's four wives. Walter Scott had come to stay there, taking Edgeworth off with him on a tour of Killarney, and a few years later, Wordsworth had come to visit, in all his 'slow, slimy, circumspect tiresome *lengthiness*', as Edgeworth had written in a letter to her aunt. It had been that place, and now it was just one more maze of wards and stairwells and hallways humming with the unmistakable smells of a hospital run by a religious order: disinfectant and candlewax, gravy and soap and starch.

For a while, he kept telling his mother how his thesis was going, and sharing with her any stories he had managed to turn up about the old house, and in these even his father took an interest, but eventually Mark ran out of such stories. Eventually, it was just him and Edgeworth's writing and the theories he needed, now, to apply to it, and when his parents asked him whether he had found out anything new about the house or the history of the town, he had replied regretfully at first, and eventually irritably, until, it seemed, they learned no longer to ask.

He did not need to be around Edgeworthstown any more to do his research. He needed to be in the library; he needed to be in his carrel. And his carrel was a long way from Edgeworthstown, and from his father's farm.

Mark's father did not expect him to come and live at home. He did not expect him to gradually take over the running of the farm. In the first place, his father had no intention of handing control of the farm to anybody – it was his life, and its daily rituals and its daily difficulties were like oxygen to him, much as he might complain of them. Nor, Mark knew, did his father honestly think that farming offered any kind of future. Especially on the small scale on which he farmed, it was impossible to make a living from it. Yet none of this kept his father from thinking that Mark should do more of what he called taking an interest; that Mark should be around more often, there for the larger jobs, there to advise his father on whether to expand the yard or to buy a new piece of machinery – or, at least, there to express approval at the decisions his father had already made on these things. He did not want an heir, Mark's father. He wanted a partner. And a life in Dublin that required Mark to be physically present in the city for only two hours a week – for the undergrad class he taught, and for the office hour he was obliged to hold afterwards – seemed to Mark's father no barrier to the kind of partnership he had in mind.

Mark was the only son. He had an older sister, Nuala, who had lived in England for years. His father had neighbours, but he would not ask them for help. He had brothers-in-law, but they lived in the town, played bridge, went with their wives to Tesco and Supervalu to do the weekly shop. They did not drive tractors. They did not haul bales. They did not talk traneens and wet clumps and oil filters and phone calls to the Met Office. And there were no brothers. His father had not been born an only child, but he was as good as one now. And he knew how to turn the tricks of an only child when there was something he wanted.

But with Mark – with Mark and the farm – those tricks were not turning, at least not as Tom expected them to turn. Mark knew this. He had seen it on his father's face so many times, on so many of those evenings when it was time for him to return to Dublin after a weekend at home. It was not anger, it was not disappointment; it was, instead, a sort of uncomprehending surprise. How could he be leaving, when things had been running so smoothly with both of their shoulders to the wheel, when there were still jobs to be done and to be discussed? How could he have failed to hear his father's many pleas for his continued presence, delivered in the guise of casual conversation since the minute he had arrived from the railway station? How could he be going when the fact of what he needed to be doing was laid out all around them in acres and herd numbers and ear tags and calendar markings for tests and marts and dehornings and cows that were due to calve?

'Jesus, I didn't think you were going so soon. And you have to be back up there?'

It was the same from his father every time. The same words. The same tone – the tone other fathers might have used upon discovering that their sons had just been redeployed to Iraq. Mark always managed, always succeeded with his tactic of being at once firm and vague, but he always knew, too, that in a week, or in a fortnight, or in a month, he would be back again, having a conversation that felt like an ulcer, making himself late for the Sunday evening train.

It was a small farm. A hundred acres, meadows around the farmyard and a stretch of bog at the far end of the lane; thirty cows or so spending their year in those meadows and in that bog instead of in the slatted shed that, Mark knew, his father wanted his help to build. A slatted shed, somehow, was the sign of a real farm, and it was essential if you wanted to get at the really good grants, but Mark scarcely knew what to say any time his father hinted at the need for one, because Mark barely knew how to build a fire, let alone a slatted shed. Was he supposed to come down one weekend and suddenly take on the skills of a builder, a carpenter, an engineer of the flow and storage of bovine sewage? You built the shed over a pit of some sort, that he knew, and you put slats over the pit, and then you kept cattle in the shed for long periods, and you fed them there, and in the pit beneath the slats you collected their shit, and at the end of the season you had a shedful of saleable animals and a pitful of pedigree manure, and the grant cheque came in the post and you went to the bank to lodge it with all the other proper farmers. And then you did something with the money – invested it back in the farm somehow, made some strategic decisions about the way the next year was going to go. You sold your animals, and you bought new ones, and you bought new machinery, and maybe you bought new land, and you expanded, you extended, you excelled, and all the other farmers and all the other farmers' sons welcomed you to the club.

But Mark was writing a doctorate on a nineteenth-century novelist, and when he finished it, he wanted to do the things that you did after you finished a doctorate on a nineteenth-century novelist: maybe write a book about a nineteenth-century novelist, maybe teach a course or two on nineteenth-century novelists, or maybe run the hell as far away from nineteenth-century novelists as he could. He didn't know. He had to get his thesis finished first, and he had to publish many more papers, and present at many more conferences, and he had to ingratiate himself with the English departments of various universities, which was something he kept meaning to get around to but had not yet quite achieved. As a teacher – or, more accurately, as a teaching assistant – he suspected he was terrible; he had recognized, in his students' eyes, the same slow dawn of scorn and incredulity of which he had been a master in his own undergraduate years. He suspected, too, that he was writing an appalling excuse for a thesis, but still he felt sure that he wanted to have a career as an academic, to spend his days reading and researching and writing, figuring things out and pinning things down. What those things were, he no longer felt sure, but they were the things he wanted to do; he knew. And he knew that what he did not want to do was to live in Dorvaragh, even half of the time, even a quarter of the time, and farm with his father, and fight with his father, and watch himself becoming more and more the image of his father every day. But still he could not turn his back on him. He could not refuse him. He tried to be honest with him – he told him, over and over, that his life would be in Dublin, and that his trips to the farm would be occasional, but they would be as often as he could manage, and that that was the most and the best he could do. He knew that, with his father, the words were not taking. But he could not find in that fact justification to stay away, justification for anything like a final break. And, besides, a final break was not something that he even knew how to want.

In all of this, Mark's mother was sympathetic. She told him to do what he had to do, to concentrate on his own work, to take with a pinch of salt his father's air of being winded by his leaving, confused by his inability to stay. And yet, after a couple of weeks had passed, she would be on the phone again, wondering when he would be coming down. In the spaces between her words he felt he could almost hear his father's breath.

'Monday,' his mother had said on the phone that morning, when he had explained to her about the deadline. 'Monday, you'll be finished? Monday we'll see you, so?'

He had said yes. Or he had made some noise that sounded like it. Then he had said goodbye and, looking to the clock radio beside his bed, he had discovered that there were technically three more hours left in the morning, despite the sharpness of the sunlight splaying itself through the blinds.

31

He had slipped back into a heavy, dream-crazed sleep, and when he had gone down to the kitchen more than three hours later, Mossy had cooked breakfast and had planned for them both what he called a knockout of a day.

And this was the knockout. A back yard in the Liberties, barely bigger than the sitting room of their flat, heaving with the sun-blistered bodies of strangers and skangers and shits like Nagle, and a bar that looked populated entirely by jailbirds and jailbait, with a few pissed grandmothers and breastfeeding infants thrown into the mix. He knew he was kidding himself to think he'd get anything done now if he went back to the flat, back to his bedroom, where he'd set up an old kitchen table as his desk, across which his notes and books and printouts lay in the kind of neat and careful order that, in truth, only meant that he wasn't working, that he hadn't been working for some time. Because there was on that desk no sign of the scuffling and flittering and leafing and scrambling it took to really get through a piece of academic work, with its footnotes and its quotations and its weavings in and out of elements from every scrap of paper touched and filed and vanished over the course of long months and years. It would be useless, Mark thought, but he would be better off there, so he drained his pint and went to say goodbye to Mossy, pushing his way through the crowd, elbows and tummies and tits and arses and pint glasses raised and pint glasses slopping.

And talking to Mossy was a girl who made Mark decide, the instant he saw her, that he was staying where he was.

Chapter Two

She was dark-haired. No: brown-haired, Mark saw, as she turned in the low slant of sun. Brown hair that looked heavy, the way it fell in its thick, loose curls. As she listened to whatever Mossy was saying now, she put a hand to her fringe, pushed it aside; she smiled, and Mark saw the gap in her smile, the sliver of nothing between her front teeth, and he swallowed.

She was tall. Almost Mossy's height, and taller than either of the girls who were with her as she talked to him, standing beside her doing things with their handbags and their sunglasses and their phones, like people who were getting themselves organized to go somewhere. Like people who were leaving.

And she was leaving. That was what she was saying to Mossy now, Mark could hear, as he came close; that she was heading, that she would see Mossy later, that he was to text her if he couldn't find the house. And then she was coming towards Mark, and when she saw him, as she passed him, she was smiling.

'Hiya,' she said, and he saw that her eyes were green. And she was gone. He nodded a response, but too late for her to see; one of her friends saw instead, and gave him a strange look. They must have been the girls Nagle had turned to when he and Mossy went into the bar, Mark realized. They must have been the ones at the next table. He tried to remember. Had he noticed her? He would have noticed her. He would have stared. Staring would have been a better use of his afternoon. Talking to her would have been better still. What had he been doing? Talking shite to Mossy, taking shite from Nagle? He raised his eyebrows as he handed Mossy his pint.

'What?' Mossy said, innocently.

'What yourself?' Mark said. 'What was that about?'

'That girl?'

'Yeah, that girl. Who is she?'

'Joanne. Comes into Laser a lot. Gets the new releases. Nice girl. Training to be a solicitor. Joanne.'

'I heard you the first time.'

'Yeah, well,' said Mossy, and he stretched. He looked lazy, unbothered, almost post-coital; either he'd slept with her already, or he was utterly confident of sleeping with her soon. Mossy scored whenever he wanted to score. Mark did not do too badly – at least, he liked to think of it that way – but Mossy was always miles ahead. It was the accent, or it was the wild head of hair, or it was the fact that he could speak Irish, or something. Mark didn't know what it was. But it worked. There were weeks when he bumped into two or three different women in the morning. Not on the same morning. But even that he wouldn't put past Mossy. Even in their first year in college, when everyone was talking about it and nobody was getting it, Mossy had been getting it. And he didn't brag about it. He barely ever talked about it. But he got it. And now it looked like he was on track with this girl. He yawned. Mark wanted to give him a dig in the stomach.

'So you're meeting up with her later?'

Mossy took a drag from his cigarette. 'We're going to a party,' he said. 'Some of her solicitor friends just bought a house out in Booterstown. Mustn't mind the place getting trashed already, I don't know. Or maybe they're just desperate for a lawsuit.' He laughed, and Nagle brayingly joined in.

'Christ, outstanding rack on that blonde friend of hers,' Nagle said, inclining his head to where her friends had been sitting. 'She gonna be at this party?'

Mark stared at him. The thought of being left in the pub with Nagle while Mossy fucked off to meet the girl was bad enough, but if Nagle was invited to the party too, Mark was going to do damage with one of those Miller bottles. This was what he got, he thought. This was what came of sitting by himself at the bar inside, moping over his thesis - moping over his *parents*, for Christ's sake - while out here Mossy and Nagle were doing what anyone with any cop-on would be doing in a beer garden on a sweltering Saturday afternoon: talking to chicks and laying the groundwork for Saturday night.

'They're all going to be out there,' Mossy, stubbing out his cigarette, said to Nagle. 'They're all going out there now to help this friend of theirs get the place ready. We'll head out there around ten.' He turned to Mark.

'Are you coming?'

'Who, me?'

'She said there was a barbecue from eight. But if I see another hot dog today I'll vomit blood. Ten or eleven will be time enough to get out there.'

'I wasn't even talking to her,' Mark said.

'Well, she said to tell you to come,' said Mossy, shrugging.

'She said to say that to me?'

'I'm texting Lockser,' Nagle said, reaching for his phone. 'That blonde bird would be right up his alley. Though he'll have to go through me first.'

'Don't text him then, you bollocks,' Mossy said, and nodded over to Mark. 'So we'll head out there later?'

'Yeah, sure,' Mark said, as a fist of anticipation opened, warm and opiate, within his chest. 'Sure we're in no rush.'

*

At Booterstown DART station, the sea was hidden behind a high wall, and Nagle complained loudly and fervently about the smell of the marsh. Two long-necked birds were moving through the rushes, making their way to the glittering pool of water banked, on the other side, by a stretch of mud.

'It's a fucking outrage,' Nagle was saying. 'You could pay two or three mil, easily, to live out here, and you open your door in the morning to the smell of shite.'

'Snipe,' Mossy said.

Nagle turned his head quickly as though he had been insulted, then seemed to think better of it and continued along the walkway over the marsh.

'There's an offy just here at the bottom of the hill,' Mossy called out to him, and this time Nagle stopped in his tracks and gave Mossy a disbelieving stare.

'We're expected to bring our own fucking booze to this gaff?' he protested. 'What are we – students?' He looked to Mark. 'No offence, Casey.'

Mark shrugged and moved ahead, leaving Mossy to listen to Nagle. He was carrying, now, none of the boozy confidence with which he'd made his way from the pub to the station in Pearse Street, none of the bluster with which he'd strode around the platform, laughing with Mossy and even with Nagle, as the heat of the day hovered still in the red brick of the old building, as blue sky glinted through the great cross-hatched barn of a roof. He had felt, then, not just glad about the prospect of the party, but smug, almost; entitled, almost. Not to the girl, but to the night, to the pleasure of it, to a house where there would be a girl he wanted to get talking to, and where he'd have the whole night to do it. That was what parties were for; that was why parties, when it came to meeting someone, were the only way to go. In a pub, you'd only ever have started talking to someone like her before the barman was stacking chairs and snatching glasses and calling time, and in a club it was always too loud, too crammed, too pointless, too dark – and he knew it aged him, seeing it this way, but he didn't care. He wanted to talk to her. And only at a party could you get a chance to talk to someone like her properly; at a party, you felt halfway to being comfortable with someone like her, even when you'd only just set eyes on them, even when you'd only glimpsed the side of their face or the curve of their ass. It was something to do with already being in a house, already surrounded by living-room furniture, by CDs all over the carpet, by books messed up on the shelves.

But now, crossing the Rock Road to the off-licence, he felt uneasy, felt conscious of all the pints, of how he must look, how he must smell. What if there were only eight or ten people at this party, all close friends, all solicitors or whatever they were, and he was about to clatter into the middle of them, with Mossy and Nagle, who were surely even more of a mess than he was? He cringed at the thought of it, and yet he kept going, hearing, as the door of the off-licence opened, the tinkling of some little bell – hearing, behind him, Mossy shouting at Nagle to quit something, to *fucking quit*! – and going on, and keeping going, because it was better than going back to his unfinished chapter and his hung-over tomorrow and the phone calls that were sure to come; it was better than all of that, it was different from all of that, and so he went on.

*

The place was a terraced cottage tucked well away from any chance at a sea view, a window on each side of a squat brown door. Nagle snorted at the sight of it.

'Six fifty, minimum, and it's a fucking gardener's hut,' he said.

'High standards for someone who just took a piss in full view of the traffic,' Mossy said. He was looking sloppy, smiling obscurely, his gaze fixing on nothing in particular, his bag of cans slung low by his side. He leaned a moment too long on the doorbell and frowned in irritation when Mark told him to leave off. Music sounded from the windows, and the busy squall of voices. They seemed all to be women's voices.

'Fuckin' Beyoncé,' Nagle said, just as the door was opened by a guy their own age in a tight striped T-shirt and cargo shorts. He greeted them brightly and immediately disappeared back into a room, leaving them to make their own way.

Inside, the place was bigger than it had seemed, and it was thronged. There were people everywhere: standing in the middle of the floor, sitting on sofas and bean-bags pushed back against the wall, leaning on low bookcases and coffee-tables and on the high silver speakers from which some female singer – maybe Beyoncé, probably Beyoncé – blared. In clusters, among the standing groups, some women were dancing. Everyone, dancing or not, seemed to be smiling, and to be confident and happy and well dressed, and to be absorbing and entertaining and exhilarating each other in conversation. The mood was not just lively, it was positively phosphorescent, delirious, delighted in the extreme: which meant that the explanation had to be somewhere nearby. And there it was, glimpsed as someone opened a door at the back of the room and quickly closed it again. A girl bent over a dresser. A couple of others waiting their turn. And the guy who had just come out of the room standing on the thresh-old of the dance-floor with a beatific smile on his lips, with a quick little tap and tug at his nostrils.

'Oh, nice one!' Mark heard Nagle roar.

*

Nobody was dancing in the kitchen, but a DJ was twitching and hovering over a pair of decks. A girl was darting around with a Polaroid camera, detonating the boxy little flash in people's faces so that their smiles rippled, for an instant, in recoil. Mark pushed through. On a radiator by the small window, a red-haired guy was slumped, sweat stains darken-ing his shirt, his tie wrapped several times around one wrist; he looked defeated and belligerent all at once, and the glare with which he returned Mark's gaze slipped off his face like oil.

'You made it!'

Mark turned. It was the blonde. The blonde friend, that was, Mark corrected himself – wanting, even in his internal commentary, to distance himself as far as possible from Nagle. She was grinning; he didn't think she was off her head, but he couldn't be sure. He smiled at her. She clapped a hand on each shoulder and kissed him, hard, on the cheek. Definitely off her head. She laughed. 'You bring your friends?'

'Yeah.' Mark waved back in the direction of the other room, slapping someone on the side of the head as he did so. He apologized. They seemed not even to have noticed.

The blonde – the blonde friend – looked down to see what he was carrying. 'Cans?' She laughed as though he'd turned up with a vault of Buckfast.

'I was going to bring wine,' he said, and it was true, he had stood for several minutes in front of the small shelf of wine at the off-licence, but had given up; for as little as he knew about wine, he had reckoned that a bottle should cost more than a tenner to be any good, and, with the dinner-party paranoia still ringing in his head, he had not wanted to show up on the doorstep offering a bottle of plonk. So Heineken it was. A lot of Heineken, which he was tired of carrying by now.

'Oh, there's loads of wine . . .' the blonde girl was saying. 'Do you want a glass?' And she turned and was gone. To the table, or the garden, or the extensive wine cellar, he didn't know. He elbowed his way through to the fridge. It was packed; there was certainly no room for six-packs. Bottles, and jars, and packets, and tubs, and as much fruit, nearly, as you'd see in one of the Moore Street women's prams, and lumps of cheese and schlongs of salami and the gold-foil knobs that meant champagne. He closed it and shoved the cans, instead, into one of the kitchen presses, between a food-processor and a little tower of painted clay bowls. Morocco. Or maybe just Spiddal. More money than sense, anyway. He snapped a can off the six-pack and opened it. When he turned, she was standing in front of him, grinning. Off her head? No time to think about that now. It was her. Joanne.

'Your stash?'

Blondie must have sent her. She was holding a bottle of wine and an empty glass, which she offered to him now. He took it. This left him with an open Heineken in one hand and a wine glass in the other.

She laughed. She was even better than he remembered. Green eyes, yes, and you didn't see those too often, and her fringe dipping low, and her skin freckled, maybe from the sun that day, and her shoulders were brown and bare. 'Glad you could make it,' she said. That gap between her teeth when she smiled.

He put the wine glass on the counter behind him. 'Just about,' he said, which made no sense, he knew, as a reply, nor was it true, but it seemed like the right thing to say, seemed to sound as though there had been other options, as though he had gone to great lengths to get there, so she should be grateful as well as glad, and should show that gratitude by, say, talking to nobody but him all night, and that just for starters.

She nodded. 'So, did your friends come, too? Mossy and . . .'

'Nagle. Eh, Niall. Yeah, Niall's not really our . . .' He stopped. There was no point in getting into what Nagle was and was not.

'Mossy's a cool guy, though.'

Mark made a noise of agreement, feeling the return of his earlier anxiety. Had he even, really, been invited to this party? Mossy had said so, and he hadn't said anything to suggest that he was interested in this girl, but then, he hardly ever did, and even so, that didn't mean she wasn't interested in Mossy, that she wasn't just killing time, now, talking to Mark so that she'd look busy, or popular, or whatever it was that women wanted to look when the guy they fancied walked into the room. Which Mossy would probably do any minute now. Mark willed him to stay away. To go into the coke room and snort himself into oblivion. To meet some other girl out there, fall on to a couch with her, take her home to the flat and screw her on their couch, on Mark's bed – on Mark's table of notes and orderly printouts, if necessary.

'Anyway.' She leaned towards him, suddenly, and he was startled – and then, all in the space of an instant, delighted, disbelieving, flattered and aroused – but she was just reaching past him to pick up the wine glass he'd put down. She filled it – really filled it – with red wine. He took a swig from his can. As he did so, she leaned in and around him again, this time with the wine bottle, and this time she looked right into his eyes, in a way that meant something – he didn't know what, exactly, but something, and possibly something good.

'Anyway,' she said again. 'So how do you know Mossy?'

Fuck Mossy, he wanted to say. 'I live with him,' he said instead.

'Loads of free DVDs, so.'

'Yeah,' Mark said. 'Though most of the stuff Mossy brings home isn't really to my taste.'

'Really?' She raised her eyebrows.

'Animals, you know,' he said. 'I mean, it's cruel. It's just wrong.'

She squinted at him for a moment, then caught his meaning; she laughed, shaking her head at him, her tongue touching her lips, in a way that made him decide. He was not going to leave this place without this girl.

'So you're . . .' He wasn't sure what he was going to say. What did he want to say to her? What did he want to know about her? Anything? Did they really have to go through the checklist of introductory prattle, talking about their jobs, talking about the neighbourhoods they lived in, talking about the last gig they'd been to – or the last gig they'd pretend to have been to for the sake of making the right kind of impression? He didn't want to have to launch into a chin-stroking commentary on whatever band he'd last seen at Whelan's, and he definitely didn't want to find himself trying to explain a PhD on Maria Edgeworth and the Realist Novel. It wasn't that he just wanted to push her up against the fridge and kiss her; he did want to talk to her, but not about anything to do with the real world, not about anything that was going to make him have to try too hard, or work too hard, or think too hard.

'So this is your friend's house?' he said.

'You don't recognize me,' she said, at exactly the same moment.

'What?' he said.

'Do you?'

He wondered how drunk she was, or how much she'd put up her nose.

'I saw you back in the pub,' he said uncertainly. 'I saw you leaving.'

'Not from the pub.' She shook her head, 'Obviously you recognize me from the pub. We're talking, aren't we?'

Mark exhaled noisily. 'I mean, yeah?' he said, and he cringed at how moronic it sounded. He was now very unclear about what was happening. He wanted to turn around and get himself another beer, but she was looking at him expectantly.

'You don't,' she said. 'You haven't a clue who I am.'

Jesus, was she famous or something? Mark stared. Maybe she did look familiar. What, was she a newsreader, or an actress – was she in *Fair City* or something? He never watched it. Well, that wasn't true: it was just on, sometimes, and he found himself following it, but no, she didn't look familiar, and he told her so. Anyway, it was a bit fucking arrogant of her to expect to be recognized. He was having second thoughts. Maybe he didn't want to push her up against the fridge after all. Except maybe to get away from her.

'But I know you,' she said, and now he felt panic judder into his perspective. Was she someone he had already slept with? And forgotten? There had been one-offs. He had been plastered. But he didn't think she was one of those. He would have remembered her. He looked at her more closely. He shook his head. She wasn't anyone she knew.

'I'm sorry,' he said. 'I don't remember.'

'Fuck's sake,' she said, with a huge grin. She gripped him by the arm; startled, he stared at her hand. 'We're neighbours. You seriously don't recognize me?'

'From Smithfield?' Mark said.

'No,' she said, taking her hand away, running it through her fringe. 'Not neighbours in Smithfield. I mean *really* neighbours. In Longford. At home. You're Mark Casey, right? From Dorvaragh?'

Mark felt himself flush. His heart speeded up. He had never met anyone in Dublin who knew him from Dorvaragh. Nobody knew Dorvaragh. It was too tiny; it was only two houses separated by a long lane. One house, really – his parents' house – since the other house, at the lane's other end, was nothing more than a ruin. It had been a cottage once, a tiny place with a roof of corrugated iron, and around it a few scraggy fields. It had belonged to an old man who had been a friend of his father's, and when the old man died, his fields had been bought by the son of the local solicitor, much to his father's disgust. His father had really hated that guy – the solicitor, not the son, though he was not exactly keen on the son either. Lynch. Frank Lynch. That had been the solicitor's name. He was dead now, but Mark's father still hated him. Mark remembered being down the fields with his father the day Lynch had been buried, and seeing the funeral procession pass slowly on the road, and watching, in disbelief and in discomfort, as his father had turned his back. It was not like his father to show such disrespect for the dead. But that was the effect Frank Lynch had had on him. Thinking about it now, Mark was disturbed to realize that what he himself thought when he thought of Lynch was also hatred, even though he had no reason of his own to truly feel that way. He had taken it on, taken it into himself, without even noticing; it was now his to pass on in turn. And yet he could barely even picture Frank Lynch's face. He could picture the son, a long streak of piss, and he could picture the mother, her skin always tanned, her cars always flash. But the father: the father was gone. And yet when Mark thought of him, a dull anger clouded his mind.

Joanne was laughing again; the sound brought him back to the room. She was standing closer to him, and he could smell her perfume, and he thought, for some reason, of leaves.

'I don't know you,' he said. 'Why don't I know you?'

'I'm a couple of years younger than you. Maybe that's why. And I didn't go to school in the town.'

'Where did you go?'

'I was a boarder in Ferbane.'

The boarders in Ferbane were rich girls. Bare brown legs and white knee socks. They used to come back into Longford on the bus on Friday evenings, spilling into the car park opposite the cathedral, kilts hitched up and blouses hanging out, and you didn't know whether you wanted them to tuck the blouses back in so that their tits would be more obvious or leave them untucked so that they looked half undressed already. Both, preferably. An assortment.

'Ferbane,' Mark said, and shook his head.

'I lived up the road from you,' she said, and she shrugged. He had to work out who she was. If he didn't do it soon, she would get insulted and walk away. If she wasn't insulted already.

'Your name is Joanne,' he said.

'Mossy probably told you that,' she said, and she drank her wine.

'You're from Edgeworthstown?'

'I'm from Caldragh,' she said.

And then it was as though he was in a field, and he had lost his footing, and he had grabbed an electric fence for support. It went through him the same way. A jolt, a quick searing of everything's edges. Caldragh was a townland ten minutes up the road from Dorvaragh, and Mark had scarcely ever had reason to be there; he was on no more than nodding terms with anyone from there. But there was one name from Caldragh that he knew. And as he looked now at the girl in front of him, and around him at the scene in which she seemed so at ease, the circle to which she seemed to belong, that name was coming in on him like a current.

'I think I have you,' he said.

'You know me?' she said, smiling widely.

'I think so,' he said. 'Joanne Lynch, am I right?'

She gave a cheer, as though he had pulled her name from a hat. 'That's me,' she said. 'I knew you'd remember me. I knew you'd get me eventually.'

'Well,' Mark said, and then he couldn't think of anything else to say, so he smiled at her, and he took a long slug from his beer.

*

When she woke the next afternoon, sprawled on top of her bedclothes, with the sunlight pressing sharp against the closed curtains and the sound of children playing in the street below, Joanne was still dressed. And she felt like she was shaking. She was not trembling – she was doing something other than trembling; she was, it seemed, jumping, jittering, without even moving from where she lay. Her head was pounding with what felt like noise, but when she groaned and the groan came out as noise, she knew that what was in her head was pain, and her mind; her mind she could not stop from slamming, catapulting, through one vivid, disconnected image after another. All she got, and she could not slow it down, was a carousel of people's faces, saying things to her that she could not hear, because although their lips moved, their voices made no sound; Mark Casey's was one of them, and she tried to slow it down there, she wanted to slow it down, because although he kept flashing through her mind now, she could not remember what Mark Casey looked like. She could not remember what he tasted like; her mouth felt suctioned of everything but its own skin. She could remember only fragments of what they had said to each other, what they had done to each other, and the fragments were all out of order, were scattered impossibly across different parts of what did not even seem like the same night. She couldn't remember how she had got home. She could remember talking to him, and flirting with him, and kissing him, and going into a bedroom with him, and doing a line, and doing another, and doing another, and at some stage going into another bedroom and finding someone already fucking someone else in there, and then what? What had they done instead? She could remember talking, a lot of talking, and sitting on his lap and holding his face and telling him things it suddenly felt like a very big relief to tell, and she cringed at that now, because she could not remember what those things were, but if it had felt like a relief to tell them, it meant that, really, they were not meant to be told at all. And she could remember his friend with the fat face coming up to them and roaring, with absolute joy, 'Blondie's snogging another chick!' and that was Sarah, her housemate, getting together with that girl she had been trying to score for ages, which was why Sarah would not be here now, to do what they always did for each other when they were destroyed the morning after: to answer the weak knock on the bedroom wall and bring in painkillers, bring in a washcloth soaked in cold water, bring in a fucking sleeping tablet so that you could pass out and be unconscious for whatever else it took to get to the end of this nightmare.

She was already dreading the next morning. She had brought home so much work to do this weekend, and she hadn't even looked at it. There was no way she was going to get it done today. If she went near it, she would probably make such a mess of it that she would be fired more quickly than if she never did it at all. It was horrible work, case notes and court transcripts, and the client, who was at the moment taking up most of the time and energy of Brennan and Mullooly, the firm with which she was doing her traineeship, was a sleazy, pompous boor. But it was a traineeship. They were hard to get. They were worth it for what, hopefully, they led to: a real job doing the kind of work you wanted to do. What Joanne wanted to get into was family law, of which Brennan and Mullooly did very little, and the partners' ideas about training seemed to revolve mainly around how much photocopying needed to be done. What legal work she was allowed to do was dull – conveyancing and probate, both of which left her buried for hours in convoluted leases and deeds – and there had been no chance, so far, to go to the courts; that privilege was reserved for the other trainee, Mona, because Mona had been there almost a year longer. Mona got all the court work, and all the coffee breaks and walks in the fresh air and conversations with other people that went with it, while Joanne stayed in the small, dusty office and photocopied so many documents that in the evenings she saw the glint of the Liffey through phantom flashes of yellow.

She could have got a better traineeship. It would have taken one phone call. During the summer when she had worked for him, her father had introduced her to one of the local councillors and made very clear that if there was anything she wanted she had only to let the councillor know.

'That man will do any child of mine a fair turn,' her father had said, and over that summer, she had learned just what her father's idea of a fair turn involved. Documents vanished. Signatures materialized. Guards came around for nightcaps; the councillor Joanne had met came around whenever he pleased. She typed up one threatening letter after another as her father dictated without even looking up from his newspaper; when people, often old people, came in for meetings with him and left looking deathly pale, it was Joanne's job to draw up their bills before they had even reached their cars. Other cases were shadier, dealt with only by her father; one had to do with land for an apartment block, another with funds from an unresolved will, another with a drink-driving case in which a local man had been killed. For the work she did, she was not paid; that was not part of the deal. Her father was giving her experience, he told her, and he was giving her contacts, and for the last twenty years, anyway, he had been giving her a roof over her head, and would she type up that letter now like a good girl and then get the solicitor in Longford on the phone.

Sometimes, especially when he had been drinking, her father told her how much it meant to him that one of his children was following him into the trade. But none of her brothers had followed him – none of them had wanted, particularly, to work that hard at school. If there had been a shortcut, their father would have bought it for them, but there was no shortcut, and so he had got Joanne.

And then one day, during that one summer she worked for him, Joanne had packed her things and walked out of his office while he roared abuse at her, and she had gone back up to Dublin, back to the terraced house in Stoneybatter that he had bought as an investment years before, so that he could play at being landlord: the house Joanne had lived in, rent-free, since coming to the city. She kept living there, always intending to move elsewhere, always intending to free herself of this one last debt to her father, but when he dropped dead of a heart attack two years after that summer in his office, she discovered that he had willed the house to her; that it was hers. And yet, in those two years she and he had barely spoken a word to one another. It was something – the silence, but also, probably, the inheritance – for which her mother had never forgiven her. It was something – or rather, something else – for which her brothers scorned her. But she was long past caring what her mother and her brothers thought of her.

When she had passed her first set of law exams, and her mother had told her to call one of her father's old friends, to get them to put a word in with one of the big firms, she had refused. She had posted the applications, and waited for the rejections to come, and they had come – the firms her father's friends would have got her into, the firms her classmates longed for, the firms she would have loved to get into herself. Her mother had told her she was ignorant. Each of her brothers had had his own take – Paul said she was stupid, Kevin said she was looking for attention, Frankie told her she was good for nothing and would end up as nothing, and that this was all that she deserved. And when the letter from Brennan and Mullooly had come, and she had gone to their offices to meet them, and Eoin Brennan had asked her whether she had any family background in the law, she had told him that her father had been a schoolteacher and that her mother had worked in a bank.

'You'll be a self-made woman, so,' he had said, winking at her, and she had shrugged, and smiled as nicely as she could.

*

She watched junk on the television all evening, the pile of untouched court transcripts dismayingly within sight. She was hungry, but there was only some cereal and milk, and the thought of getting dressed and going down to the Centra made her feel like she might start shaking again, so she ate a bowl of Rice Krispies and then a bowl of Weetabix, and as the evening wore on she repeated that pattern until she had emptied both cereal boxes. She also drank tea, lots of it, and as the nine o'clock news ended and the Sunday evening film began, she almost began to feel human again, and she stretched out on the lumpy couch, sighing in what sounded like contentment but was actually just relief.

The sound of the doorbell sent a scalding sensation through her chest and down to her fingers and toes. She stepped down the hall as quietly as she could; in this neighbourhood, pleasant as it was, it was not uncommon for a night-time visitor to come bearing a heroin habit, or a needle, or a question about a recent crime involving a heroin habit and a needle.

But it wasn't a junkie. It wasn't a guard. It was him. And so that was what he looked like. It was coming back to her, not all of it but some of it, as she peered out through the yellowed peephole, her hands pressed to the wide frame on either side of the door. She remembered him: he had waited with her at the bus stop on the sea road for nearly an hour that morning, the sharp wind bullying their bare skin, families passing by on their Sunday-morning outings. He had pulled her into him, let her have his coat, stared with her out to the pier as the ferry from England sailed in. He was dark-haired, messy-haired, and he was drunk now, she could see that, as he looked not into the peephole but everywhere else: up to the bedroom windows, down to the keyhole, left and right to the narrow street empty of everything except closing-time waifs and strays like him, stumbling home.

And then he swooped out of view, and there came the rattle of the letterbox. She pressed herself against the wall.

'Too late,' he said, and he pushed his hand through the slot. Something was scrawled on it in messy blue hand-writing, in *her* handwriting, she saw: her address. 'Too late,' he said again. 'I know you're in there. I saw your legs.'

She said nothing. She watched as he waggled his fingers in her direction, as his hand groped the air like the hand of a child playing blind man's buff. His wrist was thin. It was upturned, and through its skin she could see the blue of his veins branching up into his palm. When she reached her own fingers out to his twitching ones, she did not touch them at first, but circled them, slowly, with the curve of her hand, and cupped them, still without touching, from below. Then she raised her hand slightly. His fingers stilled. She ran a finger and thumb along each one, feeling how slender they were, how hard their bones, how smooth and cool their skin. She unlatched the door. Almost as soon as his grasp had slipped away, the rest of him was on her. He tasted of beer and smoke and of the cold night air.

Chapter Three

Joanne made it to her desk by eight, and once she had had a coffee and got down to the work of the transcripts, it wasn't so bad. She was actually interested in the case, she remembered, even if she did sympathize far less with their own client than with the plaintiff. It was a dispute over property: a man was being sued by his mother for demolishing a building at the back of her house and putting a restaurant in its place. Their client was the son, who maintained that his mother had signed the building – a mews house – over to him years previously, granting him permission to do with it whatever he pleased. The mother was in her eighties, and in the transcripts her personality came vividly through; she was determined, she was elegant, and she was proud. Joanne found herself reading the mother's words as though they were the lines of a novel with which she had fallen in love; the haughty paragraphs seemed to her beautiful, the way they rambled backwards into long-ago passages of the old woman's life. This morning she was going back over the account the woman had given in court the week before of her relationship with her son, who had been born in East Africa, where the woman and her husband, an officer in the British Army, had been based in the 1950s. Shortly afterwards, they had moved to Dublin, and her husband had bought the house on Fitzwilliam Square, and then, a couple of years later, very suddenly, her husband had died. At first, the woman said, she had 'minded terribly', and found the house with its four floors and its high ceilings and its huge windows onto the park too much to bear, but in time she had come to love it again. And she knew, she said, that her son, only a schoolboy when he lost his father, had come to love the house too.

But as he grew up, she said, her son grew fond of the old mews at the back of the house, which had never been renovated, which was still, for all purposes, a stable; downstairs, it still looked ready for a horse and carriage, and upstairs, it was just a couple of shabby rooms with a fireplace that smoked badly. Rupert did not care about the fireplace, or the damp on the walls. Rupert liked to invite his schoolfriends there, to have them gather in the narrow rooms to listen to records, or to play card games, or to do whatever it was that boys of his age liked to do. And Elizabeth – that was the woman's name, Elizabeth Lefroy – had liked to stand at her own sitting-room window and look down on the mews, and to think of the life happening within its walls, of her son and his little circle. Slowly but surely, then, her son had begun to move all of his things into the mews, to decorate the walls with photographs torn from magazines, to add his own books to the squat pine shelves. And the summer after he had finished school – the months before he started at Trinity – he had begun to sleep in there every night. Elizabeth had worried about him – that he was not warm enough, that he would wake up hungry in the night and have no fridge to go to – but her son had told her not to worry, that he could take care of himself. And then, while he was at college, he had started, on Sunday afternoons, to do this 'darling thing', she said, of inviting her over for lunch, even though there was no kitchen to speak of in the place; he had ordered in, and together they had enjoyed all sorts of dishes at the rickety little table, and all kinds of wines, and they had talked, and her son had told her about his plans for his career, and asked her to tell him things he could not know or remember about his father, and about Kenya, and about all the people she and his father had known there. She had told him these things, and he had listened to her and, she felt, they had grown closer still, and that was a joy, she said, 'a marvellous joy'. And on Sunday evenings, when she had crossed the yard to the main house – to her own house, as she had thought of it by then – she had begun to feel, somehow, as though she were the one living in the chilly little rooms, as though she were the one who was, as she put it, no longer quite at home.

The rattle of the doorknob startled Joanne. As she turned to greet Mona, the other trainee, she felt herself flush, guilty at her absorption in Elizabeth Lefroy's testimony, at the fullness with which she had been living through these moments of the old woman's life.

'Morning,' she said, too brightly.

'You're in early,' Mona said, as Joanne had known she would. She looked perfectly put-together, as always; today a dark linen suit – a new one, Joanne thought – carefully pressed, the skirt hitting just below the knee, and black patent heels, and her makeup as flawless as though she had come from a stool in the Brown Thomas cosmetics hall.

'Catching up,' Joanne said. 'I didn't get much done over the weekend.'

Mona smiled knowingly as she laid her huge leather handbag on her desk. 'Must have been a good one, so,' she said.

Joanne shrugged. 'It was fine.'

'Yeah, right,' Mona said. 'You're blushing. You're *scarlet*. Something went down.' She smirked.

It would have been easy to take it from there; to talk about meeting him, about the party, about him turning up at her door last night, about how he had come in and kissed her for ten minutes and then fallen asleep on the couch, about how she had covered him with a blanket and left him there for the night, about how bashful and sweet he'd been earlier, as she was leaving for work. He'd made her promise that she'd answer her phone when he called her later that week; he'd asked for her number, then, and discovered that he'd lost his own phone. And so he'd written her number, too, on the hand with the blurred ink.

But coke rooms and hangovers and hands through letterboxes and lost phones were not, she suspected, Mona's idea of a fine romance, and Mona would be horrified, and probably a little disgusted, by the idea of leaving a stranger on your couch and trusting him not to steal anything – let alone by the idea of letting that stranger sleep on your couch while you yourself were asleep just a staircase away. Mona was not that kind of girl. She still lived with her parents in Castleknock. The only powder that went near her nose came out of a compact marked Chanel. She expected her boyfriends to be in control and in possession of a number of things, including their own apartments, in which they did not, ever, pass out on their own expensive couches. The parties she went to were catered. The gardens she sat in were not attached to the back walls of Thomas Street pubs.

'So how was your weekend?' Joanne asked, because it seemed polite.

'Oh, you know,' Mona said, and launched into an account of how swamped the Dundrum centre had been on Saturday, and how it always seemed impossible to get her size in anything in Harvey Nichols, and how some new restaurant on Dawson Street had sushi to die for, and how she thought maybe that she was getting tired of the nightclub she and her friends always went to on Saturday night, but how there was nowhere else worth going to, really, so what could you do?

'Right,' said Joanne, summoning all her reserves of empathy. 'I suppose those places get tired fairly quickly, don't they?'

'They really do,' Mona said, spinning around in her chair and seeming about to extend the analysis, but then she took a long look at the open folder on Joanne's desk. She frowned. 'That's the transcript from the Lefroy case?'

Joanne nodded.

'Crazy old bat,' Mona said.

'She's definitely eccentric,' Joanne said, and Mona arched an eyebrow.

'I couldn't *believe* the stuff she was coming out with in the witness box. She sounded like she was high on something. You know?'

'Mmm,' Joanne said. She looked at the last sentence she had underlined in the transcript. *No longer quite at home.* She thought of Elizabeth Lefroy crossing the yard at dusk on Sunday evenings, standing in the window of her silent home, looking out at the smoke-clogged outhouse her son had made his own. She imagined her in the witness box, deep lines on her face, a necklace of dark stones – jet, she thought – at her throat, a soft cardigan hanging on her thin frame. She tried to imagine her voice. She kept hearing one that, embarrassingly, was probably the Queen of England's. She tried to be more imaginative than that, but the Queen or some woman from *Poirot* was the best she could do.

'Eoin says she drinks a lot,' Mona went on, sorting through the pages on her own desk now, putting a stack into her drawer. 'And then there's her age. Her age makes it easy for us, really.' She slammed the drawer shut, pulled her chair up tight to her desk, and turned her computer on with one gleamingly manicured finger. The previous week, Joanne had seen Imelda look at Mona's nails, then glance at her own, and then – all in the time it took her to take a document from the folder she was carrying and hand it to Mona – peer over the room to where Joanne's unpainted nails, with their calcium spots and tattered cuticles, were hammering away on her keyboard. Imelda had given her usual curt nod then, evidently satisfied that her grooming was not the worst in the office, and their morning briefing had begun.

'You know she's over eighty?' Mona said, over her shoulder, while her computer screen drifted through the slow, whirring slideshow of its start-up. 'I mean, her testimony's *clearly* unreliable. At that age, who isn't delirious? Anyway, it's poor Rupert I feel sorry for.'

'The son?'

'Yes, the son, obviously,' Mona said, turning around with an expression of disbelief. 'He's only our client, for Christ's sake!'

'Sorry,' Joanne said. 'Wasn't thinking. Not fully awake.'

Mona took a small mirror from her desk drawer and checked her makeup; seeming to see some flecks of mascara beneath her eyes, she brushed at them with the quick, delicate strokes of a fingertip. 'God, I've been awake since six,' she said. 'I hate dragging myself to the gym, but what can you do?'

'I don't know,' Joanne said vaguely, and looked down to the page in front of her, back to Elizabeth's words. *Clearly, they just meant so much more to me than to him*, she was saying. She was talking about the Sunday afternoons in the mews. Her counsel had asked Elizabeth whether she now suspected those afternoons merely to have been part of a ruse, and

Elizabeth was saying, no, that she did not think that, that she could not think her son, back then, capable of such deceit. Such capability came later, her counsel offered, and Elizabeth, then, said nothing at all.

'Actually, it was Rupert's new restaurant I ate in on Saturday night,' Mona said now.

'Nice,' said Joanne, with what she hoped would be enough enthusiasm to satisfy Mona.

'God, omakase to die for. Rupert says it's as good as anything you'll get in New York.'

'You met Rupert in the restaurant?'

Mona looked around and gave Joanne a frown that suggested she really wasn't keeping up. 'I was *with* Rupert at the restaurant. He invited me. He said it was important for us to know the kind of establishment he runs.'

'Oh,' Joanne said, as evenly as she could. Mona's little crush on the Lefroy son had been evident for a while now. Joanne didn't think Mona could be sleeping with him – she couldn't be that stupid: word would spread, it would hobble her career – but she was definitely past the point of professional objectivity, flirting with him on his visits to the office, joking with him on the phone. It was nothing new: any guy with a whiff of power seemed to get her going. It was something, maybe, that Joanne should have a word with her about – a friendly word, a word to prevent Mona from making herself look unprofessional in front of Imelda and Eoin – but, then, Joanne and Mona were not friends. If they were friends, Joanne would surely not have been doing, in her head, what she had been doing at some level all morning: mentally retelling the story to Mark. Picking out the moments, mimicking the sentences, ramping up the details, so that in her mind she saw him laugh, or exclaim, or shake his head in wonder or enjoyment or incredulity; saw him watch her as she told him the story, saw him like her for it, all the more. 'She sounds like a dose,' she imagined Mark saying of Mona, and she saw herself smiling, and eating another forkful of the dinner they would be having together, and taking a sip from her glass of wine.

'Rupert's *huge* into sushi,' Mona said then, and Joanne imagined the mileage she and Mark would get out of this statement, and how much he would appreciate that she could make that kind of joke, and then he would make a joke of his own about it in return. Though, on second thoughts, that might be awkward.

'Have you been to the other restaurant?' she asked Mona, because she wanted, somehow, to shake all of these images – Rupert, Mona, sushi, Mark's jokes about sushi – out of her head. Then, as an afterthought, more to herself than to Mona, she said, 'It's not a sushi restaurant as well, I hope.'

'Nope,' Mona said. 'It's fusion. And it's *gorgeous*. I mean, it's obvious he did the right thing with the place. I can't imagine how that old witch thinks she has a ghost of a chance to win.'

Rupert Lefroy had lived in his mother's mews all the way through his time at Trinity, and for a couple of years afterwards, while he tried to make a name for himself writing on politics for one of the Sunday newspapers. But he lacked discipline – he had admitted as much himself, in his first meeting with Eoin – and soon even the friends of his father who had been putting work his way tired of his disregard for deadlines, and of the signs, which displayed themselves more and more blatantly with every piece he wrote, that his grasp of politics, not to mention political history, was extremely selective. He moved to London and, with the bulk of his inheritance from his father, opened a restaurant in Knightsbridge, which within five years had made him 'moderately wealthy', he told Eoin. He had married a model – a catalogue model, actually: Joanne had googled her – bought a Jaguar (no googling required) and built a country house that had involved some complicated and very expensive levelling work on a field in the Cotswolds. Within another five years he was divorced, almost bankrupt, and hatching plans for a return to Dublin, which was then in the first flush of the boom.

Joanne had read both sides of the rest of the story, from the court transcripts, but it was Elizabeth's version that had stuck in her mind: delighted to see Rupert home, she had agreed readily when he explained that, for tax reasons, it would be of enormous benefit to him to be able to claim the mews as his own. He would be living in it, he had promised her, and he would not be using it for anything else; certainly for nothing commercial. The lease he had had his own solicitor draw up had included this condition, he assured her. She had trusted him, and she had not felt the need to read through the final draft of the lease, and shortly after signing it, she had woken one morning to find a demolition crew setting up in her yard and roaring at her, when she ventured out her door, to get back into the house. When the new restaurant opened a few months later, its design was hailed as a triumph of modern sophistication, mainly, Elizabeth added, by the publicists Rupert had hired to secure him ample coverage in the Dublin papers. But for her own part, she said, she had stood at her window and wept as she watched the brick walls come down and, later, the glass walls go up; watched them carry into the place a 'ghastly' steel spiral staircase without a banister. It was her one small comfort, she said, that some people from the Health and Safety Authority had forced Rupert to put a banister on the staircase after all, but it was still ghastly. And the restaurant was not a place into which she would ever venture; not that she would ever be invited. She had declared her intention to sue almost as soon as the demolition crew had gone for lunch that very first day, and she and Rupert had not shared a civil word since. It was, she said, a source of unspeakable pain to her. But she did not know what else to do.

When she read that detail in the transcript, about the lack of an invitation, Joanne had hesitated over whether to include it in the case notes. Whether or not Elizabeth felt welcome in the restaurant was, after all, beside the point. The question was whether Rupert Lefroy had tricked his mother into signing away her rights to keep the mews house the way it had always been.

'And he's put all these absolutely divine paintings on the walls,' Mona said. 'None of your Graham Knuttels.'

'Right,' Joanne said lightly, and typed a few nonsense words on to her screen, signalling with the clatter of her keyboard that the exchange was over, and that it was time to disappear into the wordless hum of work in which they were both expected to be immersed every morning when Eoin and Imelda arrived.

'Well, rather you than me, reading that old windbag,' Mona said, and she turned back to her screen.

*

Waking up that morning had not been among the more pleasant experiences in Mark's life. It wasn't the hangover, though certainly that was bad enough; he had agreed, after coming home from the party on Sunday morning, with Mossy's suggestion that they postpone the inevitable by heading to an early-house. So, the hangover was atrocious, but the hangover was not what was causing him to cringe: it was the fact of what he had done the night before, turning up plastered on Joanne's doorstep, falling into her house, collapsing into Christ knew what kind of a flailing, snoring, farting mess on her couch. He had no memory of having been awake on the couch the night before, even for a couple of minutes. Joanne had said, when she had brought him in a cup of tea that morning, that they had talked for a while before he 'dozed off', as she so delicately, so sweetly, put it; but when he asked her what they had talked about she had just given him a sort of teasing shake of the head, told him that she knew all his secrets, and then gone around the room, picking up folders and stuffing them into her handbag and cursing about the creases in her suit. And then she had left.

He had let himself out of the house half an hour later – there had been no chance of any more sleep: the self-loathing had already been too intense – and it was only when he hit the fresh air that he realized how bad he smelled. When he had found Mossy asleep on the couch in their place he had woken him with a dig in the ribs and told him that they were never going to another early-house, ever again, and Mossy had grunted and sat up and produced Mark's phone from his jeans pocket, and then he had flopped back down on the couch. Then, in the shower, there had come the next high point – throwing up all over the little corner gang of shower gels and shampoos, and for a moment Mark had considered leaving the clean-up to Mossy, as a sort of thank-you note. But it would probably be bad karma, he thought, and he needed all the help he could get.

Nor could he remember anything he had said to her at the party – at least, not after the coke had kicked in. He was not sure he wanted to remember. And he felt pretty shit about the coke as well, about having taken it with her. He felt guilty, but not guilty because he had somehow led her astray – it was obvious that she had done it before. Guilty, rather, that he had let her see him in such a fitful, shit-talking state, because that was how he was on coke, that was how everybody was, and he wished she hadn't seen him like that. He didn't know how many lines they'd ended up doing, but he knew it was more than was wise. *One* was more than wise, for fuck's sake. He'd promised himself he was finished with that shit for good. It wasn't like he did it very often, maybe once every couple of months, maybe more at certain times of the year than others; it was just that he was getting a bit fucking long in the tooth for all of that, by now; it was that he wished he hadn't had to go and make such a jabbering prick out of himself in front of her the first time they'd talked. And he couldn't remember what, if anything, they had done in the bedroom – had they even been in a bedroom? He had a vague memory of a bed, but he also had a vague memory, now that he thought of it, of someone else already being on the bed, on top of someone else. So where had they done it, whatever they had done? He had a vague memory now, too, of having spouted some stuff to her, while he was touching her, while he was getting off with her; he groaned. That was the problem with coked-up sex, or with any kind of physical contact while you were on coke: you just ended up saying – shouting – the most excruciating things. You went from being someone who knew how to make all the right moves – all the hair-stroking, all the eye-contact, all the kissing and caressing it took to get over the threshold of the bedroom door – to someone who was bellowing at a girl to know who her daddy was while at the same time trying to ignore the fact that you couldn't really get properly hard.

At least, at *least*, he had not said that to her. But it was hardly as though the question had not been, and was not still, hanging over their heads. At the party, after she had told him who she was, before they had gone anywhere near the coke, he had tried, by a series of apparently harmless questions, to work out whether she knew anything about the history between their fathers. About what her father had done to his. About how his father had reacted. About the fact that his father still held a grudge. But she had given no sign of knowing anything. She talked mainly about growing up where they had grown up, about trying to get into the pubs in Edgeworthstown, about hitching lifts to the shitty clubs in the Fountain Blue, about seeing Mark around the place sometimes, and – this part had swollen his head pretty nicely – wondering about him, wondering if he had noticed her. He could remember that part. And he could remember, too, that she had talked for a while about her father, about working for him one summer and hating every minute of it; he remembered being relieved to hear that, relieved that he would not have to listen to her gushing about the dead father she still worshipped and adored. He had been crooked, she said; as crooked as a briar and just as nasty to come into contact with. Mark had said nothing. She had fought with him, she said; he had wanted her to fiddle with a will or something, and she had refused, and had walked out of the job, and she had never talked to him again before he died. That had been an opportune moment for hair-stroking, and for a concerned arm around her shoulders, and for a comforting little hug that had had the very satisfactory ending of a long, deep kiss, and it was a couple of minutes after that, actually, that he had suggested they take a trip into the room with the mirror and the marching powder. It had got him high, the feeling of her body in his arms, her tongue moving against his, her gorgeous, full little ass in his hands, and he had wanted to get higher still, had wanted to go that high with her coming along for the ride. And so that was how it

65

had started. But where they had gone, in terms of talking and touching and everything else at which they had spent the next seven or eight hours, he didn't know. All he knew was that she had seemed pretty friendly to him this morning. She had been smiling, and slagging him, and she hadn't seemed to be pissed off with him, or wary with him, about anything he had said or done, and when he had asked her if he could call her during the week, she had given him her number, and given him this cheeky little look at the same time. So maybe, after all, things weren't that bad, but Mark couldn't believe that; maybe the reason for her cheerfulness was actually that he had given her so much ammunition against him that she felt, he didn't know, powerful or something, standing over him like that in her business suit. That suit: if he could see her again right now in that suit it would do a million good things for his mood. But he had to see someone else in a suit now. And it was not going to go well.

He looked rough enough. That was some reason for hope; his skin was pale, his eyes were heavily shadowed. So the excuse he had invented for his supervisor might just work. And in case McCarthy brought up the obvious point – that he had had a year, not just a single weekend, to write this chapter – Mark stuffed a folder of notes into his rucksack. He could offer it to McCarthy as evidence that he'd been working.

The nerves really started to hit as he walked through Front Arch. McCarthy had the power to take his funding away, and without his funding, Mark could not continue his PhD. He could not afford to. A part-time job would not pay his rent, and a full-time job would make it impossible for him to do his research and to write. He did not allow himself to think about the fact that a year of not needing to work at all had done nothing to advance his writing, and little to advance his research; that was the way with most PhD students, he told himself. Most of his peers in the department were in similar positions. And the ones who weren't just had less complicated relationships to their thesis subjects.

McCarthy was in his office with the door ajar. He answered Mark's knock with a lift of his eyebrows. 'Reporting for duty?'

To his horror, Mark felt himself blush. If he was blushing now, even before he started to tell the lie he needed to tell, what chance did he have of getting around McCarthy? He shook his head, more in disgust at himself than in reply to McCarthy's question, but it seemed to do both jobs at once, because immediately, McCarthy's face took on an expression of practised exasperation.

'You're not serious. Are you serious?'

'Sorry,' Mark blurted. 'I was sick the whole weekend. Food poisoning. I ate something Thursday evening . . . Salmon . . .' He could see from McCarthy's set jaw that he didn't believe a word of it.

'And, what, in your fever you accidentally destroyed all the work you've done over the last six months?'

Mark wanted to sit down. No, he wanted to stand. Did he? What did he want to do? He wanted to escape. McCarthy hadn't invited him to come into the office, to sit, to come closer. He was still standing at the door. And to McCarthy's question he had no answer. How could he not have worked out an answer to that question? He had known it was coming.

'You've been working on this chapter since Christmas,' McCarthy said, pointing finally to a chair opposite his desk. 'Are you telling me that a few days of puking fish has made all the difference?'

Mark had to move a couple of copies of *English Studies* off the chair in order to sit. McCarthy had told him to submit something to *English Studies* the year before, he remembered, with a pang of guilt; he had meant to get around to it, but he had never seemed to have enough time. 'It's just not ready,' he said now, and McCarthy snorted.

'It's never ready with you, Mark,' he said, putting both hands behind his head. When McCarthy did that pose – the one that made him look like he was trying to sunbathe under the fluorescent lights, tilting the two front legs of his chair up off the floor – you knew you were fucked. He was getting into withering dismissal mode. He was gearing up to tell you you might as well forget the whole thing.

'I've these . . .' Mark said, opening his rucksack hurriedly. He took the pages from the manila folder. 'I mean, it's just a draft, but if you want to see what I've been doing?'

McCarthy stared down his nose at the pages. For one awful moment, it looked like he was about to reach over and take them. That would not be good. That would be a disaster. They were appalling. There were actual doodles on them. Mark had written his name in the margins at points. His edits consisted of scribbled, furious messages to himself, often containing expletives, telling himself what a fucking idiot he was to have written this paragraph, to have started this argument, to have started this thesis.

McCarthy looked at Mark for a long moment, and he seemed to decide something. Slowly, he took his hands from behind his head and sat up straight at his desk again. He sighed. 'Look, Mark,' he said. 'You need to meet me halfway here. I have to write to the board to argue your case before the end of this month. What am I meant to say to them, when you haven't given me anything? What am I meant to put on the form?'

He didn't wait for an answer. 'You were doing so well with this thing up to now,' he said, and his tone was different; it was quieter. It was, Mark realized with something of a jolt, sincere. 'What happened?'

'I don't know,' Mark said. He hadn't thought it was possible to feel any more disgusted with himself than he'd felt an hour previously, letting himself out of Joanne's front door, but he'd been wrong. McCarthy was right. What the hell had gone wrong?

'Is there something else going on for you, do you mind me asking?'

Mark stared. 'Something else?'

McCarthy looked out the window. 'Family stuff, personal stuff, whatever.' He turned back to Mark. 'Is there some bigger reason why you can't get on top of things?'

'No,' Mark said, and now when McCarthy looked at him he found it hard to look back. 'There's nothing wrong.'

'Well,' McCarthy said, 'I'm glad to hear that, I suppose. But this block of yours . . .' He shook his head. 'I mean, it seems to me to be a problem with your subject.'

'With Edgeworth?'

'Well, with this whole idea you're trying to elaborate about Edgeworth. The one you set out in your introduction. You're arguing something about Edgeworth being wrongly perceived as a realist writer, isn't that it?'

'Yes,' Mark said, but when McCarthy nodded at him to go on, his mind went blank. 'I mean, I think she's been fundamentally misread,' he was finally able to say. 'I think she was more of an experimentalist, in her way, than has ever been understood.' He swallowed. 'I mean, I'd like to . . .'

'Oh, yes,' McCarthy said, his hands reaching back into the sunbathing pose. 'Now I remember. Outshandying Tristram Shandy since seventeen-whatever-it-is.' He coughed. Or he snorted, and he turned it into a cough. 'Well, it's different. I'll give you that.'

Fuck you, Mark thought. 'Well, I mean, she's obviously pretty different to Sterne,' he began, but McCarthy was waving his hands in the air now, and it seemed he wanted Mark just to stop.

'All right,' he said. 'All right.' He sat back into the desk and let his head drop low, as though he was tired. 'You know, Mark, this time tomorrow, I'll be in my car with the windows open and the kids watching their DVDs in the back and the wife staying quiet for once because we're finally getting out of Dublin and back down to Clonakilty.'

'Sounds good.'

'It is good.' McCarthy rubbed his hands together. 'It's a great spot. I can read a bloody book without visualizing a hall full of students staring up at me as I try to explain it. Do you know what I read when I'm on my holidays?'

'No.'

'As little as possible. Maybe a bit of crime. Maybe the papers.'

'Right,' said Mark, uncertainly.

'Do you know what I *don't* want to read on my holidays?'

Mark paused. He was conscious of having to give the right answer here. 'Edgeworth?' he eventually said.

'Close,' said McCarthy. 'Your bloody chapter on Edgeworth and her experiments. Or, worse still, your bloody notes towards your chapter on her experiments.'

'OK.'

'No offence.'

Mark shrugged. 'None taken.'

'Now, it's not as though I'm exactly going to be jumping out of my skin to read about Edgeworth the experimentalist when I get back from Cork in August, but I will. And I'll expect to read it.'

'OK,' Mark said slowly.

'It'll want to be more than OK,' McCarthy said. 'It'll want to be magnificent. And on the presumption that it will – on the presumption that you'll get out of here now and go straight to wherever you left your mojo and start working again, like you were working last year, I'll fill in this form, and I'll say I've read your latest, and I'll say you're sufficiently on track to have your funding renewed, and I'll send it to the board. All right?'

'All right,' said Mark, weakly. Then the wave of sheer relief that washed over him was met with the sensation of his skin detaching from his body and crawling right away from it as he thanked McCarthy effusively not once, not twice, but three times. 'I promise I won't disappoint, Maurice,' he heard himself say, the *pièce de résistance*, and he thought, If I had a pen in my hand right now I would use it to stab myself in the eye.

'Damn right you won't disappoint me,' McCarthy said, and he stood. 'But, Mark?'

'Yes?' Mark said, standing too, and his voice sounded very small. He should have said, 'Yeah?' not 'Yes?' he thought; it might have sounded less like he was lying on the ground under McCarthy's boot. 'Yeah?' he said then, before he could stop himself, and he heard the ridiculousness of it echoing around the room.

'Don't pull this shit on me again,' McCarthy said, as he walked him to the door. 'You're in your fourth year. You're not in a position to mess around. Do you understand?'

'I do,' Mark said, and he said goodbye. Then he spotted his bag where he had left it, under the chair he had been sitting on, and, making noises of apology to McCarthy, he had to duck back and get it, and apologize again, and say goodbye again, all while McCarthy looked at him with perfect indifference and, as he turned around to say a last - stop it! - goodbye, closed the door in his face with what definitely qualified as a bang.

In his jeans pocket, Mark felt his phone vibrate. He didn't need to answer it. He didn't need to check the number. It was Monday, and it was midday. He knew who it was.

Chapter Four

She had written novels, Maria Edgeworth, and Maura had tried to read one of them, but it had had nothing she could recognize. She liked to read, but only stories she could imagine happening around her, in her own time, in her own world. Anyway, any time she asked Mark about his writer, he said he was tired of her himself by now. He said he could not wait until the thesis was finished, until he did not have to think about her any more. And yet he could never really say when he thought that would be. Neither could he ever say, for sure, when he might able to come home again for a couple of days to help Tom with the work of the farm. Usually he just turned up, and usually just at the point where Tom's impatience seemed on the verge of darkening into real anger. He had inherited her own ability to gauge Tom's impatience at a remove, and to know when it was no longer a good idea to delay. She never asked him to come home; she would not plead. When he had to come, he came.

He was waiting at the station when she got there, sitting on a window ledge with his bag at his feet. He had cut his hair since last she saw him; it made him look like a boy again. He would soon be thirty, her only boy, and still she was driving to the station to meet him. Other women watched out their windows as their sons arrived from Dublin in their new cars, as they came for a weekend away from the jobs that had given them their houses, their dark pressed suits, their air of being older than they were. Whether she should want those things for Mark, whether she should feel disappointed in him for not having them, she could not tell. If there was a job like that, if there was a house, then the break between his life there and his life here would be clear: Tom could no longer push it, could no longer press his wanting on the situation until it yielded to him. But such a break would mean other things, too, things she did not want to picture, and so Maura never went on long with this line of thought. Mark could drive, but the train was cheaper, and handier, and that for now was probably the best way to have it, she thought. Besides, there was the drive in to meet him, the drive back to the house with him at her side. He was crossing the street to the car now, raising a hand in reply to her wave, smiling in a way that let her know that, as much as he loved her, she was an embarrassment, waving like that. He threw his bag in the back seat. He put one arm tight around her shoulders as he kissed her on the cheek.

'Well,' he said, and she started the car.

He was talkative. That was what surprised her. Usually on the way home from the station he only ever talked in response to her questions, or sometimes to ask questions of his own. But now he was full of news, volunteering stories, jumping from one thing to the next. Mossy, the lad he lived with, was going to be someone's best man in a couple of weeks, he said. The new flats in Smithfield were almost finished. In the grocery shop beside his house, he had got talking to an old woman somehow, and it had turned out she was from Ballymahon; she had known Tom's sister Rose in the domestic college in Ardagh. And coming out of the National Library the other evening he had seen Bertie Ahern and Brian Lenihan in front of the Dáil.

Maura stopped at Keogh's and asked him to go in for a batch loaf and a half-pound of ham. She had already been into Keogh's herself that morning and didn't feel like facing a second time into the bored curiosity of Annie McGurk, the girl behind the counter, into her questions about town, and whether it had been busy, and whether there had been many at the station, and how long Mark was home for this time. Annie McGurk had been in school with Nuala, which made her only thirty-one or thirty-two, but working behind that counter since her schooldays had turned her into the kind of character that was sent up, now, on television comedies. She asked too many questions, and she talked dull, mouthy circles on the same subjects all day to anyone who would listen. She would wring everything she could get out of Mark now, Maura knew. Probably he would come back to the car in a black mood, and maybe she should not have sent him in there after all, she thought; that mood was bound to come on him soon enough during his days at home. But she could not face into it herself again. She was too tired for it. She turned the car radio off and wanted nothing more than to close her eyes and get a few moments' sleep. But if she was seen sleeping in the car it would be all over the country by evening: they would say she was drinking, on anti-depressants, dying. Breda Keogh was probably watching her right now from the upstairs window.

Instead Maura fixed her gaze on Paddy Keogh's field beyond the petrol pumps, the field that had been wild, and scattered with wild-looking cattle, for as long as she had been about the place. Every other wild field in the area was a field of new houses now, and Keogh could make a fortune on his field if he sold it to the developers who were known to be interested in it, but Keogh would not sell. He would never believe that the price he was offered was the highest price he could get, no matter how high that price went, no matter by how much it climbed above the little that the land, in truth, was worth.

Maura had met Paddy and Breda Keogh long before there was any need to meet them. She and Tom had been going together for only five or six months at that stage, and there had been no reason, really, for him to bring Maura to see the place he had built up the road from his parents' old house, no reason for them to see each other anywhere other than in the dancehalls and pubs and at the pictures. But one Saturday night he had announced that he wanted to know what she thought of the house, and he had arranged to collect her from the manor the next evening and take her out to see it.

Since they had been together she had wondered what the house could be like, knowing that he had done it all himself in the two years since his mother's death; the building, the painting, the buying of the things inside. She tried to imagine it, a house furnished and decorated by a man all on his own, and she tried not to imagine what that could mean for her, what kind of place she was setting herself up for, getting closer and closer to every time she lifted her mouth to his in the front seat of his car. And so as they drove down that summer evening, the sun still high in the sky, she was as fearful as she was curious, and when he pulled the car into Keogh's yard she had looked at him and looked out at the rough-built house in front of her, the ugly extension piled up on top of what must have been an old cottage, and she had only shaken her head and tried not to burst into tears. It was not until Tom got out of the car and went into the house that she registered it, the way the door was wide open, the way there was someone already in there, looking out at her through the uncurtained window, the way that person was standing in front of shelves of what looked like sweets and chocolate bars, and reaching back, now, to those shelves to take something down. She had laughed at herself in relief, and seconds later, she had almost jumped out of her skin at a knock on the windscreen. Paddy Keogh had had more hair then, but the gap-toothed grin was the same, and the white shirt and black trousers were dirty-looking even on a Sunday. He had gestured at her to roll down the car window, and then he had thrust in at her a hand brown with sun and lined with grime, and shaken her hand so vigorously that she had wondered if the rocking she could feel was just herself or the whole car.

'This lad is the envy of the whole place with his little Anglia,' Keogh said, clapping his hand to the roof of the car. 'I'd say ye cover fierce country in her all the days we see Tom heading off there on the Longford road.'

Almost before Maura had nodded in reply he had her door open and was pulling her out; she was too surprised to resist, and found herself being ushered on through the shop door. There was a step down, and then she was in what seemed like a storeroom packed with everything anyone could ever want to buy. Plastic toys hung on strings from the ceiling beside onions and hoses and kitchen pans. Sacks of potatoes and cattle feed were lined up together along the inside wall. Women's aprons and housecoats were slung and stacked above the shelved cans and packets of food; bottles of orange and lemonade were stuffed into the legs of new wellingtons. In one corner a child's pram held boxes of carrots and parsnips, and in a set of shining metal buckets the local newspapers stood in neat, fat rolls. A machine for making ice-cream cones was the biggest thing in the room, and from its rubber-tipped handles a broken piece of Christmas tinsel trailed. Tom was hunched with both elbows on the counter, looking over his shoulder to where she stood at the door. He was buying a Swiss roll, a packet of cigarettes and a bag of Rowntree's Eclairs. When the woman came out from behind the counter to shake her hand, Maura saw that she was heavily pregnant; she looked only a couple of weeks from her time.

'You're used to seeing bellies like that, of course, lassie,' said Paddy Keogh, and Maura heard, as though on a crossed wire, the echo of the gossip about her that must have been exchanged in this very room. She imagined the snatches of information: how she was from Dromod, was a nurse in the manor; her father was dead; her mother entered knitting and embroidery into the summer shows; her brother ran the farm. She imagined them talking about how she and Tom had met at the dance in Newtown, and they had been to dances as far away as Athlone and Drumshanbo since then, as though the local dances weren't good enough for them.

Maura knew the drill: it was the same in Dromod when someone from around started going with someone from somewhere else. The particulars were quickly gathered and gleefully spread. Bits were tacked on to the stories, extra details added, regardless of their distance from the truth. She didn't care. Tom was a good man, and a good-looking man, and she was proud to be seen with him. Still, she wished Paddy and Breda Keogh would stop looking her up and down with their small little eyes.

'And you'll be gettin' used to bellies like that yourself, Tom, be the looks of it,' Keogh spluttered with laughter.

'We're not all poor cornered bastards like you, Paddy,' Tom said. Taking up his shopping, he nodded to Maura to follow him, and she said an awkward goodbye to Keogh and to the woman, who were both now red in the face and looking out after Tom. In the car, the two of them laughed like children, and it was a relief to Maura to laugh over it, because it stopped her having to think about how else she should take it, what Tom had just said. Anyway, he proposed to her the next month, so whatever he'd meant by it, it couldn't have been what she'd feared. Probably he had just thought of it on the spur of the moment. Probably it had meant nothing at all.

Mark had begun to slouch when he walked; that was something Maura noticed about him now. He carried the batch loaf under one arm as though it were a newspaper, and he had the thin plastic bag of ham bunched up in his hand. She thought about saying something to him about that slouch, but then she was wondering, instead, about those worn-looking canvas runners he had on his feet. She tried to think about when she had first seen him in those shoes, when the soles had been bright and white instead of yellow and scuffed. It seemed like years. She didn't think it was lack of money had him going around with his shoes falling off him like that. She hoped not. He had his grant coming in, and he said that was enough to live on, and he had been with Mossy in that same house for six or seven years now, and the rent, he said, had hardly gone up at all. He never seemed to be wanting for money, and apart from the shoes, which really were in tatters now that she looked at them more closely, he was dressed smartly enough. A hooded top, like he was always wearing, and his jeans looked new, and he had a nice-looking watch on his wrist.

'That Annie McGurk is a nosy bloody bitch,' Mark said, tossing the groceries into the back of the car.

'Where are you after pegging my good bread?'

'It's batch. It's meant to be hardy.'

'You wouldn't know what kind of junk your father had on that back seat when he took the car this morning.'

'It's fine,' Mark said, in a tone that suggested he wasn't interested in talking about bread, or back seats, or his father.

She drove out past the petrol pumps, past the parked cars she recognized and put faces on as instinctively as though they were their owners themselves and not her neighbours' Almeras, Mondeos, Hilux jeeps. Even at this time of day the traffic was heavy: not for a few moments was it clear enough for her to pull out on to the road for home.

'First she wanted to know how long I was back for,' Mark said. 'Then she wanted to know whether I liked being at home. Then she wanted to know if I preferred being at home to being in the city. Then she wanted to know how I could stand living up there in the city, because she could never stand it herself, living in the middle of all those strangers and hooligans and junkies, and she wanted to know did I live in a house by myself or in digs, and when I said neither, she wanted to know how I could be sure of the people I was living with, and would I not be worried that they'd steal from me, or be 'ithin in their bedrooms doing drugs or something, and then did I hear what happened to Jimmy Flynn's niece 'ithin in the town, and did I ever see drugs myself, and did I know anybody who did drugs, and did I think that the judge would go hard on Jimmy's niece for what she did, sorry, what she done, and were you glad to see me, and wasn't Dad doing a great job around the place without me, and would I ever think of moving home and . . .' He shook his head and looked out the window. 'Jesus Christ, she's a bag.'

'She's full of questions, anyway.'

'Fuckin' bitch,' Mark said, and Maura wondered if she should say something to him, but he was past that a long time now and, anyway, he was probably right.

'Jimmy's niece was caught dealing Ecstasy or something, I don't know,' she said, trying to change the subject.

'I don't know her.'

'She's younger than you. Poor Jimmy had to bail her out. I think the case is up next week. They say she'll probably be all right unless she gets Naughton.'

'Naughton is the woman?'

Maura nodded. 'She's the one is always being given out about on *Liveline*. The one that said things about Africans hanging around the shopping centre and girls dressing up like they wanted to get raped.'

'Jesus Christ,' Mark said, but he was barely listening to her now, she could tell: he was looking at his phone. He wiped the screen with the pad of his thumb and clicked through the keys. Wondering who he was making contact with, or who was making contact with him, was an old instinct Maura had learned to bat down in herself as quickly as it bubbled up; still, it did bubble up, and her mind flicked, as it used to do when he was a teenager answering the phone in the house, through a rapid list of possibilities. She knew some of his friends, heard him talking about others, had a gallery of imagined faces for the rest; the kinds of friends he must have now, the kinds of women he might be associating with, going with, sleeping with, which was something she still found strange to think. At nearly thirty, how many women would a man have slept with, these days? Was it really like the television programmes made it out to be, that parade of one-night stands, that stumbling from one hurried, noisy affair to another? No problems taking their clothes off in front of each other nearly straight away, no problems looking each other in the eye afterwards, no problems doing it at parties or in toilets or in public, even, girls not even blinking about going down on their knees and opening their mouths in the corner of a nightclub? She couldn't imagine. Before Tom, other men had slid their hands between her thighs in the front of a car, and there had been the backs of cars, too, but there were things everybody got up to and there were things you knew it wasn't permitted to do, and that night in the Abbey Hotel had been her first time, Tom her first man, and what people Mark's age did with each other now she regarded with a mixture of envy and exhaustion.

Mark's hands were freckled, already growing brown, though the summer had only just begun to suggest itself, and there was a bony strength to them, a gnarled, awkward kind of strength. For a moment Maura tried to imagine herself as a girl, looking at those hands; tried to think would she be drawn to them, would she look at them and feel herself feeling a certain way, and for that moment she thought she would, and then she realized that Mark was aware of her eyes on him.

'Mossy,' he said.

'What?'

'Mossy, texting to know if I wanted to go to a gig this evening.'

'Did you not tell him you were coming down here?'

'I don't know,' Mark said, and it was exactly as he had tried to lie to her when he was a child.

Mossy had a real name. She tried to think of it. Thomas, it must be. Or more than likely Tomás, the Irish, with the end of it sounding so much like *moss*. He was a nice lad, friendly, but watchful, from what she imagined as a wild sort of family down in Kerry or somewhere. Wild partly because Mossy had huge tumbles of curls, and a face too craggy for his age, and partly because there were a lot of them in Mossy's family, as far as she could remember, eight or nine of them, she thought. And it wasn't even that Mossy was the youngest, that he came from parents of that generation, from a mother who would do nothing to stop herself falling pregnant every twelve months; Mossy was nearly the eldest, and the youngest few were still in primary school, and Mark said they all looked alike, hair like that and hard little faces like that, all running around speaking Irish and not giving a damn. As far as Maura could gather, it wasn't religion that had had Mossy's mother going around pregnant so often: it was the enjoyment of it, of every bit of it, the bit with her husband and the bit with the child in her and the bit on her back in the hospital, even, and the bit with a whole straggle of youngsters traipsing around under her feet.

Maura would have had more. But more hadn't been possible for Maura, and that was what she had had to get used to. She was thankful, at least, that there had been one of each.

Meaning she was thankful that one of them, at least, had been a son. For Tom's sake. But for her own sake, as well. She had wanted a son. She had cried tears of real gratitude when he had arrived.

They were nearing home now. Mark glanced at each house as they passed; habit. Tom always did more than glance: Tom always stared, and from her own kitchen window she had seen others do the same to her porch, her shrubs, her freshly tarmacadamed drive. She saw them taking note of what was new, what was changing, what was theirs to mull over or to mock as they drove on. She herself glanced now at the last few houses before the lane: Bradys, with the trampoline at the back of the house for the grandchildren; Healys, with the pebbledash and the tiny windows; Murtaghs, with the beautiful curve of flowers all along the path to the door. As she turned into their own lane she knew that Mark was tensing; knew that Tom was likely to be at a gate or in a shed door now, listening for the sound of the car, readying himself to look busy and unbothered as it passed him by. All weekend he had been needling her with questions about when Mark was coming, when she had last called him, what it was that could have been keeping him away this long. He asked the same questions over and over, twice a day the same questions, maybe three times. That was habit, too, a habit she should have tried to get him out of a long time beforehand; if he asked about something often enough, it would happen. She would take steps, behind the scenes, to make it happen, for the sake of peace, for the sake of being able to go about her day. And when he asked again and again whether Mark was coming down, he was not trying to torment her, she knew: he was reaching, rather, with a muscle that had worked so often before. He was saying the words, and waiting for them to work. And now they had worked. Now she had brought him his son.

Chapter Five

In the kitchen, Mark sat with his parents over a lunch of cod and potatoes and salad, his mother pouring orange squash into the crystal tumblers she had started to use for everyday. The dog, Scruff, sat by the table, hoping for scraps. All through the meal, Tom kept up a steady delivery of local news, much of which Mark had already heard from Maura. But neither he nor his mother let on, listening and nodding and coming in with the right questions, at the right time. Now his father was talking about how Farrell, the vet, had become unpopular lately, how fewer around were using him any more, and how they were calling a new vet, a woman, instead.

'It's that or go to one of the foreign lads,' Tom said, laying butter thick across the potatoes he had peeled and crushed on a side plate. He smirked. 'There's nobody left to look after the poor fuckers of cats and dogs now that she's taken the cattle and the sheep off of Farrell.'

'Couldn't Farrell look after them?'

Tom snorted. 'Look after them with a grocery bag and a shotgun.' He tore off a small piece of fish and dropped it on the floor. 'You don't know how lucky you are, lassie,' he said to the dog.

'Tom,' Maura said, and she rolled her eyes at Mark.

They talked on through lunch and through the slices of the apple tart Maura had made that morning, and when they had drained their mugs of tea, Tom got up from the table and said he would see Mark outside. No mention of work was made. They would talk about the work as they were doing it, and with as few words as possible – words shouted from a tractor cab, nodded over quickly in the lean-to beside the barn. There was a language, and as long as it was spoken fluently the work always got done, but in fact it was less a language than a convoluted dialect, easy to slip into and almost impossible to translate. Mark watched from the table as his father stepped into the back kitchen and knew it was only a matter of hours before they would be roaring at each other, each of them unable or unwilling to understand the meaning of the other. He knew the rota, knew what needed to be done. To his father, it was a week's work; to him, it was something he intended to have over with in a couple of days. He reached for the pot and poured himself the last of the tea, and took the mug with him as he went up to the bedroom to change.

He pulled on old jeans and a flannel shirt, soft from years of washing but still stained with the shadows of cowshit. The shirt was years old, from when he was in fourth or fifth year at secondary school; everyone had been wearing them then, along with the kind of runners that were in that photograph of Kurt Cobain's sprawled feet, Kurt Cobain's dead feet. The kind of runners, come to think of it, that Mark was still wearing now. He pulled them off; they stank of sweat worn into dirty rubber. He rummaged in a drawer for a thick pair of socks.

From the window he could see his father in the yard below, working at the baler with a pair of pliers. He was tightening the pins below their metal shields, bent over the pick-up reel like a quilter tweaking his threads. By now he had lost almost all of his hair. The gleaming tan of his crown, its spray of dark freckles, was somehow disorienting. He was not old, and certainly not frail, but he carried about with him the indemnity clause of seeming an older man than he actually was; a cloud of anxiety that asked to be met with solicitude, attention, a kind of anticipatory grief. The trace of warmth on his skin, the healthy brownness of him, complicated this picture, even for all the hours working in wind and rain to which it actually attested. On the baler he worked deftly, moving between the parts without hindrance, without once seeming to linger, his tools neatly laid on the ground by his knee. Now he reached back into those tools for the thing he needed – the ratchet wrench – without even having to look.

Mark envied it in him, this ability to lock his thought down. His own attention was always darting, sputtering, untied. Reading, he would be four or five lines into a paragraph before he would think of something he wanted to see to, or listen to, or type into a search engine, and he would drift off on that thing, letting it tumble him into one new distraction after another until the clock demanded that he be somewhere, do something – and through that thing, in turn, he would almost sleepwalk his way. But his father's concentration was absolute. On a machine or on a match, he could fix and settle like this. Until the job was done or the whistle blown, nothing could pull his gaze out of its walled path of awareness, out of its still, determined hub. The rhythm of his father's hands was something Mark knew as intuitively as he knew the rhythm, even the feeling, of his own; and from where he stood, he could see exactly what remained to be done with the machine hitched to the back of the tractor, could see what way Tom would go about it, could tell where his glance fell, where his gaze fastened, where his mind pulled back for a moment, charting its next move.

And yet if he was out there with him now, they would be arguing, already, over the best way to deal with the pins. Mark would be trying to do it more quickly; he could see the short cut from here. And his father would be telling him that he rushed everything, that he could stay with nothing, that he had no patience, no steadiness, no sense.

He lifted his phone and clicked his way back into the text Joanne had sent him while he was in the car with his mother. Was he feeling better, the message had asked. He had tried to text her back, but his mother had been talking to him, asking him questions about Mossy, and he hadn't been able to think of anything to write; he had wanted his reply to be something funny, something wry, something that would cast him in a better light than the state she'd seen him in that morning. But his mother wasn't talking in his ear now, and he still couldn't think of the right thing to say. What was funny? What was wry? Should he ask her out now, or would that look like the action of a desperate fool? Should he tell her he was down home, or would it be presumptuous to think she was even interested in where he was? He stared at the message for another moment and then, snapping the phone shut, he left it on the dresser and went downstairs.

Chapter Six

He was there now, and that was what mattered. Tom had waited for him all weekend, and Maura had given him stories about college work and scholarships and money that had to be applied for, and he had accepted it all, and he had started the work by himself on Saturday morning, mowing the first few meadows, getting the grass into rows, going through them with the tractor and the old Claas baler. It was a sight, too, to think of that baler as an old one: when Tom had bought it, only ten or twelve years ago, he had been the talk of the country, he knew he had, but now it was a rusting, unreliable heap of a thing, and the last few hours had been spent fixing it up after another ordeal driving around an uneven field. Now, though, he had it ready to go, for another while at least. The hardest fields, the fields that dipped too sharply and went too suddenly into bogland at the edges, he had left for Mark to do; he preferred Mark to do them. Tom himself would go around the meadow with a pitchfork, making sure the rows were even, watching the bales as they came.

The weather was promised good for another two days; then the rains would come from the north and stay heavy on their part of the map over the weekend at least. The summers were getting worse. Tom knew he was not imagining those summers years ago. They had been long and hot and sometimes desert dry, but there was no point in talking about those summers now. They were gone. Mention of them in Keogh's of an evening drew only a silence that never seemed friendly. There were things nobody thanked you for reminding them of. There were years that had somehow slipped so far into the past that it was better not to mention them. People had been around then who were gone now, children had been small then, neighbours had been neighbours. Nobody around the place had been happier then, as far as Tom could remember it, but they acted now as though they had been happy in a way that they would never be happy again. It was best to leave it. People needed to have their ideas about what was gone; they needed them to hold on to.

For the week they would work together on the remaining fields, and then there would be the work of gathering the bales and of stacking them in the hayshed. There was other work, too, that Tom needed help with after the hay was saved; work he could do by himself, but that went more smoothly and more pleasurably with Mark at his side. He had been angry over the weekend, annoyed that Mark had not come down sooner, but he looked back on that anger now as though it had belonged to someone else. He checked the pins again and listened for the sound of the back door.

There had come two children, no more. It was enough and it was not enough; it seemed at once a blessing and a snub. All around them were families of four and six and even ten children, families crammed into cars and tearing around gardens; families too big, often, for the houses they were born into. But families that said what needed to be said about their fathers, that settled things into place for the years too far away yet to see. Tom and Maura had first a daughter and then a son. There had been only the beginnings of others. Two before Nuala, and another – late on, so late that it had been a shape, that Maura had taken to talking to it, even to naming it – around a year before Mark. And no more afterwards. Mark, the doctor had told Maura, was the last one there could be.

Nuala, to Tom, had been the same person all her life. She had seemed on her guard with him in the hospital when she was one day old, and she was still that way. The whole time she was small, all through her schooling years, then all her weekends home from college, she had been like that with him. Talking to him only in half-sentences. Giving him only half the story, and probably less than half the truth. Maura saw it in her too, said Nuala was secretive with her as well; said it was her age, but she said that about her no matter what that age happened to be. And in no time at all that age was almost the age Tom had been the year Nuala was born, and she was moving to London, coming home to see them only once or twice a year. She phoned often, and she and Maura had their chats, and on the phone to him she always told him a few things he liked hearing about her life over there, and asked how things were with him, but when she visited, he seemed never to have a conversation with her that lasted longer than their conversations on the phone. Always, she seemed only in the door with her suitcase – and now with her husband, a quiet English fellow called Denis – before she was heading off with the cases again, off to the airport, back to London.

The longest she had been home was for her wedding in the local church a mile from Dorvaragh. In the car that had talem them there, Tom had told her not to be nervous, and she had shown him how to fix the rose in his buttonhole. The air in the car had been struck with her perfume, and the skirt of her dress had spread out over almost the entire back seat, part of it resting, rustling, on his knee. The makeup she had worn made her skin look different, gave it a different colour and a new smoothness; her lips looked wet and glistening, and her eyelids were painted silver as a coin. All morning the house had been full of women bent down in front of mirrors, racing between the bedrooms and the sitting room with dresses and shoes and boxes in their arms. As the car pulled up to the church porch, Nuala had squeezed his hand once, and then she had opened the door for herself, before the driver could come around to her, and stepped outside. Tom had felt her shaking as he walked her up the aisle.

Mark was born three years after Nuala. His stare as Tom took him from Maura for the first time was steady and clear; Tom had carried him to the window and pointed down to the car park, down to where he had left the car; it had been the blue Escort, that time, with the dog-bone grille. The child had a red face like a drinker and a head of dark spikes. A broken vein above his left eye would, Tom thought, take years to fade away. From her bed, Maura called him back from the window. She was worried about draughts.

Almost from the day he could walk, the boy wanted to be outside with Tom. He was a strong child, sturdy, and he was infatuated with the things of the farm. Hearing the splutter of a tractor engine, he would rush to the window, demanding to see it, offended if it could not be seen. To be allowed in the cab of his father's tractor, to grip the cold metal of the steering-wheel, to press the black plastic dome of the horn; these things sent him into a chattering frenzy, or else into a spell of speechless delight. With the animals he was fearless. He would walk up to a cow and swipe at its legs with a stick he had pulled from the ditch, or a length of piping he had picked up in the yard. He would grab at its udders, imitating what he had seen Tom do in the milking shed. The cows were content in their routine, and used to handling; they tolerated the boy's noisy proximity, his prodding and pulling, his lunges at their throats, their nostrils, their tails. But it was not safe. It could not have been more dangerous. One kick from a cow lunging in to protect her calf could leave the child useless for the rest of his life.

Those first years, when he was small, there was pleasure just in watching him among the animals, the fields, the sheds that, before him, had only ever meant work or worry. To see this boy stride around the farm, even if he was hardly taller than the sheepdog, even if he was in short trousers and red wellingtons, even if he had a head of curls like a girl; even for all this, the sight of him there was like a prayer lodged in the mind and answered with every thought. Tom took Mark everywhere – to the mart and its chaos, to the creamery and its dirty white puddles, to the slaughterhouse beside the army barracks, where the workers crossed the yard in butchers' coats stained crimson, sucking on cigarettes and talking the ordinary talk of the day. He took him up to visit Tommy Burke, who farmed at the other end of the lane and who Tom had known since he was a boy himself, and soon Mark was walking over the lane to Tommy alone, staying for hours around the yard and the sheds, just as Tom had done at his age. Mark plunged into this world and asked few questions, showed little sign of being cautious or uncertain or afraid. It was as he had been that first day in the hospital, the solid way of looking, the air of already knowing it all. Of being born to it, and for it. Tom did not say this to Maura, or to anyone, because it was not the sort of thing that could be said aloud, that phrase, that set of words, but once it had rung in his mind, it continued to sound.

School was what changed Mark. It took a few years, but the change came, and then it worsened with each new year. The friends, the football matches, the long evenings at the kitchen table with his books and his pencils and with Maura close by; he saw it as a chore to have to go out on the farm. Then he was in the secondary school in Longford and then he was in Trinity, gone altogether except for the odd weekend.

The farm would be his, of course; Tom had long since sorted all of that out. He would have loved to know for sure that it would be farmed, but he could not insist on that, and he did not know how to ask. He knew there was the matter of Mark's college career, something he did not fully understand but had to pretend to understand unless he wanted to get the sharp end of Maura's tongue; she was always telling him that he was too selfish when it came to Mark and to what Mark was entitled to do with his life. He knew by now to keep quiet on it, and not to ask too many questions, and not to point out – and he was only saying – that Mark seemed to have only a few hours a week when he really needed to be up in Dublin, and that he had his whole, long summers free, and long breaks at Christmas and Easter as well, and it was just the case that there was a farm down here with his name on it, a farm that was coming to him, and Tom couldn't see how that farm could not be compatible with those few hours a week, those few months a year, that Mark had to spend up in Dublin. He could be saving himself a fortune on rent, for a start, and if he would only do the training course for young farmers that they ran in the Teagasc place in the town, he would be in line for all sorts of grants and subsidies. There was a desk up in his room, and he could work on his studies every evening if he wanted to – he could work on them any time he liked; Tom would not disturb him. And since he was so interested in the one from Edgeworthstown who had written books, it seemed only natural that he would need to be around here anyway, instead of in Dublin. Mark kept talking about the library, how he needed to be near to it and working in it and able to go into it any time he liked. But he was entitled to borrow some huge number of books from the library, hundreds of them; he had told Tom that a couple of years ago, when they were talking about Trinity one time. And there were a couple of trains a day up to Dublin now, and back again, and of course he could buy himself a car. Tom would buy him a car. He was always offering. But Mark always had some way of putting him off. He didn't need it, he kept saying; he preferred the handiness of the train, preferred to be able to sit on the train and catch up on work.

Work. Tom knew what work was; knew what the work really worth doing was, too. Work in rain or shine, the work of keeping a good farm on the go. He knew Mark liked to read, liked to write, and Tom liked to read, the odd time, himself, but there was no way you could think of that, truly, as work. There was pleasure in it, sure, but not like there was pleasure in the work he did every day: the pleasure of seeing a field well fenced, or freshly baled under a clear blue sky – or of a whole herd of cows come safe and well after a calving season. Tom knew that, and Mark would know it, before too long. Things would sort themselves out in the years ahead. You could say no to a car, but you couldn't, not really, say no to your own place. The thought of it gave Tom a glad feeling, a safe one. When the back door banged, he started at the sound. In all of his thinking he had almost forgotten that Mark was actually there. It was nearing evening. They needed to begin.

Chapter Seven

It was after ten when they finished work that night. Though it had not seemed dark in the meadow as they gathered the last bales, the view from inside the kitchen showed that night had come. Mark could see his reflection in the glass against the darkness; he looked hard-faced, he thought, wild-haired, his shoulders hunched. He looked like what he was, a farmer's son, and he looked, too, like a farmer's son who was himself becoming a farmer. He looked like one of the farmers his own age who lived nearby. John Flood, or Noel Flynn, or, he thought with a start, Frankie Lynch, boys who had grown up as he had, driving tractors before they were out of primary school, knowing every dip in the land, every drift on the wind, every eye in the herd. Now they all looked the same, no matter how much or how little money they had behind themselves and behind their farms. The same way of walking, the same way of standing, the same way of looking up slowly and assessing whatever met their eye – a woman, an engine, a sky. The eyes were always slightly hooded, the shoulders always slightly tensed, and the mouth hung heavy; the lips looked weighted, somehow. In the window's mirror, Mark saw that young farmer staring back at him, one big hand clamped to the edge of the sink, streaked with muck and oil, and the other slamming a delicate cup down as heavily as a stake, exhaling hard to push the strain of the whole long evening away.

'Now,' said his mother, putting a plate of chicken and chips on the table behind him.

'Thanks,' Mark said, and walked to the place she had laid for him across from his father.

It had been a beautiful summer's evening. It had been hard to want to be anywhere else, looking out at the meadows stretching golden against the sunset, and at the small lake beyond them, and at the bruised blue and grey of the hills on the horizon. But then one of the chains on the baler snapped, which meant that Mark had not been watching the feed of grass closely enough. It would set them back an hour. From the tractor cab he could see his father's face as he stood, watching, with the pitchfork in hand.

There had been an argument. Mark was accused of laziness and sloppiness and, finally, of ignorance – in his father's book, a truly unforgivable trait, though also, Mark suspected, a word whose meaning his father did not precisely understand. Tom was asked, again and again, to get out of the way; out of the *fucking* way, actually, which did nothing to calm his temper. Mark was asked to stop cursing, Tom to stop roaring – that had been the contribution of Maura, who had come out to help rake the hay into rows. Maura had been asked to stay out of it. The chain had been repaired, the clumps of hay raked into another row, and the evening had looked just as beautiful, still, but filtered through a gauze of unease. Inside those houses on those hills were people, and people made everything difficult; tripped over one another and tripped one another up. So, it didn't matter how beautiful the place was, or the evening. It was just a rare few hours of sun in a place where, usually, the bogland would suck you in up to your sorry knees. That was all.

Over dinner, his mother asked questions about the ground and the hay and the forecast for the next day, his father gave short answers, and Mark devoted his thoughts to a steady stream of images of Joanne Lynch without any clothes on; to what she might whisper, what she might urge. He caught his father looking at him as though knowing exactly what was running through his mind.

'I'm going to start on those last two fields as soon as the sun is up tomorrow morning,' he said, and his father shook his head.

'There's not that much rush on them,' he said, filling his glass with milk. 'A normal hour of the morning will be time enough. Anyway, you want to wait for the sun to take hold.'

'I want to get through them,' Mark said.

'So you're in a hurry,' his father said sullenly, and beside him at the table his mother sighed.

He was upstairs trying to read shortly afterwards when a knock came on the bedroom door. He closed the book. *Belinda*. It was not difficult to close. It was the one Edgeworth book he had never been able to get into.

'Come in,' he said, though his father was already in.

'You're working,' his father said, nodding to the book.

'Not that hard,' Mark said, and cleared his throat just as his father did exactly the same thing. Mark began to crack a smile at this synchronicity, but stopped himself: it was pointless; his father would not have noticed the coincidence, he would wonder why Mark was smiling. It was best to wait for his father to say what Mark knew he was going to say.

'Would you be interested in going down to Keogh's for a while?' Tom looked directly at Mark for just an instant, then to the book where it lay on the bedspread. 'If you're not too busy with your studies.' He did not wait for Mark to reply. 'You're hardly working this late, anyway, are you? That's bad for your eyesight.'

'No, that's something else,' Mark couldn't stop himself saying. His father gave a short laugh, but looked uncertain.

'I'll be going in a few minutes,' he said, and closed the door.

Mark picked up his phone. *Down home*, he typed. *Thanks for this morning*. He deleted that. *Thanks for the weekend*, he typed instead. *Give you a call later in the week?* He signed off with his initial, though it was hardly necessary: she had his number, she would know it was him. *Just thought about you long and hard*, he typed in then, just for the sake of seeing it on the small grey screen; he deleted it, and sent the rest of the message. Immediately, he panicked that he hadn't deleted the last line; it was stupid to worry about it, but it would have been just his luck.

There were only the regulars in Keogh's. Tom and Mark took the usual spot at the bar, beside Charlie McCabe the postman – or the retired postman, as he was now. Charlie shook hands with them both and asked Mark what he was up to in the city, these days.

'This and that.' It was the same answer Mark had given Charlie the last time he had met him in Keogh's, and probably, he thought, the time before that as well. It was all that was required. If he had launched into a description of what he was really doing, or of what he was supposed to be doing – his thesis, his supervisor, the manuscripts, the letters – Charlie would look uncomfortable very quickly, and his father's evening would be ruined.

'You've a good loch of those meadows taken care of, by the looks of it.' Charlie turned to Tom instead.

Paddy Keogh himself was behind the bar, and as he placed three fresh pints in front of them he came easily into the conversation; he had saved his own meadows the previous week, he said, as soon as the first sign of the good weather had arrived.

'*Ara*, I should have waited like yourselves, lads,' he said, 'but I'm not near as brave or as patient as the two of yous.'

'Bragging prick,' Tom muttered, as soon as he was out of earshot, and Charlie laughed.

'He hasn't a whole lot to be bragging about when it comes down to it,' Charlie said. 'There was hardly a blade of those fields dry when he sent the sons in to get hay out of them. Sure, that rain there the week before last.'

Tom nodded. 'Greedy.'

'Greedy. They have the meadow destroyed, dragging bales out of it before the ground was hard enough.'

'Aye.'

'Better to do it like you done it, Mark, not a bit of hurry on you at all.'

In reply, Mark gave Charlie the vaguest of nods. It was an established rhythm. There were set subjects, set questions, set responses; a set way to move your head, to shrug your shoulders, to turn slowly towards the door and keep an eye on whoever was coming in. When you laughed, when you really laughed, you turned your whole body in on itself, hooped over, like you were trying to keep the laugh where it was, trying to keep a hold on it. Even after several pints, these rules stayed in place; those who did not observe them were outsiders, or troublemakers, or drunks. Those were the people who were likely to shout, or to sing, or to send a pint glass clattering to the ground; to make a show of themselves. There would always be someone to see them to the door and, more often than not – what else were you going to do with them? – to their cars.

Mark had been coming here with his father since he was five or six years old. Younger, even. You didn't bring a child into the pub at night, but on Saturday and Sunday after-noons his father would drop in for a pint, and would bring Mark with him, buy him a mineral and a bag of crisps. There was a video game underneath a screen set into a low table, and when Mark was a teenager, Keogh had put in a pool table, so that it became the place to spend as many nights as you were let, swaggering in front of local girls. Girls he wouldn't even look at now.

She would never have been one of them. The Lynches never came in here; her parents went only to the hotel in Edgeworthstown, and the sons went drinking there too, in one of the bigger pubs. Joanne would have gone to Longford, to Fallon's, maybe, or Valentine's, or Eamon's, if she had gone through that grunge phase, which everyone around the place had. She would have looked much the same at sixteen or seventeen as she did now; in a way, she still looked that age. It was hard to believe she would be a solicitor in two years.

'Charlie's in bad form,' his father said.

Mark was surprised to see that Charlie was gone. 'It's early for him to be off.'

'Ah, he's a bit depressed, I think,' said his father, with a gravity that made Mark want to laugh aloud. In his father's mouth the word 'depressed' sounded as though it were being tried out for the first time. His father was eyeing him now as he waited for a response.

'I suppose he could be. Retirement's meant to be very hard,' Mark offered.

'Ah,' his father shook his head impatiently, 'it's not the retirement. Sure he's still out in the car the whole day long. He's still driving the same route, chatting to the same people, having the same crack, and then in here for his few pints in the evening. Only thing that's missing is the letters. I'd say if the post office got wind of it they'd give him the letters to hand out too.'

'It'd be cheaper for them,' Mark said.

'It's not the retirement, you see.'

What is it, Mark knew he was meant to ask, but something about his father's tone made him wary: it was too careful. It was the tone he used when he was trying to lead the way to a conversation that was more about himself than about anybody else.

'It's the son,' his father said, and Mark could have laughed out loud. So this was where it was going. This was what the conversation was to be about. Charlie McCabe ran his farm by himself, too; he had one son, too, who was hardly ever down home, who was high up as an engineer with Google, Mark had heard. He seemed like a nice guy. Charlie talked about him all the time, about some promotion he'd been given, about a trip he was taking, about the restaurants he took his parents to when they visited him in Dublin. There was no way that Charlie's son was ever coming down to work the farm, and there was no way, either, that Charlie expected it. For Mark, resentment began to settle in its familiar grooves. He was tired, he had worked all day; he was not in the mood for his father's guilt trip, and even less so for one that was bowled at him sideways, pretending to be something else, pretending to be concern for poor old Charlie, who tipped around that farm fine on his own.

'What's the problem with the son?'

'Ah.' His father shrugged. He seemed to have changed his mind.

'Go on, you've started now,' Mark said forcefully, and gestured to Keogh for another two pints.

'Jesus, don't call Keogh over here,' Tom said quickly.

'He's not coming over. He's ignoring me like he always

does, the fucker,' Mark said. 'And anyway, what's so terrible that you don't want him to hear? Brian McCabe is sick, is that it? He's dying?'

'No, but Charlie thinks he's a gay.'

What washed over Mark was strange and not exactly soothing: guilt and mirth and sadness and relief. Guilt at having jumped the gun so much; relief at escaping the conversation he had thought he was in; mirth at the image of his father and Charlie mulling together over the question of what Charlie's son was or was not. And, too, Mark couldn't believe he hadn't copped it before now about Brian McCabe; of course he was gay, of course he was, and happy as fuck about it too. Living the life. Always well dressed. Always well groomed. And always with that gaze, Mark thought now, with a jolt of self-satisfaction, which was a bit more interested than it ought to be. Well, fine. Mark wasn't going to object to being eyed up, no matter who was doing it. He knew he wasn't as safe in his own looks as he had been a couple of years ago. He told himself again that he'd have to start going to the gym – he told himself this a couple of times a month now, but never acted on it. He'd have to. He had seemed for a while to be getting away with the pints and the chips and the kebabs, but the signs were starting to show. He had the beginnings of a gut. Already, there'd been more than one grey hair. That was the road to thirty. Brian McCabe was thirty-four or thirty-five, and he looked a hell of a lot better than Mark.

'Charlie says there's never been a girlfriend,' Tom broke into his thoughts, 'and sure you'd know well just by looking at him. Sure he was done up there on Christmas morning like a man going to his wedding.' He finished his pint. 'And,' he added, 'he used to be a great lad for the choir.'

'He had a good voice before his balls dropped,' Mark said. 'That doesn't mean he has a preference for other people's.'

'Other people's what?' said Tom, as Keogh came over and asked if they were ready for two more.

'Other people's balls,' said Mark, and he nodded to Keogh, whose mouth opened and closed for a second before he moved off to get the drinks.

'Ah, Jesus,' said Tom, but he was laughing. He waited until Keogh was out of earshot again before continuing. 'Charlie's awful worried about him, though. Ah, poor ould Charlie, you wouldn't wish it on him.'

'He'll manage,' Mark said. 'He's not going to be any less fond of him.'

'No, but . . .' His father sighed. He was in uncertain territory now, Mark knew. 'It's not easy for him,' Tom said at last, and groped around in the pocket of his trousers for his cash.

'I'll get this,' Mark said. 'Charlie'll be grand. Sure what difference does it make to him?'

'Jesus, it makes a lot of difference,' his father said, almost in a whisper, and he looked around him before he went on. 'Won't everyone about the place be talking about him?'

'Isn't that what we're doing now?'

His father paused. 'It is, but we're Charlie's friends,' he said, frowning. 'He can't count on everyone else around here to his friend.'

'He can't control it, so he should forget about it,' Mark said, and his father looked at him as though what he was saying was madness.

'And of course he'll never get married now, and there's an awful lot to worry about, you know, when you have a son that way.'

'Like what?' Mark said, knowing the answer.

'Like . . .' His father stopped.

'Like AIDS, you mean,' Mark said, and his father clicked his tongue.

'Would you shut up about AIDS,' he said, under his breath. 'I don't want that fucker Keogh knowing Charlie's business.'

'You're the only one thinks it's Charlie's business,' Mark said. 'There's no reason why Brian McCabe would get AIDS, any more than I'd get it or anyone else would.' From the way his father started beside him, Mark could tell that he had provided him with cold comfort. 'And there's no reason why he shouldn't have as good a life as anyone can have. He can't get married, I'll grant you, but not everybody wants to get married. And anyway, that might change. For Brian, I mean. In a few years, he might be able.'

His father said nothing. A conversation about gay marriage was hardly what he had had in mind when he had come into Mark's room and invited him to Keogh's. Then again, it was not something Mark himself had had in mind. It was time to change the subject. He lifted his pint. 'So Charlie shouldn't be worrying himself. Let's leave it at that. Brian always seems happy to me.'

Tom was still quiet. 'Do you know him well?' he said eventually.

'I see him around here the odd time.'

'You never see him out and about in Dublin?'

'No, you needn't be worrying,' Mark said drily. 'I never see him out and about in Dublin.'

'I'm only asking.'

'Yeah,' Mark said.

They were silent for a long moment, during which Mark wondered what, after all, it would be like to be with Brian McCabe. Because the more he thought about it, the more he reckoned McCabe probably was into him. It could be worse.

McCabe was a good-looking guy. If it had to be someone, if it had to be some guy, he wouldn't mind it being McCabe.

'There's the farm, too, of course,' Tom said, his voice stronger, surer now. 'Charlie's getting to the stage where he could do with his son to help him. Not much chance of that buck coming down and putting on his wellingtons.'

Mark felt his jaw clamp. He had walked into it. 'Ah, for fuck's sake,' he said, loudly enough for the three or four drinkers in the bar to look up and take notice. 'Don't start.'

'I'm only saying it's hard on Charlie.'

'Charlie seems to manage well enough by himself.'

'Ah, you think that.'

Mark sighed. This was going exactly where he had suspected it would go. And there was a long way to go yet. They always stayed until closing time on these nights in Keogh's. He could try to shut the conversation down, or he could face up to it. It was probably time he told his father a few things. It was time he spoke to him directly. He cleared his throat. 'Charlie's son has his own life, and his own career, and I'm sure Charlie is glad about that,' he said.

'Ah, he is, he is, of course he is,' Tom said. 'Apart from the worry of the other thing.'

'So why would he want his son to give his own life up to run a farm of less than sixty acres?'

'He could run the farm and still have his own life. The farm wouldn't stop him.'

Mark snorted. 'Brian McCabe is a software engineer in one of the biggest companies in the world. He lives in an apartment on one of the most expensive streets in the city. He goes to New York and London and God knows where else several times a year. He eats in the best restaurants and drinks in the best bars.'

'I thought you said you didn't see him in Dublin?'

'I don't.' Mark sighed. 'I'm just saying, that's the kind of lifestyle you can expect someone like him to be having.'

'Because he's queer?'

'Because he's rich.'

'Ah,' Tom shrugged.

'And so, tell me, how would a life like that be compatible with running a farm like Charlie's? How would he do both at once? Spend every weekend to his oxters in cowshit, is that it?'

'There wouldn't be any need of that.'

'So how?'

'There's ways.'

Mark laughed. 'Tell me the ways. Go on. I'm interested.' At this, he saw, his father himself grew interested.

He turned to face Mark. 'There's jobs around here too, you know,' he said.

'Not jobs that Brian McCabe would want,' Mark said slowly. 'Not jobs that anyone, really, would want.'

His father was unruffled. 'Athlone or Sligo, then,' he said. 'There's everything there – they've factories, businesses, universities, the whole lot. A man could easily be living down here and doing whatever he wanted to do with the time he wasn't at work.'

'It's not the same.'

'How is it not?'

'It's just not.'

'And that's a great answer,' his father said, a line he had been using on Mark since he was a child. He was on his feet and heading for the toilet before Mark could reply.

'Two more, Mark?' said Paddy Keogh, who had, Mark realized, been standing close enough to hear the last few minutes of the exchange. Charlie McCabe had a gay son now, whether he liked it or not.

'Two more, please,' said Mark.

'That's the stuff,' said Keogh, with a slow smile. 'But if I'm not mistaken, it's your father's round.'

Chapter Eight

On warm summer evenings a crowd always surrounded the pub on the corner of South Anne Street, not trying to get in, but taking pleasure in being outside, drinks in hand, soaking up the last of the sun. Suit jackets were shrugged off, ties were loosened, the work day done, the night stretching out ahead. The atmosphere was at its most elated on Fridays, when a communal sense of liberation descended, so that proximity could lead to banter, and banter could lead to bed, but evenings like this were so rare in Dublin – so balmy, so beautiful, the low sunlight burnishing the deep red brick of the buildings – that a weekday could seem like a Friday, and nobody would say a thing to shatter the illusion.

Inside it was cool and dim, and few of the tables were occupied. The pub was made up of several small rooms, and a rickety staircase, lined with old photographs of writers and musicians, led to more narrow rooms and a second bar. Mark moved through them quickly, his gaze taking in every table. Several of the drinkers looked at him, out of boredom or curiosity, as he passed. She was not upstairs. He checked downstairs again, stuck his head into the snug at the front of the pub. He had to elbow through an animated throng at the door, and then he saw her. She was in a skirt, and heels, and a shirt with the sleeves rolled up. She was talking to some guy who hadn't taken off his jacket or his tie. She looked up and saw Mark, and she excused herself from the gathering and came towards him, smiling, the beginnings of a blush spreading on her face.

She leaned in for a kiss, not on the lips but on the cheek; he was thankful he'd figured that out in time.

'So you're good for another winter?' she said.

He didn't have a clue what she was on about, but he wasn't going to let her see that: he'd muddle through it, whatever it was. He didn't want his first sober words to her to suggest that either she was making no sense or that he was a bit slow. 'Yeah,' he said enthusiastically.

'So everything's saved?'

Shit, he thought. This one he couldn't just nod and guffaw his way through. 'How do you mean?' he said apologetically.

She laughed. 'Some farmer you are. The hay, obviously. That's what you went down to do, isn't it? You saved the hay?'

'Oh. Right. Yeah. All in safe and sound.' And that's the last thing I plan to say about hay for at least another twelve months, he added silently. 'Drink?' he said, and she said yes.

'Don't go away,' he said, as he turned.

As the booze kicked in, he started to lean back into the evening properly, to watch her as she talked, to take pleasure in the sight and nearness of her, instead of trying to think of the right thing to say. She was talking, now, about the case she was working on – something about feuding Ascendancy throwbacks, as far as he could tell – and she was gesturing like crazy, which gave him an excuse to look at all of her. He looked at her arms, trailed by freckles, a mole nestled in the shadowy veins of her inner elbow. He looked at her throat, smooth and lightly tanned, and at the top two buttons of her blouse, how they were undone, and how, intermittently, an arc of dark lace at her left breast revealed itself, hid itself, hinted at itself. She had a small nose, and she was wearing lipstick, but it seemed to be the same shade as her lips – or was that the point of all lipstick? The green of her eyes was flecked with copper. As she talked, she turned her palms upward, spread them wide, stiffened them as though to catch something falling from above.

'She's unbelievable,' she said – he raced backwards through the last couple of things he'd heard, and worked out that she was talking about her colleague.

He nodded. 'She sounds it.'

She jiggled the ice in her glass. 'So, how about you?' she said, glancing at him. 'What have you been up to?'

What had he been up to? Tugs of war with his father over every little thing. Tense encounters with his mother as she tried, like always, to encourage him to do two contradictory things: go back to Dublin as soon as he wanted and yet stick around in Dorvaragh for another few days. And there'd been the night in Keogh's, and a conversation with Sammy Stewart from over the road about baler pins, and a conversation with another neighbour about what the neighbour referred to as 'global warning', and there'd been farcical attempts to read.

'I got a bit of writing done,' he said.

'Oh, you got your chapter finished?' Joanne said. 'You were talking about it the other night.'

'Which night?'

'Both of them,' she said, laughing, and Mark groaned.

'Sorry to have inflicted that on you,' he said.

'No,' she shook her head. 'I actually found it really interesting. I don't know anything about Maria Edgeworth.'

'It's pronounced Mur-eye-a, actually,' he said. 'Like pariah.'

She looked at him for a moment, and he wanted to kick himself. It was an automatic thing by now, correcting people when they said the name wrong – almost everybody did – but he wished he could have held back, just this once. 'Sorry,' he said. 'Force of habit.'

'That's OK,' she said, and sipped her drink.

'And nobody knows much about her. I don't know much about her myself.' He attempted a laugh. She returned it.

'It's gas to think someone like her lived in Edgeworths-town, though. I mean, from what you were saying the other night, it sounded like she was a pretty big deal.'

'Yeah, she was, then,' Mark said, and he knew what was coming next.

'I mean, you were saying that she was good friends with Jane Austen? And that she had a thing with, what do you call him, William Scott?'

'Walter Scott.' Mark winced, but not at the mistake, which was kind of hilarious, and something he would have enjoyed if he hadn't been seething at himself over the drivel about his research that he had obviously, once again, been spouting. It happened every time he talked about it with a few drinks on him: he homed in on the most obvious claims to fame in Edgeworth's biography and blew them up to be much more significant than they actually were. Look, this woman from up the road knew Wordsworth! And Austen! And Erasmus Darwin! And *Virginia Woolf*, for Christ's sake, and *Turgenev*! And she had an affair with *Walter Scott*!

When, in fact, all there had been with Wordsworth was one very boring-sounding afternoon in 1829 when he had swung by Edgeworthstown House unannounced, as part of his tour of Ireland, and afterwards Edgeworth had written to her aunt complaining that he was too fond of the sound of his own voice. As for Austen, that had been no friend-ship, either, even though Austen herself had sent Edgeworth a copy of *Emma*; Edgeworth had dumped it on a friend because she could find no story in it, nothing close to life, and because it had in it some unconvincing detail about soup. As for Darwin, he was just part of her father's crazy circle of friends and, anyway, he wasn't the right Darwin, just his grandfather, and yes, what Turgenev said about Edgeworth's novels had been impressive – that if she hadn't written about 'the poor Irish of the co. Longford and the squires and squireens', he might never have written the Russian equivalent – but then, there was reason to believe that Turgenev might not have said that at all, that someone writing an obituary had just made it up. And while Edgeworth had definitely been close to Scott, the theory about their actually having slept together was just a rumour Mark had heard at a conference or, more accurately, in the pub after the conference. Anyway, the point was, he got excited about all the wrong things in Edgeworth: not the novels, not the tales, not the innovations in realism and autobiography about which he kept prattling on to McCarthy. Instead, he found himself getting fixated on the fact of all the famous people Edgeworth had known. It was pathetic. It was just another aspect of the stupid provincialism with which he'd chosen the subject in the first place. It was as though he was writing some kind of nineteenth-century version of a celebrity magazine as his thesis.

'Sorry,' he said. 'I tend to talk a lot of crap about it when I have a few jars in me. I'm a bit bogged down in it all at the moment.'

'Oh, yeah,' she said brightly. 'That's another thing you were telling me about. How her father was obsessed with the bog. How he went digging in it for dinosaur skeletons or something. Or did I imagine that?'

'Oh, God,' said Mark, his hands over his face, and she laughed.

'Well, it all sounds pretty interesting,' she said, with a magnanimous little shrug that made him want to kiss her, and he realized that he could, that there was nothing to stop him, and so he did, putting his lips gently to hers, not taking too many liberties with his tongue, which was probably closing the gate after the horse had bolted, given what he remembered of Saturday night, and when he pulled back again she touched his cheek, and said she was going in to get them another round.

*

He was coming around for dinner, and she was nowhere near ready. She was just in from work, she had nothing in the house. It had been a stupid idea, inviting him to come around this evening; it had been a drunken idea, something that had made sense while she was sitting with him on the footpath outside the pub the night before, watching the sky change colour with the sunset, talking to him and kissing him and noticing the way his eyes kept flickering down to where her bra showed. But it was not an idea that made sense now. For a start, she was not a cook. She sat heavily on the couch in the sitting room and moaned in Sarah's direction. Sarah ignored her. Her attention was fixed on the television screen.

'Tasha's meant to die in this tonight,' she said solemnly.

'She doesn't die,' Joanne said. 'She just gets lost in the bush for a while.'

'Ah, fuck you,' Sarah said. 'I was looking forward to that. Can you stop telling me spoilers from the Internet?'

'I'm fucked,' said Joanne. 'How the hell am I going to come up with something for dinner?'

'I've had mine, don't worry about me,' said Sarah, gesturing to an empty plate on the coffee-table. 'But I'd murder a cup of tea.'

This was how they lived. A Boston marriage, Sarah called it, and then Joanne's part of the gag was to tell her she should be so lucky. Since their last year of college, when Sarah had moved into the house in Stoneybatter, their evenings and their weekends had melted into a comfortable routine; dinner in front of the television Monday to Thursday, sometimes, they went for a pint in Walshes down the road. Always, they went into town on Fridays and Saturdays, usually with different sets of friends, but always, at some stage, crossing paths with each other. After the pub on weekends, there was often a house party somewhere. And then on Sunday nights, as they grimaced and brooded in the face of the coming week, they'd have an Indian takeaway and a bottle of wine.

'I'm making dinner for Mark,' Joanne said, and Sarah gave a whoop of innuendo.

'Don't,' Joanne said. 'Did you hear anything from Deirdre today?'

Sarah shook her head. Deirdre was the girl she had got together with at the party on Saturday night; Joanne knew that Sarah had been out with her again on Sunday night, and the next night. She had just qualified as a solicitor; Joanne knew her to see from Blackhall Place. Sarah had been into her from the first time she had met her with Joanne, in the Stag's Head one night after Christmas, when a load of trainees had met up for a drink; Sarah was tagging along, and clearly bored, until Deirdre arrived and squeezed in at the table beside her. After that, Joanne had been under orders to text Sarah whenever a trainee get-together was planned. There weren't that many – everyone was usually too exhausted – but there had been one about a month ago, when Sarah had been talking to Deirdre for hours. And then there was the party, when one or the other of them had finally made their move. Which was something about which Joanne was still not quite clear.

'So, wait,' she said now, and Sarah looked at her warily. 'You never told me the full story about how it happened the other night. Who kissed who?'

Sarah shrugged and pointed the remote at the television. But she did not change the channel. 'It was a mutual decision,' she said. 'We both wanted to.'

'That was handy.'

'I could say the same thing about you and Farmer Joe. Handy. The two of you were definitely handy.'

'Shut up,' Joanne groaned.

Sarah stretched. 'I'm only messing. So, he's coming around tonight, is he? Do you want a hand with dinner?'

'No, you're all right,' Joanne said, as she got up to go to the kitchen.

'Good,' Sarah said. 'I'm knackered after those bloody Koreans.'

Sarah taught English to Korean students in a language school on Dawson Street. She had studied English at Trinity, and every year she made noises about going back to college to do a master's in something related to her degree, but she had just watched another round of application deadlines pass by. She complained incessantly about the students yet always warmed to a few of them, and they seemed fond of her, piling her with gifts of flowers, or packets of biscuits, or magazines they thought she would like. That she was considered the target readership for magazines filled with real-life stories about broken marriages and botched surgery caused Sarah real dismay, but she ate the biscuits, and she placed the flowers in vases around the house.

There was a particularly gaudy arrangement on the kitchen table now.

'Can grass *be* blue?' Joanne shouted back to the sitting room. There came no reply. She plugged the kettle in. As it boiled, she looked through the cupboards over the sink and then through the fridge. There were eggs, and noodles, and a head of broccoli that looked past its time. She scanned a recipe book, but everything seemed to require ten different spices and at least one type of vegetable she doubted it was possible to get in Ireland, let alone in the Centra around the corner. The kettle clicked. She made two cups of tea and brought them to the sitting room.

As she walked in the door Sarah gave her a doleful stare. 'You didn't tell me that Maxwell was going to die instead,' she said.

They watched the ads in silence until the next show began. It was a regional news round-up, opening with an item about how another Viking settlement had been found on the site of a motorway. Bare-chested men in mud-caked trousers flung clay up from a deep trench into a wheelbarrow. A woman with streaks on her face drank from a bottle of water. Three yellow excavators crawled over a vast brown field, a valley of dirt scattered with barrels painted like barber poles.

'The diggers will win,' Sarah said, as she reached for the remote. She found another soap, an English one, and she lay out on the couch.

It was time, Joanne knew, to start cooking if she wanted to have dinner ready for eight. But she found herself resisting: she didn't want to shop for food, didn't want to cook, didn't want to go upstairs and shower and change before Mark arrived. She wanted to flop down on the armchair and watch junk television with Sarah all night. She wanted to drink tea and eat biscuits and not bother with dinner.

'Get moving,' Sarah broke into her thoughts. 'Lover boy will want to get his hands on more than that mouldy broccoli.'

'I'm going,' said Joanne. 'I just want to see how this bit ends.'

'He finds out about the brain tumour,' said Sarah, through a yawn.

*

As Joanne returned from the Centra she met Clive Robinson. He was thinner now, and his hair had gone completely white. As soon as she saw him she felt herself blush: he had been one of her favourite teachers in Trinity, and in front of him she had always felt shy. But when he smiled at her and exclaimed her name, she relaxed and felt glad to see him. They stood in under the awning of the butcher's shop and he showered her with questions, asking about her job, her exams, her friends from college. When she told him that she was working on the Lefroy case, he looked at her in surprise. 'That's the woman in the house up on Baggot Street?'

'Fitzwilliam Square,' Joanne said. 'Yes.'

'But she sounds like a wonderful woman!' Robinson said, with a slow shake of his head. 'I'll tell you, there aren't too many women like her around any more.'

'She's really fascinating,' Joanne said.

'Indeed,' said Robinson, carefully. 'I honestly don't know how your employers can live with themselves, lending an ear to that hooligan of a son of hers.' He was smiling again, if only faintly. 'But you like the work?' he asked then, coming back to meet her gaze. 'You think you've found your trade?'

She wanted to tell him everything then. The way she could hear the old woman's voice coming through the transcripts, her diction, her strange formality, her old-fashioned words – words that nobody bothered to use any more, words that nobody Joanne knew had bothered to use in the first place. She wanted to tell him about the nights she had stayed late over the case notes, and the afternoons she had had to grit her teeth and listen to Rupert's bullshit, and Mona's drivel, and Eoin's and Imelda's comments on Elizabeth.

'The work is fine,' she said.

'I'm done with my trade now, of course,' Robinson said.

'You're not teaching any more?'

'A whole year without it now, and I don't miss it at all.' He gardened, he said, and he read, and he went almost every day to the Markievicz pool; it was nice and quiet in the afternoons. His children took him abroad on holiday twice a year. His grandchildren lived nearby, and they called to see him.

'Or to see the cats.' He smiled. 'I'm never sure which it is.'

'It sounds like life is good.'

'Well, it is.' Robinson nodded, but then he stopped, and looked out to the traffic on Manor Street. On the footpath beside them, a boy passed on a bicycle too small for him. As he pedalled, his knees were almost hitting his hands.

'I find, though, that there are still things I wish I could do with my days. Still things I wish I had the time to do.'

Joanne hesitated. She knew it was important to look at Robinson as he spoke to her now – he seemed to need to tell her something – but, like an itch, she felt the urge to check her watch. She forced herself to smile into Robinson's eyes instead. 'Like what?' she said, and he shrugged.

'Oh, whimsies,' he said. 'I've started out on another book, if you'd believe it.'

'That's great,' Joanne said, hearing in her voice a note that was too bright, too eager. 'What's it about?' she said. She had tried for seriousness, but this time the words came out sounding wary.

'About discordance,' Robinson said, sliding a hand into his jacket pocket. 'About how we deal with discordance, within experience, I mean. How we reshape our world of experience when things within our experience turn out not to be what we'd expected. Our lifeworlds, and how we reconstitute them when we're in that bind. You remember all that nonsense, about lifeworlds?'

'*Lebenswelt*,' Joanne surprised herself by saying. Where had that surfaced from? She remembered hardly anything of Robinson's philosophy classes, much as she had loved them at the time. But *Lebenswelt*: *Lebenswelt* she could remember, for some reason. Probably, she realized then, because he had said it in English five seconds ago.

'You're driving home, and it's night-time, and suddenly a car comes around the corner with its headlights glaring, and you're blinded for a second,' said Robinson. 'Or you drive around the corner yourself, and instead of the clear way home you were expecting, there's a roadblock, and you have to find your way back along an unfamiliar route. Or you ingest some santonin – ever heard of that?'

Joanne shook her head.

'Turns everything yellow. Not to be recommended. Or, say, you burn your fingertips, and suddenly nothing feels the same. And what I want to know is, how capable are we, really, of dealing with it, of taking it up and synthesizing it into a new concordance, a new idea of what's normal? Not only on these small scales, but on much larger scales – on a global scale, if I have the guts and the longevity to get around to addressing that.' He shrugged. 'Sorry,' he said. 'Here I am again, rattling on.'

'No, no,' Joanne said. 'It does sound fascinating.' And the way he glanced at her then, with a half-smile, and the way his eyes fell away again to the ground made her want, for a moment, to cry.

'It's something to do,' he said, and he looked down to the plastic bag she was carrying, the groceries and the wine she had bought in Centra. 'But I can see you are busy,' he said. 'I won't keep you any longer from your night.'

'It was really lovely to see you,' Joanne said, and they shook hands, and he offered to see her as far as her door under the shelter of his umbrella, because it was raining now. But Joanne said there was no need, that it was only a drizzle, that she lived only a couple of steps away. At the house, as she opened the front door, she could hear Mark in the sitting room, talking to Sarah. She found herself impatient for the sight of him. Her heart was jumping in her chest as she came down the hall.

*

'I thought about joining a monastery once,' Mark said, as they had dinner. Somehow, they had got to telling each other the hymns they'd been forced to learn in primary school, and he'd made a joke about how he hadn't expected to spend their third date talking about 'Ave Verum', and how maybe for their sixth they should go to Glenstal Abbey for a mass at dawn. And now this. Which was presumably another joke. But he wasn't laughing, and he didn't seem to be expecting Joanne to laugh. All of his concentration seemed to be focused on getting an equal amount of meat and potato and mushroom on to his fork. He chewed slowly.

'I'm serious,' he eventually said.

'Fuck off,' she said, and it came out sounding harsher than she had meant it to. 'What are you talking about?'

'I read a piece about a monk from Glenstal in the paper, when I was an undergrad, and I thought it sounded pretty cool,' he said. 'I didn't want to bother with the religious side of it. I just wanted to be somewhere where nobody could reach me. Where I could just get on with doing what I wanted to do. I liked the idea of this very silent, steady routine.'

'You wanted to be a *monk*? So . . . are you religious?'

He shook his head. 'Not even slightly.'

'So you wanted to be an atheist monk.'

He shrugged. 'I doubt all the monks in there are that cracked on religion,' he said. 'The guy I was reading about spends most of his time writing.'

'Writing what?'

'Chick-lit.'

'Ah, come on.' Under the table, she hit his knee with hers. 'You're taking the piss.'

'No, no, no, I'm not,' he said. 'I mean, I am about the chick-lit. But I just liked the idea of this guy, writing away in there without anyone to bother him.'

'Right.'

'And then I decided I didn't want to get up every morning two hours before dawn. And that I'd get my essays written between nights on the tear the way everyone else did.'

'And that you wanted people to bother you.'

He laughed. The laugh of someone who hadn't thought of it that way before. 'I suppose,' he said, looking at her. 'Some people.'

They sat in silence for a moment. In the sitting room, Sarah roared with laughter at something on the television.

'Should we bring her another glass of wine?' Mark said. 'Or should we go up and join her?'

'No,' Joanne said. Often, before, when she and Sarah had

invited somebody around to the house, dinner for two had turned into drinks for three, and it had always been a laugh, but not tonight; tonight, that was not what she wanted. 'Let's stay here for a while.'

'Thanks for dinner,' he said, and she smiled at him. On his forehead, between his brows, she noticed three pock-marks. Like the skin had once been a pool of something; like it had bubbled as it dried.

'You scratched your chicken pox,' she said, putting her fingers to the marks.

'Oh,' he said, and he breathed out a laugh. 'Yeah. My mother was raging with me. She said she'd buy me a new tape if I didn't scratch them.' His fingers were over hers, stroking her hand. 'But I couldn't resist and I scratched them when she went into town to get me the tape. By the time she got back they were gone.'

'You brat,' Joanne said, and she traced her fingers over his lips. 'What was the tape?'

'Billy Joel,' he said. 'She came in and took one look at me and pegged the tape at me in the bed. I listened to it for weeks.'

'And you got holes in your head for keeps.'

'Yeah,' he said. 'Ah, well.'

She stood and gathered their empty plates, taking them to the sink as he refilled their glasses with wine.

'You don't have to go down home this weekend, do you?' she said, sitting back down.

'Not for another while.'

'They don't mind?'

'They mind but they'll manage.'

In the pub the night before he had talked to her about the farm and about his father. It was a story she recognized. It was her brothers' story, her cousins' story, the story of every son with a father who owned meadows and animals and haysheds. It was hers, too, if she substituted her father's practice for his hundred and forty acres, his clients for his cattle and sheep. She'd said that to Mark, and he'd seemed glad that she understood, grateful, but he had not asked any questions, had not shown an interest in hearing any more. It seemed strange to her, but it made sense, too. He had just returned from two days of dealing with his father, of working with him, of fighting with him. He probably hadn't wanted to talk about family – anybody's family – or about home.

But she found herself wanting to talk about those things now, for some reason, and she had said it before she could stop herself. That she had not been home herself in several months. That she didn't miss it. That it would probably be months before she visited again; probably Christmas.

'Which is the biggest fucking nightmare you can imagine,' she said, feeling how the wine massaged her into fuller sentences, bigger descriptions, than would normally occur to her. She was glad to have them. She was glad to be telling him this. 'My brother Frankie spends the day on the couch reading old issues of the *Sunday World*, and my other brothers bring their awful wives and their awful children, and my mother acts like she's run off her feet trying to look after everybody when actually she's in the kitchen topping up her gin and bitching at me not to ruin the turkey. What do I know about turkey?'

'Who knows anything about turkey?' he said, and she laughed.

'Exactly. So that's Christmas, and I come back here as soon as I can, and then every April I go down as well. Every April, I should say, I get guilted into going down.' She paused. It seemed suddenly very important to find the right tone. But whatever that tone was, it seemed out of her range.

'For my father's mass,' she said, and it came out in a blurt. 'I can't stand going down there, but I can't not be there for that. That just wouldn't look right. You know?'

He nodded, but he did not say anything; he did not ask her to go on. She looked at him. She wanted, she realized, for him to ask about her mother, to ask what it was about her mother that bothered her so much. She wanted him to draw her out, to let her tell him things, to let her vent – to let her get upset, even, if it came to that. She wanted his eyes on her, she wanted his hands on her, stroking her, giving her the attention he had given her a minute ago, giving her more of it, pulling her close. She wanted to say, My mother, I don't think she ever actually loved me. It sounded like something a teenager would say. She wanted to say, My mother, she saw me as a nuisance, as a rival, as a drain on her money and her nerves. She wanted to tell him how her mother had always sided with her father. How she had told Joanne she was only a stuck-up little bitch for throwing everything back in his face. You've always thought you were better than us, her mother had said to her, the night Joanne had announced that she wouldn't work for her father any more. But she'd never thought that. She'd just thought, for a long time, that something was missing in her, or that something was wrong with her, because she felt so different from them all.

'I'm sorry about your father,' Mark said, and he touched her hand, but not like she had wanted him to; too briefly, too lightly, his hand already back in his lap. 'That must have been hard.'

'It was hard because it was sudden. I didn't think I'd miss him.'

'Of course you miss him,' Mark said, and the smile he gave her had something unsettled in it, something awkward. Of course it has, she thought, here you are, trying to talk about emotions with an Irish man. It doesn't matter that he's an Irish man who writes about books. It matters even less that those books were written by a woman. He's still an Irish man. So change the record. Change the mood, if you want to keep him in this house with you, if you don't want to ruin the entire night. She shook her head, vigorously, as though shaking something away from herself.

'Anyway,' she said. 'Nobody wants to talk about that old stuff.'

'I don't mind,' said Mark. 'Talk about anything you want to talk about.'

'Well, I don't want to talk about my father, really,' she said, and she heard how unconvincing the words were. 'I don't know where that came from.'

'I don't remember much about him,' Mark said, and he was looking not at her, but at the table, at the crumbs scattered where his plate had been. 'He and your mother used to call up to our house sometimes at Christmas, but that was when I was very young.'

'My father always fancied himself as some kind of local politician,' she said, and Mark glanced up at her; he looked as though he might laugh. But he did not. 'Except he wouldn't have been able to play politics half as well if he'd been on the inside of it instead of fiddling it from the outside. So he probably did do that kind of thing. He probably did go around bringing Christmas boxes to his constituents. Kissing babies.' She poked Mark in the side. 'Kissing you.'

'Jesus,' Mark said, and as she leaned in towards him, he looked startled for a moment, but then all the watchfulness went out of his eyes, and he met her mouth with his own.

*

Upstairs, he looked at her very steadily. As he kissed her, he touched her ass and her thighs, her belly and her breasts. Her dress was light cotton, hardly more than a sundress. He threw it to the floor. She could feel him against her, that shape against denim that had drifted through her mind when she was meant to be thinking of other things. His mouth was against her, wetter now, and harder. He seemed, as he pushed against her, to want to lift her, and in turn she pushed against him, trying to keep her feet on the ground. He lowered one bra strap, kissing her shoulder, and then the other, and he reached behind her to unfasten the clasp. She pulled away from him and sat on the bed; she watched his face and watched his eyes. His hands came for her, and she caught them, and held them, and felt the strength of them, and he let her guide them, let her show him how to touch her so lightly that he must hardly have felt her, must hardly have realized the warmth and the dampness of her skin. He wanted more. His breath fought her. His body tried to press on her. With his hands, he traced her all over, traced circles on her breasts and lines on her throat and a feather-stroke up inside each thigh. And when his eyes said enough, she felt how the sweat had pooled at the base of his spine, and she drew him to her, and she let herself be drawn.

When she woke again near dawn it was to the sound of his voice beside her; he was mumbling to himself in his sleep. She tried to make it out, but it was nonsense, just noises, not even words. She shook him and he woke, gasping. His breath was stale on her face as he asked her the time.

'Time to be asleep,' she said, and she curled her body back into his.

Chapter Nine

And time for work was three hours later. Mona was already in the office when Joanne got there, standing by the coffee machine, clicking a stiletto heel on the tile floor. Her shoes had red soles that glinted like nail polish.

'Yes,' she said, when she saw Joanne glance at them.

'Yes what?' Joanne said, as she slumped into her chair.

'Yes, they are.' Mona made a face of mock alarm.

Joanne nodded. She knew what this meant. It meant that the shoes were new, that they had cost a fortune, and that there was something about the red soles that she was meant to understand. It was a moment, she knew, when energetic admiration was expected of her, but she felt too exhausted even to lift her gaze from the floor back to her computer screen. Two bottles of wine in the middle of the week was something she could no longer do without suffering the consequences. A sharp arc of pain was strung between her temples, and Mona's perfume, hanging on the air like pesticide, was not helping. Neither was Mona's excitable presence, as she darted now from one filing cabinet to another, pulling out folders and slapping them on to her desk. She sat down to her computer. She stood up again. She went over to the bookcase by the window and took up a thick hardback. She leafed quickly through it, consulted a page, slammed it shut. She picked up her phone. She put it down.

'You're busy,' Joanne said carefully.

'Oh, God, I'm run off my bloody feet,' Mona said, and then she laughed, and looked back at her shoes. 'I really shouldn't have bought these. But I couldn't resist.'

Joanne nodded. 'What are you working on?'

'Oh, everything,' Mona said. 'I have to get a full day's work done in half a day today. I have a lunch meeting with Rupert.'

'So you're taking a half-day?'

Mona looked to her screen. 'Eoin sanctioned it. He said it's important that we give Rupert the time he needs. Even if it's in an informal setting. There's still a lot of background we have to make sense of.'

'Don't we have all the background we need in the case notes by now?' Joanne said, but Mona kept her eyes on her screen.

'Don't ask me, ask Eoin,' she said. 'I'm just doing what I was told.'

Joanne sighed. What this meant was that Mona's work-load for the day would end up being hers. She had too much to do as it was. But she would have to agree. Mona had been there longer than Joanne. She claimed seniority – as long as it was understood that seniority, in this instance, was not a matter of age.

'You're not going to walk all the way to the restaurant in those heels, surely,' Joanne said. 'It's a fair trot to Fitzwilliam Square.'

Mona looked at her as though she were mad. 'I'm not meeting Rupert at his restaurant,' she said, in an incredulous tone. 'Rupert can't be seen at his restaurants at the moment. The paparazzi are staking them out. Didn't you know?'

'I have to say, I didn't.'

'Well, yes, they are,' Mona said, turning fully around in

her chair now. 'That creep over at the *Herald* has a total vendetta against Rupert.'

Joanne felt the beginnings of a smirk. She turned it into a cough. One photograph of Rupert Lefroy had, indeed, been taken outside his sushi restaurant and carried alongside coverage of the case in an evening newspaper, but the coincidence of a high-profile American actress having eaten there on the same evening could hardly be ignored. Neither did Joanne imagine that a scattering of bored newspaper photographers, fitting the job between an ad shoot and a football match, could be described as paparazzi.

'I'm sure Rupert is well able for them,' she said, and Mona nodded.

'Well, yes, he's used to this sort of thing,' she said. 'But, still, I hope they're not waiting for us at the Shelbourne.'

'The Shelbourne's hardly out of the way.'

Mona ignored this. 'So I'll need you to step in on some stuff for me,' she said, pulling her chair back up to her desk. 'There's a big section of the transcript that I haven't even looked at yet, and Eoin wants notes on it by this evening. It's that old bat again, Rupert's mother. I'm sorry to land you with more of her ramblings.'

'Fine,' Joanne said, and clicked into her email window. She had no new mail. She clicked out again and into one of the websites she kept open, but hidden, on her screen for much of the day; she knew Mona did the same. On a good day, Joanne only ever dipped into the virtuous sites – the newspapers, the things it was not so bad to be caught on by Eoin or Imelda, since you could be looking up court reports or precedent cases – but today was not turning out to be a good day, and she let herself fall into a rabbit hole to numb the brain: news items on celebrities, photographs of them walking in the street with their boyfriends or girlfriends or babies, links that led to more photographs, more snatches of gossip, to reader comments that were, more often than not, defamatory. Maybe, if Eoin or Imelda walked past, she could say she was researching Internet litigation. Eoin might buy it, but Imelda would know a gossip website when she saw one.

But Eoin was in court, and Imelda was staying safely in her office, and Mona was absorbed in the work she had to get finished before lunch. And so Joanne clicked on, and found out what was happening in the world. A teenage film star was pregnant. A model had been filmed taking cocaine. Mel Gibson had gone apeshit and said something anti-Semitic to a police officer. Paris Hilton had been spotted with her dog. It was junk. It was mindless. And when next she glanced at the clock it was almost lunchtime.

It never ceased to amaze her how easily and rapidly time seeped away when she went online. She opened the Lefroy transcript and looked at the last notation she had made. She stared at it, struggling to place herself back inside its world. *Check?* her own handwriting read, in block capitals. No arrow, no word circled, nothing to make clear what needed to be checked, and how, and why. She read the paragraph again. Paddy Glackin, the barrister for the plaintiff, was setting out the grievances of his client. Mrs Lefroy had sent her son to the very best schools. Mrs Lefroy had supported him through his years in college. Mrs Lefroy had paid for his master's, the master's he had never finished, and when he had gone into journalism, she had supported him then, too, making sure there was money in his bank account, making sure her son had the means to live the lifestyle he wanted to be seen to live. She had paid for the mews house to be painted and decorated, so that he and his friends would be comfortable there. She had bought him his first car. She had never been anything but supportive of her son, Glackin went on, even when he had broken her heart by moving to London. And when she had signed over the lease of the mews on his return to Dublin, she had done so in good faith, in the belief that he needed a home, that he had tax difficulties, that he was under pressure. And because Mrs Lefroy wanted her son to have a place of his own, because she did not want to see him suffer, she had signed the deeds transferring the property to him, and very soon afterwards, said Glackin, she had discovered what kind of a son she truly had. She had had her eyes opened, said Glackin, to the true nature of their bond.

Joanne rolled her eyes. Glackin was fond of his melodrama. She skimmed the passage again and again, and still she could not see anything she needed to check; still she could not spot the detail about which, on a previous read, she had written a note to herself. She looked back to the previous page. It was more of the same; Glackin setting out in agonized detail the depth of the son's betrayal. How lonely the old woman was. How badly she had been let down. How she had lost her husband so many years ago, and was no longer in touch with her daughter. 'And now this, Judge,' Paddy Glackin had said. 'And now this.'

She stopped. She read the paragraph again. She opened the folder of case notes and searched through the very first details they had gathered from Rupert. He was one of two children, he'd told Eoin; his sister, Antonia, had moved to New York many years ago. He had said nothing else about her; had Eoin *asked* him nothing else about her? Apparently not. And all through the court transcripts Joanne had read nothing, until now, of a daughter; there had been no mention of another child at all.

Joanne looked across the room. Mona was gazing at her computer screen with an absorption Joanne recognized; it was now her turn in the rabbit hole, clicking and staring her way through the links.

'Hey,' Joanne said, and Mona turned her head in surprise.

'What?' she said.

'What's the story with the daughter?'

Mona looked blank, then wary. 'What daughter?' she said slowly.

'Mel bloody Gibson's daughter – whose daughter do you think I'm talking about?'

'I don't know,' Mona said, clicking hurriedly into a Word file.

'The Lefroy daughter,' Joanne said impatiently. 'There's a daughter. In the notes from the opening consultation.'

'Oh,' said Mona, her expression breaking into bright relief. 'The sister. Oh, yeah.'

'Antonia.'

'Yeah, Antonia.' Mona said. 'Why? What about her?'

'What *about* her?' Joanne almost shouted. 'What became of her? There's not even one other mention of her in the case notes.'

Mona shrugged. 'I guess she's not important.'

'Of course she's important,' Joanne said. 'How can we expect to know the whole story about a case involving two members of the same family if we don't find out everything we can about that family?'

'Oh, for God's sake, we don't need to know anything more,' Mona said, turning back to clatter at her keyboard. 'We don't need help, remember. Rupert is the one who's clearly in the right. Eoin's said it over and over again. Our case is as good as won.'

'But we should have looked into the daughter. If the other side haven't brought her up, hasn't made something of her, there must be some reason for that. Mustn't there?'

133

'Don't go making work for us,' Mona said, in a warning tone.

And then Imelda's door opened, and Imelda stepped into the room. She glanced at Mona – glanced down to where Mona's feet were hidden by her desk – and looked to Joanne with a frown. 'I was sure I told you to look into that sister of Rupert's several weeks ago,' she said, her eyes on the file open in front of Joanne. 'Is that not the case?'

'No,' Joanne said nervously, and she heard Mona exhale between her teeth.

'Well, my mistake,' Imelda said, handing her the phone. 'Get on with it.'

'It's six in the morning in New York,' Joanne said.

'Ring her during lunchtime, then,' Imelda said. 'You don't have anywhere you need to be, do you?'

*

Antonia Lefroy picked up on the second ring. It was still early in New York, but she did not sound wary as she said hello, and neither did she sound as though she had just been woken. She sounded confident, capable, used to dealing with interruptions.

'Ms Lefroy?' Joanne said, and heard in her own tone the very nervousness and uncertainty she had expected in the other woman's.

'This is she.'

'My name is Joanne Lynch. I'm calling from Brennan and Mullooly Solicitors, in Dublin.'

'Hold on, please.'

There was a pause. Joanne heard a quick solid noise, like the movement of an object, or the sound of a door closing. When Antonia came back on the line her breath was close to the mouthpiece, and it came out in a long sigh. She was expecting bad news, Joanne realized. Who could receive a call from a solicitors' office in another country and not expect bad news?

'I don't want to worry you, Ms Lefroy,' she said. 'Nothing has happened. Nothing is wrong.'

'I'll be the judge of that, I think,' Antonia said tightly. 'This is to do with my mother and my brother, I suppose?'

'Rupert is our client. Your mother is suing him—'

Antonia interrupted. 'Yes, I know all about their little tussle. I read the papers. Or I should say the paper. It hasn't been reported anywhere other than the *Irish Times*, I hope?'

'The *Sunday Independent* did something last weekend.'

'Oh, for Christ's sake.' Antonia clicked her tongue. 'Sordid, I suppose?' She didn't wait for Joanne to reply, but told her to go on.

'Ms Lefroy, there are a couple of things I'd like to ask you,' Joanne said.

'Such as?'

'Things to do with your mother, and your brother, family . . . history things.' She winced at her words. At the other end of the line, she heard a clipped laugh.

'Family history things?'

'I'm sorry,' Joanne blustered. She felt a wave of relief that she had waited until the office was empty to make the call. 'Ms Lefroy, in her testimony, Mrs Lefroy has described her relationship with you as being estranged.'

'I didn't read that in the papers.'

'It hasn't made it into the papers.'

'And you're calling me to see if you can change that, I assume?'

'I'm not a journalist, Ms Lefroy.'

'You don't sound much like a solicitor either, I have to tell you.'

'I'm a trainee. I'm working on your mother's case.'

'My brother's case, from your perspective, surely.'

Joanne swallowed. 'Yes.'

'And what do you want from me?'

'Well, I was hoping . . .' Joanne stopped. 'I was hoping you could fill in for us, a little bit, the background to your own . . . estrangement . . . from your mother. How that came to be the case, and why. What happened, you know.'

'I see.'

'I mean, I know it's very personal information . . .'

'It certainly is.'

'But I think it's also essential to the progress of your brother's case, if we are to represent him fairly.'

Antonia laughed curtly. 'What makes you think I'm on my brother's side in all of this? What makes you think I believe Rupert to be the one in the right?'

Joanne hesitated. She had been getting into the swing of things, and now she felt uncertain again. She cleared her throat. 'I'm sorry, Ms Lefroy,' she said. 'It's just . . . with the implication that you and your mother no longer get on—'

'You assume that I despise her just as much as my brother does. That I have just as great a desire to see her shamed and ruined.'

'Well, no,' said Joanne. This woman had just as much talent for melodrama as Paddy Glackin, she thought. The combined force of the two of them in the courtroom would be too much to bear.

'Do you have a mother, Miss Lynch?'

Joanne stammered. 'Do I?'

'Of course you do,' Antonia broke in impatiently. 'You sound about eighteen years old. You probably still live with your mother.'

'No, I don't,' Joanne said, more sharply than she had intended.

'So you are estranged from her.'

'I'm sorry?'

'You no longer live in the same house as your mother. Therefore you and she must be estranged. Am I correct?'

Joanne frowned. 'I don't think . . .' she said, but then she couldn't find anything else to say. 'I don't think so,' she said after a moment.

'Because you see, Miss Lynch, from my mother's point of view, that is all it takes to become estranged. The mere fact of geographical distance between us, and of lives lived separately – of a life, on my part, lived on my own terms – that is enough to constitute an estrangement. That is why she describes us as estranged. Do you know how many years I spent living in the house on Fitzwilliam Square?'

'No,' Joanne said. 'We don't know anything about you, actually. That's kind of the point.'

'Thirty-nine.'

'You're thirty-nine?'

A long pause confirmed the error that Joanne already knew she had made. 'I'm sorry,' she said. 'I mean . . .'

'Flattery may get you everywhere in your chosen profession,' Antonia said, 'but no. I am not thirty-nine. I am well past it. What I said is that I lived in my mother's house, with my mother, for thirty-nine years.'

'Oh,' Joanne said. She wrote 39 in her notebook and circled it twice. *Not age*, she added, and immediately put a line through it. 'I'm sorry,' she said again.

'Sorry for what? Don't be sorry for me. I've been out of Dublin ten years now. My life has never been better. I've lived in London, and now I'm in New York, and I'm doing what I want to do. And I'm still in touch with my mother. Has she told you that? I'm still in touch with her very regularly, in fact.'

'She hasn't said anything about you.'

'Well, there's a reason for that. My mother has not forgiven me.'

'For moving away?'

'For moving out of her house,' Antonia said. 'My mother was used to having me in that house with her. To cook for her, and clean for her, and keep the place going for her, like some kind of Victorian maid. And now that I'm no longer where she liked me to be, my mother prefers to pretend that I was never there. That I never existed. And yet I still visit her at least once a year. Which is more than my brother did when he was living abroad. It was only when his money ran out that he decided to do that.'

'Sure,' Joanne said, and circled some more random words on her notepad. 'I'm sure everything that's happening between them must be difficult for you.'

'Not particularly,' said Antonia. 'I left Ireland to make my own life. I had to become immune to caring about certain things.' She sighed. 'But I'm afraid I still don't know why you called me. Would you be so good as to tell me? What is it, exactly, that you wish to find out about my brother? Do you even know the answer to that question yourself?'

Joanne did not respond.

'Well, let me help you,' Antonia said. 'Let me tell you, first of all, that my brother is a compulsive liar. You probably know that already.'

'Well . . .'

'Of course you do, you're representing him. But let me tell you something even more complicating – which is not going to help you, I'm afraid. Not only is my brother a compulsive liar, and a consummate one, but he learned how to lie from my mother. She will tell you that black is white, and he'll tell you white is brown. Are you beginning to understand me?'

'I think so,' Joanne said slowly, though that was not quite true.

'Good. Then what you're beginning to understand, Miss Lynch, is that representing my brother is about as easy a task as it would be to represent my mother.'

'I see.'

'So good luck with it. And, please, don't call me again. I have nothing to tell you. My mother may say that she is not in touch with me, but she is, and I don't trouble myself to think about her reasons for saying otherwise. I don't see myself as estranged. I see myself as away.'

With a dignified click, she hung up. Joanne stared at the phone. She was not sure what had happened. She glanced again at the useless notes she had taken. Her heart was thumping. Imelda would be back from lunch any minute, and she would see all this as dynamite: how Elizabeth had treated her daughter, how domineering and selfish she had been as a mother, how she had refused to let her children build lives of their own. Imelda would bring it to their barrister, Linda O'Halloran, as further ammunition for Rupert's case, for the argument that his mother was merely bitter at his display of independence, merely jealous of the success he had made of the mews house, all on his own. And then there was the detail about Elizabeth being a consummate liar. The second part of that detail – the part about Rupert being a talented liar too – Imelda would ignore: it was irrelevant for the purposes of their defence, she would say. But Elizabeth's lying: that, Imelda and O'Halloran would whip up into a savage attack on the old woman's character –

on her unreliability – on her claims to have been a good mother, a mother who wanted only honesty and decency from her son. If Elizabeth Lefroy could not act honestly herself, O'Halloran would address the courtroom, on what basis could they attach so much as a shred of credibility to her accusations about her son? It was all there. It lay sparkling on a platter, waiting to be snatched up and thrown. Once again, Joanne imagined Elizabeth on the witness stand, her eyes dark, her posture defiant, her chin held high. The jet beads at her throat.

She had never even seen the woman. She had only read her words in the transcripts; she had not even listened to the tapes. And she had heard only poor accounts of Elizabeth by now, from her son and from her daughter, and whatever about Rupert, she believed what Antonia had said about her mother; she had heard nothing to doubt or to treat with suspicion in Antonia's tone. So why did she keep thinking of her? Seeing her standing there, wearing those beads? She would hardly even *know* jet beads if she saw them. She would not recognize them if they flew off their string and struck her in the eye. And yet, as she heard footsteps on the stairs now, she ripped from her notepad the pages on which she had scribbled during the phone call and tossed them into the bin. Her heart beat so hard she felt it almost as pain. When Imelda came in, Joanne turned to face her, then looked immediately away.

Imelda came over to her desk and tapped a fingernail on the wood. 'So. You got her? Mademoiselle Lefroy?'

Joanne nodded. 'I called her,' she said, as casually as she could. 'It wasn't very useful, I'm afraid.'

'How could it not be useful? What did you ask her? What did she say?'

'She says she's not estranged from her mother,' Joanne said, looking at her computer screen, watching as, noiselessly, another new email piled its black weight on to the top of her queue. It was spam. 'She says she phones her mother often, says she visits her once a year, says she worries about her all the time. She says the problem is her mother is confused, that's all. That the mother doesn't really know what she's saying when she says that she and her daughter are estranged. That she doesn't really know the meaning of the word.' With a tiny click, she deleted the email.

Imelda, seeing the motion of her finger on the mouse, frowned. 'She's saying her mother is senile,' she said, with a wave of her hand. 'Well, we've argued that already. No harm in arguing it some more.'

'No.' Joanne shook her head. 'She says her mother is just getting old.'

'Oh, for Christ's sake,' Imelda said sharply. 'Don't give me semantics. She's saying her mother is no longer the full shilling. We can definitely use that. We need her over here for next week's hearing. Get her on the phone again.'

'No,' Joanne said, and she felt sweat break out on her skin.

Imelda laughed. '*No?* I'm sorry? Did you just say no?'

'I mean, no, I don't think we can use her. I don't think she'd be useful to us.'

'Why?' Imelda snapped.

'She hates Rupert. Says he's a liar.'

Imelda shrugged. 'So? We can put up with that.'

'She says he stole from her.'

Imelda's face changed. A stare, still, but not just a cold stare: something dawning in it, something uncomfortable. 'For Christ's sake. Stole what?'

Joanne looked at the screen. The bank website she'd been on earlier was still open. 'Money. A lot of money. Says he forged cheques. Says he used her bank card.'

'She says he did this or a conviction says he did it? Which is it? Is there anything to prove this actually happened?'

'Not that I know of,' Joanne said, feeling weak.

'Not that you *know* of?'

'I mean, no. No, there isn't. Nothing ever came to court. She never took it that far. Antonia. She didn't want to go through a court case with her own family.'

Imelda raised an eyebrow. 'Are you sure this woman is actually related to the other two?'

Joanne forced a laugh. 'I know. It's funny, isn't it?'

'What's funny?'

'Just . . . how different they are.'

Imelda sighed. 'She's different enough from Rupert to cause us some serious problems if Paddy Glackin gets his hands on this. I can't understand why the mother's solicitors haven't been on to her. I can't believe they wouldn't chase her up. We should have chased her up ourselves weeks ago.'

'But she's not going to be of any use to us,' Joanne said, her hands and her armpits clammy. What was she doing? Whatever it was, she had to go on with it now. She had to see it through. 'She says they haven't been on to her, her mother's solicitors, I mean,' she said. 'She was just as surprised as we were. But that has to be good for us, right?'

'Does it?' Imelda said, warily, looking at Joanne. 'Go on.'

'It just means they don't have a clue what they're doing, really.' Joanne tried to laugh, but it came out as a gasp. 'I mean, doesn't it?' she said, and in her voice she could hear the plea. She forced herself to look Imelda in the eye. She forced herself to look sure. She forced herself not to faint, because that was what she felt like doing, as Imelda eyeballed her, seemed to assess her, seemed to make a decision on whether she could be trusted or whether she needed to be fired.

'I think you're right,' Imelda said eventually, slowly, and Joanne exhaled.

'You don't think we need her?'

'I know we don't need her. I know that Elizabeth's solicitors do. But, as you say, they don't have the intelligence to look for her. So why should we help them?' She picked up the transcript from Joanne's desk; it was open at the page on which Joanne had written *Check*. 'Check what?' she said.

'Check the daughter,' Joanne said. 'Check Antonia. That was what made me realize it was something I had to do.'

'Good job,' Imelda said, after a pause. 'But now it's your job to forget you ever spoke to Antonia Lefroy. If Glackin and his all-stars dig her up, we'll deal with that bridge when we have to cross it. But we're bypassing it now. Do you understand me?'

'Yes,' Joanne said, and Imelda nodded.

'That's the girl,' she said, and turned towards her office. 'Now, would you ever make me a cup of tea?'

Chapter Ten

Mark checked his watch again. Joanne had said the judgment was likely to be given by four. She was nervous as hell; he had asked her to text him and tell him how things went. He hadn't heard from her all day, which didn't worry him, because over the last few weeks, work had become so busy for her that she hardly ever had time even to send him a text. One of her bosses, the woman, had decided she liked her, or trusted her or something, after the incident with the phone call to the woman in New York, and had given her a whole load of new responsibilities, with the consequence that Joanne was knackered all the time. She went into the office every morning practically at the crack of dawn, and she stayed every night until nine or ten. She had worked three Saturdays in a row now, and last Sunday as well. She had said it would definitely ease off when this case was over, and he hoped so: he didn't think he could stand it much longer.

They had not even been seeing each other for two months yet. It was way too soon for this kind of stress; her snapping at him out of exhaustion, him getting resentful because she was never around. He was being as understanding as he could, was trying to fit himself into her schedule as much as he could – was trying to look after her a bit, walking her home, or cooking her dinner, or getting her DVDs from Mossy, even though she was too shattered even to open them. He listened to her talk about her work, not just before they went up to bed, but in bed; the deadlines she was worried about, the research she had to do, the notes she had to write up. And, over and over, the case that was in the High Court, the old woman and her son, the feuding Anglos. They might as well have been squashed in beside him in the bed. He couldn't escape them. But now he was going to escape them; he was determined. When the judgment came through, whatever it was, whether it was in favour of Joanne's firm or not, he would go to the wine shop on Dawson Street, the one closest to Trinity, and buy a bottle of champagne. He didn't exactly have the money to be spending on champagne at the moment but he didn't care. He wanted to celebrate. He wanted to turn up on Joanne's doorstep and bring her flowers and drink the champagne with her and take her to bed. And take her out somewhere the next night, and the next. He wanted to do what people did with their girlfriends, or with the girls they were seeing; not just the sex – though he was ready to get back to that as well – but the other stuff, the dinners, the films, the dates. He looked at his watch again. Half an hour to go.

He hoped the case would go the way she wanted. Not that he was entirely certain which way that was. She'd told him about the phone call to the old woman's daughter, and about how she'd given a different version of their conversation to her boss; he'd been impressed by her gumption, but also more than a little uneasy about the whole thing. It wasn't that Joanne wanted to protect the mother from the daughter, he thought, but that she wanted to protect the mother from herself, somehow. She'd been a dominating old shrew, and Joanne saw that, saw the madness in how the mother had behaved, trying to turn her daughter into some kind of Miss Havisham, or worse. She agreed that the mother was completely in the wrong. And yet she felt sorry for her. So she had hidden the things the daughter had told her and spun them into something else. She didn't know why she had done it, she told him; it had just felt like the right thing to do. And he felt nervous about it. He'd felt nervous about it for the past month. He couldn't see how it could possibly benefit her to conceal evidence like that – not just to conceal it, but to manipulate it – and he worried that it was going to backfire on her drastically, that her bosses would discover that she'd essentially tricked them out of calling a witness who sounded like she could be very valuable to them, with everything she had to say about the old woman; that he'd soon be seeing Joanne in bits, sacked, disgraced, shit-scared about her future. But nothing like that happened. It went completely the other way. Yes, she was in bits, after a week or so of the new workload, but she was in bits in the way that, according to her, was actually good for your career. If you were drained and pale and hollow-eyed, if you were all skin and bones, then you were doing something right as a trainee solicitor, it seemed; you'd go far.

It had to be to do with her own mother, he knew, all this stuff with the old woman and her daughter. A first-year psychology student could have worked that out. Mark didn't ask her about her mother. He knew that he should. He knew that, whatever it was, the problem between them, the estrangement, it was painful – probably much more painful than whatever was going on between the other pair. He knew that if things got serious, they would have to talk about all of that stuff, but for now he just wanted them to get to know each other, to enjoy each other, without having to drag their families into it, without having to look at each other in terms of who their parents were, and what their parents had said and done.

And he knew he was being naïve. He knew he was

procrastinating, as usual. Because the fact was, things were already beginning to feel serious between them. He found himself, constantly, thinking of things he wanted to tell her about, places he wanted to show her, things he wanted them to share. Even slogging through his thesis chapter over the last few weeks, he'd been thinking about her; wanting to talk to her about what he was finding in *Harrington*, about what Edgeworth was doing with form there, about what she was doing with the line between the real and the fabricated. Joanne was always too worn out, obviously, for him to inflict on her an excited monologue about Edgeworth and self-reflexivity and autobiographical interpolation, and about how she used these things to play with what people expected fiction to be, but he wanted to tell her anyway. He wanted to tell her about what he was working on now, as he waited for her to text, about what he was trying to concentrate on – about why Edgeworth's irony in *Castle Rackrent* had backfired, about how everyone thought she was giving just a straight account of mad old peasants and ruined old estates, when in fact she was doing anything but. When, in fact, she was writing something so batshit insane, in technique and voice, that she barely even wanted it to be read as a novel at all. But Joanne would have other things on her mind. And, if he was honest with himself, he had other things on his mind. Though it was not yet four, he packed up his books and his notes.

As he walked down Dawson Street his phone vibrated in his pocket. The case must have ended early. But it was not Joanne, it was his mother, and he cursed as he remembered that he had agreed to go home this weekend. Now that the meadows were bare of grass, they needed to be spread with manure, and his father was wondering, his mother said, whether Mark would come for a couple of days and get the job done. So you're literally asking me to come down to shovel shit, he wanted to say. But he just said that, yes, he would try to get down, and his mother had sounded so grateful that he'd felt more guilt than frustration as he hung up. Now he looked at the screen as it flashed again with *Home*. He didn't answer. He stuffed the phone back into his pocket and stopped to look at the display in the bookshop window.

Joanne understood that he had to go down home sometimes. She had grown up on a farm. She knew what it was like. She knew what it was like to have a father who expected things. Though that was something else he had not asked her about much. It had come up a couple of times, usually when she was drunk and running off at the mouth a bit – which meant, he knew, that it was probably something she really needed to talk about, that it was on her mind, but it was territory he didn't want to get into with her. Not while she was drinking. Or not while she was sober.

She seemed to have no idea of what had taken place between their fathers years ago. She showed no sign of knowing that they had been friends once, his father and hers, or something like friends, and that they had fallen out badly. But she would have been young when it happened; six years old, maybe, or seven. There would have been no reason for her to notice. It would not have mattered in her house the way it had mattered in Mark's.

His father never talked about the Lynches now. He did not curse them. He did not articulate the things he felt about them. And his father was not, Mark thought, afraid of them. He just wanted to act as though he did not have to share a world with them. Yet that was impossible. He could not ignore them. And it did not take the sight of Lynch's widow Irene, or of one of his sons, or of their big farm at Caldragh, or of their jeeps on the road, to remind his father of that fact. He needed only to drive half a mile over his own lane. He needed only to see the fields and the yard and the fallen-down cottage where, for nearly fifty years of his life, he had spent a large part of every day. Where he had worked with the man who had treated him like a son, old Tommy Burke; the man who had told Tom, always, that one day those fields and those gates and that cottage would become his own. It was the old story, Mark thought now, but it was a story that was never going to disappear. There was a book of essays by Declan Kiberd in the bookshop window; he stood and stared at it for a moment. It was a book he should have read. He thought about going in and buying it. But he had only thirty euro in his pocket and he needed it for the champagne. He walked on.

Tommy Burke's farm up the lane had hardly been worthy of the name, just the cottage, with two or three rooms in it, and a few acres not much better than bog. Tommy was a bachelor, maybe thirty years older than his father. Mark could remember him only faintly – a flat cap, a battered old suit and battered old boots, a lot of rotten teeth, and a smell that became so familiar it was almost charming. Mark had never known what it was, that smell, until a few years ago when the smoking ban had come into effect and he had walked into a pub in the middle of the day and felt his nostrils twitch at the bang of stale booze, of spilled pints, of Guinness soaked into the carpet; the smells that there was no longer any smoke to hide.

His father had believed, for a while, that he had been named after Tommy; that was how close he had felt to him when he was a boy. He had told Mark about it; how he had spent so many hours every day with Tommy, helping him out on the farm. How he had annoyed his own father, the grandfather Mark had never known, by wanting to work with Tommy rather than with him. For Mark, Tommy was just there, and then one day he was just not, and he could still remember the shock of seeing his father cry at Tommy's funeral. It had been like watching a wall of the house fall away.

Frank and Irene Lynch had been at that funeral. Frank Lynch had laughed when, imitating his father, Mark had laid his hand out for a shake in the graveyard. Lynch had put his hand on Mark's head instead, had ruffled his hair, had told him that he had to be his father's companion now. His father had said that he was more of a hindrance than a help. Lynch had laughed again and said that he didn't believe it for a minute, and then he had moved closer to Mark's father and the two of them had got into a long conversation about the other people who were standing around the grave.

It was probably the last civil conversation his father and Lynch had ever had, that one; afterwards, very soon afterwards, the trouble had begun. At the time, to Mark, it had seemed just a blur of shouting and cursing. Of silences at the dinner table. Of slamming doors. It was only years later that he understood what had happened; understood just how deeply his father felt he had been betrayed. Tommy had promised his father the farm. He had involved Tom in decisions about the future of the place. He had encouraged him to graze his own cattle on the land behind the cottage. He had encouraged him to save hay from the meadows. And he had never bothered himself to make a will.

Tom had asked Frank Lynch to look into the matter of the will, and when it emerged that there was none, he asked Lynch to advise him on what would happen next. Lynch told him that, by law, everything would go to Tommy's nearest surviving relative, and that he would be happy to find out who that was. Shortly afterwards, he phoned Tom to say that the relative had been found: a cousin in Chicago, whom Tommy had never met. Lynch wrote to the cousin, and the cousin wrote back to say that he was touched and honoured by the inheritance. He was proud of his Irish ancestry, he said, and he was praying for the soul of his cousin Tom. And as soon as the ownership was legally transferred to him, he was putting the farm up for sale, and in this he wanted Lynch to act for him, because he could tell by the tone of his letter, by the kind sympathies it had expressed, that Lynch was an honourable man. When Lynch phoned Tom the same evening, it was to tell him that the auction would take place in Tommy's yard. When Lynch's secretary phoned Tom the next morning, it was to instruct him to remove his cattle from Tommy's land. Bewildered, Tom refused. Overnight, Lynch had the cattle taken from the land. Mark would never forget his father's face that morning when he came in the back door. It was rage and it was incomprehension. But most of all it was fear. His hands were shaking too much for him to be able to pick up the phone. Maura had to make the call. The cattle, it turned out, were being held in a pound near Cavan. There would be a fee for their return, and if they were placed back on the estate of Tommy Burke, the further consequences would be much more serious.

At the auction, Tom tried to bid, but he could go nowhere near the price offered by the highest bidder. The highest bidder was eighteen years old. He was not yet out of secondary school. But he won the place easily. And to Frankie Lynch's credit, he had come over, after the bidding had ended – Mark had seen it – and tried to shake Tom's hand. But Tom had turned. The older boy had looked at Mark and shrugged before going back to where Frank Lynch stood, chequebook in hand.

She wouldn't remember it. There would have been too many people who despised her father, too many people he had wronged, for her to make note of anyone in particular. And by the time she had come to her own conclusions about the crooked fucker that her father was, the falling-out with Tom would have been far into the past.

The bell over the shop door rang as Mark pushed it open. He walked to a shelf of foil-topped bottles as though he knew what he was doing. When the guy behind the counter called over to offer his assistance, Mark explained to him what he had in mind.

Chapter Eleven

Elizabeth Lefroy turned out to look nothing like Joanne had imagined. There were no scarves and jewels and shawls. She wore a simple dark suit over a cream blouse, with a gold pin on the lapel. She wore glasses, and her silver hair was pulled into a tight bun. She was tall and thin. She resembled, more than anyone, the nun who had been principal of Joanne's boarding school.

Joanne sat with Imelda, facing their barrister, Linda O'Halloran, and took notes as Glackin, the barrister for the plaintiff, made his closing arguments. He took his usual approach, clearly trying to wring as much pity as possible from the judge. This woman was broken, he appealed in his final summation. This woman had been betrayed at a time of her life when she should have been looked after, should have been thanked for all she had done. She was just another of the elderly Irish men and women, he said, who were now at risk of being abandoned and forgotten by her state. He warned, too, against the temptation to scapegoat a woman like Mrs Lefroy, the widow of a British army officer, for her connection to a time that was now past, to punish her for things that were long over, for having led a life with privileges and power that some would resent. He had shown beyond all doubt, he said, that Elizabeth Lefroy's son had broken the law, had changed and indeed destroyed a property without the consent of that property's rightful owner. That was what the case came down to – a simple matter of permission and authority and of trust.

'Of trust,' he said, eyeing Rupert Lefroy, and he thanked the judge.

'Jesus Christ,' breathed Imelda, as Glackin took his seat. 'That's a trip to the parish pump the judge isn't likely to forget.'

Linda O'Halloran stood. She demolished Glackin's arguments in minutes. She mocked their provincialism, exposed their presumption, and reminded the court that the case was a question of property law; that her client had broken no law and transgressed no authority. Sympathy and sentiment, she warned, had no place in a court of law. It did no disrespect to a person to follow the rule of law, regardless of the age or the stage of life of that person; on the contrary, one did disrespect to a person to assume that, just because that person happened to be an elderly woman, she should be treated differently, should be afforded certain liberties.

'There are loyalties, there are longings, and then there are laws,' O'Halloran said, as she addressed the judge for a final time. 'We all have mothers. Most of us love our mothers, want the best for our mothers; many of us have lost our mothers, and would do anything to have them back with us. But, Judge, we must be wary of the dangers of sentiment. We must listen to the facts. The facts are: my client was given this property to do with as he pleased. It was a useless property, nothing more than a shed, and he made of it a booming business, a contribution to his city and to his community. We have heard his testimony, which has been honest, patient and full of reason. We have heard, too, the testimony of my client's mother, which has been – as have been the questions and statements of her counsel – emotive, unreasonable and contradictory. This testimony has made much of the matter of duties, of obligation, of what is right and proper, of where our loyalties should finally lie. My loyalties lie, Judge, with the law, the law as it is set down in the statutes of this country – with laws that are fair, and reasonable, and which have the best interests and the rights of the people of this country at their core.'

Throughout this speech, Joanne kept an eye on Elizabeth Lefroy, seated close to the back of the court. Elizabeth had been watching O'Halloran with an expression of intense focus. Her chin was drawn high, her mouth was closed, her eyes were bright. As she listened, only the muscles of her face seemed to react, twitching and tightening. There was nothing, in that face, of the woman ruled by her emotions, maddened by her jealousies and paranoias, who was being described by O'Halloran. Elizabeth's testimony that morning had been the testimony of a woman who wanted no sympathy from the court, who would dismiss such sympathy were it to come her way. Paddy Glackin was an idiot, a country barrister of the kind Joanne knew so well, appealing to the lowest sentiment, pulling on heartstrings. And that rubbish about England – where did he think he was, the local clubhouse? Was he forgetting that the judge in front of him was as much of a West Brit as he was likely to encounter in a house like Elizabeth Lefroy's or anywhere else? It was the final proof that Elizabeth had no money. Even the pension that Rupert claimed to be giving her would get her a barrister with more style and more clout.

O'Halloran sat down. She raised her eyebrows at Imelda. She did not look to Joanne or back to Rupert. Then, things moved quickly. The judge spoke briefly before granting judgment in favour of Rupert. Elizabeth was instructed to pay his costs. At the verdict, Elizabeth's gaze shifted to her son, who was frowning and nodding hard. Afterwards, he left with Mona and Imelda. Joanne watched as his mother talked quietly to her solicitor. When Elizabeth was alone, Joanne stood and approached her.

'Excuse me,' she said, hearing her voice at an unnatural pitch. She cleared her throat. 'Mrs Lefroy?'

Elizabeth glanced up sharply; she had not expected her thoughts to be disturbed. But her expression was not unfriendly. She looked interested. She looked intelligent.

'Yes?' she said lightly. 'Was there something more you needed from me?'

'I just wanted to say I'm sorry for what happened.'

The old woman seemed startled. 'Aren't you with my son?'

'I'm sorry?'

'You are one of the solicitors who represented my son?'

'Yes,' Joanne nodded, but halfway through the nod she shook her head. 'Well, I'm training with them.'

'I see,' Mrs Lefroy said slowly. 'Well, my dear, you know it won't do you any good to be seen talking to me. I think it's best if you go on.'

'Of course,' Joanne said, her cheeks burning.

'My son gets what he wants,' Mrs Lefroy said, standing. 'It was foolish of me to imagine that that would not always be the way.'

'Will you be . . .' Joanne said, and she stopped. What was she going to ask the woman – whether she would be OK? What kind of answer did she expect to get? 'I'm sorry,' she said, and took a step back from the table.

'I'll get on with things,' Elizabeth said, and Joanne was struck by how much like her daughter she sounded. 'And as I've said, my dear, I think you should do the same.'

She nodded again, by way of goodbye, and then she stood and left the courtroom. Joanne packed her notes into her briefcase and followed the same way. By the time she reached the outer hall, she could see that the press, television cameras and all, had descended on Elizabeth. At the main door, she squeezed past, and stood on the steps below to watch the jostling and the shouting. What she had forced herself to push out of her mind since earlier that day was now crashing back in. It was demanding her attention. You don't have anything to worry about, she told herself again. But she did. She knew she did.

It was while she had been getting ready to leave the office that morning that she had thought of it. She had forgotten it; she had forgotten to watch for it, forgotten to notice that it had not come. She had been too overwhelmed by too many other things. She had been searching for something in the bottom drawer of her desk. Whatever she was looking for was not in the drawer, but the box of tampons was there, and when she saw it, she understood with a shock that almost forced her from her standing. It had been too long. It had been, she thought, her mind reeling backwards over the weeks, almost a whole two months. She took it up, the half-empty box, and stuffed it into her handbag, telling herself that she would need it, that it had just been the workload and the exhaustion. That, now the Lefroy case was ending, the cramps and the bleeding would come. But at the same time as Imelda called to her to hurry she was counting backwards again, counting the times, counting the possibilities. They had always used condoms. She had not got around to going back on the pill; she had meant to go to her doctor about it, but she had been too busy, there had never been the time. And she thought that they had always been careful, but she knew the truth of it was that she could not be sure. There could have been an accident. They might have been too drunk to notice. There might have been a night when he had taken too much of a risk, staying too long in the luxury of her, not pulling out in time to put the condom on. You were not supposed to do it – she had known that since she was a teenager – but surely everybody did.

'You're making us late, Joanne,' Imelda snapped, and they were gone.

Rupert was treating them to celebratory drinks in the Shelbourne, and afterwards he was taking them to dinner in the restaurant where the mews house had been. He was in exuberant humour, and so were Mona and Eoin and Imelda. Joanne watched, laughed when she had to, and drank three glasses of red wine. There was no reason not to, she told herself; there was no reason why she could not have as much wine as she pleased. Still, after the third glass, she made her excuses; she was sorry, she said, but she had someone to meet, she had already made plans. Rupert had his arm draped easily over the back of Mona's chair as she left.

At the chemist on the corner, Joanne bought what she needed, and when she got home, she dumped her things in the sitting room. She went upstairs without a word in response to Sarah's greeting. She had taken pregnancy tests before. They had always been accurate – that is, they had always been negative. This time, as she stood in her best suit in the upstairs bathroom, the two pink lines were as clear and as definite as the tracks of two tyres through a fresh fall of snow.

From downstairs, she heard Sarah shouting her name. She walked to the bathroom door without feeling that she had the use of her legs.

'What?' she shouted downstairs, and her voice did not sound like her own.

'You're all on the six o'clock news!' Sarah shouted back up to her. 'You, and Mona Manolo, and yer man she's shagging, and his mother, and you all! Come down and look at yourself! You've made it, my girl! You're the news!'

Chapter Twelve

The baby was born in May. It was a girl with nobody's eyes and nobody's shock of fine red hair. There had been red hair way back on the Lynch side once, Joanne said, but none of them that Maura remembered had ever had that colouring.

Of course, that would be another doubt in Tom's mind, she thought, as soon as she laid eyes on the baby. That would be another reason for him to refuse to have anything to do with his grandchild. She was a lovely little thing, really, as lovely as a newborn could be. She still looked battered and bewildered from the fright of being born, and naturally Joanne looked like a frightened child herself, propped up against the hospital pillows, the gown hanging off her, her cheeks blotched almost purple. By the bed, Mark sat trying, Maura could see, to appear calm, but his eyes were jumping out of his head. He was talking too much, talking non-sense; she could see he was bothering Joanne, crowding her with questions about the child's scalp and the child's feet and the plastic bracelet around the child's wrist, and about Joanne's pillows and whether they were hard enough, or soft enough, and about whether the child would need to be fed again soon, or whether they should wait until they heard her cry.

'She's grand, Mark,' Maura said, and the two of them looked to her anxiously, imploringly. You, both their stares seemed to say. You know what to do with one of these. You had one. You had two. You know the rules. Show us. Tell us. Make this thing possible for us to do.

But then, just as quickly, they looked away, to the child again, and they were focused tight in on her as though on a button they were trying to unfasten; pulling the white cap back down over her head, taking the little hands and hiding them under white cotton cuffs, touching the tiny, crumpled face and willing it to smooth into contentment. And at that kind of willing, that kind of wishing, they would spend, probably, most of the rest of their days. She would be back in a couple of minutes, Maura told them, and she stepped out into the narrow, nurse-bustling hall.

Maura had worked in a hospital with mothers and babies for nearly half her life. When they had taken children out of women with forceps, or when they had broken women's pelvic bones, or when they had taken stillborns away in tin buckets, thrown them out with the slops, she had not thought of any of it as inhuman, as horrific. It had merely been the way. Still, when her own time had come, with Nuala and then with Mark, she had gone not to the manor in Edgeworthstown but to the big hospital in Mullingar, where everything was new and the doctors were young and the maternity wards were like something out of a film. But still it had felt like a slaughtering to bring each of them into the world. Still there had been the forceps, and the blade to make room for Nuala's head to come, and still there would have been a bucket, or something like it, if anything had gone wrong. She had lost one, but that had been before she had gone her full term; for that, she had been alone. That had been a boy, and he had been given his father's name.

In the hall she tried to call home again. Tom never picked up the house phone anyway, so she did not know why she was hoping for anything different today, but she let it ring, let it ring until the climb and trill of it started to sound shrill, hysterical, unreal. He could be out on the land or in the yard, or he could be away in the jeep or on the tractor, but he could just as well be there, in the sitting room, staring at the phone as it rang itself out. He would fight her to the last on this, she knew. He would stand his ground. But she would stand hers, and though it was always important to give him the appearance of having got what he wanted, the truth of it was that she always won.

He had not reacted well to the news of the pregnancy. Neither of them had. She was not proud of how she had behaved, of what she had said to Mark, of what she had said about Joanne. But she had apologized, and quickly, and that had been the important thing. She had meant none of it. Mark turning up like that one Saturday in November, with the girl she knew only as the Lynch daughter in tow: it had been too much of a shock. Tom had been at the mart in Granard, and all she had been able to think about, at first, was how she had to get Mark and the girl out of the house before Tom returned, so that she could break the news of their involvement to him in her own way, in her own time. But there was more to it, she had known from their faces, almost as soon as they had walked in the door; she had known right inside herself what it was. So when Mark had told her, it was no surprise, not really, not after she had seen the paleness of the girl's face as she stood by the range and looked at the floor. Maura had imagined this conversation, or some version of it, all through Mark's teenage years. Once he was in his twenties she had not worried about it in the same way, and now he was heading for thirty, it should not have been a problem at all, not really, but there was the matter of the girl. And so, Mark had told her that the girl was pregnant, and well pregnant, and that they were moving together into her house in Stoneybatter and making it into something of a home. That the girl was a solicitor, or training to be a solicitor, and had worked it out with her employers: they would keep her on, on condition that she worked right up to the birth and went back again very soon afterwards. And Mark had his grant, and the money he was making from teaching, and that, along with Joanne's pay from the solicitors, should be enough to get them through the first year.

'And then?' Maura had said, and through the crack in her voice there escaped the sourest of laughs. 'And after the first year is done, what the hell do you propose to do?'

Mark looked stricken. The girl would still not meet her eye. 'We'll manage,' he had said. 'We're just trying to work out how to get through the first part for now. It's all ... it's all very new.'

'The first part,' said Maura, shaking her head. 'Jesus tonight.'

'Mam,' Mark said quietly. 'Please.'

She had looked at him, standing beside the girl at the range. They were both too awkward, too nervous, to sit down, and Maura was not in the humour, now, to try to make them more comfortable. The girl was still early enough along not to need to be petted, anyway, not to need to get off her feet. She was younger than Mark. She looked like Irene: the strong bones at her cheeks, the high forehead, the freckled skin. But she was like her father in the eyes.

Tom would take this badly. How would she get this story under control by the time he returned? And then, she had realized with a sickening lurch, there was no way to get this under control, no way to manage it. No way to turn it into something other than what it was.

'And what does your mother think of this, Joanne?' Maura had asked, and she saw how the girl started.

'She doesn't know yet,' the girl had said.

'She'll get a right land, I'm sure, like myself,' Maura said, and she sighed.

'I know that.' For a moment, Maura had thought the girl was going to cry – in fact, Maura had thought the girl should cry – but the tears did not come. What had come instead was the sound of Tom's jeep on the drive.

The hours afterwards were not something Maura liked to remember. Tom had looked at Maura suspiciously as soon as he walked in. Joanne had been introduced, and there had been for Maura the pain of watching confusion spread over his face, of watching fear set in. When Mark had told him about the pregnancy, all he had said was 'What? What?' over and over again, and he had looked to Maura, the way he always did when he wanted something fixed or something righted or something arranged; he had looked to her, waiting for her to make it go away. And then he had gone very quiet, and very still, and he had looked first to Mark and then to the girl. 'You'd better sit down, so,' he had told her.

When she had sat, she had sat in Tom's seat, the one beside the range, but that had hardly mattered any more.

The call had come to the house before seven o'clock that morning. Maura had answered it, her heart pounding. It was Mark. A baby girl, he said, just over seven pounds. A little mite, Maura had answered, shocked to find herself in tears.

He didn't think she had felt like a mite to Joanne, Mark had said in return, and Maura could hear the shock still in his voice. He had been in there with her. Of course: that was how it was done now. Well, he had seen something that he would never forget. Maura was seized with a longing to comfort him but then she was surprised to find herself thinking, instead, of Joanne. She would see them at the hospital in a couple of hours, she said.

She had got there by noon. She had brought a bag filled with the things she knew Joanne would need – not just Babygros and nightgowns, but sanitary pads, and nipple pads, and creams, and a few new pairs of underwear. It had been a short enough labour, seven hours, but one of the nurses had told Maura that it had gone very hard on Joanne. 'And on Dad too,' she had added, for a moment confusing Maura, who had thought of Tom, and of how she had gone back up to the bedroom that morning to give him the news, and of how he had just turned away from her in the bed.

He would come around. He would come here. She was sure of it. She would see to it. Joanne would be here for another night at least, and when Maura came back the next afternoon, she would have Tom with her if it killed her. This was his granddaughter. He would just have to get used to it. His son had a daughter now, and that was a great thing, at the end of the day, and she wanted desperately, she realized – again surprising herself – to see her husband looking on as their son held his child. She wanted it so badly, so strongly, that she knew it must be some instinct. And so Tom would be here. He would manage. Whether Irene Lynch would also be here was irrelevant. They would manage that as well. In a small metal cot by a hospital bed, their granddaughter was sleeping and crying and staring. Tom would be meeting her. He would be here.

*

Tom planned to be out on the land all day. There was work to be done. The fields needed to be dragged and rolled, the rushes cut from out of the thickening grass, the ground spread with fertilizer and readied for the haymaking months ahead. It was work that he could not easily do alone, but it would have to be done alone. As he was dragging the chain harrow out of the ditch where it had been left after the work of the previous spring, Maura came out to the yard to tell him she was leaving for Dublin. She asked him again if he was sure that he would not go with her.

'Of course I'm sure,' he said. 'Who else do you think will do these jobs? Am I meant to go up to Lynches' and ask one of the sons to roll these fields for me so I can go up to Dublin to gawk at a child?'

'She's your granddaughter, Tom,' Maura said, but she was already leaving, closing her jacket and checking for something in her bag.

'I'm sure she's very lonesome for me,' Tom called, as she opened the door of the car. 'Or for you. I'm sure she'll thank you for taking the trouble to go up and see her.'

Maura turned. 'Mark might thank me,' she said, and she looked at him with some question in her eyes. 'Do you have any message for him at all?'

'No message,' Tom said, and turned back to the machine. The chain harrow was tangled and seized. It would take an hour or more of careful work to set it right. As he fixed his pliers around the first link, he heard Maura's engine cough itself up to a rev, and then she was gone. He stood up and stretched, noticing how clear and blue the sky was, what a warm day it was shaping up to be. It was a May morning, and he had the place to himself. It was peaceful. There were far worse places you could find yourself.

When he had finished with the chain harrow, and was laying its rusted lengths out behind the tractor, Sammy Stewart came around with a saw he wanted Tom to have a look at. It was a knack Tom had picked up when he was a young man, how to listen to a saw, how to look at the blade as it ran and as it was still, how to know what part of it to take out and clean or screw tighter, what part of it to leave alone. Sometimes strangers came to the house and paid him to fix an engine for them or to have a look at a lawnmower or a strimmer, but he wouldn't take money from Sammy. Things went back too long between the pair of them. Sammy knew that too.

'Maura's not around today,' Sammy said, as he put the chainsaw down on the ground between them.

Tom looked at him to see if he showed a sign of knowing anything. 'She was talking about heading into Longford to get a few things,' Tom said after a moment, and Sammy nodded.

'I thought I saw her on the road there,' he said.

Tom went down on his hunkers to take a look at the chainsaw. The chain could do with tightening, and the filter with a clean, but apart from that it barely needed to be seen to at all. He looked at Sammy. 'There's hardly a hilt wrong with this engine at all.'

Sammy seemed surprised. 'I thought I felt a pull on it yesterday evening when I was using it.'

Tom stood and yanked the starter cord. The noise of the saw scared a clatter of birds out of the trees over the yard. The engine ran clear. Tom knocked it off again and took it across to the fence, to where the lower branches of the trees along the meadow drooped and jutted in towards the yard. On one of them, he tried the saw, leaning back as he did so, away from the yellow dust that leaped up around the blade. It sliced steadily through the damp green wood of the branch and Tom stood back to watch it fall. 'You must have been imagining things,' he said to Sammy.

Sammy shrugged. 'Must have been.' He took the saw and

cut away another chunk of the same branch. It fell like a shot bird into the nettles clumped along the edge of the meadow.

'Well, that's grand, Tom,' Sammy said, as he turned off the saw.

'It'll last you another while yet.'

'I was in Keogh's before I came here,' Sammy said then, quickly, and Tom heard how careful his voice had become. So he knew.

'Is that right?'

'Paddy Keogh has the whole story, Tom. I'm just telling you, now. I thought you'd want to know.'

Tom nodded. 'Thanks.'

'So congratulations to you.'

Tom put his toe to the quietened blade of the chainsaw. The dog, who had disappeared at the first sound of the cutting, had come back to stand between the two men, her tail still low but wagging warily, and she stepped forward now to sniff at his boot as he took it back from the saw. 'Did Keogh say where he heard it from?'

'No, Tom, and I didn't ask him,' Sammy said, his voice full of apology. 'You know that he'd only be dying for me to ask him that kind of thing. It'd make him feel important, to have people coming in and telling him the news, and for him to be giving it out.'

They stood in silence for a moment.

'Lookit, Tom,' said Sammy then. 'Fuck Paddy Keogh.'

'I'd say it made his morning.'

'I'd say it did, the fucker, but sure lookit, isn't it a sad state of affairs when you have to be waiting on another man's news for there to be a bit of excitement in your own morning? Jesus, when you think about it, it's little Paddy Keogh has to be grinning about. You don't see any sign of one of those useless fools of his to be giving him any grand-childer.'

'Still,' Tom said, and wanted to say more, but nothing clear would come. 'Still,' he said again, and he looked to where the tractor and the chain harrow were parked outside the shed. The harrow was laid out behind it like a quilt. Have you your own harrow ready, he was about to say to Sammy, but then heavily, dramatically, Sammy sighed. Tom felt his throat tighten as he looked towards him.

'Frank Lynch is dead a long time now, Tom,' Sammy said. He shook his head. 'You don't find the years going by. Mark a father. My God.'

Tom said nothing. Sammy knew what had happened with Lynch. Sammy had been Tom's friend. He had listened. He had given his advice. He had turned his back on Frank Lynch in solidarity with Tom. But he had said, also, that it was the fault of none of the rest of the family. That Irene was a good woman. That the lads were decent. He had never mentioned the girl. The girl would have been too young, and there would have been no reason for Sammy to know her.

'Tom,' said Sammy, breaking into his thoughts. 'I have two grandchildren. Alan has them over in Prague. The little fella is three and the girl is just gone a year now. You remember the boy being born.'

Tom nodded. 'I remember it well.' Sammy had come to the house that morning, the horn blowing, the window down, nearly – to Tom's discomfort – crying as he shouted the news. A boy. A boy had been born. Their son was a father. In a few days, he and Helen would be going out to Prague to see the child for themselves. He could hardly wait. Later, Helen had told Tom and Maura that Sammy had nearly driven her demented over those few days. Wanting to ring Alan and his wife every half-hour. Wanting Helen to go on to her email to see if there were any new photographs of the child. Wanting to see if any earlier plane tickets could be got.

'Anyway,' Sammy said, 'they're home here to us as often as they can. And they think they'll be able to move back here in a couple of years.'

'That'll be grand for yourself and Helen,' Tom was able to say.

'It will,' Sammy said. 'But those children won't be as small then as they are now. And those years when they were small and all that won't come back to us again, no matter how close they build their house to us. I'm awful sorry I don't see more of them sometimes. A lot of times, to tell you the truth. Do you know?'

'I do, Sammy.'

'The young fella talks to me over the phone at the weekends. David. Jesus, I don't know what kind of accent he has on him. You wouldn't understand the half of it. Granddad, I want to go with you on the truck, he says to me.'

'The tractor,' said Tom, and he was able, at least half able, to laugh.

Sammy pointed to the old Ford, half buried under logs in the turf shed. 'Do you mind the time Mark was up with you on that yoke over there?'

'Couldn't get him off the thing,' Tom said. 'That was the sort of him.'

'And a wee girl, of course, you won't be putting a wee girl up on a tractor,' Sammy said, and then he laughed. 'Or maybe you might, if the mother will let you, but, Jesus, it's nice to have them around you all the same, Tom. The small ones.'

Sammy bent to take the saw up again. As he lifted it, he shook his head. 'Jesus, you wouldn't know the years going by, Tom. Do you know?'

Was he drunk, Tom found himself thinking, but pushed the thought away. It wasn't right, it wasn't kind: Sammy was a good man, had always been a good friend. He was carrying the saw to the car now. After he had stowed it and slammed the boot down, he turned back to Tom. 'That lassie could be nothing like her father, Tom,' he said.

Tom looked at him. 'The child?' he said, and Sammy shook his head.

'No, Tom. The girl. Mark's girlfriend. Or his partner, I suppose.'

It was the first time Tom had heard her referred to like this. He swallowed. 'The mother, you mean,' he said.

'The mother. What's this it is?'

'What?'

Sammy looked at him. 'Her name, Tom,' he said.

'Oh,' Tom said. 'Joanne.'

'Joanne. And any name on the child yet?'

Tom shook his head, more vigorously than he had meant to. It was a shock to hear that said. The child would be named.

'No name,' he said.

'No name only Casey so far,' said Sammy, and laughed.

'Jesus,' said Tom, 'I hope so.' And that was another shock, as it hit him: there was another Casey, now, in the world. Another of them. Another of his own.

'Ah, I wouldn't worry about that, Tom,' Sammy said. 'It was the same with David over there. Alan and Teresa weren't married that time and I was wondering would she want to give him her own name, but they don't really seem to. They seem to want to give them the father's name.'

'I see.'

'And I was saying, you know, that the girl, she might be very different from the father.'

'She might,' Tom said, wanting to talk about anything else.

'Sure face it, Tom, she must be, if Mark wants anything to do with her.'

'I don't know,' Tom said. 'It all happened very quick.'

'Everything happens very quick, Tom. That's what I'm saying to you. The years. The way they go.'

'Yeah.'

'Lookit, Tom,' said Sammy, as he opened the door of his car, 'the child is here now. Would you go up and have a look at her?' He sat into the driver's seat and gestured back to the boot with his thumb. 'Thanks for looking at that engine for me.'

'There wasn't too much wrong with it, now,' said Tom, and Sammy shook his head.

'It needed to be looked at, Tom,' he said, 'and you were the only one who'd know what to do with it. I'll see you some night in Keogh's.'

Tom nodded. 'Good luck.'

As Sammy headed off, his old Volvo estate bumping over the uneven ground leading from the yard to the drive, Tom thought he heard the sound of the phone from inside. But when he went closer to the back door he realized that he was imagining it. Nobody was looking for him. Nobody was standing at a phone some place where he couldn't see them, waiting for him to pick up. He whistled to the dog and headed down the yard towards the lower fields.

Chapter Thirteen

Mossy turned up in Holles Street on Sunday, hung-over, carrying a bunch of flowers and a knitted baby's hat in the shape of a strawberry.

'For fuck's sake,' Mark laughed when he unwrapped it. 'Where did you get this thing?'

'The Avoca shop,' Mossy said, acting offended.

'So you were drinking in O'Neill's for the cure this morning?'

'Stag's,' Mossy said sheepishly.

'Don't mind him, Mossy,' Joanne said, fixing the hat on the baby's head. 'It's gorgeous.'

Mossy sat with Aoife a while, holding her up too close to him, like he was afraid she would roll out of his grip. She couldn't focus on anything yet, the nurse had told them, but she seemed to see his curls; she stared up at them. They sat there talking for a few minutes, and then there was a knock on the door, and there was Mark's mother, smiling as proudly as though she were bringing a newborn of her own in to show them, and there was his father behind her, looking down at the floor.

As far as Mark could gather, his parents had been to one o'clock mass in the cathedral in Longford, and then they had been for their lunch in the Longford Arms, and then they had driven in the direction of home, his mother at the wheel. And when she had come to the turn for their lane, she had not taken it, but had kept going on the Dublin road.

'And here we are,' she said, not to him but to the baby. 'What do you think of her, Mossy?'

'Ah, you couldn't resist her,' said Mossy. He smiled up at Maura, and he looked, then, to where Tom still stood at the door. 'I'd better let her introduce herself to her granddad,' he said, and he offered Aoife out in his arms.

'Tom,' Mark's mother said, a dip of pleading in her tone, and his father walked into the room. He stood at the bottom of the bed for a moment, clearly not knowing what to do. Then he shook Mark's hand, stiffly, without looking at him, and Joanne's hand, in the same way. And then, finding himself beside Mossy, he shook his hand, too.

'Are you going to shake this one's hand as well?' Mossy said, and everyone laughed, and Tom looked as though he might laugh too, but he did not, and still he did not take the baby. He walked over to the window and looked out at the car park below, his back to the room.

'Did you see anyone you know at one o'clock mass?' Mark said, after a long moment. It was the standard question, the question his parents always asked each other, the question everyone asked everyone else at home, but it was the wrong question, he knew, as soon as it was out of his mouth. He saw his father stiffen.

'Ah, you know, the usual,' his mother said quickly. 'Lots of people asking for you. Lots of people wondering how you were getting on, Joanne. And lots of people sending their congratulations.'

'Breda Keogh was very worried about you,' Mark's father said then. They all looked at him in surprise.

'Breda Keogh wasn't at one o'clock mass, sure,' Maura said, in a clipped tone. She glanced at Mark, and he saw the anxiety in her eyes. They both knew that whatever reason his father had for making this his first comment could not be a good one.

'I was talking to her in the shop,' Tom said, half turning, addressing himself not to Maura but to Joanne. 'She was terrible worried about you when she heard you were after having the baby.'

'Really?' Joanne said uncertainly.

'Oh, yes,' said Tom, his voice beginning to rise now. Mark's heart sank. It meant trouble when his father's voice began to swell like that.

'Very worried about the babby,' Tom went on. 'She said, sure that babby couldn't be due for another month or six weeks yet, could it now, Tom? She said it could only be seven or eight months since she heard the news. Oh, she was terrible worried. Terrible concerned at it being premature.'

Nobody spoke. Mossy and Joanne were looking at Tom, waiting for him to go on, waiting for him to make clear whatever it was he was trying to say. Mark and Maura did not look at him. They looked at each other. Maura knew what his father was saying, Mark could see – that terrible strain on her face – and he was coming to understand it too.

'Tom, stop that,' his mother said. 'Sure Breda Keogh doesn't even know Joanne.'

'Oh, Breda knows everybody,' Tom said, in a sing-song voice.

'Breda Keogh's a poisonous bitch,' Mark said, and he walked over and took the baby from Mossy. He moved in close to his father at the window, holding the baby up to him so that he could not ignore her. The baby began to whimper.

'Mark,' Joanne said, from the bed, but he only pushed the child in closer and closer to his father's face.

'Look at her, Dad,' he said, and his father's gaze flickered and flitted before coming to settle on the top of the baby's head.

'Isn't she a lovely little one?' his mother said, with great deliberateness. 'Tom,' she said, when Mark's father did not reply, and then, finally, his father nodded.

'Good luck to the both of yiz,' he said, with great solemnity, looking only to Mark and the child.

'Thanks, Tom,' said Joanne, from the bed.

'She's a lovely little one,' Maura said again. 'Give her to him, Mark, will you not?'

'Mark,' said Joanne. 'That window. I don't want her near to that draught.'

*

She cried every night for almost every last minute of the night, and she cried in the early morning, and for a good part of the day. In theory, that was no surprise. That much they had been warned about. But the exhaustion, and the drudgery, and the fear of getting something horribly wrong: nobody had described any of that. Nobody had described the way everything would shrink to this pinprick. It all became about getting this unknowable being, this powerless and yet infinitely powerful little reptile, through the day and through the night when day and night scarcely seemed divided. The hours seemed to stop passing, becoming just a wall of insomnia and of the same actions repeated over and over until all awareness of a world outside fell away, came to seem like a rumour they both remembered hearing, but which they never had the time, never a moment, to sit down and straighten out. Of course they went into this world, of course they had to; once or twice a day one or the other of them went down the street and around the corner to the Centra, which sold milk and bread and nappies and formula at extortionate prices, but it was a five-minute walk, and it passed in a daze of thought and confusion and absorption in whatever scene they had just left behind: what hour of screaming, what fragment of silence, what rash, what shiver, what colour of puke, and what the next hour would bring, what needed to be done, what needed to be guarded against.

She was doing wonderfully. Those were the nurse's words. The nurse came once a week, and when she was in the house the baby somehow seemed to know it, seemed to put on her best show: her quiet gaze, her gorgeous yawn, her delicate, almost fey little squirm in your arms. The nurse said she was strong, she was healthy, she was growing at exactly the right rate, that the formula seemed to be suiting her, although it would be even better, of course, if the milk could be coming from Mom.

'I have to go back to work in a month,' said Joanne, once again. She had told the nurse this already; she had told her several times. She had told her mother, too, and Mark's mother, and the nurses in Holles Street. Everybody seemed to be very concerned about the benefits of breastfeeding. Everybody seemed to think that surely something could be done about the terrible shortness of Joanne's maternity leave. Everybody had a solution, but nobody, as far as Joanne could see, had breasts throbbing and leaking with milk. And nobody had case files building up on a desk on Ormond Quay. She knew that the work she had to do was mounting, that Eoin and Imelda had not hired anyone to replace her during her leave; for the sake of less than two months, said Imelda, it would not have been worth their while.

She had worked in the office until the weekend before the birth. The narrow stairs with the rickety steps made sure that she started and finished each long, grinding day with the awareness of how responsible she was for the life curled up inside her beneath a layer of skin. Mark's mother had lost a baby at the bottom of the staircase in Dorvaragh, she had told Joanne. She would not wish the pain or the shock or the guilt of it on anyone, she had said. This had been while Joanne was growing bigger, growing slower, around the eight-month mark. Mark's mother had been full of the kind of advice that had made Joanne wary of even stepping outside the door.

Now it was about Mark's mother and Joanne's mother that the nurse was asking, about how far away they lived, about the great help they must be, about what a godsend they would prove to be in the months ahead. As she spoke, the nurse lifted one and then the other of the baby's legs, pulling each one gently, as if to stretch it out. What was that for? Was that meant to be some method for encouraging limbs to grow? Much of what the nurse did on her visits seemed mysterious. There was a lot of pressing and listening, tapping and weighing, and there was very little of the nurse telling them the things they had to do. They never felt, after one of her visits, that they were any closer to knowing what the trick to all of this might be.

'You'll need your mom on the other end of the phone when this mom goes back to work,' the nurse said to Mark.

'Yeah,' said Mark, in a tone as close as he could manage to the sheepishness that, he felt sure, the nurse wanted to hear. But he didn't want to sound sheepish. He resented feeling as though he had to. And if she said 'mom' in that mid-Atlantic twang one more time, he would snatch Aoife right out of her arms.

'Oh, it'll be a right land for your daddy,' the nurse said to Aoife, dipping her low so that her gaze roamed around the room. 'But he'll get used to it, won't he? He'll just have to, won't he, pet?'

Beside him, Joanne sighed. He looked at her; she looked away. She was sighing not out of irritation at what the nurse was saying about him, he knew, but out of misery at what she was reminding them of: the fact that, very shortly, Joanne would be going back to work. This was not something Joanne wanted to talk about. Every time Mark tried to bring up the subject, she started to cry. She seemed unable to bear the idea of returning to the office, and of being away from Aoife, and of starting up again with those twelve-hour days of slaving away for Imelda and Eoin, and of coming back in the evenings at a time when the baby would long since have gone down. He could understand it. The truth was, he would have hated to leave the baby too, even for a day. But how he was going to manage by himself was something he could barely imagine. He could give Joanne a run for her money when it came to anxiety and paranoia. The things that could go wrong. The damage you could accidentally do. The things that it could take you ages to spot, and by then it would be too late. And the madness. The slow, creeping madness. He could feel it already quite firmly beginning to take hold. It was sleep deprivation, he knew that. But it was also the lack of what used to be reality: adult conversation, meaningless diversion, normal everyday crap. He missed it. No, that was not true; he did not have time to miss it. He could barely even remember it. But he was going demented without it. He was a worker at a conveyor-belt. He was a horse with a thousand acres to plough. He was a rat in a lab.

'You are a useless, self-pitying, fucking arsehole, and I wish to God I'd never set eyes on you.' That was Joanne's take on what he was. It was not constant, this perspective of hers; it was not always that she felt this way, but it seemed to be most of the time now. She was just tired, he knew. Was the word 'harried'? He thought so. But that word seemed tied to 'harridan', which was something, he knew, he was absolutely not to call her. But, Jesus, if it wasn't tempting sometimes. She was still sore, he was aware of that, and she was shattered, and she was as scared of the baby as she was infatuated with her. And Mark knew, from what he was feeling himself, how these states of mind fed on and compounded each other, how the fear rendered the adoration the most terrifying thing you could feel, how the adoration warped and whittled the fear. You were afraid, half of the time, even to move.

But still. This was his baby too. This was his daughter. And it was hard to hear Joanne talking to him like that. It made everything even more exhausting. And part of the trouble was that he was certain, now, that he loved her. Loved Joanne. There hadn't been time for it to happen the way it usually did. There hadn't been that sinking from lusting to liking to loving. They had been seeing each other, and fucking each other, and getting on with each other, and suddenly they had been staring at each other in the kitchen of her house in Stoneybatter, Mark holding a bottle of champagne, Joanne holding a pink thing that looked like a pen, and then Joanne was crying her eyes out and Mark was hearing the blood thump in his ears. They had gone back and forth for hours – would she keep it, would she have it, would they stay together, would they forget this had ever happened, would they have any money, would they have any future, would he please put down that fucking champagne. And, apart from the detail about the champagne, that had been the pattern of their conversation for days afterwards. For weeks.

He had not pressured her either way. He had not told her what to do. He had not told her what he wanted – not that he knew what that was. It was only when Joanne made her decision that he realized what he had wanted: when she told him she was keeping the baby, he was stunned by the relief that coursed through him. It was ludicrous, wanting it so much. He had no proper job. He had no money. No way of providing for a child. And with Joanne, he barely even had a relationship. They had been sleeping together for not much more than a month: how could she be pregnant? But she was. And, yes, she told him, yes, it was definitely his. 'I knew that,' he said, but what he was thinking was that it had not even occurred to him to ask the question. How good could he possibly be at planning for the future – for somebody else's future – if he wasn't quick enough, even, to think of that? But there was no time to dwell on anything: soon she was showing, and soon she was growing big with the child. And there had been arrangements to make, and their parents to deal with, and a house to get in order, and a birth for which to prepare. And of course there had been talk of love. Professions of love. Moments of love. But Mark had never been really sure that he could feel it.

But now he was sure. And it made no sense. Because she was like someone else. Since the last weeks of the pregnancy, really, she had not been herself, what with the fearfulness and the tearfulness and the preoccupation and the panic. And the irritability. And the anger. He knew it had to pass. He knew it had to be normal. It was fear that something would happen to the baby, that she would somehow be neglected, or damaged, or lost. And that was a fear Mark understood.

In the hours after she was born they were both dazed, struck incoherent and disbelieving as though by a sudden loss rather than a gain. They had sat together on the bed in Holles Street, the plastic curtain drawn around the tiny space that had become charged with the shock of their now being three: Mark on the edge of the mattress, Joanne, flushed and wet-haired, propped up against the pillows. And the baby. For over a day, the baby without a name. Then, Aoife Luisne Casey, named after nobody, named for nobody but herself.

Aoife came to them at six in the morning. She had spent a whole night in the struggle towards them. Or away from them. Which was it? Which had she wanted? When they slopped her on to Joanne's chest, Mark had stared at her and tried to steel himself into feeling whatever it was he was supposed, at that moment, to be feeling. This being, this screaming little being, she was his. She was theirs. What were they supposed to do with her? What were they supposed to do for her? Were they supposed to show her how to live?

Now she was quiet in her mother's arms, sucking steadily and intently on her bottle. It was a Sunday morning. What Sunday morning, what month, what time of year? Nothing came quickly enough to his mind any more. It took a minute to work it out. It was June, it was summertime. The blinds of the sitting room were still closed. It could be any kind of day out there. At the window, he pulled the cord to reveal a pale blue sky, a dazzle of sunlight, puddles of water on the cement of the back yard. The feral cats that gathered there scattered at the rattling of the blinds. White plastic garden furniture lay around the place, old potted plants that had long since withered and died. Two bicycles were propped up against the red-brick wall, rusted now, tangled with overgrown ivy and with each other.

'We should bring her for a walk today,' he said, turning to Joanne, who looked at him with puffed and wary eyes.

'Bring her where?'

'To the Phoenix Park. Or into town, along the quays.'

Joanne shrugged. 'Maybe, after her nap.'

He began to get the pram ready. A bag with her nappies, with wipes, with all the things they would need if she got hungry or cold, or if it rained. Another bag with bottles, something to keep them warm, an extra soother, Sudocrem. Deep inside the pram's hood, his mother had pinned a religious medal. Some saint. He didn't know which one. He didn't know his saints. He knew that Anthony was for lost things, and Jude was for lost causes, and Dymphna was for the mad. But it couldn't be any of those. He put a hand into the hood and searched for the medal; finding it, he leaned towards it, squinted to see who it was. Brigid. Of course. Brigid of the chubby little crosses made from rushes. St Mel, growing confused in his old age, had accidentally ordained her a bishop instead of an abbess. It was weird, Mark thought, the useless things you remembered from school.

'No,' Joanne said suddenly, from the couch. 'Forget the park. I couldn't be bothered. Anyway, it's probably going to rain.'

'I'll take her,' Mark said, but Joanne shook her head.

'Leave it,' she said. 'It's too much hassle. If you want to be helpful, go out and get something for dinner.'

In Centra he bought steaks and potatoes and a bag of frozen peas, and nappies and baby powder and baby formula and baby shampoo, and a box of cereal for the morning, and a bottle of wine for whenever they would ever again get to sit down together and drink a bottle of wine. And walking back up Arbour Hill he saw that Mossy was at the door. He called up to him, shouted to him not to ring the doorbell. By some miracle of St Brigid and St Jude and St Dymphna, Aoife might have gone to sleep, and if Mossy woke her, Joanne would go mad. But then he realized that in his pocket his phone was ringing, and it was Mossy: Mossy, who'd worked out already that it might not be such a good idea to make a racket at the door. Mark waved, and in a minute he was hugging Mossy, like a drowning man being pulled from the sea.

*

The summer passed. It was only a clutch of weeks, seeming longer and more beautiful before it began. Soon what sunshine came was not warm but autumnal, and the light lasted each evening for a shorter and shorter time.

Joanne had been back at work since early July. The hours were long, as she had known they would be, and as winter began to draw in, she woke up every morning wishing it was night and that she was walking up Arbour Hill, looking at the crooked number 4 on their front door, coming into the house to the smell of food and to the light on in the hall and to the fire lit in the sitting room. There was so much that she wanted to do with this house now. It had hardly been a home at all before Mark and the baby. It had been somewhere she inhabited, like a student flat. Now she saw it differently. She wanted to paint the hall a bright colour and to put down new floorboards. To rip up the ugly old carpet in the sitting room. A room had to be made for Aoife; the whole house needed light and air and space. For years before she had moved in, her father had rented the place to students, and it still had that look to it. She had not had the money to do it up when she inherited it, and she did not know where that money would come from now. But she would find it. She would have to. Soon, Aoife would be old enough to see this place with her own eyes. Joanne did not want her to see it the way it was now.

If she got home before seven, Aoife would still be up. She was a joy at that hour, cheerful, affectionate, loving the sight of her mother come home. She smiled in huge gales of happiness and grasped at the strands of Joanne's hair. In a corner by the sofa they had laid a soft mat on the floor and scattered soft toys and other things around. She was still too young to play with them, but she seemed to like being surrounded by them, seemed to like being there on her back, taking slow account of them.

Joanne liked to be there to bathe her before bed; to sit her into the soapy water and watch her pleasure at the warmth of it, to watch her squirm and kick and stare as she relaxed her way towards sleep. She would carry her, wrapped in a towel, into the room where she and Mark slept, and she would change her into a clean nappy and a Babygro. Then she would lay her down under a pink crochet blanket. It had been Joanne's when she was a baby; her mother had kept it all these years, had brought it into the hospital to them on that very first day. They had a nightlight of gently turning sheep and moons and stars. The baby's eyes followed the twirling reflections on the walls and the ceiling, like the ticking hands of a clock. Joanne watched her, often, as her eyes closed. As the child slept, she clutched with one hand the top of the blanket. The other hand was always thrown wide. Often as she watched her sleep or drift into sleep Joanne felt again the dread she had felt during the pregnancy, during the labour, in the impossible first weeks. How would she do for this person all that needed to be done?

She still could not think of herself as a mother. Six months on, it was still too strange. She had expected the change to be monumental. In other women, it seemed to have been. She had no close friends with babies, but she had talked online to women who were giving birth around the same time as her, and their emotion seemed to be so much more intense than Joanne's. She worried from time to time about this. But what she felt for her baby, felt, at the same time, right; felt normal. She loved her. She would have killed for her. She found it painful to look at her sometimes, she was so beautiful; she found it painful to realize how transient this beauty was. It would grow into another kind of beauty, she knew, but the baby face, the baby smell, the body that could be bundled and carried in the crook of her arm – already that body was no longer light enough to be spirited around as in the first days and weeks. Already she was growing heavy.

Joanne felt that somehow she must be getting it wrong. None of the mothers online seemed afraid of their babies, as she sometimes was. They seemed hysterical with pride and obsessive interest, and with worry and anxiety when the child was ill or not sleeping, but they never seemed less than sure of who they were: mothers to these new boys and girls. They displayed photographs of their babies on the forum; they displayed names and dates under the comments and questions and answers they wrote. They advised one another, congratulated one another, backed one another up. Joanne rarely posted anything on the forum now but when she did it was short, a request for advice on some specific thing.

She found herself longing, sometimes, for a neighbour. Someone she could have coffee with in the mornings. It was madness. She had neighbours, and she never spoke to them, except sometimes to the old woman who ran the sewing business next door. She did not want to have coffee with that woman; she did not want to answer her questions, take her advice. The woman had some huge number of grandchildren; she was too full of information, she irritated Joanne. And even if there had been a neighbour she wanted to talk to, she was never at home. At least, not at an hour when she would drink coffee. At that hour, and most hours, she was in the office, doing three times as much work as she had done before the birth, working on a case involving two property developers who were accusing each other of fraud. It was boring work, and it was distasteful, and it seemed endless. She despised each of the developers equally.

'You're not always going to have someone to feel sorry for, you know,' Mark said one evening, as she complained about the case.

'I know that,' she said irritably.

'Anyway, it'll be over soon. That case. Won't it?'

She shrugged. 'They're running circles around each other in court. It could drag on and on. Our guy is lying just as much as the other fella.'

'You're not helping the other fella to lie this time?'

'No.' Joanne smiled.

'No secrets from Imelda? You haven't found out that the other developer has signed everything over to his second family and just neglected to mention it?'

'Come on.'

'Come on yourself. I can't believe you got away with that stuff last time. It's amazing what you lot get up to. Corrupt,' he said, and he laughed.

'That's not true,' Joanne said, and Mark raised an eyebrow at her.

'It's not,' she said again.

'No, you're right, of course it's not,' he said, standing. 'I'm knackered. I have to go up. Are you coming?'

'I'll be up in a minute,' she said, but more than a minute passed before she followed.

*

After the birth they did not have sex, not properly, for months. There were stitches, there was soreness, there was blood and, besides, bed had become a place to collapse into, already asleep, and nothing else. But one evening as she stood over the cot watching the baby drift into sleep, he came into the room behind her and put his arms around her, and she felt him, and she turned. She worried at first that the noise would wake the baby, but she soon forgot that anxiety and they moved on each other like they had before there was any of this, any house together, any baby, anything besides their separate selves making pleasure for each other and for themselves. Her breasts were still bigger. She was as turned on by this as he was. She was hungrier for him, she realized. The hormones must still have been at work. She wanted him on her. She wanted him to make noise with her, to make her make noise, however much the baby heard. He was beautiful to her again as he had been that first night, those first weeks. His dark eyes. His calm face with the fine bones. His lean body, his sallow arms. The hard knuckles of his hands.

*

They had been down to Longford a few times since the baby was born. Always, they had stayed with Mark's parents, but Joanne's mother wanted to see Aoife too, and she did not feel comfortable coming to Dorvaragh, so they would go to Caldragh for an afternoon, watch Irene fuss over the baby, answer her questions about feeding and sleeping and waking. Even during short visits, Joanne would grow weary of her mother: her snippiness, her bitterness would come out with a sly comment here, a loaded question there. Mark said she was overreacting, but Joanne could hear what her mother was saying to her, and she wanted, always, to get away. Aoife, though, seemed to like Irene. She was quiet with her, she smiled at her; one day, lying in her arms, she began to make an absurd, burbling sound. The three of them had stared at her, panic-stricken for a moment, until they realized what it was. She was laughing. It was the first time. Her mother, Joanne could see, was lit up with pride. Back in Dorvaragh, Mark kept trying all that evening to get the child to laugh again, to put on a show of the ridiculous, tiny chuckling for his parents, but she would only smile. Maura said it was good enough, that she would laugh for them in her own good time. Tom, Joanne had thought, had been disappointed.

Tom had seemed to grow used to Joanne, and to the baby. He was still not talkative, but Mark told her that that was just his father's way. Despite herself, Joanne was fond of him. Sometimes she saw him watching her and felt certain he wanted just for an easy conversation between the two of them to begin. But if she tried to start one, he would seem uncomfortable, would excuse himself saying that he needed to see to something outside, or that there was a call he needed Maura to make for him. He seemed never to make his own calls.

Christmas approached. On Grafton Street, the lights were already up in early November. Aoife was too young to notice any of the gifts they would buy her, any of the decorations they would hang in the house or point to in the streets, but there would be a first Christmas for her only once and they wanted to make something of it. Maura and Tom wanted them down home for the day, as did Joanne's mother, but they had decided they wanted to spend it in their own home. When Maura and Irene both pleaded, Joanne and Mark decided he would take Aoife down to Longford for a couple of days before Christmas; Joanne would still be at work. They bought a tree in the square at Smithfield and draped it with tinsel and baubles from a stall on Henry Street. Mark put fairy lights over the doorway and the window in the sitting room, and Joanne bought Aoife a huge stocking in Arnotts, and even before the middle of December, they had filled it with toys. For New Year's Eve, they planned to close out the world. They would light candles, have a fire going, roast a chicken, drink champagne. Maybe it would snow. Probably it would just piss rain. But that was OK. It would be some time away from the office. The steps of the Four Courts would be quiet, except for the odd drunk, except for the homeless people wrapped in blankets or in sleeping bags. These would be their days, hers and Mark's and Aoife's, to stay home, to stay inside. To stay inside and have the last hours of what had been for them such a year.

Chapter Fourteen

'The shortest day,' said Maura, as she handed Mark a mug of tea. 'They'll all have been out at Newgrange this past couple of hours.'

'I'd forgotten about that.'

'You and Nuala used to have to write about it for your homework every year at this time when you were in primary school.' She bit from a slice of toast spread thick with butter and marmalade. The rumpled cotton of her night-dress showed beneath her dressing-gown. Around her eyes, the lines seemed scored more deeply than they had the night before.

'They built it in alignment to the solstice,' Mark said. 'The sunrise today comes in through a roofbox and lights up the whole passageway. They've people buried in there. They don't know who.'

'Must be some sight,' Maura said. 'I'd love to get in to see it some day.'

'Only clout would get you in this morning,' Mark said. 'It'll be all politicians and journalists blocking the place up for a gawk. I'm surprised any light gets in at all.'

'Only clout would have got you in there the first time round,' said Maura.

Mark leafed through the pages of the local newspaper he had spread on his side of the table. It was all court reports and office-party photos and advertorials; there was a whole page about the cathedral in Longford and about how busy the priests were in the run-up to Christmas. 'During this very busy season in the hustle and bustle of Longford, be sure to drop into St Mel's Cathedral and be confronted by serenity,' the piece ended. Mark had long been meaning to call into the small museum at the back of the cathedral: he had heard that the nuns at the manor had donated a couple of boxes of old letters and documents from the Edgeworth family's time. He should go in to have a look at the stuff, he knew. There might be something he could use. He would get around to it eventually.

'She's sleeping late,' his mother interrupted his thoughts.

He nodded. 'She always does, in this house. I don't know why.'

'Country air.' His mother smiled. 'You should bring her out for a walk in it later.'

Mark nodded. 'I want to go down to see what Dad's at in the fields. I'll bring her in the pushchair.'

'Well, wrap her up warm,' his mother said. 'I don't want Joanne blaming me if you bring her back to Dublin with a cold.'

'Joanne's not going to do that,' Mark said, glancing across the table.

'I wish you could all be here for the day itself,' his mother said. 'I'd love to see her face when she gets her Santy presents.'

'Come on, she doesn't know Santy from Adam, Mam,' Mark said, and he closed the newspaper and folded it away.

'Still,' his mother said. 'You'll be missed.'

It was strange being in Dorvaragh with Aoife and without Joanne. He was acutely aware, for some reason, of the child's breathing as she lay in the cot at the foot of his bed. That was his old cot. His father – under orders from his mother – had taken it down from the attic and assembled it in Mark's old room. Mark found himself looking at it as though he might somehow remember it, which was impossible; of course he could not remember it. Still, the worn smoothness of its wooden bars seemed familiar, somehow. That morning as he had watched Aoife sleep he had reached over and gripped one, held it tightly, the way he must have done thirty years ago when his hands were as small as Aoife's were now. But nothing had come back to him.

An hour later he put Aoife in the pushchair and walked down the lane. From the gate to the lower fields, he could see that his father was fencing, using a sledge to hammer a paling post into the soft ground along the drain. Behind him, more posts jutted awkwardly from the transport box fixed to the tractor. Mark opened the gate and made his way over the bog, the thin frame of the pushchair jerking and rattling across the bumps. Seeing him approach, Tom stopped work. He was sweating, and one cheek was dirty with peat. He had taken his coat off and thrown it across the tractor's front wheel.

'These're the sleepers?' Mark asked, as he drew up beside him. He recognized the wood from the haul Tom had bought from the railway station in Longford a few years previously.

Tom nodded. 'Time to be doing something with them,' he said.

'The ground must be hard enough, this time of year?' Mark said, studying the spot where the last post had gone in. He pressed his foot to it. It felt nothing like bog. 'Jesus, it's like cement,' he said. His father shrugged.

'Bloody cattle are breaking out over this drain on me all winter,' he said, and took up the sledge.

'Right,' said Mark, and he bent to check on Aoife. She was gazing at her grandfather from beneath her fleece hood, her cheeks so flushed they seemed chafed. Her nose had started to run; he pressed a tissue to it, and she tried to turn away.

'They buy those in from Poland now, you know,' said Mark to his father, over the noise of the sledge as it came down on the wood.

Tom stepped back to examine the post. He drew the back of his hand over his mouth.

'Do they,' he said, lifting a bottle of orange from the transport box. He took a long drink, his head back, and glanced at Mark as he replaced the cap. 'Poland. Didn't that used to be Russian? Communist, like?'

'Communist, yeah.' Mark pushed at the post with one hand; it seemed secure. 'Heavy work,' he said.

'Mmm.' Tom scratched his head. 'Them posts aren't from Poland anyway.'

'No,' Mark said uncertainly.

'Matt Francis gave them all to me for fifty euro there, a few summers gone by.'

'I remember.'

'They were pegging them out 'ithin at the station.' Tom took up the pointed iron bar he used to make holes for the posts. He aimed it at a new spot and broke ground. 'Ah, old Mattie Francis looked after me, though,' he said. 'I've been using these sleepers for fencing ever since. This is the last of them.' He gestured back to the pile on the transport box. 'Don't know what I'm going to do the next time.'

Mark made no effort to reply.

'Hardly go to Poland,' Tom said then. 'Hardly go over to the Reds for a few posts of timber.' Mark saw that he was quietly laughing. He let himself laugh, too, at the sight of it.

'Hardly,' he said, and he tucked Aoife's blanket more tightly around her legs.

'None of those boys would give me too much of a bargain, now, I think,' Tom said. 'I see them in the bank of a Friday evening lodging more money into it than the whole town put together. Clever as fuck, them boys. You ever see them in there?'

'Who?'

'Them Polish lads. In the bank. Jesus, they do be lodging thousands. Thousands. Every week.'

'I doubt that,' Mark said, and he handed his father the shovel. 'I doubt they're all doing that well.'

'Ha?' Tom stuck the shovel into the ground. 'Sure when do you ever see them? You don't see them working fifteen hours of the day above at the piggery. Or beyond where Corrigan is building all the houses. I'm telling you. They're making serious money,' he said. 'Serious.'

'Fifteen hours a day, though.'

'Ha?'

'Who'd want to do that sort of work even if it was well paid? Which I guarantee you it's not. Not a chance.'

Tom looked hard at Mark and nodded, once to him and once towards the pushchair. 'She'll get a cold out here,' he said.

'She's all right,' said Mark. 'Well wrapped up.'

'It's colder than you'd think.'

'I'm going to drop her back up to Mam now anyway,' Mark said. 'Do you want a hand with the fencing?'

Tom turned back to the shovel. 'Whatever you think yourself,' he said. 'It'd be no harm to get as far as the lower bank before dark. This day won't be long more in it. Midwinter's day, is that right?'

As Mark took the handles of the pushchair, Maura's car appeared at the gate. She blew the horn once and kept going in the direction of Longford. She had told Mark at breakfast that she was doing the last of her shopping today.

'That's that,' Tom said. 'Go on up to the house with the child. I'll manage.'

'If Mam's back early, I'll come down to you.'

'Early? We'll hardly see her again till tonight.'

'Take it easy with that sledge, won't you?' Mark said. His father waved him off.

Mark had stayed in the house with Aoife all afternoon. She had been cranky, and when he had put her down for a nap she had slept for only a few minutes; he had allowed her to sleep too late that morning. He had sat with her in front of the television, and stood with her at the window, and when she would not settle, he decided to take her for a drive in the car. That sometimes worked, sometimes helped her to sleep. As he drove, he did not think about where he was going. It was only when he hit the outskirts of Longford and the traffic began to crawl that he realized he was headed for the town. He kept driving. She was quiet in the back of the car, and he wanted to keep her that way.

The evening was darkening fast and as if to speed the darkness in, to smooth its way, rain was beginning to fall in a steady drizzle. He parked on Ballymahon Street, competing for the spot with another driver – another father, he could see from the brood in the back. He met the man's stare but did not react; there was no need. He was the one with a baby carrier strapped in the back, even if the man in the other car could not see this.

He was not sure he had bundled Aoife up warmly enough. But it would have to do. There was a thick blanket on the pushchair anyway. He unstrapped her from one seat, lifted her out and strapped her into another. Some of the people who passed gave him a glance – looked at him, then down to the pushchair. Most paid him no attention at all.

At Killashee Street, he met Gary McGrath. They had been classmates in St Mel's, the boys' college at the edge of town. McGrath had done his apprenticeship as an electrician straight after school, had started his own business at the age of twenty or twenty-one. He looked much the same as he had in Mel's, except that his hairline had begun to recede. He grinned when he saw Mark and clapped him on the arm.

'Caser,' he said, using Mark's old nickname. He gestured to the pushchair, his eyebrows raised. 'So it's true?'

'Yeah.' Mark nodded, trying to look casual. 'Sure you know the way.' What way? he thought. What did that even mean?

'Let's have a look, so,' McGrath said, and he bent down to the baby. 'Oh, hello.'

'Is she awake?' Mark asked, though he knew she was. He had checked on her not two seconds previously. What was this, was he trying to look to McGrath as though he was barely even aware of what his own baby daughter was doing in the pushchair? As though he didn't care?

'God, she's lovely, man,' said McGrath, still bent down over Aoife. 'She's a beaut. How old?'

'Seven months now,' said Mark. And then he felt it. He was proud. He was as proud as he had ever been. This was what he had wanted. To stand on a street corner with Gary McGrath, or anyone from Mel's, or anyone from around, and show them his baby daughter. He was surprised at this. He had never felt like this in Dublin. He should have come into Longford sooner, he thought. He should have raced down here with the Moses basket the minute she was born.

'A beaut,' McGrath said again, straightening up. 'Jesus, you're a dark horse, aren't you?'

'Ah.' Mark shrugged. He wondered how much McGrath knew – about Joanne, about how soon they had got pregnant, about everything. He felt himself wanting to tell him, to fill him in. They used to be the best of friends. He wished he had kept in touch with him more. He would like nothing better now than to go somewhere with McGrath for a pint, to watch the old easy understanding on McGrath's face, the slow nod, hear the stories spilling out of him, too.

'Do you have time for a pint?' McGrath said.

'No, no,' Mark said. 'I just can't, I mean, now.'

'Sure, sure,' McGrath said quickly.

'With the baby and everything.'

'Ah, you're dead right,' McGrath said. 'And, anyway, I'm meant to be fucking shopping. I have the whole rake of them at home to buy for yet.' He laughed. 'It's an awful fucking nuisance, Christmas, isn't it?'

'Disaster.'

'But if you're around later, we'll be up in the Rising Sun for the dinner, myself and a few of the lads. Sure drop in if you're done with your shopping.'

'Will do.'

'Your messages,' McGrath said, with a laugh.

'Yeah.' Mark laughed back, and they shook hands as they parted.

On Main Street he met his mother coming out of the entrance to the shopping centre. She was tired, he could see, and she was carrying too many bags. He took some of them from her and packed them under the pushchair. She had been to her usual spots: Kenny's for jumpers for himself and his father, the bookstore, the shop that sold candles and ornaments and other kinds of crap.

'Are you sure you want to have her out in this cold?' his mother said.

'She's all right,' said Mark. 'Sure you can throw one of those Kenny's jumpers you're after buying across the push-chair if it gets any colder.'

'Don't you be so bloody smart,' his mother said, but she took his arm, and she was laughing. 'Come over with me to one of these shops across the street,' she said. 'There's a few things I was looking at as a present for Joanne.'

'You don't need to get Joanne anything,' Mark said, but he was already crossing the street behind her.

'Of course I have to get her something.'

'Why?' he said sharply.

'Because,' she said, in an imitation of his sharpness, as they reached the shop door. She looked down pointedly to the pushchair. 'And that's the end of it.'

The shop was narrow and brightly lit, clothes lining each wall and splitting the walkway between the walls. It was busy, women looking intently through the racks, touching things, pulling things away from the rails. His mother did not hesitate: she headed straight for the middle aisle. The clothes looked all right, Mark noticed, with some relief. They seemed, at least, to be in the colours Joanne preferred to wear: browns and greens and greys, nothing too colourful, nothing too sweet.

He looked for somewhere to put the pushchair; it would not fit between the aisles. There were already two parked by the counter.

'Leave her by the door there,' his mother said, looking back to him. 'She's asleep, isn't she?'

Mark nodded.

'She'll be all right.'

'I'll keep an eye on her,' the woman behind the counter said.

'Thanks,' Mark said, and his mother beckoned him over to look at a shirt she had taken from the rack. It was pink, probably the one colour in the shop that he could not see Joanne wearing. 'It's grand,' he said.

'Really?' his mother replied, grimacing, and put the shirt back on the rail. 'I don't know if it's the right colour for her, really.'

Then why did you show it to me? he wanted to say, but he left it. It was becoming clear to him what was going to happen. This was a woman shopping, and a woman shopping meant looking at things you had no intention of buying, things you didn't even like, just for the pleasure of looking at them and pawing them and putting them back.

'Sorry,' Mark said, as he jostled a woman going through the rack behind him.

'Hello, Mark,' she said, and he turned almost in fright. It took him a moment to recognize her. Pamela Doherty. She'd been on his school bus, and when she stepped on in the morning, every boy down the back took a good look at her: some of the girls, too. Every morning her brown hair would be damp and loose. She had been friendlier, more easy-going than a girl that good-looking should, by rights, have been. She was still good-looking, but harder-looking, too; there was something forced to what prettiness was still there. She was groomed. Tanned in the middle of December. Wearing a suit you'd wear if you worked in a bank.

'Pamela,' he said, and nodded with a breath of a laugh. 'How's things?'

'Not too bad,' she said, and he noticed her accent – Edgeworthstown pure and undiluted, the bit of a rush on the last word. 'What are you up to, these days?'

'Ah.' He shrugged, and gestured back to his mother. 'Helping out with the Christmas shopping, you know.'

'Good man yourself.'

'And you?'

'I'm working in the bank,' she said, and he congratulated himself silently on having got it right. 'Pain-in-the-arse work but it pays the bills.'

'Lot to be said for that.'

'Sure is. And you're in Dublin, aren't you?'

'Yeah.'

'At Trinity, isn't it?'

'That's it.'

'Lecturing?'

He hesitated a moment. It was always the same dilemma, when someone from home asked him what he did; whether to clarify for them the difference between being a lecturer and being a teaching assistant – which felt, most of the time, like being a jumped-up grinds tutor, only on less pay. He nodded. 'Yeah. Lecturing. Pain-in-the-arse work too.'

'But, wow,' she said, raising her eyebrows. 'That beats anything that's going on around here. A lecturer at Trinity. I mean, fair play.'

He shrugged. He could feel himself flushing. He glanced down at the thing she had in her hands. It looked like a piece of underwear, silk, a slip or a top or something that made him think of what she must look like naked, what she must have looked like naked back in the school-bus days, at sixteen. He felt as though the walls of the place were closing in on top of him. 'Well,' he said, 'good to see you anyway.'

'Yeah.' She smiled. 'Might see you around over Christmas. You be in Valentine's on Stephen's night?'

'I'd say so, yeah.' Mark heard in his voice a local lad's confidence that he did not have.

'See you so.' Pamela winked at him, as he nodded a goodbye.

His mother was down at the back of the shop now; she could not have heard the exchange. Still, she glanced at him quizzically as he joined her. 'Who was that one?'

'She used to go on my bus,' Mark said. 'Doherty. You don't know them.'

'I do know them,' his mother said, and craned her neck to get a better look.

Mark took an intense interest in the blouse his mother had in her hand. 'That one's nice.'

'I don't know,' his mother said. 'It seems a bit skimpy to me.'

'Whatever you think.'

'What about this?'

It was a cardigan in dark grey; long, plain. Joanne would wear it. He touched it. The wool was soft and smooth. 'Looks nice,' he said.

'It'd want to, for the price of it.' She showed him the tag and he did the taken-aback look he knew she was expecting. 'Cashmere,' she said. 'Still.'

'It's too much,' he said. 'That blouse you had a minute ago would do fine.'

'Would it?' She did the uncertainty dance now, with her mouth and her eyes, looking between this rail and the other one, sizing each piece up, frowning, chewing her lip. 'Which of them do you think she'd get more wear out of?' she said.

Mark tried to picture Joanne, first in the blouse, then in the cardigan. The blouse would be sexier. But the cardigan was something she'd come in and put on in the evenings, something she'd wrap around herself. Then again, that would mean the cardigan would be covered, soon enough, in baby puke. Just as he was about to say this to his mother, he heard Aoife's cries. 'I'll be back in a minute,' he said, and as he pushed his way up the shop, past what seemed like thirty women, the baby's cries grew louder and more urgent than seemed possible: had she not just woken up? Had she actually been awake, crying, all that time, and he had not heard her? He made his way through, and every woman seemed to glance at him disapprovingly as he passed. Except Pamela Doherty. What was on her face was not disapproval but disbelief, and laughing disbelief at that.

As he took the handles of the pushchair and steered it out of the shop, Pamela was still watching him, a faint smile on her lips, her eyebrows raised. He nodded to her, another goodbye, and she nodded back, but he could see it on her face: all that he had not told her, all that he had not admitted to, all that he had tried to hide.

It was raining outside, and the night had fallen completely now, the Christmas lights high over Main Street in their gaudy yellows and greens and reds. The sound of the rain splashing against the footpath seemed to calm Aoife, and he stood by the bright shop window with the slickly dressed mannequins, rocking the pushchair back and forth, until his mother emerged with a shopping bag and they headed for their cars.

*

It happened again that night. The wailing drifted into their room, angry, jagged, catching on itself like an engine trying to start in the cold. Maura pulled on her dressing-gown, left the room without turning on a light. She called out to the child as she moved along the landing.

Then Tom could hear Mark's voice along with hers,

puncturing the clamour of the child's hunger. A door opened and the cries grew louder for a second, nearer, then more distant; they were taking her downstairs. Tom lifted himself slightly to look at the clock; it was almost six. He stared into the half-light of the room. Already his mind had stretched open to sleeplessness, to the blankness of an hour too early to use. He thought about going down to the kitchen, but Maura would be fussing over the child. The tiles would be cold under his feet. He pushed his knees together and drew them closer to his chest; he pressed the quilt between his shoulder and his chin. He wondered if the dog, in the back kitchen, would be confused now, if the noise had made her think it was time to get up, time for the day's work to begin.

Footsteps sounded on the landing again, and the bedroom door opened quietly. A blade of light fell over the pillow beside him, then vanished as Maura shut the door. He kept his eyes closed as she eased back into the bed, kept them closed as she pulled the quilt to her. He did not open them until he felt her shuddering her way back to sleep. Then he heaved himself out of bed and dressed quickly in the clothes he had taken off the night before. As he closed the door behind him, he heard a sudden rustle of the bedclothes. Maura, he knew, had jolted awake again.

The child seemed to be quietening as he made his way down the stairs, and when he reached the kitchen the crying had stopped completely. Mark stood facing the window, the bottle jerking in his hand as the child sucked. He looked at Tom's reflection and nodded a greeting.

'Did she waken you?'

Tom shook his head. He looked at the tiny Christmas tree with its scattered ornaments, its thin lengths of tinsel as frayed as old twine.

'I'd be up soon anyway,' he said, pulling at a small silver bell on the tree. It came away in his hand. He set it down on the counter beside the sugar bowl.

Mark glanced at the clock on the kitchen wall. 'You must be busy,' he said evenly.

'Busy enough.'

'Six o'clock in the morning in the dead middle of winter?' His voice was careful.

'What needs doing needs doing.'

Mark said nothing. He held the bottle away from the child for a moment, watching as she dribbled milk on to her chin, her mouth moving as though the teat was still in it. He wiped at the white spittle with a cloth. She whined.

'Can't you let her suck at it when she's hungry?' Tom said.

Mark raised the baby high on to his shoulder and rubbed her back, the white folds of her sleepsuit sliding up and down with his hand. 'She makes herself sick if she drinks it all at once.'

Tom watched Mark's fingers travel over the child's shoulders, the skin of her neck, the fluff of her hair. She burped. He lowered her back into the crook of his arm, touching her lips again with the cloth. As she started to kick and whimper, he eased the teat into her mouth. She sucked. Her eyes were wide open and locked on Mark's.

'When's her mother coming down?' Tom said.

Mark looked at him. 'Joanne,' he said. He did not answer the question.

'Yiz won't be here for the Christmas,' Tom said, and Mark shook his head.

'We won't,' he said. 'We'll be down again after Stephen's Day.'

'Yeah,' Tom said. He handled the small bell again and

placed it on a branch of the tree. As soon as he took his hand away, it fell. He caught it before it clattered to the counter, closing it in his fist. The child watched him. For a moment, he thought about offering her the bell. But she would probably just choke on it. He put it back on the counter.

'She doesn't see too much of the mother, I've noticed,' Tom said.

Mark raised his eyebrows. 'What?' he said. 'What are you talking about?' There was a warning in his tone.

Tom let the silence stretch out another moment before giving an answer. 'Joanne,' he said then, and Mark exhaled. 'She doesn't be up at Caldragh too often when yiz are here. Herself and the mother don't get on, is that it?'

Mark sighed. 'It's complicated,' he said, looking at the child.

Tom laughed. 'Nothing's complicated with Irene Lynch. Nothing was complicated with the husband either. Either they had a use for you or they didn't.'

Mark shook his head. 'That's your concern, not ours,' he said. 'Not mine and Joanne's. We don't know anything about what happened between you and her parents.'

'You don't know?' Tom said. 'You know bloody well. You were here, weren't you?'

'I was a kid.'

Tom snorted. 'You had eyes. You had plenty of sense.'

'Well, Joanne doesn't know anything about it,' Mark said. 'It has nothing to do with us. And it definitely has nothing to do with Aoife. So leave it. Forget about it.'

'I haven't much of a chance of that now,' Tom said, and he let Mark see him looking at Aoife as he spoke.

'Cut it out,' Mark said, and his voice was quick, hard.

'I'm only saying what everyone around here is saying.'

'Fuck everyone around here.'

'It's easy for you to say that. We're the ones that has to live here after you making a show of us. Your mother and me.'

Mark seemed to shiver. Then he moved forward so quickly that Tom began to raise his hands to protect himself. But Mark went past him, heading for the stairs, and Tom caught sight of himself in the window's black mirror, his hands hanging uselessly in the air. He turned. Against Mark's chest, the child was fumbling with her fists, moving her head from side to side. Mark pressed his lips to her hair.

'That's enough, now,' Mark said quietly. 'Don't say any more.'

'I'm only saying what's the truth of things,' Tom said, slamming a hand down on the counter.

'You don't know anything about truth,' Mark said. 'You've been living in your own world for years.' He sighed. 'I'm going back upstairs,' he said. 'You should go back up too.'

'I have work to do,' Tom said, but his heart was beating hard. He wanted to take a hold of what was happening. He wanted to turn it back. Mark's footsteps sounded on the staircase, and then there was nothing in the room but the buzzing of the fridge and the fluorescent light overhead. Tom found that he was shaking. The light was making his eyes ache. The drip of the tap was itching his brain. He walked quickly out into the back kitchen, where the dog was awake and waiting. He thrust his feet into the cold tubes of his wellingtons and pulled on his coat and cap. Stepping outside, he blew on his hands and rubbed them together before reaching for the stick that stood in its usual place against the wall. Above him, in a sky still far off dawn, the stars glinted like shards of steel.

Chapter Fifteen

Mark brought Aoife back from Longford with a cold, and that was their Christmas, nursing her through it and catching it themselves. Joanne had only a few days off from work, and she returned to the office more exhausted than she had been leaving it on Christmas Eve. She hoped they would send her home when they saw the state of her – the red nose, the streaming eyes, the scarf muffled around her throat, the scraggy tissues tucked in her cuffs – but they did not. There was too much to do. Instead, they all caught the cold too, and blamed Joanne.

With the new term in Trinity, Mark began to teach a second class. It was on something more closely related to his thesis, something into which a couple of Edgeworth's novels fitted, and he was glad about that. And though the pay was meagre, the extra money was good to have. While he was teaching, Mark left Aoife with Eileen, the woman who ran a dressmaker's shop in the house next door. She refused to take any money. It was only a couple of hours, she told him, and she would be more than happy to have Aoife for the whole week if he wanted to go off and work at a proper job. Joanne had roared with laughter when Mark told her the story that evening, and he had laughed too, but in a different way. A couple of days later, he had brought up once more an idea that he had aired several times since Aoife's birth. He thought he should look around for a second job, he said, something that would help them to be more secure. They were always talking, he reminded her, about how they needed to start up a savings account for Aoife.

Joanne shook her head. 'Yes, but you don't have to get a second job for us to do that. We should do that anyway. Even if we only put a tenner a week into it, we should be doing it now.'

'But a tenner a week is going to get us nowhere.'

'It won't always be that little,' she said. 'I'm saying that the point is to save, not to wait until we might have more to save. And, anyway, we've talked about this before. If you work full-time too, the cost of putting her in a crèche is probably going to cost us double what you earn.'

Mark gestured to the door. 'But Eileen says—'

'Come on, Mark. We're not going to leave her in a dressmaker's shop all day. That's not going to work. It's probably not even safe to leave her in there as little as we do. As soon as she starts crawling, we're going to have to find somewhere else. Eileen might have reared her kids among pins and scissors and plastic bags, but we're not going to.'

'She doesn't leave her in the shop the whole time.'

'She leaves her by herself?'

'She leaves the door open between the shop and her sitting room.'

'We're going to have to get someone to come here and mind her while you're teaching,' Joanne said. 'Could you see if one of your students will do it for a few quid?'

Mark exhaled in loud protest. 'I don't want any of my bloody students poking around my own house. They look down their fucking noses at me enough as it is.'

'What's wrong with this house?'

'I didn't mean that,' Mark said tiredly, and he shook his

head. 'I don't want to have this conversation now. I'm too knackered after work.'

Joanne opened her mouth to respond, but she left it. There was no point. It would collapse into an argument and they would go to bed in a cloud of irritation and resentment. She did not want that. She did not want to bring that into the room they shared with Aoife. She wanted nothing to press in on her sleeping child; nothing but her dreams.

They did not argue often. Usually, in the evenings, they were almost too tired to talk. Usually they watched television until bedtime, or Joanne went online and looked at gossip sites and discussion forums, or Mark read his students' essays and sighed and cursed and clicked his tongue as he scrawled all through their pages in indignant red pen.

Joanne tried to read. There were novels she wanted to get through. They had been sitting on her bedside table since the final months of the pregnancy. She brought one down to the sitting room occasionally and sat with it for a while, but the paragraphs seemed to dissolve as she read them; she kept needing to go back to the start. Or the television would distract her, or she would think of something she had been meaning to look up on the Internet, and she would put the book aside. She always meant to get back to it. She always took it back upstairs with her and tried to read it in bed. That lasted for about the length of time it took for her eyelids to blink once, then again, and then to close.

Mark did not fare much better, but most evenings he sat for a while with a book, looking at it, writing in its margin with a pencil. He said he could not work otherwise; that he could not absorb the information. So he scribbled, and annotated, and underlined, and while he read he frowned and squinted in a way that she told him was certain to damage his eyes.

'No, that's something else,' he always joked when she said that, and she always told him he was hilarious.

One night when he had fallen asleep on the couch with a book in his lap she reached over and took it from him. It was one of Edgeworth's, the only one Joanne had heard of. *Castle Rackrent.* She did not know why she had heard of it: she had not read it. It had never been assigned to her in school or in university, and she had never come across it by herself. She should read it, she thought; she should know more about Mark's writer. Besides, it was set around Edgeworthstown. It might be interesting. It might be just the thing to help her to concentrate again.

She fought the impulse to skip the introduction; there could be something in it, she told herself, that she needed to know. She read Edgeworth's birth date, her death date; she did the calculation in her head. Eighty-two. A great age, she thought, and realized that those were her father's words, the words he had often used to describe someone who was old. You didn't say they were old; you said they were a great age. And when they were dead, you said that they had lived to a great age. That was a way of saying it was no big deal that they were gone. That they'd hung on for long enough. That their family had nothing to be crying about. That crying over such a death, at such an age, was just a little bit rich. Joanne's father had been fifty-eight when he died. That had not been a great age.

She skimmed the next paragraph; it mentioned the American revolution. It mentioned the French one. It mentioned Rousseau. Then she read the line about how Edgeworth's father had employed her to write his business letters, to help him deal with his tenants and listen to their pleas, and she read it again, and then with Mark's pencil she placed a little exclamation mark in the margin beside it. She skimmed on through the dates and the placenames and the titles of books, and she read a couple of lines about Scott, and she read about how Edgeworth did her writing in her sitting room with a crowd of children playing all around her. She underlined that part and gave it an exclamation mark as well. *You think you have it tough*, she wrote, beneath the exclamation mark, and she could not help it, she laughed to herself. She looked over to Mark where he slept, and wanted to wake him, to show him what she had done, to enjoy the joke with him there and then, but she left him sleeping. She left the joke for him to find for himself, some time when he would go back over the book, some time when he would find her writing in the margin and stare at it for a moment and then laugh. And when she would come in from work that evening, or when he would come in to her, he would ask her, in a voice pretending stern-ness, to guess what he had found. And she would have for-gotten about it then, and they would laugh about it, and they would kiss. She thumbed forward twenty or thirty pages, into the novel itself. She wanted to leave him something else to find. She glanced at a paragraph: it was something about a house being full of people and heat and smoke, something about a man hiding in a bed. On the facing margin, Mark had left a note in pencil himself. *Anecdote*, he had written. *Effect of the Real*. Beside it, Joanne wrote, HELLO BABY. She put two *X* marks underneath. Jesus, she thought then, looking at the words, you're acting like an idiot. You need to go to bed. She closed the book, left it back on the couch beside Mark, and stood up, stretched and loudly yawned. At the noise, Mark opened his eyes as though in fright.

'It's OK,' Joanne said, smiling at him. 'It's only me.'

'I knew it was you,' he said.

When Mark got a text inviting him to Niall Nagle's stag party, Joanne encouraged him to go. It would be a weekend in Glendalough in late April. He would be on a break from his classes by then, she said. It would be good for him to get away. And the case she was working on, the one with the developers, would, with any luck, be finished by then. It would be a good time for her to have a weekend alone with Aoife. 'We can bond,' she said, lifting Aoife from the playmat on to her lap, bouncing her up and down. 'Isn't that right, Aoife?'

'I think you're meant to have bonded with her by now,' Mark said wryly.

'Ah, you know what I mean,' Joanne said. 'A girls' day out. And you can have a weekend with the lads. Are you seriously going to argue with me on this?'

'No.' Mark shook his head. 'I'm not stupid.'

'Good,' Joanne said, and curled herself forward around Aoife. 'We'll have a great time.'

'I don't know why Nagle's inviting me,' Mark said, frowning at the screen of his phone. 'We're not exactly friends. I'm probably going to be the only one there who's not on the way to CEO of some bank.'

'Mossy will be there, won't he?'

Mark laughed. 'Mossy could end up running a bank yet.'

'Just text Nagle back and tell him you're going,' Joanne said. 'Before I change my mind.'

On the Friday night after Mark had gone to Glendalough, Sarah and Deirdre came around for dinner. They had accepted the invitation on condition that Joanne would not cook. They brought takeaway from the Indian on Manor Street, and two bottles of wine. They also brought a tiny birthday cake for Aoife, who would turn one in a few weeks, and who was still up when they arrived. They played with her, and fussed over her, and from her bag Sarah took a wrapped gift and placed it on the carpet in front of her. Aoife stared first at it and then at her mother. Joanne opened the gift. It was a set of board books. Bending down to Aoife, she pointed to things on the pages: a cat, a giraffe, a dog. Aoife looked at the pictures as though they were photographs of people she was expected to recognize. She took the book from her mother and chewed its spine.

'Definitely another PhD student in the making,' Deirdre said.

Over dinner Deirdre, who had qualified as a solicitor the previous year, talked about the firm she worked for, a new outfit in Smithfield that sounded like a dream to Joanne; they specialized in family law, which was what she wanted to get into, and the partners were young and sounded decent and smart. Deirdre said the vibe in the office was always good, even if everyone was worked to the bone. She promised to introduce Joanne to one of the partners. There was a staff night out planned in May, she said, and Joanne should come as her guest.

'You can pretend to be my new girl,' she said, ribbing Sarah.

'For that to work, they'd have to know you actually have an old girl,' Sarah said drily, and for a moment nobody spoke. Sarah shook her head quickly then, and reached for the wine.

'Sorry,' she said to Joanne. 'That's beside the point. Deirdre's right. You should go along and meet her bosses. I'm sure they'd be impressed. You can tell them you just helped yours to win another case.'

'For all the good it will do,' Joanne said. 'Any job I get after I qualify is likely to be with Imelda and Eoin. Your firm will have its own trainees to promote.'

Before Deirdre could argue, Joanne asked Sarah about her group of Koreans this year, and Sarah rolled her eyes and launched into a long and comical description of her students, the questions they asked her and the gifts they gave her. But it was definitely going to be her last year teaching Koreans, she said, with an almost bashful glance at Deirdre. She was going to go back to college in the autumn. 'And I mean it this time. I've applied and everything,' she said.

'That's brilliant, Sarah,' Joanne said. 'What are you going to do?'

'Journalism,' she said, and Deirdre gave a mock groan.

'Another hack hanging around the Four Courts,' she said, as Sarah swatted at her. 'That's all we bloody need.'

'It's great, Sarah,' Joanne said, and poured them more wine. 'You were always too good at English to end up just teaching it.'

Deirdre snorted with laughter. 'There's something not quite right about that sentence,' she said.

'Oh, well,' Joanne shrugged. 'Here's to you anyway.' She raised her glass to Sarah, and they clinked.

When they had finished eating, they moved to the sitting room. The *Late Late Show* was on, and they half watched it, passing occasional comment on the host and the guests. Deirdre and Sarah were merry by now, and Joanne knew that she must be well on too, but she didn't feel it: as usual, she just felt tired. She was furious the first time she caught herself secretly longing to leave the girls by themselves in the sitting room and go upstairs to bed; it was rude of her, and more than that it was pathetic, she told herself. It was the thinking of someone who was too old and too boring to be open to even the mildest kind of fun. But as soon as she had thought that, she was thinking that if she excused herself to go upstairs and check on Aoife – which she would have to do soon anyway, which she would be expected to do – she could stretch out on the bed, just for a moment.

She shook herself, trying to wake up. She did not want to go to bed, no matter what her body was telling her: she wanted to be here, spending time with her friends, friends she loved, friends she hardly ever saw now. She wanted to throw herself into the conversation they were having – the conversation in which they thought she was participating – about the politician who was on the television screen now, and what a moron he was, and how insincere, and how dangerous, despite his homespun banter and his cartoon moustache. She wanted to talk about this with them, and to share with them the stories she'd heard about this politician, about other politicians; she wanted to express disgust like they were expressing it. She wanted to care. And she did care. She cared very much. She could not look at that guy, she had never been able to look at that guy, without wanting to tear that ridiculous moustache from his face. He was a gombeen man, and he thrived on it, and because of it he got away with things for which he should have been fired, and that was outrageous, just like Deirdre was saying, just like Sarah was repeating. Joanne agreed. But even as she was agreeing, she was thinking that it really didn't matter what a politician did, or what he said, or what he lied about, or what he had on his upper lip. Or, rather, it mattered, but it didn't matter as much as other things did. And she was furious with herself when she found herself thinking that, too, because if there was one thing she didn't want to be, it was that kind of woman, that kind of mother, who thought that nothing in the world mattered except the shallow little breaths, the muffled little heartbeat of the person sleeping a fragile sleep in the room upstairs. But nothing else did matter, or nothing mattered as much. Was that true? Was she still so completely hormonal? Was this thinking going to stick? Was she going to shrug at everything except her daughter's existence for the rest of her life? She couldn't do that, Joanne thought, she couldn't live with herself, and yet she didn't see how she had a choice.

'Oh God, stop *lying*, you fucking weasel,' Deirdre shouted at the television screen, and Joanne stood and said she had to nip upstairs for a second.

'Just need to make sure she's still alive,' she said, raising her eyebrows, as though to suggest the tediousness of the chore. 'That kind of thing.'

'Don't fall asleep up there, now,' Sarah called after her, and as Joanne stepped into the hall, she could hear that Aoife was awake. She tripped on the stairs. It must have been the wine.

The next morning, she took Aoife into town and bought her things. She bought her clothes in Dunnes and toys in the Early Learning Centre, and she went into Habitat and got some picture frames for her bedroom, and she took her into St Stephen's Green and wheeled her around the flowerbeds and across the little bridge. She felt invisible; a woman with her child. There were so many of them around. Grafton Street was packed. She ducked up past Kehoe's to get away from the crowds.

They had lunch in a café on Dawson Street. The waitress brought her a high chair so that Aoife could sit at the table with her. Afterwards, Joanne took out the little wooden farm animals she had bought her; they kept Aoife occupied long enough for Joanne to read almost a whole article in the Saturday magazine. Then she packed the animals away, and left the newspaper behind, and they walked out again into the sunshine. Joanne decided to walk through the grounds of Trinity, to find a bench and sit to soak up the day's warmth.

Clive Robinson had aged so much in the space of a year that she barely recognized him. He must have been ill, she realized. He was walking towards the Berkeley Library, looking unsteady on his feet; maybe it was the cobblestones, but everybody else was walking on them perfectly well. She wanted for a second to avoid him, but she could not: he had seen her, and he was coming over. She waved and pulled the pushchair closer. As Robinson reached the bench, he pointed to the child with one hand and extended the other towards Joanne. He could not have looked more surprised. 'This is news,' he said, and he touched Aoife's hair. She frowned up at him. 'Bless every hair on her head,' he said to Joanne. 'She is yours?'

'Mine.' Joanne nodded, and they smiled at each other for a moment and then both looked down to the pushchair. 'How are you?' she heard herself ask in the very instant she warned herself, silently, not to ask that very question, and she cringed. She thought she saw him laugh a little as he sat on the bench beside her.

'How am I?' he said, and he made a face at the baby. 'I'm seventy.' He shook his head. 'This is what seventy looks like.' He turned to her. 'I've seen better years, but I'm here. And you? Are you well?'

'I'm fine,' Joanne smiled. 'This is Aoife.'

'Aoife,' he said, and he looked at the baby as though seeing her for the first time. 'Which one was Aoife, again?'

Joanne hesitated. 'I'm sorry?'

'In the myths. Aoife was in the Children of Lir, am I right? Isn't that where you find her name?'

'Oh.' Joanne nodded as though in agreement. 'Right.' In fact, she and Mark had not even considered the meaning of the name when they chose it. It had been one of the few they could agree on. But she wasn't going to let Robinson know that, she decided. The legend was a better story. 'We did wonder whether we'd have to give her three brothers,' she laughed.

Robinson looked at her for a moment, and she knew she had said something wrong. 'But Aoife was the wicked step-mother in that story, wasn't she?' he said, with the apologetic half-smile she remembered from whenever she had made a fool of herself in class. 'Fionnuala was the girl, if I remember. And Fiachra, Conn and Aodh were the sons. Poor creatures. Nine hundred years as swans. Imagine their loneliness.'

Joanne searched for a response. 'It can't have been fun,' she said, eventually, and she blushed at how inane it sounded. But what was she supposed to say? He was talking about a fairy story. He was feeling sympathy for people who had never lived. She looked around the square. 'It's a lovely day, isn't it?' she blurted.

Robinson leaned back into the green slats of the bench. 'Spring again,' he said.

Joanne felt relieved. They were back on some kind of normal track. She could manage this. 'Are you busy, these days?' she asked, and Robinson smiled and shook his head.

'I'm doing very little,' he said. 'Doctor's orders.'

'I see,' she said, trying to sound at once discreet and surprised. What was the etiquette in this situation? Were you meant to ask outright?

'It *is* cancer,' Robinson said, as though answering a very specific question. 'But it seems the doctors got to it in time, and that I'm off the hook for now.' He glanced at her. 'Though I'm aware that it doesn't look that way.'

'Oh, no, no,' Joanne said, in a rush. 'I mean, you look thinner than before, maybe, but,' she nodded vigorously, 'you look good.'

'There was radiation therapy, there was chemotherapy,

and there have been drugs,' Robinson said lightly. 'The drugs have not been allowing me to sleep so well, I find. But that's not a bad price to pay for life, is it?'

'Of course not.'

'Which you, more than any of us, should know,' he said, looking at her almost mischievously.

'Oh, yes,' she said, though it was clear that she did not know his meaning.

'New motherhood.' He put a hand to the pushchair. Aoife was leaning out of it, staring at the passing pigeons. 'New life, in exchange for an end to nights of any sleep worthy of the name. Isn't that how it goes?'

'Oh, yes,' Joanne said, with altogether more certainty. 'Yes, it definitely is.'

'I remember those nights. Of course, my wife did most of the work – that was the way then – but still, I remember.' He laughed. 'My God, the stamina these little creatures have for their own discontent.' He leaned to look at Aoife again. 'It's remarkable, when you think about it. We spend our first years in this world furiously refusing the luxury of what we'll spend the rest of it longing to do.' He sat back on the bench. 'Sleep, that is.'

'Her father helps out a lot, though,' Joanne said, after a long moment of silence. 'I mean, her father actually looks after her most of the time. I'm at work.'

'That's admirable,' said Robinson.

'He's doing a PhD in the English department here, actually,' Joanne said, and she pointed to the arts block, as though Robinson needed the illustration. 'On Maria Edgeworth and Walter Scott.' She thought for a moment. What was it about those writers, exactly, that Mark was working on, again? Robinson was sure to ask her. 'Their novels,' she added pointlessly.

'I see,' said Robinson, but he did not ask for any more details. He seemed to have no interest. And she wanted him to be interested, Joanne realized. She wanted Robinson to ask about the man she had met, the man she had made a child with. But he just sat beside her and lifted his face to the sun. He closed his eyes. From her pushchair, Aoife called out.

'We're going in a minute now,' Joanne said to her, and Robinson stirred beside her.

'I don't want to hold you up, my dear,' he said quietly. 'You go on ahead. I'm just going to catch my breath here.'

'Oh, no, there's no rush,' said Joanne. 'I was talking to the child.'

Robinson opened his eyes and peered at Aoife. 'Do you have good conversations, the two of you?' he said, and Joanne wondered which of them he was addressing. 'And you have an interesting case to work on now?' he said then, and this time he was looking directly at her.

Joanne shrugged. 'Not really,' she said. 'A lot of the work is very dull.'

'Ah,' he said.

'Of course, I'll be done with my traineeship soon,' she said. 'I'm hoping then to get into a firm that works more directly in the areas that interest me.'

She expected him to ask what those areas were, but he did not. His interest in things seemed as thinned as his body was. She felt suddenly intensely sorry for him. There was no way he could not realize how much he had changed in himself, how diluted the energies of his mind had become. As though the shelves of a library had been ransacked. It's not fair, she thought, and for a moment she thought she might even say this to him, but it was out of the question. It would not help in any way. It would embarrass them both, and he would look at her . . . he would look at her, she thought, much as he was looking at her right now. Was she imagining it? That he was looking at her so knowingly, with something so much like tolerance? As though he could hear or read what had been going through her mind? He had always seemed capable of that. She told herself to snap out of it, to stop wallowing in this nonsense, and she found that he was still regarding her, and smiling at her, in exactly the same way.

'You're interested in family law, I recall,' he said, and she was taken aback. He had remembered. So his memory was not the wreck she had imagined; he was not the poor senile old dear she had been picturing and so energetically pitying. He was just as sharp, just as good on the small details of other people's lives as he had ever been, even if he had shown no interest in the man who had fathered her baby. Maybe he simply had good manners, she told herself. Maybe he just knew when to keep his nose out of things that were none of his concern.

'And now here you are,' he said then. 'Here you are with a family all your own. Isn't it strange? After all?'

She waited for something, some nub of wisdom, to follow in the wake of this, but there was nothing. He looked now as though he might be growing sleepy in the sun. But then he shook himself and sat up.

'You heard, of course, that the woman on Fitzwilliam Square sold up?' he said, in a much more strident tone.

Joanne considered pretending not to know who he meant. But it was obvious. 'Elizabeth Lefroy sold the house?' she said.

'Yes.' Robinson nodded. 'I think for a huge sum. You know how much those houses are selling for these days.'

'I didn't know,' Joanne said, almost stammering.

'I imagine the legal fees would have been significant,' Robinson said. He glanced her way. Joanne felt prodded on to the defensive.

'Well,' she said, 'hardly to the tune of that kind of amount.'

'I expect there would have been some profit,' Robinson said mildly, glancing to the lawn. 'But then again, I imagine that the woman just wanted to get away. In light of what had happened, I imagine she could no longer be happy in that house.'

'No longer quite at home.'

Robinson looked to her. 'I'm sorry?'

Joanne shook her head. 'Something from her testimony. I remember noticing it at the time. Sorry,' she said, as though she had interrupted him.

'Yes, that is a nice phrase,' Robinson said, his hands laid flat on his thighs. How thin his legs were. 'A very nice way of putting it indeed. And true too, I imagine. True too.'

'It was all very sad, what happened,' Joanne said, and he looked at her kindly.

'Oh, it was far from your fault, my dear,' he said, patting her hand. 'When you get to your family law, there'll be time enough for it to be your fault.' He smiled, showing his slightly browned teeth. 'So you go easy on yourself until then.'

Aoife was asleep now in the pushchair. Joanne tried to see her through Robinson's eyes. The red hair, that was from way back on her side, she imagined telling him. The full lips: those were Mark's. The nose was Joanne's, and the pale skin too. The striped tights and the purple suede booties and the corduroy dress with the green cat stitched into it somehow suggested a more colourful life, a life of more treats and more excitement than was actually the case; they were all gifts from friends, and Aoife had never worn them before. Joanne had chosen them in the bedroom that morning, for their big day out. And the way she had thrown her head back in sleep, the way she had flopped her hands forward, that was the absolute surrender that made Joanne want to pick her up and carry her everywhere for the rest of her life. That was the ability to trust that she must have inherited from somewhere deep inside her father, because it was not anywhere on her father's surface, and it was not anywhere in her mother at all. And that's my daughter, Joanne imagined herself saying to Robinson, but he was not even looking at the child now: he was staring over to the arts block, to its cement terraces blotched with the varying darknesses of age and wear. And it was time to go home, with the green cat, and the purple booties, and the little hands thrown down like rejected toys. Beside her, Clive Robinson looked ready to fall asleep himself, to doze off right there, and to stay until someone came and found him, until with a nudge someone woke him – what would they call him? Professor? Darling? Dad? – and took him home.

'We'd better go,' Joanne said, calling him nothing at all.

'Of course you must,' said Clive Robinson, and he stood with her and kissed her cheek, and on his breath she smelt the thing she had imagined to be happening to his mind. And though she wished he would sit down again, and not tire himself, he stood and watched and waved as she walked away, until she had gone around the corner of the old library and out of his sight.

She searched her bookshelves for it that evening after she had put Aoife to bed for the night. She had loved it in college; she had read it several times. She found it on the bottom shelf, hidden under an old photo album. She poured herself the last of the wine that Deirdre and Sarah had brought the previous evening, and she curled up on the couch. Her phone beeped and she read the new message from

Mark, *Having good time. How is Aoife?*, and she texted back to say that Aoife was asleep and that she was reading. *Xx*, he texted back, and she thought of the note she had written on his Edgeworth book, and wondered if he had found it yet. She put the phone down. She opened Robinson's book. She turned to the first line. *Never are the philosophical problems of identity and difference so poignantly formulated as when they bear on the dimensions of social life*, she read, and she saw how she had underlined the sentence several times, in different colours; how she had pushed at its meaning for herself again and again. *What does it mean to belong to a family, to a group of friends, to an organization?* she read. *How is it possible to say 'we'? Who counts as a stranger? What is it to be truly conscious of ourselves, let alone of someone else?*

Joanne looked at the words, and she looked at the traces of herself as she had been years previously, reading them, noting them, needing them. She needed them now, she felt; she needed them once again, but she did not know how. She did not know why. She read on, but the rest of the paragraph pulled her into territory that she was no longer certain how to traverse. As they always did now, the words began to slip from their moorings. The sentences began to slide off a ledge. She went back to those first lines and used them to steady her grip. She let them lead her on. After a couple of pages, as she had known they would, her eyes began to close. She went upstairs, taking the book with her. In the room, Aoife's nightlight was throwing coloured stars to the ceiling, like confetti to a summer sky. She left it on. Some time during the hours to come, it would turn itself off.

Chapter Sixteen

It was on the following Saturday afternoon that Maura's car met with an overtaking van on the Longford road. Joanne and Mark had come down to Dorvaragh that morning. Maura intended to throw Aoife a birthday party; there was a cake in Longford that she wanted to pick up. As she had been getting ready to leave the house, Aoife had woken up from her nap. 'Sure come with me for the drive,' Maura had said to Joanne. 'There must be a few things you need to get in town.'

The miracle, everyone said afterwards, was that Aoife had escaped without so much as a bang on the head. Everyone talked about the new child seats, how sophisticated and modern they were, and quite a few people talked about mercy, and about how at least the little girl had been spared. But the truth was that Aoife had simply been lucky. That she had, purely by chance, been sitting at exactly the right distance from both sides of the car to stay shy of the inward crumpling. That she had been tiny enough not to have her neck broken by the car roof as it was thrown sideways against the wall. Mark pictured it for a long time afterwards, what the police and the firemen had told him about lifting this little red-haired thing clean and clear out of the wreckage – although it wasn't that clean, he knew. They would have had to cut through the crushed metal of the roof before they had got that far, hoping to Jesus she would not die of some unseen wound or bleeding before then. But they described it to him as though it had been a sort of religious experience for them, getting this pale, quiet baby into their arms, not crying, not calling for her mother – and they told him this, he knew, so that he would think she had not suffered, that she had not seen anything, that she had not been hysterical with fear and incomprehension at anything she had seen. He thought, afterwards, about the use of that word 'clean' – because they had used it, more than one of them, the priest who had been there, too – and what it was meant to signify. That she had no blood on her. That she had no wounds. But also that she had not been touched by the blood of her mother. The blood of his mother. And at this he stopped himself. At this he knew he had gone far enough. This was more than they had told him. More than they had given him. What they had given him was this child, lying now in this pine cot, sleeping now, impossibly soundly, beneath a knitted blanket and a flannel sheet. Her cheeks were fiery red. Her forehead was damp. But it was normal, he told himself. She was teething.

PART TWO

Chapter Seventeen

With Mark gone back to the city, there was less for Tom to do in the morning. Tea could be made in a mug, the used bag tossed into the small bin on the draining-board. A slice of bread with butter and marmalade was enough for breakfast; the smell of bacon and pudding browning on the pan seemed too heavy now on the air of the small room. Afterwards, he would rinse the mug and the spoon and the plate and the knife and put them back in the cupboard, ready for the next morning. At midday he would make himself another mug of tea and eat a sandwich – baked ham well sharpened with salt – and later he would boil four potatoes, empty a can of baked beans into a saucepan, and fry a pork chop in a dark, spitting pool of butter and oil.

There were no longer enough scraps from the table to feed the dog. She followed him around the kitchen. He began to buy cans of dog food in Keogh's. There was more than a euro in the difference between the cheapest and the most expensive. The brand he chose had a dog like her pictured on the label.

He spent most of the day outdoors, moving between the hayshed and the yard, the byre and the fields. He drove around the lower meadows and into the bog, over the back lane to call on Sammy Stewart or Jimmy Flynn, over to Keogh's to shop for groceries. If he sat into the bar for a pint during the day, he took the newspaper with him. There were seldom many others there and they talked to him only of farming and of football, of the going prices for land or for animals, of the weather and how it had been. He had his pint, and he left, and he found something to tip around at for the rest of the day. The dog went everywhere with him, riding high in the cab of the tractor, her back pressed warm against his.

In the evenings, soap operas came on the television. He began to follow some of them. The Australian one after the news was for youngsters, he thought, but he liked looking at it, liked the scenes of fighting and smiling and fussing played out against the backdrop of the beach. The tumbling blueness of the waves and the sky filled the television screen. The girls were impossibly good-looking, blonde and suntanned, wearing short dresses and swimsuits. They were all very young. There was one older woman in it, and she, too, was very attractive, but she was made out, most of the time, to be a sort of laughing-stock. She gossiped or eavesdropped or interfered, and her actions always backfired. When the programme ended, always with a mystery or a surprise, he would go to the kitchen and cook his dinner, standing over the range until it was ready, turning the meat and stirring the beans, putting a plate in to warm when the potatoes yielded to the touch of a fork.

He ate at the kitchen table, drinking a glass of milk with his food. He spread butter thickly across the steaming potatoes cracked open on the plate. He sprinkled grains of salt and watched them melt. The dog sat at his feet. From the other room he could hear the drone of the television, bursts of talk and music and applause, and the louder blasts of the advertisements. When he had finished eating, he washed and dried the things he had used and returned to the armchair. Before the news at nine o'clock there were two English soaps and one set in Dublin, moving between offices and sitting rooms and pubs. In these, the women were older, their clothes duller, their mouths downturned, their accents either sullen or shrill. The men sat nursing pints in bars that were too quiet to be real. Outdoors, the skies always looked swollen with rain, but no rain fell. The young people's lives were ruined with worries about sex and money and family. The old people worried about petty things, sick pets and broken ornaments and the carry-on of drunken neighbours. Their worries were there for the sake of comedy. He sometimes laughed.

While the news was on a second time he would make a mug of tea and cut a slice of sweet cake or apple tart from the biscuit tin over the fridge. He would feed the dog, scooping the glistening meat out of the can with a spoon he rinsed afterwards in boiling water. He put the empty can in a plastic bag and hung it on the doorknob. He took his tea and his slice and sat back down to watch whatever it was they had on after the news. He never changed the channel after nine. Before Mark left he had paid for the television to be hooked up to some huge number of American channels, as well as to the English ones, which had never come properly into the house with the old aerial. Mark had shown him how to use the new machine under the television, the slim white box with the three buttons and the dial that you had only to touch lightly to operate. But when he had tried to work it himself, the first evening on his own, he had only been able to get channels with no picture, in some other language. At first he thought it was Irish.

He left one of the lamps on in the kitchen at night. The dog slept on an old rug under the table, and he liked to leave her a dish of water. He locked the front and back doors and climbed the stairs in darkness. In the bathroom, he took his dentures out and left them in a plastic mug on the washbasin. After he had used the toilet, he did not bother to zip his trousers back up or to redo his belt. He did not flush: it could wait until morning. He did not like the sudden noise in the quiet and the dark. He undressed at the foot of the bed. He turned the light out. The sheets were cold. The pillows held his head in a firm embrace. Some nights, through the window, he could see the roof of the hayshed and the tops of the garden oaks etched hard against the moonlit sky. When the moon was small, he could see only vague shapes, and sharp stars, and on other nights, he could see nothing but the blackness of the air. Sleep was slow in coming, but it came. He went towards it. He took no interest in his dreams.

Chapter Eighteen

Mark heard from his sister now more often than he would have liked. They had little to say to each other, but between them, they worked out a bearable routine. Nuala asked the same questions; he gave the same answers. Nuala asked about their father, knowing that Mark would have talked to him earlier; Mark knew that Nuala would have been talking with him too. She asked about Aoife. She asked how Mark himself was doing. In those first days, those nine days, she had asked about Joanne. But even then, Mark had known that all Nuala really wanted to talk about was their mother. She was panicking, Mark knew. He was going through it too. Trying to claw everything back into view and into focus, trying to recall everything, to preserve it, to have it for keeps – and she was losing it. Forgetting it. Realizing that she could no longer hear, clear in her head, the sound of their mother's voice. That she could no longer remember the set of their mother's face. And so every phone call became a clutching after one more memory, one more detail. Had their mother said this that time one Christmas, or had she said that? What did Mark remember of their holidays in Spiddal? What kinds of books had their mother been reading over the last few years? What had she liked to listen to on the radio? Was RTÉ still making episodes of the thing she used to listen to when Nuala was a child?

Harbour Hotel. No. It was long gone. And Mark could not

bring himself to look through the pile of books on their mother's bedside table – still on the bedside table – so he could not answer that question for Nuala. These were, anyway, little things. He knew that. Nuala knew that. But they were the clippings and the shavings and the locks of hair that Nuala needed for the collage she was trying so desperately to make and to control. Sometimes on the phone she would let out a sob, or a sigh that Mark knew to be chased by tears. But usually she was steady, almost chatty, briskly asking and avidly gathering, as though she were doing market research, as though she had a quota of answers to get and spaces to fill. Which she did, Mark knew. As did he. The difference was, he already knew he could not think fast enough, could not hold everything together. Everything had never been held together in the first place. It was gone. The parts were gone. To try to gather them was to try to gather leaves from an autumn five, ten, twenty years ago; there was the sense that countless things had fallen and scattered, but nothing to grasp at, nothing to sweep.

Because Mark was forgetting things too. Already his memory was deciding that some things could be discarded, that some things could fall out of view. On this, his memory was not consulting him. There was nothing Mark felt willing to discard. But it was just one more thing he could not control, and what he could not explain to Nuala was that he felt miles away, even, from being able to worry about that, much less panic about it. None of this was in his control, but some of what he had to get up to, face up to, was more consuming than anything else. And what he had to face up to, every day and every hour, was the fact. And at the fact, Mark felt as though he was still staring, still trying to make it real. Still trying not to be as startled by it every morning as he would have been if he had woken to find a stranger in his room.

And so there was no time to cry over what was going, over what was slipping away. The business of being the self that could cry over such things, that could exist after a fact like that and react with sorrow or anger or fear: all of that would have to wait. All of that he could not do. Not yet. He was not yet ready to realize that he was alone.

Alone. He was not alone. He had a father who called him every day, a father he had to call every day. He had a sister. He had friends, who tried to do the kinds of things they thought friends, in such a situation, were meant to do – although some of them vanished, some of them could not face him, call him, text him, even, to say a version of the same old lines everyone felt they had to say. And he had Aoife. A daughter. A child. Sixteen months old, with her mother's quick, vivid glance. A challenge and an interrogation, meeting with him every morning, looking at him over the bars of her cot. She watched him as he came towards her, she watched him as he walked away from her at night. She watched him as she sat at the kitchen table, as she stood, demanding, beside the fridge. She watched him as she walked, as she wobbled. As she sat in front of the television programmes he hoped she would watch. Before, those pro-grammes had only ever been on for an hour a day. But this was not before. This was now, or this was afterwards, and in now, or in afterwards, he depended on cartoon animals and animated trains for distraction, for relief, for help in spinning the hours into a pale, dulled haze. But she did not watch these programmes, not really. She watched him.

She had three words. The name she called him, which made her sound like a little Dubliner hollering for her da. 'Boy', the name for the blanket she carried with her as she walked – it had looked angelic and soft when they had bought it, in its whiteness and its satin and its fleece, but now it looked like a month-old lump of snow. And she had 'mere', which meant 'come here', which was Mark's signal to follow her, go to her, take her hand and walk with her to the fridge, the toybox, the staircase, the front door; c'mere, it said, and do what I want you to do. Do what has to be done. Do the thing that has just occurred to me and is full in my mind's eye as the only needful thing in the world. Look sharp about it. Or be with me as I do it, as I get it, as I turn the dial or climb the step or push the door to make it happen. To make it begin.

He spent his days with her now, mainly indoors. Mainly in the house on Arbour Hill. Because of her, there was need of a routine. He took her for her walk. They came home and ate breakfast. She played, walked through the rooms, waved things at him, gave him her bright, urgent orders. He changed her. For a long time as he changed her, he found himself on the brink of turning to Joanne to make a comment about the smell or the colour of the child's shit. He found himself, more than once, beginning to turn his head towards the bedroom door, towards the other room, towards the rooms downstairs. As the child watched him look there, she looked there too.

Money was not short. They were fine. The mortgage was long paid on the place. His funding was safe for next year – McCarthy had phoned early on to assure him of that, and what was left would stretch. The money his mother had left him came through in a cheque, and for months he let it sit in a drawer. Eventually he opened a savings account for Aoife. It was something he and Joanne had meant to do. Now the account was there, and it had more money in it than any bank account Mark had ever had, but by the time she used it, he knew, it would pay for maybe a couple of months in America on a J1. Or a second-hand car. Or a master's in something useless, if they still had degrees in useless things by then. But they would. There would always be degrees in useless things.

*

The Phoenix Park was depressing. Homeless people slept there. Rent-boys worked there. The pope had blessed the country there. Animals lay in filthy cages in the zoo there. But it was a park. It was Mark's local park. And the park, he decided one morning, was where you were meant to go on your morning walks. Not the square in Smithfield. Not the footpaths along Manor Street. In the park, with trees and greenery and water, and sunlight reflecting off them all. 'We're going out to see the sunshine,' he told Aoife, and she frowned and tugged at his hair.

They passed the disused travel agent's, and the hair salon already busy with women sitting under driers, and the four squat cottages at the foot of the hill. He felt the pushchair jolting, and he knew that Aoife was pointing to something, kicking her feet, saying one of her words. It was impossible to hear her. At this hour, these streets were at their worst; hardly wider than country lanes, bloated with rush-hour traffic. From narrow junctions all along Manor Street, drivers tried to edge into the main flow, surging forward, stalling, ignoring the horn blasts. Ahead of Mark on Arbour Hill, a lone cyclist was forced in tight to the kerb by traffic, one foot on a pedal and the other stepping its way along the pavement. A siren dipped into the clamour of horns and engines and car radios. The bells from the nearby church rang for nine, and an instant later, the jingle for the hourly news sounded from inside the car that Mark was passing. The driver pounded both hands on the wheel and swore. Ahead, several sets of lights changed to red at the same instant. So imperceptible had the crawl of the traffic been that it was only in its sudden seizing up that it made itself known. Mark walked on.

People were still sleeping on benches in the park. It was too early to expect them to be up and moving in towards the city. An old man lay on a bench, a piece of clothing bundled up as a pillow, his feet on the armrest as though he were basking in the sun. Farther on, a couple lay locked together under a blackened blanket, cider cans on the ground beneath the bench, like skittles toppled in a game. Sometimes, especially during the winter, passers-by would leave things under the benches: packets of crisps, or sandwiches, or cartons of milk. There were no offerings today. After he had passed, Mark reached into his pocket, thinking to leave them some coins, but he found nothing that could be of use – a clothes-peg, a penny, a soother. He moved on towards the pond.

He settled the pushchair at a bench in front of the spot where the ducks seemed busiest; they were surfacing, circling, fussing. Aoife was straining against the straps, calling out. It was her new word, her fourth word. Up. He unstrapped her and lifted her out as she squirmed. She started, in her hurried, half-balanced steps, towards the water, towards three fat ducks, which were ignoring her, picking at themselves with their beaks. She squealed, and still they ignored her, and she turned to look back at Mark, and to wave her arms at him, and to smile a smile of such unbuttressed glee that he found himself feeling, for an instant, almost sorry for her. They're ducks, he found himself wanting to say to her; dirty, probably diseased ducks, and they're ignoring us, and if you go closer they'll scatter and get as far away from you as possible, and yet, from the look on your face, they're the best thing in your life right now. In your little life.

The ducks moved off into the middle of the pond. Aoife watched them and turned to him with a question on her face. He knew what it was.

'Ducks gone,' he said, in the tone he used to tell her that something – a yoghurt, a drink, a game – was finished. Her reaction to this tone was the same as always. She shook her head. She peered at him as though giving him one more chance to change his tune. She swung an arm towards the ground as though throwing something. The action unsteadied her. She jolted on her feet.

'Ducks gone,' he said again, and she began to whine. A low whine at first, a warning – there was still time to repent, it seemed to say, there was still time to get the ducks back, to set everything right with the world – but as he came towards her it rose to a wail, and as he bent to her she was howling, flailing, battling against him. Her cries spread out over the water of the pond, and the ducks lifted too, into clumsy, irritated flight, and he rocked her, and shushed her, and bundled her into the pushchair. Already the park was growing busier – other pushchairs, other parents, other howls about other heartbreaks, other eyes lighting up at the sight of other indifferent birds. On the bench where they had been sleeping, the man and woman were awake now, sitting at a distance from each other. Their hands, wrapped around new cans of cider, were the same deep red as their faces, their coats looking too heavy for the warm day it was turning out to be. They could have been in their thirties or their fifties; it was impossible to tell. Both of them had eyes of an intense, bright blue. But they did not look at him. They looked elsewhere. She to the ground. He to the sky.

*

Later, as Mark sat in front of the television, Sarah phoned to ask him to come to dinner with her and Deirdre in their house in Phibsborough the following evening.

'Tomorrow?'

'Yes, tomorrow. You don't have anything else on, do you?'

'Not that I know of.'

'And how's Aoife?'

'She's asleep upstairs. Finally.'

'The little pet. You can bring her, needless to say.'

'That's all right. Eileen will watch her.'

'Aw,' Sarah said.

'You wouldn't say that if you were here with her all day.' He smiled as he spoke, but he could hear that she was not smiling; he could hear her suck her breath in suddenly, and he knew an apology was tumbling his way.

'Oh, of course, of course, of course you need your time to yourself. Don't mind me. Sure we'll see lots of Aoife. We'll all have a day out or something soon.'

'What should I bring? To dinner.'

'Just yourself.'

'No. Come on. I'll bring wine, obviously. But do you want me to bring dessert?'

'Bring wine, then,' Sarah said. 'But there's really no need. We have plenty.'

*

Eileen worked in the space where the shelves and counters of a grocery store had once been. Fabrics were piled high on chairs, and rails held trousers and dresses and skirts waiting to be altered. Aoife reached for a small plastic lunchbox full of coloured thread and emptied it on the floor, sitting down heavily among the spools to grab at them and arrange them around herself in some unknowable order. Mark apologized for the mess, but Eileen shook her head.

'She's doing no harm,' she said. 'She'll be fine here for the evening, and don't you worry your head about her at all.'

Aoife did not react to his leaving, at least not that he could hear as he walked down the street. The evening was still warm, the brick of the terraces glowing a rich, baked red. Something flashed through his mind: red brick burnished on the street outside Kehoe's that July evening the year before, but then a taxi was passing, and he was hailing it, and there was need to think of other things, the address for Sarah and Deirdre's house, the speed with which the driver pulled away, the fact that he had forgotten, after all, to buy a bottle of wine.

The driver, thin and sickly and wearing a thick gold chain, asked him questions about his job and his holidays and how long he thought the good weather was likely to last. 'Christ knows we deserve some kind of fucking summer,' he said.

'We do,' Mark said, and for the rest of the drive they were silent. When they got to Phibsborough, Mark directed him through the narrow streets, and when the driver pulled up outside the house Sarah, in a blue summer dress, was at the front door, waving. She hugged him tight in greeting.

'I'm so glad you're here,' she said, and from the tone of her voice he knew it was going to be a long night. She was already close to tears.

He considered, for a moment, asking her to pretend that everything was normal, but he knew this was something he could not do. He pulled himself out of her embrace as gently as he could and smiled. 'I forgot the bloody wine,' he said.

'Oh, Mark,' Sarah said, and she put her arms around him

again, and kept them there until Deirdre came into the hall to coax her away.

*

Joanne had lived for nine days after the accident. She had come closest to consciousness just before dying. The doctors had given him reason to believe that she would survive, but on the Thursday, after he had watched her eyelids flicker for more than an hour and believed that her eyes were about to open and that they were about to hold the sight of each other clear in their minds again, something burst or blocked or broke apart in her brain stem, and in place of the beautiful, minimalist music of her pulse came the falsetto siren of its absence. He had been with her when the last signals to her brain had stalled and stumbled and bubbled away into nothingness. He had been holding her wrist firmly enough so that she could feel it, if she could feel anything, which they said she could. He had been talking to her, silently, and his mind had been not in the present, not in this actual, living moment, but in some daydream of the future, some fantasy of weather and brightness and sound, some symphony of his words and hers and the still unarticulated words of their daughter, some place far from silence. He had been with her, he had told himself over and over afterwards, but he had not: he had been somewhere else, somewhere impossible, and while he was in that elsewhere, she had stopped and turned and dissolved into an elsewhere that was beyond even his dreams.

He had stayed with her afterwards, after they had made clicks on the machines and slid tubes out of her skin and closed the plastic curtains around them and placed sorry palms on his shoulders. He had been in the present then, in the moment of its happening, and he could not escape, and when the nurse had come in a while later and whispered that Joanne's family were in the hall, and that it would be good to let them say goodbye, he had been almost glad of the movement, of the encounter, of the onward rush.

When he walked into the house that evening, his father, standing at the kitchen table, had looked at him for a long moment, his mouth as heavy as though it were hung with a hook. Then he had turned away and faced the wall, crying, his whole body twitching like that of a young dog in its sleep.

*

Deirdre was the cook. The food was good, a vegetable lasagne and a side dish of lamb. They had not known whether Mark would prefer meat or no meat, Sarah said, and they had not liked to call him to ask, to put him on the spot. Mark began to respond that this was ridiculous, but found himself saying, instead, that it was thoughtful. 'And they're both delicious,' he said. 'Thank you.'

'We didn't want to put you on the spot,' Sarah said again.

'You're so good. Thanks.'

'So,' Sarah said, after she had refilled their wine glasses.

'So.'

'You're back in the land—' She stopped suddenly, shaking her head, her eyes wide. 'Jesus, Mark. Sorry. I mean . . .'

'I know what you mean, it's all right.'

'Back among us.'

'Yeah.'

'Does that feel better?'

He shrugged. He could see that Deirdre was watching Sarah, willing her to stop asking questions, to stop pushing in this direction. She, meanwhile, was pushing just as hard in the opposite direction, changing the subject every time

Sarah tried to ask him how he was. Neither tactic helped. To be too much pitied, or to be too carefully respected. Though he could tell that the food was very good, he did not want to eat. The wine seemed to him as bitter as cough syrup, yet Sarah had already commented on how delicious it was. He drank it anyway. Deirdre refilled his glass.

When he and Joanne had been thinking about godparents for Aoife, they had considered Sarah and Deirdre, had wondered if that would work. But while they were talking about godparents, they had realized that they were talking about a christening, and they had remembered that they did not believe in any god, and so there had been no christening. But Sarah and Deirdre had meant enough to them for it to have seemed right to ask them.

And now he wondered why they were friends. But he had wondered it about everyone who was left. Even Mossy. Mossy who came to see him every day, Mossy who fed him in the evenings sometimes, even though Mossy, unlike Deirdre, could not cook. It was true, it had taken Sarah and Deirdre until now to invite him to dinner, but he knew why that was, too. They had been afraid. In the first weeks, it was too soon. In the next weeks, everyone thought he wanted to be left by himself to get used to things, to cry his tears, to climb his walls. And then it was inching into being too late, and people started thinking that they had missed the boat, that they should have contacted him weeks ago, and now they were too embarrassed to get in touch. But that was not fair on Sarah and Deirdre. They had been in touch. They had called around. Sarah had always been crying so much that it had been an irritant more than anything to have them in the house. But they had made the effort. They had let him know that they were there.

Still, he could see it in them. It was something he had

noticed in other couples too. He had seen it, even, in his sister and the way she looked at him, and then looked at Denis, her husband. Unsuspecting Denis, unaware that he was suddenly being surveyed as something precious, something almost unreal.

Sarah and Deirdre were doing exactly the same thing. In quiet moments during the lull in a conversation – or even during a conversation – he would see one of them watching the other. One of them staring at the other, with a kind of melancholy. The first few times he had noticed people doing this, he had thought there must be something wrong in these relationships, that there had just been some row or difficult conversation, being carried now into the rest of the evening, into interactions outside the privacy which was just their own. But it kept happening. He kept catching it. And eventually he realized what it was. One half of the couple was looking at the other, thinking that one day the other would die. That they themselves would be left without them, that they themselves would be left, the way Mark was left. And what would it be like, they were thinking, how would they cope? What would this house be like with only one person in it? What would the dinner table be like when there were visitors, with only one of them to carry the conversation through the night? What would it be like, that world outside, knowing that this other person was not in it, not out there doing their usual things? That door, if the other person were never again to walk through it, would it look different? These rooms, this furniture, what would they mean?

He felt suddenly very tired. He had had trouble sleeping since the day of the accident, but now he thought he could lie down on the couch across from the dinner table and pass out for hours, for the whole night, for days. It exhausted him to listen to the conversation, to take part in it, and at the same time, to take part in the unspoken conversation, to watch and know and understand what was happening in the spaces in between.

'Are you all right?'

It was Sarah. She looked, Mark noticed with a twinge of alarm, close to tears again. 'Are you feeling bad?' she said, and reached out for his hand.

'I'm fine,' Mark said, feeling guilty at having allowed his face to give so much away. He squeezed her hand. 'I'm just a bit tired.' It was tiring in itself, this swinging between being sick of someone and being fond of them.

'Of course you're tired,' Deirdre said, and she gestured to the couch. 'Why don't you sit down? We can have dessert over there.'

'Thanks,' said Mark, and as he rose from the table he could see that more glances were being exchanged between the two women. There was, he realized, something in the air, something other than the awkwardness he had felt all evening: an agitation, a restlessness, almost a panic. Was it that they wanted him to be gone? That they could not take it any longer, this sadness he must be trailing around with him – this grief he was forcing them, by his presence, to see and to feel?

'I won't stay late,' he started to say, but as he glanced at them he could see that he had got it all wrong. They were smiling at each other, almost glowing, sharing some secret, some private joy, and in the instant before they became aware that he was watching them, he realized that there were always new ways to feel it, the loneliness. It was not just bottomless, or endless, it was also inventive. It was smart, self-generating; it was various. *The drunkenness of things being various*: a line from a poem came into his head, and he blinked at it, dismissed it. Was it that they wanted to be

alone? But he had only just arrived. They were still, technically, in the middle of dinner. That was rude, he thought,
and then thought, You're such a fucking moron. He could
not be sure, actually, that he had not said it aloud. They were
both staring at him. He was standing in the middle of the
room.

'We have something to ask you,' said Deirdre, at exactly
the same time as Sarah said, 'We have news.'

'Really?' Mark said, and he stammered.

'Yeah,' said Deirdre, with a laugh.

'Oh, right,' said Mark.

They stood in silence for a moment.

'I hope you're not going to ask me to help you have a kid
or something,' Mark said, and he tried to laugh. It was meant
to be a joke. He had wanted to say something that made him
sound less nervous, made him feel more in control. But as
soon as he had said it, he knew it was the wrong thing. At
first, they both looked stricken, and then Sarah's face moved
into deeper upset and Deirdre's into what he knew to be
annoyance, though they both moved very quickly to cover
these expressions. His face burned.

'You're not . . . ?' he said, and felt stupider still as he saw
how absolutely they refused his suggestion. They shook their
heads as though he had confused them with two entirely
different people. So it was not that he had blurted out
precisely what they wanted from him, not that he had
trodden on their announcement in that way: it was worse.
He had crossed some line of propriety, of correctness; he had
exposed himself as the narrow-minded boor who was still, in
some part of himself, unused to the idea of them – two
women in a relationship, two women sharing a bed. He was
still a gawking schoolboy, ready at any moment to be found
out, likely at any moment to make a comment that would

give him away. And now he had done it, and they were looking at him so strangely. They were seeing him. They were judging him.

'Sorry, sorry,' he said. He put his head into his hands. When he looked up, a man on the television was pulling a foal out from between a mare's bloody haunches. The foal was covered with yellow slime. It seemed impossibly long. At the table, Sarah and Deirdre were silent. Then Sarah rose from the table and came over close to the television, settling into the armchair opposite Mark.

'God, I hate those animal programmes,' she said.

'Yeah.'

'They'd show anything on the telly now.'

'Seems so.'

This time the silence between them seemed deeper. On the television, the foal was already staggering to its feet, black blood still matted to its hair, the man holding it by the back legs, steadying it, before letting it go. It was much ganglier than calves were at birth.

'Mark, we're getting married, Deirdre and I,' said Sarah. 'We're only asking a couple of people to be at the ceremony, and we want you to be there. As our witness. Would you do that for us?'

He looked at her. She was smiling, she was nodding; she was beginning to cry again. Wait, was that why she had been crying all along? Not out of sadness for him, or about him, but out of whatever rush of happiness and excitement she felt about what she had just told him? There was no time to think about it, and of course it was not good-natured, good-hearted, to think something so selfish as one of his friends told him something so good, but still as he widened his eyes and lifted his hands and got up to meet and return her messy embrace, he was thinking it, and chiding himself for thinking it, and replying that he was damn well bloody entitled to think of it, all at once.

'Congratulations,' he said, and held and squeezed and patted Sarah as she laughed and cried. 'Congratulations, Deirdre,' he said, over Sarah's shoulder.

'Thanks,' Deirdre said, and came over to hug him too.

After a lot of this, hugging and smiling and laughing and saying the same thing over and over, they all sat down. Sarah was wiping her eyes, and Deirdre was exhaling and shaking her head, as though what they had all just done together had been strenuous, as though they'd hauled a heavy piece of furniture up a narrow staircase.

'It's brilliant news,' Mark said again, and the women both smiled their hectic smiles.

'Isn't it?' Sarah said, and she clutched at Deirdre.

'Can you get married here?' said Mark, and their smiles dipped and wavered.

'Not officially,' said Deirdre, and Sarah nodded. 'It'll be a commitment ceremony.'

'Just as good,' said Mark, and instantly regretted it. Deirdre was regarding him that way again, careful and serious. But she said nothing.

'Of course I'll be there,' he said. 'Thank you so much for asking me to come.'

'And you'll bring Aoife, of course,' Sarah said. 'She can be our flower-girl.'

'Oh, yeah,' Mark said, not knowing what else to say. Maybe it was, once again, the wrong thing to say, but it was good enough, and once again there was hugging and kissing, and Deirdre went to the fridge and took out a bottle of champagne.

'Is it . . . ?' Sarah looked at him, and looked to Deirdre.

'Is it what?' Mark said, and then realized what she was asking: 'Is it OK to open a bottle of champagne?'

The thing was, he didn't know the answer. The answer he had to say out loud was that of course it was OK to open the bottle, that it was more than OK to open the bottle, that if Deirdre didn't hurry up and open the bottle he'd snatch it out of her hands and burst the cork off it himself. And as he nodded, frowning as though there could be no question as to the rightness of this, and as he watched the bottle tilt and Deirdre's fingers working at the foil, and as the cork hit the bathroom door, and as the liquid spilled and steamed and bubbled outwards, there seemed nothing wrong. It could not be wrong to do this, to celebrate with friends, to toast them, his glass held high. It felt easy. It felt doable. He managed it. He drank the champagne, and kept the panic down.

The mare was now licking her newborn foal clean, her huge tongue sweeping the rough, sodden hair and replacing the thickness of the birth fluids with the bubbled sheen of her own saliva. Mark glanced at Sarah. She was watching him.

'You can talk to us, you know,' she said, smiling sadly.

'I know.'

'About anything.' She leaned in closer and pressed her cheek to his temple.

'Even foaling,' he was about to say, but instead he raised his glass again. 'To the two of you,' he said.

*

He was woken early next morning by his phone. *Home.* Outside, it was not yet fully bright. In her cot, Aoife was starting to stir. Mark silenced the ringing and took the phone out to the hall. When he put it to his ear, his father was already saying hello.

'Hello,' Mark said. 'What is it? Is everything OK?'

'I don't know,' his father said, sounding irritated. 'You were the one ringing me.'

'What?'

'You were ringing me. Weren't you?'

Mark sighed. This had happened at least once a week since he had bought a mobile phone for his father. 'I wasn't,' he said, sitting on the top stair.

'Sure who else would be ringing me on this thing?'

'I don't know. It wasn't me.'

'You must have hit the number by accident. You must have had it ringing in your pocket. Didn't you tell me the phone could do that? And use up all your money?'

Mark opened his mouth to explain, but thought better of it. 'Yeah,' he said, rubbing his eyes.

'You'd want to be careful of that.'

'I know,' Mark said. 'Thanks.'

'So what did you want anyway?'

In the bedroom, Mark could hear Aoife starting to whine. He stood, but did not move from the landing. 'I didn't call you, I'm telling you.'

His father said nothing for a moment. 'What are you at up there anyway? Are you up?'

'I am now. So is Aoife.'

'And what are ye at for the day?'

'I don't know,' Mark said. 'I haven't thought about it yet. What are you doing yourself?'

'The usual,' Tom said. 'Only I'm headin' up to Stewarts' for the lunch later.'

'Lunch?'

'Yeah,' his father said. 'Didn't I tell you I have the lunch with them every Sunday now?'

'Right,' Mark said. He had not known it was Sunday. He had not known what it was.

'Helen says I'm welcome up there for my lunch every day if I want it.'

'You hardly want that,' Mark said.

'Indeedin I don't. She'd make you feel like you're at confession. Never fuckin' stops with the questions.' Tom drew breath suddenly. He rarely swore in conversation, and Mark knew that he was uneasy now in the echo of his own language. The kindest response would be to laugh. He stayed silent.

Tom cleared his throat. 'So are you doing anything yourself for the day?'

'No.'

'Didn't even know what day of the week it was, I'd betchya.'

'I did know.'

'Aw, now. I'd wager you weren't too sure.'

'Near enough.' Mark was quiet again for a moment. 'You're getting on all right down there, so.'

It was Tom's turn to be silent. 'Flynn has red water in the herd,' he said eventually. 'There's an awful amount of them with it, he says.'

'That's a nuisance.'

'Bloody curse.'

Down the line, as his father sighed, Mark heard what sounded like a car passing. 'Are you outside?' he said, unable to keep the surprise from his voice.

'Down at the road.'

Mark took the phone away from his ear and checked the time. It was just past six o'clock. From the bedroom, Aoife's whining grew more insistent. He walked to the door, and she seemed to sense him: she began to howl.

'I'll have to go,' Mark said. 'I'll talk to you later.'

'That's Aoife I can hear, is it?'

'I'll talk to you.'

*

His father was coping. Adapting, that was the word. Fitting himself to the shapes of things; steeling himself to the day. Moving through the world – his world – as though he recognized it. As though it recognized him. He seemed to be up every morning at dawn. He called Mark twice a day. His voice always sounded calm. It always sounded sure.

All summer, Mark had watched him. He had spent the first months after the funeral in Dorvaragh with him because he knew he had to be there. Nuala could get away from her job in London for only so long, and the two of them had decided – during one of the very earnest, very focused conversations they seemed capable of during those first weeks – that Mark should stay around. There was no other way, they agreed, of knowing how their father would manage once the shock of what had happened began to fade. There was no other way of ensuring his well-being. He was a man alone in a house in which he had not been alone for more than thirty years, and he could not be expected to face that. It was a change, and he would have to be eased through it. Carried through it.

As for you, Nuala had said to Mark, and Mark had told her not to go there. Not to go on. He was staying at home for their father, he said. He was staying at home because there was a summer of work to be done. What he did not say was that the house in Stoneybatter was not a place he could be. Not yet. Dorvaragh was familiar in some way he did not have to think about. And there was Aoife. Around the work of the farm, a steady routine for Aoife began to mould itself, and for a long time Mark could not imagine having to start with another. So, for almost three months, he stayed.

The work was his father's succour. It was his centre. The hay and the cattle and the machinery seemed not just to ground him, but to fill him with some kind of optimism, to fuel him with something like zeal. In the mornings he was like a child as he chattered to Mark about what needed to be done, what approach would be best, what problems might arise. As they worked he consulted Mark on everything. He came to him for the kind of advice that, before, he had always been the one to impose. When relatives and neighbours came to visit, as they did often, Tom talked to them of the farm, and the men nodded and gave their own stories of work finished and unfinished, and the women talked of how good it was to be busy, to have something on which to focus the mind.

Mark watched. He worked, and he did everything that needed to be done, but more than that, he watched. For the first time in his life, he realized, he was trying consciously to learn from his father. He was trying to understand how to manage in his father's way. But the work kept failing him; the work kept leaving him with himself. It did not take him over the way he needed; it did not burn his thoughts away. Almost every day after he came back in from the farm, he would take Aoife up in his arms and carry her out to the car. He took her to places he had been as a child. To the wasteland of Barley Harbour. To the bog lakes at Currygrane and Gurteen. To the old farmyards at Carriglass, where the developers had started work on the new hotel. To the low peak of Corn Hill. Outside the building that had once been Edgeworthstown House, he sat in the car and watched the old people shuffle between the smoking hut and the porch.

When they returned to Dorvaragh, his father would have some kind of dinner on the table. It usually involved black pudding and potatoes and baked beans. Mark ate it. Aoife ate some version of it. If his father asked where he had been, he told him he had been to Longford, or to some other town. At night, while they sat in front of the television, his father would talk about the farm. He would look to Mark for answers. Mark would try to watch the programmes, but the storylines always seemed impossible to grasp.

In August, the house in Stoneybatter began to press itself on his thoughts. He began to feel guilty about it; he imagined its rooms growing dusty, growing stale. And he imagined, sometimes, that Joanne was in those rooms, waiting for him, somehow. Confused about where he and Aoife might be. When he left for the city, he told his father he would return to the farm every weekend that he could. His father had nodded, and tapped his stick against the ground, and gone down to the lower fields to check on a fence that the cattle had been breaking through, a fence they had repaired together the previous day. 'Call me when you get there,' he said to Mark, as he went. Mark had been on the road five minutes when his father phoned to tell him that the fence had held.

*

Later on Sunday Mark took Aoife to the swimming-pool. It was something he had been meaning to do. He found the tiny swimsuit someone had given her as a gift long before she was big enough to wear it, and he found his own trunks, baggy and grey. He stuffed a couple of bath towels into a bag. They walked into town along the quays.

In the changing room, a single long bench faced the showers. Under the flow nearest the door, an elderly man stood with his back turned, his head facing down, sodden trunks clutched in his right hand. The water slapped onto his freckled shoulders, the paps of his elbows, the bumps of his spine.

As Mark got her into her swimsuit, Aoife shouted and pointed to the old man, to the water leaping off his skin. While Mark undressed, she wandered closer to the showers and stood watching, her hands loosely clasped behind her back. When beads of water hit her skin, she flinched, but she did not come back to Mark.

Mark inflated the plastic armbands he had bought at the entrance desk. 'Come over here,' he called to Aoife. She shook her head vigorously and pointed again at the old man.

'Aoife,' he called again, and in the same instant, the man turned. He was cupping his dick and balls – washing them, Mark thought, he hoped. He dropped both hands by his side now, and he gazed at the child. His beard was full, though narrowed and pointed now by water, and his heavy eyebrows, too, were slicked down. He was almost bald. As he stood watching Aoife, the flow from the showerhead stopped.

'Hello there,' he said. Aoife continued to stare. Mark stood and brought her back to the bench where he had laid her clothes. She let him carry her, but when he tried to get her into the first armband, she snatched it from him and threw it to the floor.

The old man stepped forward and picked it up. 'You need to let some of the air out,' he said to Mark.

'Thanks,' said Mark, taking it from him.

'Once you get it up to the elbow, you need to open the little valve there, and let some of the air out so that it'll go over,' the man said, squeezing water out of his trunks. 'Then you blow it back up the whole way.' He shook the trunks briskly and walked to the other end of the bench. 'You'll pull the arms off her otherwise,' he said, and wrapped a striped towel around his waist.

'Thanks,' Mark said again. He opened the white rubber valve on the side of the armband and let out some of the air. Aoife complained as he pushed it up her arm, and when he put his lips to the valve and blew until he could feel the plastic hardening, she tried to shake him off. When he reached for the second armband, she turned her back on him, and when he pulled her to him, she began to scream. He put both arms tightly around her, turned her away from him, and held her still. She screamed more loudly and kicked her legs. Her fingernails dug into his forearms.

From the old man came a high-pitched laugh like a woman's. 'She's a devil,' he said. He was dressed. It hadn't taken long. He wore brown linen trousers and a short-sleeved shirt. He stepped into leather sandals.

Aoife let her whole body go limp. Mark kept his hands on her as she slid to the floor and lay there, sobbing furiously. He shrugged and looked to his neighbour, who gave him a grin. The man slung a string bag over his shoulder and pulled at his beard. 'Her first time at the pool?'

Mark nodded.

'She'll love it,' the old man said. 'Once you take her in.'

'I don't know,' Mark said, and when he reached down to Aoife she lashed at his face with her hands. The sharp edge of her armband caught him on the cheek.

'Ouch,' the old man said, wincing.

Mark had done it before he thought about it. He found himself with a hand tight on each of her arms. He pulled her to her feet. He whipped the armband off her arm, not stopping to let any of the air out, and Aoife screamed. 'Stop it,' he said to her, and she widened her eyes at him, and raised her cries to a higher pitch. She slumped to the floor. Sweating, his face feeling flushed, Mark looked to the man.

The man looked at Aoife. His face was cautious. He stepped forward a fraction, then stepped back. He cleared his throat. 'I expect it's all just a bit too much for her,' he said, over the noise of her cries. 'She is very young.'

Mark could not speak. The man checked the bench behind him and pulled the strap of his bag more firmly on to his shoulder. 'Have a good swim,' he said, touching his temple in a light salute, and he was gone.

Mark realized that he was cold, and that Aoife, kicking and thrashing on the tiles, would be even colder. He picked her up; she resisted him. He bundled her into a towel and sat her on the bench. He crouched in front of her, rubbing her shoulders through the towel, trying to soothe her where the plastic of the armband must have pinched and dragged.

'I'm sorry, baby,' he said, and she howled at him.

'I'm sorry,' he said again, and she shook her head, her face glooped with snot and tears. He sat on the bench beside her, and leaned in close to her, and she grabbed him by the cheeks with both hands and dug in her nails. It hurt. He didn't stop her. He didn't pull away. She continued to cry, and to scream, and to the sound of it he felt his chest cleave; he felt himself cling to her cries as they climbed against the distant echoes of the pool. His teeth were clenched. His eyes were locked on hers. It was not cold enough for him to shake as much as he did. When she finally quietened, he lifted her, and dressed her, and dressed himself, and he wheeled her out into the street. By the time they were back on the quays, she had fallen asleep, her thumb in her mouth, her hand clamped to her hair.

Chapter Nineteen

Tom tried Mark's number again. This time there was no ringing sound at all, just Mark's voice, sounding lazy, saying to leave a message, and then there was a beep, which was Tom's signal to hang up. He would not talk to something that was not listening.

At first, Mark had answered the phone every time Tom called. They had talked several times a day, something Tom considered essential. There were things he needed to check with Mark, things he needed to tell him. But over the last couple of weeks, Mark had started to pick up only now and again. Some days they did not talk on the phone at all; some days Tom could not get him. He had been busy, he always said, when they finally spoke: something had happened with Aoife, or there had been some issue to do with his studies. Was there anything urgent, he always asked Tom, and Tom never knew where to begin. Everything on the farm was urgent; nothing could wait a couple of days.

It was over two months now since Mark had gone back to the city. He had been back for a weekend only once, the first one after he had left, and since then there had been no visits. He had too much on his hands, he said. He could not get away. There was too much to be sorted out in Dublin, and he was still trying to get Aoife settled. He would be down, he always said, the next weekend. But then the next weekend came, and he was not there. Tom was not going to call him and beg him to come. That had never been Tom's style.

He needed to talk to him, but he could wait no longer. He would have to go ahead on his own. That afternoon he drove over to Brady's place, the new showroom he had built the year before. Brady himself greeted Tom when he walked through the glass doors. When Tom told him why he had come, Brady murmured approvingly.

'You know, you're dead right,' he said. 'Sure, the farming is hardship enough. We'll get you well kitted out.' He reached up to a shelf over the till. He lifted down three or four thick books and put them on the counter. On the cover of one, a huge John Deere pulled a round baler.

'The new catalogues,' Brady said, patting them. 'All the specs, as they'd say.'

Tom felt suddenly nervous. He looked at his phone. He had tried Mark again before getting out of the car. There had been no reply.

'The old mobiles are handy, aren't they?' Brady said, and he began to talk of the tractors he had, of engines and air compressors, drills and suspensions.

Tom nodded like a man who had long been hungry for the day when these things would come. 'You've some place here,' he said to Brady, looking to the high roof, the skylights streaming sun, the huge machines arranged like mannequins around the floor. Outside, the cheaper equipment was marked in neat rows.

'It'd fuckin' want to be,' Brady said, laughing. 'The fuckin' price of putting it up. Jesus, it's like Knock. Or Old Trafford or something.' He looked up to the skylights, to the blue sky beyond. 'Isn't it?'

'It's something like it all right,' Tom said.

'It was the young fella was at me to do it. Sure they're all like this now, all the good places around the country. Sure you have to keep up. What I had here for the last twenty years, sure it was nothing better than a hayshed.'

'Ah, you're dead right,' Tom said.

'You've seen some changes around this part of the world, I'd say, no more than myself,' said Brady, and he walked over to the huge tractor in the middle of the room. 'Now,' he said, putting his hand to the tread of the high front tyre. 'If you want the best of everything, this is the lassie to climb up on.'

Tom laughed with Brady as he rubbed the tyre vigorously, slapped it. 'Get up on her there, sure, can't you?' said Brady, but Tom shook his head.

'No thanks,' he said, and he saw how Brady's face became careful. 'What's the next one you have after this one?'

Brady nodded. 'Right you are,' he said. Tom followed him outside.

'Now this one,' Brady said, as he walked ahead, 'this one is an unbelievable tractor for the price.'

*

He had the whole lot picked little more than an hour later. Everything he wanted. Brady slid a docket across the counter, printed with the name of the shop, and with the price of each machine written on it in Brady's crooked hand. 'Now,' he said. 'And we'll call it that.' He pointed to the figure on the bottom of the docket. 'Sure, you're buying in bulk,' he said, spittle springing to his lips with his laugh.

'What about cash?' Tom said, and Brady froze for an instant. He looked again to the number he had written down. He looked to Tom.

'All cash?' he said, frowning.

'About the half of it,' Tom said. 'I've the rest in a cheque.'

Brady glanced out to the yard. 'You're a hard man,' he

said, and he pulled out another docket. He scribbled on it intently. He totted the figures up, tapping them with the tip of his pen. 'How's that?' he said, and his face was serious as he slid the paper across the counter to Tom.

Tom looked at the price. 'Now, you can do better than that for me, Gerry,' he said, and he stepped back.

'Ah, now, Jesus,' said Brady, but by the way he glanced out to the yard, Tom knew he would come down again. They went back and forward, and Brady sighed and chewed his lip and shook his head, and when they finally shook, it was on a price Tom knew was a good one, and Brady asked Tom where it was he had the new farm.

Tom looked at him, surprised. Then he remembered: he had told Brady he was stocking a whole new place. 'Ah, I'll be keeping them up in the sheds at home for a while,' he said, the words tumbling out in a hurry. 'I haven't the new yards ready for them yet. And you don't need to worry about delivering them. The son will be down from Dublin tomorrow and myself and himself can come in to you and drive them out. It's just as handy.' He thought of the neighbours watching: Keogh behind the shop door, Jimmy Flynn maybe going past on his blue Ford as Tom and Mark turned the new tractors in at the lane.

'Grand, so,' said Brady. 'You're out near Edgeworthstown, isn't it?'

'Dorvaragh,' Tom said. 'Just ahead of the crossroads there as you go out the Bal road.'

'I thought so all right,' said Brady, and he looked again at the cheque Tom had handed to him. 'Tom Casey,' he said. 'Sure I know you, of course,' and there was in his voice the note Tom heard in most voices now: the commiseration; the fascination. And as soon as the next thought flashed into his mind he hated himself for thinking it: that there might have been more off the price still, had Brady recognized him, had he made the connection sooner. He was shaking his head to get rid of the idea when he realized that Brady was studying him.

'I have you now,' Brady said. 'Didn't you buy that Massey from me there a few years before?' He did not wait for a response. 'That Massey was a very nice little runner,' he said. 'At the time. But, Jesus, you'll get better satisfaction out of these two.' He laughed. 'And you never thought of trading her in? You're a man in a hurry.'

'Ah, I'll keep her,' said Tom.

Brady nodded. 'Fair enough, Tom. No harm in having her around the place. Sure, maybe the son can run her around.' He winked at Tom. 'Ha? Don't let him get his hands on these beauties.'

'Ah,' Tom shrugged. 'It's a lot of interest he'll have in them anyway.'

'I doubt that,' Brady said. 'Unless he's blind altogether.'

'We'll see,' said Tom, as Brady handed him the receipt. 'Thanks very much.'

'Thanks yourself,' Brady said, offering his hand. 'And the very best of luck to the two of ye with the new place.'

*

The phone on the kitchen counter rang that evening as Tom was sitting down to his dinner. He was over to it and had the receiver to his ear before it finished the second ring. It was Mark.

'I was trying to get you earlier,' Tom said. 'What were you at?'

'Work,' Mark said. He sounded tired. 'And then Aoife.'

Tom cleared his throat. 'Working on the Edgeworthstown one, was it?' he said. He hoped Mark would recognize the generosity of the question, the interest it showed in his life. His heart speeded up as he waited for Mark's reply. It took a moment to come, and it came flat.

'Yeah,' Mark said. 'Edgeworth, yeah.'

Tom nodded. In his mind's eye he saw the old manor at Edgeworthstown, the porch with its two black pillars where he used to wait in the car for Maura to finish her shift. When first he started to call for her, when first they started to go together, it was like picking her up from school. There was always a nun watching from the door. And Maura would come down the steps like a schoolgirl, her coat over her uniform, the thin strip of her handbag swinging from her shoulder. As she slid into the car, there was her perfume and her bare knees and her sideways hello. Granard and Longford and Mullingar for the dances then. As far away from Edgeworthstown as they could. Wanting something different.

'Anything new with you?' Mark said then.

Tom hesitated. 'Aoife's asleep?' he said, looking at the clock over the range. It was seven.

'No,' said Mark. 'She's here beside me. She's watching one of her DVDs.' He seemed to yawn. 'What did you do yourself today?'

'Ah,' said Tom. 'Just tipping around. You know yourself.'

'Yeah.'

He took a long breath. Now was the time. Now was when he would have to tell him. He should have told him already; he should have phoned him from Brady's again and again until he answered. 'I went up to Brady's for a while to look at a few things,' he said.

'To Brady's?'

'Aye,' Tom said, carefully. 'He had me looking at all his new machinery.'

266

Mark clicked his tongue. 'That bollocks. He got the timing as wrong as he could get it with that place.'

In his chest, Tom felt a jolt. 'How do you mean?' he said, and he knew it sounded too anxious. 'He says it's doing well,' he added then, more lightly.

'Well, he'd say that,' Mark said, in the same tone full of scorn. 'But if he thinks anyone's going to be stupid enough to shell out for his overpriced rubbish the way things are going now, he's mistaken.'

'What do you mean, the way things are going?' Tom said.

'Do you not listen to the radio? The country is fucked.'

'What the hell do I want with the radio?' Tom said, and what came into his head was the radio that Brady had shown him in one of the new tractor cabs. You could plug all manner of things into it, Brady had told him. There was nothing you couldn't play through it, he had said. Tom had not asked him what he had meant.

'Yeah, well,' Mark said, and he sighed. 'Anyway. Sorry. I just never trusted that guy Brady, that's all. The prices he charges are ridiculous. But I suppose there's nowhere else to go if you need a part.'

On his forehead and underneath his arms, Tom felt himself sweat. His heart was thumping. 'Yeah,' he said, and he wanted to hang up the phone.

'So what was it you were looking for from him?'

'Ah,' Tom said, and as he shrugged, his shoulders felt like someone else's. 'Just a few bits for the Massey. Nothin' much.'

'It's giving you trouble?'

'Ah,' Tom said. 'The usual.'

'I'll take a look at it for you when I get down again,' Mark said.

The room felt darker to Tom. It felt as though it had

begun to move. 'You'll be down soon?' he said, and he put a hand on the counter to steady himself.

'Next weekend, maybe,' Mark said. 'I've a lot of work now.'

'You won't be down this weekend coming?'

'Tomorrow?' Mark said. 'Ah, no. No way. Sorry.'

'It's all right,' Tom said, quietly.

Mark said nothing for a moment. 'We can get through a lot when I'm down next weekend,' he said then. 'You must have a cattle test coming up this month some time, have you?'

'No.'

'But they're always around the end of October. Did Farrell not send you a card?'

'I had one earlier in the month,' Tom said, his voice so loud that the dog raised its head. 'I'll let you go.'

'All right,' said Mark, and he sounded uncertain. 'Sure if you need help with that tractor before the weekend, I'm sure Sammy could help you.'

'I'm sure he could,' Tom said. 'I'll let you go,' he said again.

Chapter Twenty

It was not that Mark had been lying to his father. He had meant to get down to Dorvaragh the following weekend. It had seemed possible when they spoke on the phone: there had been the stretch of another whole week ahead. But by Wednesday it was obvious that he could not be out of Dublin, not even for a couple of days. There was too much to do. He was on a roll with a new chapter: if he left it, he would lose the rhythm of it. He could not afford to be away.

He could barely even afford, he felt, to be out of the house; even going to the library was a disruption, but it had to be done. Other things had to be cut back on; it was not always feasible to take Aoife for a walk in the morning. She was always in better form if he did, so he felt guilty, but he found that he wanted, needed, to get down to work earlier and earlier, and the walk always wound up taking an hour at the time of day when he felt his mind was at its sharpest. It made more sense just to put her in front of one of her DVDs. He had it down almost to an exact system by now. Each episode of the things she watched was twenty minutes long. She sat or stood in front of the television, absorbed, staring, dancing along, and she whined only if she caught sight of him, so he worked on his chapter in the kitchen. If she came in, whining, he would give her Cheese Strings, or a yoghurt, and he would carry her around for a while, or he would change her nappy, if it needed to be changed, and then he would put her in front of the television again. And that would take her up to her nap time, when she usually slept for almost an hour, and after her lunch, she was happy to watch the DVDs again. He had accumulated a huge pile for her – Mossy let him borrow them from the shop for nothing – and she barely had to watch the same thing twice in the same week.

Eileen from next door called around sometimes in the evening. She brought bread she had baked, or apple tarts, and sometimes she brought little presents for Aoife. Aoife loved her. She always wanted, the moment she set eyes on her, to play with her or to sit on her knee. She offered Eileen her toys; she shouted and pointed to the characters on the television screen as though wanting to introduce Eileen to her friends. Mark saw the way Eileen looked at the kitchen table now, covered as it was with his books and notes, and the way she looked at him as he sat there; he knew she disapproved. But it was only for a while. In a week or two, he would be done with this chapter, and things could go back to normal. He would take Aoife out walking, out playing; he would take her everywhere. Eileen always offered to take her into her own house and watch her if he needed to work, but there was no need, and he told Eileen so, and he thanked her. Even though he was busy, he wanted Aoife with him in the house. He knew it was important for her to have him there, in the next room. He wanted to be able to see her, to hear her, to hear the chatter and jangle of her programmes, even if the theme tunes seemed, by now, to be burning themselves into his inner ear.

If he had to go to Trinity to check on a reference or borrow a book, he brought Aoife along: it was a chance to take her out in the fresh air, and it was a diversion for her. They were used to the sight of her in the library by now: the security men greeted her at the entrance, and often someone came over from the reference desk to talk to her, to offer to keep an eye on her while Mark went down to the stacks or up to the fourth floor to get what he needed. They had a pile of children's books she could look at, and it didn't matter, they said, if they were torn or if she drew on them with the crayons they gave her: that was what they were for, those books. But he couldn't remember seeing a child in the library before: he couldn't remember, before Aoife, standing at the circulation desk and looking down to see, behind it, a baby sitting on the thin green carpet, scribbling with a red crayon on the page of a picture book. Though maybe he had not been looking, back then.

By Friday, he had a rough draft of the chapter and he wanted McCarthy to look at it. He left Aoife with the librarian and went upstairs to the English Department to leave the pages with Grace, the secretary. But when he walked into her office, Grace handed him an envelope. Mark looked at it, surprised. His name was written on it in black ink. 'This isn't Maurice's handwriting,' he said.

Grace shook her head. 'No.'

'Then who?'

'Do you know Professor Clive Robinson?' She pointed to the ceiling. 'Used to teach in the philosophy department upstairs. He's retired a couple of years now, but he's still around a lot.' She laughed. 'Institutionalized.'

Mark did not reply. The name meant something to him, but he did not know what, not at first. At first, all he knew was that the sound of it took the air from his lungs and replaced it with a soreness; the soreness that meant Joanne. She had studied philosophy, but that was not it, that was not all – and then it came back to him. The day in the house in Stoneybatter: his first day to go back there after the crash.

The day after his mother's funeral. Joanne was still in Beaumont, still hooked up to the machines. She would need things, Mark had told himself; she would need things soon. He had gone back to the house to get her night clothes, and sweaters, and her iPod and some books. She would need books to read, he had told himself, and he had looked to the locker on her side of the bed. There were some novels, and a law textbook: Joanne had marked whole pages with yellow highlighter. And there was a philosophy book, and it had been heavily underlined too. Mark had been surprised by this. He knew Joanne had studied philosophy for a while in college, but she had never said anything to suggest that it was of interest to her still. He scanned the back cover: the book seemed to be about consciousness. He had stared at it. What had been her interest in consciousness? Had it been something to do with her work? He looked at the author's name and read his biographical note. And it had been this guy. Clive Robinson. Mark had not heard of him before. He left the book on the bedside locker and threw a couple of the novels into a bag. He did not know where those novels were now. He did not know what he had done with that bag of things.

'Mark?' Grace said, and he looked at her. Her face was a study of concern.

'I don't think I know him,' he said.

Grace smiled. 'Well, he dropped that in for you. Asked me to make sure you got it. I was going to post it out to you, but I thought . . .'

'Did he say what it was about?' Mark said, indicating the envelope.

Grace shook her head slowly, sadly, the way she always shook her head at him now. It had been months since he had seen the old brusque Grace. 'Maybe he heard about what happened.'

Talking to you, it wouldn't have taken him long to find out, Mark wanted to say, but he just nodded. 'Anyway, thanks. You'll give that draft to Maurice?'

'I will, of course,' Grace said. 'He'll be amazed you have another draft in to him so quickly. I know he's hoping to get a chance to talk to you about the other one.'

'Well, I'm around,' Mark said. 'Tell him I'll come in whenever he wants to talk to me. I can come in again tomorrow if it suits.'

Grace looked uncertain; she looked, Mark realized, embarrassed. 'I think he's away tomorrow,' she said, and she frowned down at the diary which lay open on her desk. 'I think he has a conference in Galway. But I'll be sure to tell him you're ready to talk to him.'

'Very ready,' Mark said, pulling on his backpack.

'How's Aoife?' Grace smiled.

'She's great,' Mark said, and he left the office before she could ask any more.

*

On the front of the card there was an image of a moon in a pale sky, its light mirrored and muddled in an ocean. The writing inside was neat and slanted, the same black ink covering almost all of the white space. He looked first for the signature, and it was the name Grace had given him, and below it was an address and a phone number.

Dear Mr Casey,

You will not know me. I was a teacher and, I dare to presume, a friend of your Joanne. It was with great sadness and shock that I learned of her death from our department secretary this week. Please forgive my not having written sooner.

When last we met, Joanne mentioned that you were writing

your doctorate in the School of English. I hope that this letter will reach you from there. Joanne was a favourite of mine, always a favourite. It was a joy to see her so recently, and to meet with your little girl. That was in the spring, and I realize now that it must have been very shortly before the accident. The things we cannot see. Joanne seemed to me very happy that day. Her pride and delight in your daughter was clear.

I am rambling. Your Joanne knew that this has always been something to which I have been prone. If ever you feel like being in touch, I would like that. The number and the address are below. Again, I am sorry for your loss, and sorry, too, that words cannot be of use in trying to make sense of such a thing.
Sincerely,
Clive Robinson

The address was in Ranelagh; Ashfield Avenue. Mark looked again at the card's illustration. The moon was a clumsy thumbprint in an insipid sky. He turned it over; it had come from the National Gallery. In their first weeks together, he and Joanne had gone there on a date one weekend afternoon. They had seen something about Beckett, some grouping of paintings and drawings that, supposedly, Beckett had liked. This was the kind of worthy thing you did on a date early on, when you were still trying to impress each other, still telling each other stories about the kinds of people you were. When you were not facing into having a baby together after having been together for only a matter of weeks. And later, if you got to that later, you would see through those stories that you'd told each other, but by then it wouldn't matter, either because you no longer cared about each other, or because you really did, because you no longer cared about anything else. Sometimes, Mark didn't know if he and Joanne had even reached that point. Twenty months:

was that enough time? To really know each other? She had never mentioned this guy to him, for instance, this Clive Robinson. Or maybe she had. Maybe she had, and he hadn't heard her. Or remembered. Or maybe he had heard her, and remembered for a little while, and maybe, now, it was gone. Maybe it was just one of the countless things he had been unable to keep.

*

His father called three times that afternoon, but Mark did not answer. He was in the kitchen, reworking his chapter, making notes on a letter from Edgeworth to Scott. He thought now that he had taken an entirely wrong approach in the draft he had just finished, the one he had delivered to McCarthy; he had failed, in that draft, to place enough emphasis on Edgeworth's correspondence, on particular letters she had written to Scott and to her aunt. He was becoming certain, now, that it was in the letters – in their style, in their curious marriage of formality and gossip – that he would find the key to everything he wanted to do in his research. He wanted to gather the letters, as many of them as he could, and he wanted to read them all the time. He had been avoiding them, procrastinating on getting around to them, for months – for years – and now he had found that they were what he had been looking for all along. There was such pleasure in hunting through them. In matching up the phrases between one person and another. In finding their intimacies, in finding their news. He wanted to start the whole thesis over now, not just this chapter – he wanted to do the whole thing differently. That night he stayed at the kitchen table, working, until he was disturbed by Aoife's cries from upstairs. He was surprised to look up and discover that, outside, it was almost dawn. He did not go up to her immediately. He needed to finish a sentence before he could do that: he knew if he walked away from it he would never be able to make the point in the way it needed to be made.

After he had fed Aoife, he put her in front of her DVD and went upstairs to take a shower. He needed it. He felt sticky from having sat up over his work all night, and he knew he must smell bad. When he stepped out of the shower, he could hear Aoife screaming downstairs. He wrapped a towel around himself and hurried down to her, calling to her, his heart racing. When he saw that she was not hurt, the relief that coursed through him was like physical pain. Her DVD had ended, and he had not been there to change it: that was all that was wrong. That was why she was crying, shouting, standing in front of the television, banging at its screen with the remote. He went over to her. He lifted her, and he took the remote out of her hand. Then he saw that it was not the remote. It was his phone, and as he looked at it more closely, he saw that the screen was displaying the tiny graphic of a handset, which meant that it was on a call. Slowly, cautiously, Mark lifted the phone to his ear. It was his father's voice he could hear. He was saying hello, over and over. Mark slipped the phone back into his palm and pressed a button to cancel the call. In his arms, Aoife howled and pointed to the television. He sat her on the couch and changed the DVD; she calmed. In his pocket, he felt the vibration of his phone. He let it ring out.

*

He went to the library later to borrow another book of letters. On his way there, he called into the DVD store. Mossy took Aoife in his arms and talked to her; he took her to the back of the store, where they kept the children's films. Aoife reached for the cases and flung them to the floor. Mossy picked them up and asked her which ones she wanted. She did not answer him, and Mark chose three for her.

'You don't want anything yourself?' Mossy asked. 'There's some good stuff just in, new releases.'

'I've plenty to keep me going,' said Mark.

Mossy scanned the barcodes. 'I might call out to you this evening, if you're not busy. I could bring some takeaway around.'

Mark swallowed. 'I've to get pages to McCarthy in the morning,' he said. It was not true, but he did not want to give up the evening. 'Thanks anyway, though. Another time.'

Mossy clicked his tongue. 'Are you serious? Again? That guy's taking the piss, man. Does he not realize he needs to cut you a bit of slack at the moment?'

'I don't need anyone to cut me any slack.'

'It's only common fucking decency for him to take the pressure off you for a while. It seems to me like he's doing the opposite. What's his problem?'

'Leave it,' Mark said, an edge in his voice that he had not intended; he saw surprise cross Mossy's face. 'Sorry. I just mean it's fine,' he said. 'I'm fine. I'm the one who wants to get the work done.'

Mossy said nothing for a moment. 'You mean McCarthy's not setting you the deadlines?' he said then, slowly.

'I'm giving him the stuff, and he's getting back to me,' Mark said. 'It's the way I want to do it at the moment. It's fine.'

Mossy regarded him. 'And you're getting good feedback on what you're giving him?'

Mark nodded firmly. 'He says it's really going places.'

'All right, man,' Mossy said, sighing as he handed him the DVDs. 'But even so, you want to take it easy.'

'I'll give you a call in a couple of days,' Mark said,

strapping Aoife into the pushchair. 'I've got to get to the library before it closes.'

'Take it easy, man,' Mossy said again, coming around the counter to bend down to Aoife, who reached for his face and shouted an indecipherable word of delight.

*

He had only intended to leave Aoife with the librarian for a few minutes. He needed to quote a letter from Scott to Edgeworth, and it was in one of the books that was too old and precious to be lent out. It would take no time, he told the librarian. But he found himself quickly sucked into other pages, into other books, into looking again at other letters he had read before and forgotten. It was not until the security guard came to say that the library was closing that he realized how long he had been. It was almost five; an hour had passed since he had left Aoife. He packed up quickly and went downstairs.

She was still where he had left her, sitting on the floor behind the reference desk, her pushchair parked nearby, but he could see that she had been crying. The woman he had left her with looked harassed.

'Thank God,' she said, as she saw Mark coming. 'We didn't know where you had got to.'

'I was just over in Early Printed, I'm sorry,' Mark said. At the sound of his voice Aoife threw her crayon aside and began to cry.

The librarian shuddered. 'I'm afraid she's been very upset here by herself,' she said. 'I really thought you would be only a couple of minutes.'

'I'm sorry,' said Mark, as she let him through the low gate at the side of the reference desk. 'I lost track of time.'

'Well, maybe a library is not the best place for a little one after all,' said the woman, and she avoided his eye. 'We've been very busy here this last hour and, as I said, she was very upset.'

Mark saw the irritation on the faces of people queuing at the circulation desk. 'I'm really very sorry,' he said again, as he lifted Aoife up. 'It won't happen again.'

'I'm afraid it can't happen again,' the librarian said. 'I shouldn't have taken her in here in the first place. I just wanted to help, and she is such a lovely little one, but we can't take this responsibility.'

'I understand.'

As he went past the queue with the pushchair he kept his gaze straight ahead, not wanting to meet anyone's eyes. When he felt a hand on his arm, he flinched. His first impulse was to keep going, but it was McCarthy. He nodded down to the pushchair.

'Babysitter cancelled on you?'

Mark shrugged. 'Babysitter ran out of patience,' he said, glancing back to the circulation desk.

'Well, it livened up a day in the doldrums for them.'

'She caused a bit of a scene, I think,' Mark said, and he bent to offer Aoife her soother. To his relief, she took it. 'She can really tear the place down when she's in the mood.'

'You can swap her for my thirteen-year-old any time, if you really want to see what a kid looks like when they're in a mood.'

Mark laughed. It struck him how much he had come to like McCarthy over the last while; how strange it felt. A tension seemed to have fallen away between them. Now that McCarthy could see he was really serious about his thesis, Mark thought, he was treating him with new respect. Talking to him more on the level. Mark appreciated it.

'I'm really looking forward to having a chat with you

about the chapter I'm working on,' he said. 'I've decided to take it in a whole different direction.'

McCarthy blinked slowly. 'Oh, yes,' he said. He took a few steps forward and, as Mark kept pace with him, pulling the pushchair backwards, something occurred to him. He raised an eyebrow at McCarthy, who looked back almost apprehensively.

'Grace told me you'd be in Galway at a conference today,' Mark said.

McCarthy frowned. 'Galway?' he said, and shook his head. 'Wild horses wouldn't drag me to a conference in Galway. Where the hell did Grace get that idea?'

'I don't know. She just told me that was why you wouldn't be around when I asked if she could give me an appointment with you today.'

It was something he had never seen before: a blush on McCarthy's face. It started in his hairline and spread right down to the collar of his shirt. Mark could not work out what was happening. He knew he had caught McCarthy out somehow, but on what? Was he having an affair with Grace or something?

McCarthy sighed almost frantically in the direction of the circulation desk. 'Jesus, what is the hold-up?' he said, looking at his watch. 'Some of us have trains to catch.' He glanced at Mark. 'If you can come in to me next week some time I can have a talk with you about that draft. Or those drafts, I should say. Didn't you give me more than one?'

'Two, yeah, but you can pretty much disregard them,' Mark said. 'I'm planning to give you a completely new one by Monday.'

McCarthy nodded, but he did not look impressed. 'Monday?' he said, and peeled his sleeve away from over his watch once again. 'You're hardly going to get me a whole new draft by Monday.'

'No, no, I definitely will,' Mark said, feeling his excitement over the chapter begin to swell again. 'I just need the weekend to get some shape on it. I was over looking at a couple of the letters she wrote around the time of *Ormond*. I really think they're going to bring the whole thing together. I think—'

'Look, Mark,' McCarthy interrupted sharply. But he did not go on. He seemed uncertain. As the queue inched towards the desk, he stepped out of it suddenly and let the people behind him move ahead. He put a hand to his chin.

Discomfort crept up on Mark. He moved the pushchair into the space between two bookshelves and turned away from it. 'You have read the drafts I gave you?' he asked, and immediately regretted the words. They sounded childish, petulant. 'It doesn't matter if you haven't,' he said hastily. 'Like I said, I'm going to rework it anyway.'

'I've read the drafts, Mark,' McCarthy said. He sighed. 'I mean, I've tried to read them. They're not easy to follow. They don't really seem to make a whole lot of sense.'

Mark opened his mouth to speak, but McCarthy held up a hand to stop him. 'I think you need to take a break from the thesis for a while, Mark,' he said quietly. He sounded as though he did not want to be saying this at all. 'I think,' he looked towards the pushchair behind Mark, 'you have a lot on your plate at the moment, and nobody expects you to be able to do it all.'

Mark stared. 'You're telling me to stop working on my thesis?' he said. At his tone, two women in the queue looked to where he and McCarthy stood. 'You're my supervisor, and you're telling me to jack the fucking thing in?' He laughed, and the women turned quickly away. McCarthy looked extremely unhappy. As Mark watched him fiddle with the books he was carrying, shifting them under one arm and then back under the other, something else dawned on him. 'You told Grace not to make any appointments for me, didn't you?' he said, bending low to force McCarthy to meet his eye. 'That's why she gave me that story about Galway. Am I right?'

'Mark, as your supervisor I have responsibilities towards you,' McCarthy said quietly. 'I knew a meeting with me would be disappointing for you because of what I would have to say to you about your work. I wanted that meeting to happen at the right time. I didn't want you to be rushed into it. I was hoping you would be able to get a bit of distance from the draft.'

Mark grabbed the handles of the pushchair and jerked it out of the aisle. 'I won't bother you again,' he said to McCarthy. He turned his back and moved on. McCarthy called after him as he went, but he did not follow. As the grey-haired security guard saw Mark approach the exit, he left his booth and, with a smile down at the baby, held open the door.

*

When he answered a call from his father that evening and told him that he would not be coming down that weekend, Mark did not mention his work. He did not want to hear his father's attempts at conversation about Edgeworth, as though she were someone he often bumped into buying groceries in Keogh's. Aoife had a bad cold, Mark told him, probably something she had picked up in the swimming-pool, and he did not want to put her through the journey until she was better. Had he taken her to the doctor, his father had wanted to know, and he had said he had. Dr Gorman was as good as they came when it came to getting rid of a cold, his father said, and Mark said he was sure that was true, but Dr Gorman was in Longford, not in Stoneybatter. If he wanted, said his father, he could probably get Aoife an appointment today or tomorrow. He did not want to make the trip with her, Mark said again, and his father said again that it was not even a two-hour journey, and that Aoife could sleep in the car. She was not sleeping, Mark said, and his father said that sounded very serious, and that a second opinion could hardly hurt, and again he said that Dr Gorman was the only doctor he would ever trust with a child who had a cold. That's because Doctor Gorman was the only doctor he knew, Mark said, and then he said that Aoife was crying, even though she was not, and that he had to go.

'I'll be down next weekend,' he said. 'I promise.'

'I'll call you again later on,' his father said, and he did, but Mark did not answer the phone.

*

Clive Robinson's house was third in a neat red-brick terrace. The path to the front door was narrow and short; four steps did it, and then Mark was looking at the doorbell, and at the brass knocker in the shape of a lion's head. He chose the doorbell: it seemed less intrusive – until it rang, sounding like church bells at close range. After a moment, a shadow moved behind the stained glass of the door panel, and came quickly closer. There was the click and scrabble of the latch being turned.

His first thought was that he had known Robinson all this time, and had somehow forgotten it; he must have met him somewhere with Joanne. The familiarity of the face with its grey beard set his mind rifling through the possibilities:

had there been a walk through college, a lunchtime sitting on the lawn when this man had stopped to talk to Joanne, when she had introduced him to Mark?

'Yes?' said Robinson, in a tone of careful surprise.

'Hello,' said Mark, and nodded, though he did not know at what.

'From the swimming-pool, yes?' said Robinson, and then Mark remembered where he had seen him before. He almost laughed at the coincidence, until he saw that Robinson was not similarly amused. In fact, he looked frightened.

'How did you get my address?' said Robinson. In an attempt to reassure him, Mark held up his hands, but this seemed to further alarm Robinson, who moved to shut the door.

'I'm Mark Casey,' Mark blurted loudly, and after a moment, that seemed frozen, he watched the plates of Robinson's face shift and resettle. 'Thanks for your card,' he added, talking too quickly, running the words into each other. 'The one about Joanne.'

Robinson stared. 'Come in,' he said eventually, and gestured, in a dazed sort of way, into the hall. 'Come in,' he said again, and as he stepped back, there was a howl and a sudden flash of black at his feet: a cat, bolting away up a staircase now, stopping to survey them both with a resentful glare.

'Castor,' Robinson said apologetically. 'Named by my wife. She liked all that French lot.'

He showed Mark into a small sitting room. Leather armchairs faced a delicately tiled fireplace, and to one side of it, an old writing bureau. The mantelpiece was cluttered with cards for a birthday, two of them homemade by children. Wild flowers stood in a painted clay vase. Where there must once have been double doors, the room gave through to a large kitchen, another cat sleeping in the sunlight on a table piled with papers and books.

'Please sit,' said Robinson, and took a newspaper from one of the leather armchairs. 'There's coffee, just made,' he said, 'and also, of course, tea. Would either interest you?'

'Coffee would be good,' Mark said, and he watched as Robinson moved around the kitchen, taking down mugs and pouring in the coffee and the milk.

'I really should have thought to ask whether you take milk before I put it in,' he said, as he came back into the smaller room. 'But, as you'll no doubt have noticed, it's something of a surprise to see you. To meet you. Even though, of course, I'm delighted you've come.'

Mark nodded. He should say something about the swimming-pool, he thought. He should say that he had never lost his temper like that with Aoife before, that he did not intend to lose it again. That he had never before done something like that to her – whatever it was he had done, shaking her or snapping at her or being rough with her, whatever it was that Robinson had seen, that Robinson had watched.

'I hope I'm not disturbing you,' he said instead.

'Not at all,' Robinson said, lowering himself into the second leather armchair. 'I'm just so surprised that we've met before. Without even realizing.' He attempted a smile. 'And your daughter, whom, of course, I had met on an earlier occasion, but, well, babies.' He shook his head. 'They change so rapidly.'

'She's grown a lot since April,' Mark said.

'April?' Robinson looked confused.

'You said in your letter that it was April when you bumped into Joanne.'

'Did I?' said Robinson, looking no more certain.

'You said in your letter it was April,' Mark said again.

'Well, yes, I suppose it must have been.'

'You said, too, that you and Joanne had a conversation,' Mark said, and he took a deep breath before going on. 'What did you talk about, do you remember?' This time, while he waited for Robinson to respond, he found himself holding his breath. He sat perfectly still. He did not want to miss a word that Robinson might say about Joanne. He did not want to miss the slightest twitch of expression on his face as he thought about her, as he talked about her. Anything that was about her, that was to do with her, he wanted to see it, he wanted to know it. He wanted to hear about her; he wanted news of her. It did not matter if that news could only be of the past; just for a moment, it would come to him as something new, something living, and he wanted it more than he wanted air.

'April, yes,' said Robinson, thoughtfully. 'They were taking a walk around Fellows' Square. It was a Saturday, a cold day. The little one's cheeks were bright red.' He looked at Mark as though he had suddenly remembered something. 'What is it, your daughter's name?'

'Aoife.'

'That's right.' Robinson nodded. 'Aoife, from the Children of Lir.'

'No,' Mark began to say, but he stopped himself. He found that he did not want to admit to Robinson that he and Joanne had not taken Aoife's name from any myth or legend, that they had chosen it only because they both liked it. He did not want Robinson to think less of Joanne for this. But, it struck him, what if Joanne had, indeed, told Robinson that they had chosen the name for some such reason? Would she have done that? Was Robinson someone she had so desperately wanted to impress? The vision of him sodden and dripping in the shower stall came to Mark: the withered skin at his elbows, the hard, stark bulbs of his knees. Or, he thought then, could Aoife's name have held some meaning for Joanne, a meaning she had never shared with Mark, a meaning she had for some reason kept to herself? What else did Robinson know about her? What else had she told him that she had never told Mark?

'It struck me that day,' said Robinson, looking to the empty fireplace, 'that she was very content, your Joanne. Richly content, I would say. She seemed very different from the young woman I'd met, oh, I suppose, two years previously.' He frowned. 'I think it was about that. Since I'd seen her.'

Out of the questions that spilled into Mark's mind then, he could not choose just one to ask. Where had she been that day? What had she talked about with Robinson? Where had she been going when she saw him? What had she been doing – what had been going on in her life? Had he met her yet, had they been seeing each other? He calculated; no, two years back from April she would still have been innocent of him, still clear of everything to do with him – every connection, every moment afterwards that would lead to Aoife, and to all that went with Aoife, and to being in a car with his mother on the Longford road on a Saturday afternoon in April. Two Aprils ago, she had been free, Joanne. She had had a chance. But Robinson was saying she was different then – that she was not so happy, was that what he had said? How could he tell that she was happier the second time? Mark tried to picture her, walking with the pushchair through campus: what had she been doing there? Taking a break from shopping? Sitting on a bench to eat lunch, or read the newspaper, or throw crumbs to the pigeons on the lawn while Aoife reached out for them and squealed? He stared at

287

Robinson as though the folds of his clothes, the curl of his beard, the grip of his fingers on the coffee mug would give the answers. Joanne, alive and content, on a Saturday in April. Which Saturday, of the few that had been left to her? What had she been thinking that day? What had she been planning? And where had Mark been while she was doing it?

'You were at a bachelor party that weekend, if I remember correctly,' Robinson said, and Mark looked at him, startled. Had he spoken aloud? Was Robinson responding to what he had said? But he knew he had been silent. Robinson was just doing what Mark wanted him, after all, to do: putting together the pieces of the day. But it was painful to be reminded of how he had spent that last weekend, of how he had wasted it: getting pissed in Wicklow for two days on Nagle's stag party. Joanne had encouraged him to go; it didn't matter how he felt about Nagle, she said. Nagle had invited him, and Mossy would be there, and it would be fun, and he should go, she said. She could look after Aoife by herself for one weekend. You need the break, she had said to him. Just go.

'In Glendalough,' Mark said. 'A friend of mine from college.'

'Beautiful spot,' Robinson said. 'Once you get away from the business end of it. High up in the valley, you could forget you were part of this life at all. Though I doubt the bachelor party was spent in the quiet of the valley?'

Mark managed a laugh. 'It wasn't exactly monastic,' he said, and that hurt as well, because as soon as he said it he was back in the kitchen with her that first night she had cooked him dinner, that first night she had led him up to her room, and he thought now it had been a mistake, after all, to have come looking for details of her that were new to him, when he was barely able to manage the details he already had.

'And your research?' Robinson said, out of the silence. 'Joanne mentioned that you were working on Scott? I know only what Bertrand Russell said of him, I'm afraid, which is only the painfully obvious. "Scott is the author of *Waverley*." Which is not the same as Scott being Scott.'

Mark felt at once panic at not understanding whatever it was that Robinson was talking about – could he be raving? – and relief at being able to close it down with an entirely different subject. 'It's actually Edgeworth I'm working on,' he said. 'Though she and Scott were very good friends.'

'Ah,' said Robinson. '*Castle Rackrent*. I think old Thady Quirk is one of the most memorable of characters, don't you?'

'Oh, yeah,' Mark said, without enthusiasm. He did not want to talk about Thady Quirk. He wanted to talk about Joanne. Or at least he had thought he did until a minute ago. 'Thady's a gas man,' he said, and immediately cringed.

But Robinson nodded. 'An utter cliché, but like so many clichés, an absolute truth.'

'Right,' Mark said uncertainly.

'I mean, they're still everywhere in this country, really, aren't they?' Robinson said airily. 'I believe they're referred to as local characters.' He looked at Mark more closely. 'You're from the country, aren't you?'

'I'm from the same place Joanne was from,' Mark said.

'Really?' Robinson looked surprised.

'Yeah. Longford.'

'Oh, well,' Robinson said, 'I don't mean to suggest you have them only in Longford. Or in the country, for that matter.'

Mark frowned. 'Have who?'

'Oh . . .' Robinson waved a hand. 'Ignore me. I ramble. My children tell me that all the time. Their mother did too.'

He looked at Mark suddenly, a flutter of panic on his face. 'God!' he said. 'I'm afraid I've completely neglected to tell you how sorry I am about your mother. I do apologize.'

'It's all right,' said Mark.

'Indeed, it's quite unforgivable.' Robinson shook his head. 'Not even in the card, if I remember?'

'Really, it's not a problem,' Mark said. 'Thank you.'

Robinson weighed this for a moment. 'And your father?'

'My father's fine,' said Mark. 'As fine as can be expected. He's busy.'

'The only way,' Robinson said. 'Partly because it's the only way to get other people to leave you alone. That's what I found.'

'This is it,' Mark said. He wanted, now, very much to leave. The conversation had seemed never to go beyond an awkward and useless skimming of facts. Robinson had told him nothing, given him nothing that he could take home and add to the store of kept traces. It had been a wasted journey. He made a move to stand, to announce that it was time for him to go, but then Robinson sighed deeply and looked over to him, nodding slowly.

'I'm afraid it's just a matter of forward equilibrum, you see,' he said.

'Yes,' Mark said carefully.

'Time marches on, and you're best to go along with it.'

'You are.'

Now Robinson stood. Leaving his unfinished mug of coffee on the floor beneath the armchair, Mark did the same. 'Thanks for seeing me,' he said.

'I'm very glad you came,' said Robinson. 'Though I'm afraid I haven't been very good company for you.'

'No, no.' Mark shook his head energetically. 'I mean, you have. Of course you have.'

'I'm always like this when I'm working, I'm afraid,' Robinson said. 'And now more so than ever, because I don't think that what I'm working on is going anywhere. I always think that, but this time I'm sure.'

'I'm sorry to hear that,' Mark said. 'I know the feeling.'

'To feel it at my age is infinitely worse,' Robinson said, seeming sharper suddenly, and he led Mark to the hall.

'What's it about?' Mark said.

'It's nothing I really want to talk about,' Robinson said, as they reached the front door. 'I hope you don't mind. I remember telling Joanne about it, actually, that day I bumped into her.' He frowned. 'Or maybe it was another day.'

'I'd love to hear about it,' Mark said.

'I just think it's something I'm going to have to abandon,' Robinson said, reaching to the latch. 'I'm sorry.' He shook his head. 'Little point in talking about what's already lost.'

Mark opened his mouth to reply, but the words would not come. He walked through the front door to the path outside. He turned and offered his hand. They shook.

'Thank you again for coming,' Robinson said. 'I'm so sorry about what has happened.'

'Don't give up,' Mark managed to say. 'On the idea, I mean. I'd like to read it eventually.'

Robinson looked at him oddly. Giving Mark the slightest of nods, he closed the door.

Chapter Twenty-one

All that week, a fist of frost held the land in mute sub-
mission. The low fields, and the bog they sank into; the
bushes of berries and the brittle trees that lined the laneway
to the house; the trimmed hedges of the garden and the
livid briars of the yard – all stood stiffened as in a spell.
When Tom hauled open the high iron door of the hayshed,
the machinery within glinted, seemed to quiver, in the sudden icy shaft of light from the moon. He pushed out a sigh,
and the shape of his breath hung white for a moment in
the blind air.

Twice a day now – just after it came light in the morning, and again by evening, as the first scarves of dusk settled
into the corners of the meadow – he would come to stand
here, with the sheepdog panting gladly at his back. He
would keep one hand on the cold rim of the door as his
gaze travelled over the hulking forms of the tractors, their
sheet-glass cabs, their pristine surfaces, the huge black
haunches of their tyres, on to the hexagonal baler, the red-
skirted mower, and the other equipment filling the space in
which, that summer, he and Mark had stacked two hundred
bales. Whistling to the sheepdog, he moved in to walk
among the machines.

The tractor seats were still clothed in clear plastic. A film
of yellow oil still coated the blue axle of the seed-spreader.
The inner lip of the baler still held a fine dust of brown

hayseed from August. All was exactly as he had left it that morning. He whistled a shorter note to the dog and strode back out into the yard, tapping the side of each machine with his stick as he went.

Chapter Twenty-two

Traffic was already terrible by the time Mark backed the car out of Sitric Road and down on to Arbour Hill. Friday evening at rush-hour: there could be no stupider time to head west. It moved at a crawl down to the river and out the quays past Heuston, and it did not ease until he was on the M4.

He did not mind the drive in the dark. There was a comfort in the straightness of the road and the width of it, and the yellow glow of the streetlamps overhead. There was a sense of ditches and fields and forest at the edges of every-thing, and the small squares of light that were the windows of houses. On the car radio, the talk was of hope and change in one country and of everything going to fuck in another. He was still waiting for it to make a difference to him, this disaster that everyone was talking about, still waiting for it to make his life impossible, this collapse of everything, this end of everything. Apparently the country was dying on its feet. But things seemed strangely the same to him.

He let himself sink into the chatter. At some level, he realized, he was listening to everything, but there was a filter, or there were only some words about which he cared enough to make him listen. They mentioned Garryowen, and he looked to the radio in surprise: he had been rereading the Edgeworth story of that name the night before. But it was about Garryowen the rugby club. Then, job losses, and something about a vaccination. Banks needing billions. An item about the computer games on the market for Christmas.

When the news came on he switched to a CD. The drive-time programme, with its arguments and commentary, was one thing, but he still did not want to listen to the news. There was almost always a certain kind of headline, and he did not want to hear it; yes, they sounded sorry, yes, they sounded sad, but to them it was just another news story. And to someone else, it was just the start, and it was something he did not want to think about. The CD did nothing to offend. In Edgeworthstown, a guy he had gone to school with was smoking outside the Park House. At the chipper, the evening buses were pulling in. Headlights swooping, rucksacks lifted, boot doors popping open. Students home for the weekend. He glanced in the mirror to check that Aoife was still asleep.

Keogh already had the Christmas decorations up in the shop. The bollocks, he imagined himself saying to his father. It would be a way in. It was the way in he had been looking for, he realized, all the drive down. None of the items on the radio programmes would have given them anything to talk about; none of them was useful enough in that dull, pragmatic way. Besides, he would not be stupid enough to try to have a conversation with his father about anything that had happened outside his father's world. Paddy Keogh having a Christmas tree in the window and blue icicle lights hanging down from the eaves at the beginning of November was good enough. A mean-looking little runt of a tree too, he imagined himself saying, crooked as a whin, and don't you know well it was the cheapest he could get? The cheapest? Tom would ask, in mock disbelief. Surely you don't think he paid for it? And the back and forth would be under way, and somehow they would keep going from there. Mark felt his language sit

295

into the groove he had made for it, somewhere along the line; the mould he had taken from his father. The conspiratorial mutter, the accent thick again on the tongue, the head nodding or shaking along with every second sentence. The vocabulary of half-phrases, of words that meant nothing and meant everything. He passed the last houses before the lane and looked up ahead to the farm.

Light. The hayshed door was a square of yellow light against the darkness. The surprise of it almost caused Mark to miss the turn for the lane. The lights were never on in the hayshed. Even if an animal was sick, or a calf being born, everything happened in the low houses to its rear. Mark had not thought that there was even a light to switch on in the hayshed. What would it shine on? From where? The shed should have been packed from wall to wall, and right to the roof, with the summer's round bales. There should have been no room for light.

He resisted the temptation to drive right around to the farmyard; his father would expect Mark to come straight into the hayshed and help him with whatever the problem was. The last thing he wanted to do was to spend the night standing and kneeling in straw and shit and in the dust of the hay, watching an animal kicking and dying and staring at him out of one frightened yellow eye. He would have to face it in a couple of minutes, but not yet. Not now. He parked outside the house.

Aoife whimpered as he heaved her out of the seat. He tugged her dress down over her nappy and tried to get her to take her blanket, but she was too cranky. He draped it over his shoulder, smelling its beautiful tang of sleep and powder and piss. It needed a wash.

The front door opened, and his father was there. 'Well, button,' he said to Aoife, taking a step forward with his arms outstretched towards her. He nodded to Mark. 'Well. You got down.'

'She's not awake yet,' said Mark, nodding a greeting in reply. The dog was sitting alert in front of his father's chair, her tail thumping the ground, a question in her eyes.

The place looked different, but not in a way that he could place immediately. All the furniture seemed to be exactly as it had been, and even the small things – teapot, sugar bowl, bread bin – were in the same places they had always been, yet the place seemed somehow stripped back. There was something spare about it that made it seem not neat or tidy but instead held in some kind of quietness, some kind of shock. The smell was different: frying-pan grease and cooked meat and something else, too, something artificial and high on the air.

As his father shut the door to the hall Mark turned to him. 'Why are the lights on in the shed 'ithout?'

His father came over to the couch and reached a hand out to Aoife, laying it flat on the crown of her head. 'She's tired from her journey,' he said.

'She's not tired, she's still half asleep,' said Mark. 'She slept the whole way down. It'll be a nightmare to get her down now again.'

'What do you think of this lassie, Scruff?' his father said to the dog, kneading its ears. It panted with pleasure. On its breath, Mark caught the smell that was hanging in the air: dogfood from a can.

'What's going on in the hayshed?' he said to his father.

'Ah . . .' His father shook his head as though whatever it was did not matter. But when he looked at Mark, his eyes were shining. In his chest, in his arms, Mark felt wariness thicken and deepen.

'I'll show you in a while,' his father said.

'Show me what?'

'Just . . .' his father shook his head again. 'Something I want you to look at.'

He seemed pent up with something, seemed almost high, as though one nudge or one question would tip him into giddy laughter. When Aoife whined, Mark was glad of the chance to look towards her and lift her. 'I might as well bring her upstairs,' he said. 'It's late.'

His father reached a hand out to Aoife again. This time she stared at him. 'I don't think she knows me at all,' he said.

'She's just sleepy.'

'It's all set up for you anyway,' his father said, nodding towards the ceiling. 'I put the electric blanket on the cot and all.'

'Thanks.'

'Sure I might as well go out to the shed and you can come out to me when you're ready,' his father said. The dog was at his feet, tongue out, tail dancing. They looked one with the same excitement. They looked like two friends who had discovered what it was that wagged the whole world.

*

The sight knocked the breath out of Mark. He steadied himself against the wall of the shed.

'What the fuck is this?' he started to say, but his father was already walking over to one of the tractors, a red beast of a thing with a curved bonnet and a front weight block like a fist.

'What do you think of this lassie?' his father said, clamping a hand to a front tyre that was almost as tall as him.

Mark stared. His mind would not work. 'Are you going to fucking live in it?'

Tom laughed and moved on to the second machine. It

298

was also colossal. It was of a green so bright and lurid it could have belonged to a float in a Paddy's Day parade.

'Where the fuck did you get these from?' Mark tried again. 'What the fuck are they for?'

'Gerry Brady'd be able to tell you all about them,' his father said. 'I can't remember the half of it. But you'd want to hear Brady, the way he goes on about them. Hydraulic this and telescope that, and some new type of transmission, and wait till you see the way the cab 'ithin is laid out.' He gestured up to the door. He was lit up like a bride. 'Go on there, get up into her. She's like an airplane in there, I'm telling you.'

The step up into the tractor cab was spotless. The interior was so luxurious that Mark almost laughed. The seat on the old Massey had been like a small metal stool; this one looked like a recliner, with a cushioned cover and a headrest and armrests, and beside it, a jumpseat that folded neatly down. The gears and the controls were laid out like a buffet, presided over by what looked like a computer screen. The steering-wheel extended from the floor on a muscular base; the dash itself was a sleek black panel of glass. As Mark sat, his mind hurtled through attempts at calculation. A figure came and he stared at it. It was disgusting. But it was probably close to the truth.

'What do you think of that, now?' his father said, stepping up and looking into the cab. He touched the jumpseat. 'There's room enough in it for the two of us.'

Mark said nothing. He stared at the sleeping darkness of the dash.

His father gestured towards it impatiently. 'Turn her on, can't ya?'

It was quieter than Mark expected it to be: a low, confident thrum. On the dash, the needles of two dials blinked into life; a monitor between them told him the time was close to ten. He looked to the other screen: it was a GPS, showing the road and the lane in storybook colours, an eager red ring marking their spot.

His father leaned in closer. 'That's the command centre there, now,' he said, pointing to a cluster of gears. 'And this is a panorama cab you're in. And you see that plug there?' He pointed somewhere under the steering-wheel. 'Do you know what you can put into that?'

'No,' Mark said warily.

'Your laptop,' his father said, in a tone of absolute triumph. 'You plug your laptop into that, or your phone, and you can do whatever you have to do.'

Mark killed the engine. Every little dancing and flashing piece of red and yellow circuitry vanished back to where it had come from.

'And all those controls, the most of them is electronic,' his father said. He shrugged with the same glad air. 'Ah, it's beyond me, I'm afraid, though.'

Mark looked at him. 'Then what are you doing with it?'

His father seemed ready for the question; he seemed amused by it. He shrugged again; a dance of the shoulders.

'The horsepower on this thing must be ridiculous,' Mark said.

'I couldn't tell you, to be honest. Brady would tell you.'

'It must be near three hundred,' Mark said.

'Chancy but it is.'

'And what – you buy two of the fucking things in case you need one to pull the other out of a bog hole?'

His father grinned as though he were being teased about a new girlfriend. 'Ah,' he said. 'In the long run, I'm telling you, they're worth it. Sure, the farming is hardship enough.'

Mark got out of the cab, jumping from the first step to

land heavily on the floor of the shed. It was a habit he'd had since he was tall enough to get out of a tractor cab without being lifted; he'd imagined himself to be MacGyver, or Magnum PI, or one of the guys from the A-Team. And he'd imagined this while he was jumping out of a scrawny Massey Ferguson from the arse of the seventies, all the time wishing his father would buy a new tractor, a modern tractor, so that he could really pretend he was an American detective on a souped-up set of wheels. Now the souped-up wheels were everywhere he looked in the hayshed, huge, obnoxious in their streamlined sheen, and all he could feel was a plummeting dread.

'He gave me the topper and the conditioner nearly for nothing,' his father said, gesturing to the corner of the shed, where there stood two more new machines. 'I haggled him down till he was nearly crying. He couldn't get over what I got him to agree to.'

Mark heard himself saying the words before he had given them permission to be sounded. They sprang forward of their own accord. 'Which was?' he said, an edge in his voice like a warning.

His father had never been willing to talk to Mark about money. He might tell him the price a cow had got at a mart, or the price of a machine he was mulling over in the *Buy and Sell*, but anything more than that, he would not share. Anything more than that, he kept private. He did not even tell Mark's mother. Who was spinning into view for Mark now as he looked at what his father had done. Or something belonging to her was spinning into view. Something she had left behind.

'Where did you get enough money for this?' he said, and even before he had finished the question he was certain of the answer.

His father's face changed. In seconds it seemed to age all over again. 'I made my money,' he said, and he turned away.

'You used Mam's money,' Mark said, and he grabbed his father's arm. 'Didn't you?'

His father shook him off. 'That's none of your concern.'

'Is it none of my concern either what you did with the bales?' Mark stepped around to face him. 'Where are they?'

His father said nothing.

'You sold them?' Mark demanded.

His father's voice was whittled with scorn. 'I hardly fucking gave them away.'

Mark stared. He stared at the back of his father's head, a whorl of grey around a scalp of brown. He stared at his hands, the hands that had rested on his daughter's head half an hour before. Her tiny head. His heavy hand. He stared at the dirt on the shoulders of his father's overalls, at the ridged nape of his neck. The skin was browner there still, weathered by more years, more summers than Mark had known, than his mother had got to know, than Joanne had come anywhere close to knowing. Over his father stretched the parts of the shed that Mark had never seen before. The high corrugated arches of the roof. The rafters, rusted and shadowed. The cobwebs hanging low, heavy and clumped as nests of bees. The mottled concrete of the corners, naked to the air for the first time in years. His father had never let this space go empty; he had always filled it with hay again before the back walls ever had a chance to show. Now the tools that had always been kept by the door were thrown in a heap on the ground: the graip and the pitchfork, the billhook, the sledge, the shovel with its reddened handle, the yard brush, the loy. Mark stared at them.

'The cattle,' he said, and his father shook his head.

'There'll be other cattle,' he said in a low voice.

*

Mark found what he was looking for without difficulty. Yet still it was not what he had expected to find. It was in the old biscuit tin where his mother had always kept bills and other envelopes, lying over a pile of mass cards. A sad-faced Jesus tilted at him as he lifted the receipt from the box. It was thin, pink, folded once; it was covered with his father's writing. The name of his father was the first thing he saw. The name of Joanne's father was the second.

He blinked. He squinted. He could not be seeing what he thought he had seen. But it was there. His name. *Frank Lynch.* And then, Mark saw, there was something else after it. Some squiggle, some symbol, some mark. He stared at it, willing it towards meaning, and then he got it. He untangled it. *Jr. Frank Lynch, Jr.* It was Frankie's name: it was what he would have been christened. It was also a name he had never been called for as long as Mark had known him. But Mark's father must have felt the need for some kind of correctness as he filled out the docket. Some kind of formality. *Received from Frank Lynch, Jr,* the crinkled sheet was inscribed, and half-way down, the blue ink in which his father had written *Cows (18 Chr, 5 Her, 4 Fr) / Heifers (9 Chr, 3 Her, 1 Fr) / Bullocks (9 Chr, 1 Her, 2 Fr)* had faded to nothing but pressure on the page, and *Calfs 24 (16 Chr, 4 Fr, 4 Her), 1 Chr Bull* and *Round Bales 342 (186 Hay / 156 Silage)* were in black ink, stronger and surer, as was his father's signature, and the date, October 15th. And the price, underlined twice like a word on a placard.

It had been years since Mark had gone with his father to the mart in Edgeworthstown, years since he had stood, stick in hand, beside the closed gate of a cattle trailer while a buyer handed his father a cheque. A pound a pound, the price had been then, and the men would joke as they shook hands; the buyer would say that the trailer was only half full with the cattle, that he had thought they would pack it out, and his father would retort that the cattle were only half price; the buyer would tell his father not to go too far away on holiday with the money he was giving him, and his father would promise to send him a postcard. Often, when Mark was young, the buyer would pat him on the head and tell him that he'd know how to spend the money for his father, or something like that, and his father would say that he would know well. And the men would laugh, and Mark, not even fully understanding, would laugh too.

And the child that Mark had been would have been able to see, now, that this price was too low. It seemed three grand, maybe even four grand short of what it should have been. The cows were all young and strong, the calves well fed: he had seen them coming on all summer. And the bullocks were heavy bastards, and the bull – the bull was built like the truck he had arrived in. Mark closed his eyes. He saw the empty fields, the empty sheds, the empty stalls. He saw the empty mornings, and the stretch of the days, and the dog racing around looking for the last of the scent, looking for something to worry, something to watch. When he heard the door from the yard, when he heard the tread of his father's boots in the back kitchen, his first instinct was to stuff the receipt back into the biscuit tin and throw it back into the press. But he stopped himself. He stopped his own arm as it twitched and as it climbed. He turned.

*

There were things that seemed unsayable; things that seemed impossible to push over the surface of thought. There were truths, or what seemed like truths, lodged in the walls of the mind; there were summations, pronouncements, accusations, formed and moulded and added to over months and over years, curling and stretching and nestling in the spaces they had made for themselves.

The extraordinary thing was how they turned out, all of these things, not to be hiding after all; not, after all, to be anywhere out of reach. They turned out to have been waiting, to have been poised. They came to each man's lips like lines that had been long ago learned for a play never staged; they came into the room like over-praised children, sure of themselves, proud of their presence, never for an instant imagining that they ought not to be there. Never for an instant intuiting that they might have burst in too soon or too loudly, in too large a number.

Mark went first, because Mark had the evidence; the pink slip of paper that seemed, in the moment that he held it up to his father, sharpened to a switchblade's edge. In that moment, in a rush of self-certainty that was almost like joy, Mark thought that there was nothing his father could say, nothing his father could send at him that he could not swipe aside and send shattering against the wall.

But he had forgotten. How had he forgotten? His father was so good at this. He glinted at the scent of it. He was an athlete, opening with light shots, weighing the return. His father saw where his opponent was willing to go; he saw, with a sliding thrill, the terrain they thought they could handle. Then he went deep, went fast, moved as though on ice through convolutions of his own invention, through spirals that could not be anticipated and could not be stopped; he was fluent, exhilarated, alight. When he shouted, when he sneered, when he spat out his verdicts and his vehemence, he was like a man thirty years younger; like a man younger than his son. Mark stared at him. It was almost wonder that he felt for him, watching how he soared. It was a kind of pride, a kind of awe.

In the grip of what felt so much like hatred, it was a kind of love.

When there was silence, and when it settled in the room among the rubble of their words, Mark stood and took his car keys from the counter. At the stairs, he listened to another type of silence, and then he made his way to the door.

'Watch her,' he said, without looking at his father. 'I'll be an hour.'

His father did not ask him where he was going. His father knew that he could not be seen to care.

Chapter Twenty-three

Tom's heart hammered in his chest as he listened to Mark drive away. He had said everything he had wanted, for so long, to say, yet his mind still whirled through new ways of saying it, through other ways of telling Mark how it was. He took the whiskey from the bottom cupboard, uncapped it, then screwed the cap on again. He had a headache, he realized. Whiskey was not what he needed. He filled a glass of water and looked for the painkillers.

Mark understood nothing. He understood nothing about the farm, and he understood nothing about what Tom had been through with it, and he understood least of all that Frankie Lynch had done them a favour by stepping in and buying the cattle. This was no longer a country to try to run a herd of animals in. Any fool could see that. The best thing to do was to get out now at the best price you could, and keep the head down for a while, and then, when the air calmed and the place settled into whatever it was going to settle into, to get back in at your own pace. It was what people were wishing they could do with their houses and their sites now, what Frankie Lynch's brother, the builder, must have been wishing he could do with the field of houses he had built up at Glen. But those other people had not got in quickly enough, they had not heeded the signs, and heeding the signs was what you had to do.

Besides, he had wanted a change. It was not that he found

the work of the farm demanding; he could manage it alone. He always had. That was part of what he had been able to make clear to Mark tonight, that he had always had to do everything alone, that even on the rare occasions when Mark was around, he was no real help, doing only the bare minimum and getting away again as soon as he could. Mark had disputed this, but it was indisputable: it was fact. He had no interest in the place. He looked down his nose at it all. And yet he thought of himself as having some claim to it, some right to tell Tom what he should and should not do with his own money, his own herd, his own land. He was a grabber, pure and simple, and it had been time for that truth to be told. It was not fully true what Tom had said about being happier to see the herd going to Frankie Lynch than to think of it falling to Mark, but it made little difference, Mark having so little interest, and he was glad that he had said what needed to be said about the laughing stock Mark was making of himself, and of Tom, with what he called work, with his excuse for a job; sitting all day in front of books and papers like a boy getting ready for his school exams. He had been in college now nearly longer than he had been in school, and with nothing to show for it; he spent his time thinking and reading and writing about the one part of the place's history that nobody around the place gave a damn for. He was living, like a squatter, in a house that Frank Lynch had paid for, a house that belonged, now, not even to Mark, but to the child. And he was smothering the child, stopping her growing up the way she should. She could barely even talk, could barely mumble anything other than a few baby's words. There had been more, and some of it had gone on to ground, maybe, that would have been better avoided, but still Tom was glad to have it said. It was better out. He was tired of carrying it around.

He had not found the work of the place too much; that was not what had happened. It was more that he had found that it had begun to matter to him less and less after the summer, as the months began to slide in towards winter. To take hay to the manger every evening seemed a nuisance; instead, he piled it with bigger loads twice or three times a week. If he did not change the straw bedding in the calf house, there were no consequences: the animals did not complain. He noticed damage to the fences he had put up over the summer in the lower fields, but he put off the work of fixing them, letting the bullocks and the cows mix freely, which was something he had never before allowed.

Late in September, he realized that one of the Friesian cows was missing. He was not sure how long she had been away from the rest of the herd; he had not checked on them in a couple of days. When he found her, she was lying in the shelter of a tree, and when he hunted her up, he saw that she was badly lame. He cursed at the sight of her, limping and straining; he should have spotted it in her earlier, should not have left her to suffer like that by herself. He saw, too, that she was run down: she looked thin and weary; her eyes were dull. He brought her up from the fields to the yard, talking to her as she made her slow way, telling her, more than once, that he was sorry not to have looked after her sooner. When Farrell came to inject her, Tom saw the way he looked around the place, at the tools left on the ground, at the gate fallen off its hinges, at the troughs more full of leaves and twigs than they were of water.

'Where have you the rest of the cattle?' he asked Tom, after he had finished with the Friesian.

'The lower fields below,' Tom said, as casually as he could.

'I might as well have a look at them while I'm here,'

Farrell said, and he walked on to the gate before Tom could say anything to stop him.

'They're awful lean, Tom,' he said, when he had looked at the herd.

'That's the breed of them, Mick.'

'It can't be the breed of all of them,' Farrell said. 'And there's scour in them. They need dosing for fluke.'

'Right enough,' Tom said. 'I'll take care of that.'

Farrell looked to the road. He sighed. 'Look, Tom,' he said. 'I'm coming to this place a long time, and I know you well and I knew poor Maura well, may God have mercy on her. You know well I'd never do anything to cause you trouble. But there's people passing on that road every day mightn't go so easy on you. These cattle are scrawny. There's men getting reported for cruelty for far less. Do you know what I'm saying to you?'

'Say no more,' said Tom, and he pulled at the twine on the gate so that it fell open.

'If you need any help with them, Tom,' said Farrell, 'anything at all . . .'

'I'm going to book them in for a test with you next week, Mick,' Tom said. 'I'll be needing that done.'

'Anything, Tom,' Farrell said, and he walked up the lane to his van.

After Farrell had tested the cattle, Tom called the *Leader* and placed the ad. It went in the following Wednesday, and the house phone rang that afternoon. There was a moment of silence when Tom realized it was young Lynch who was calling about the herd, and when young Lynch realized it was Tom he was talking to, but it was money they were talking, and talk of money could only keep going, could only pick up where it left off.

Lynch took them away in five loads, and it was only when he was rounding up the last dozen, the heifers, that Tom noticed a Charolais heifer standing apart from the rest. When he walked over to tip her along he saw that her hips were down and her udder had filled. The heifer looked at him. He saw her sickness and her fear.

'Ah, lassie,' he said, and he patted her on the neck. Behind him, shouting, cracking his stick, Lynch was running the rest of the heifers into the trailer through the cattle pen.

'Look at this one, what she's at,' Tom called to him, pointing to the Charolais.

Lynch squinted over at the heifer. 'She's calving?' he said, in surprise. Tom nodded.

'She has the right idea,' Lynch laughed, and he started towards her. 'More for her new master. Come on.'

Tom looked at him. 'Sure you'll leave her here for today itself?' he said, as Lynch swiped at the heifer's hind legs.

'I'll have her up at my own place before she gets too much further into it,' Lynch said. 'Sure it's only a couple of miles.'

'You'll leave her here for to calve, at least?' Tom tried again, and when he heard the plea in his own voice, he took his stick and hit the heifer more sharply than Lynch himself had. She staggered towards the trailer.

Lynch stilled her, moving her slowly and carefully on to the ridged ramp and into the trailer. 'That's it,' he said, in a low voice. 'Good girl now. That's it.'

The heifer stood uncertainly on the trailer's edge, still trying to keep apart from the crush of animals jolting and mounting each other in the small space, each of them staring to the side in the same frightened way. Knees buckled and necks lengthened, but there was barely room enough, even, for a tail to swish at a fly.

'She'll be all right,' Lynch said, turning to Tom. 'She has a couple of hours to go yet.'

'That lane,' Tom began, but he stopped himself.

Lynch needed a hand to raise the ramp and shut the trailer on the animals. 'Good suspension on this yoke,' Lynch said, gesturing to the trailer wheels. 'She won't feel a thing.' He dug in his pocket and took out an envelope thick with the burnished brown of fifties. 'Now,' he said as he handed Tom the wad, 'nothing left to worry about, only how to spend it.'

He climbed into the cab and was gone, the trailer jangling over the rocky surface, the yard ringing with the bellows of the heifers. Tom followed him down the lane as far as the house, watching the dust risen by his wheels.

At first it had been strange not having the herd, but in truth the shape of Tom's day changed very little. He walked the farm as much as he had before Lynch took the cattle; some weeks, he walked it more. He still started out in the lower fields, testing the ground, checking the bog holes, examining the fences. Then he would walk back up the lane and past the house to the yard where the calves had been housed until they were old enough to be let out to grass, and where the yearlings had pucked and chased one another through the long garden. He would look into each of the sheds and then, setting the radio going in the old Massey, he would work for a few hours at something in the small shed he had years ago turned into a workshop for himself and Mark; he would hammer at something, do something up, make something that would be useful in the yard. Before, there had always been a chainsaw or a hedge-trimmer to fix for someone, but nowadays hardly anyone left them in; it might have been that they were buying new ones instead of getting them repaired, but Tom knew it was more likely that people still thought it was too soon to ask him to do a favour for them, to do a job. And yet nothing could have been further from the truth. If he could have found fault with his own chainsaw or trimmer, he would have taken them apart just for the pleasure of dismantling them and finding the problem, putting it right, piecing the whole lot neatly back together again, but they were running perfectly. The saw went through wood like water. The trimmer put a shape on ditches that would nearly win you a prize. Only the old Massey was giving problems, the clutch worn down again, the gearbox sticking badly, the lift losing strength. It was on a wet morning, wrestling in the tiny cab to open up the floor and get at the gears, banging his head and his elbows every time he budged, that Tom cursed and thrashed and twisted his way towards the decision that landed him in Brady's showroom two days later. In his coat pocket were Lynch's envelope of cash and a cheque written on the savings account he had had with Maura.

So Frankie Lynch had done him a favour. But Mark would not see it that way. Mark would only see it in his own way: childish and suspicious and wild. It shocked Tom how far from calm in himself Mark still was. He had come on nothing at all since the summer. Standing there tonight, with the receipt from the sale in his hand, he had been like a young lad in a tantrum. Sense had needed to be talked into him. Now, half an hour later, Tom knew he had gone too far with some of what he had said to Mark; with what he had said, especially, about Joanne. It had not been fair; it had not been true. But it had seemed as though only strong words would force Mark to face up to the facts of how things really were.

And it was not as though the things Mark himself had come out with were fair or true. No father should ever have to hear such words from his son.

Tom knew where Mark was gone, and he knew he should be worried. But he could not bring himself to worry. He could hardly bring himself to care. He felt himself hoping only that Frankie would do him another favour by telling Mark more of what Mark needed to hear.

*

'Mark,' Irene Lynch said, when she answered the door. Her face registered surprise only for a moment; very quickly, it turned to fright. 'Is everything all right? Aoife?'

'Aoife's fine,' Mark said. He wondered what time it was; had the clock in the car read half past ten just now or half past eleven? Irene was ready for bed. Her dressing-gown hung off her; she had grown even thinner. Her slippers were large: the sort of novelty slippers your children gave you for Christmas. Mark shook his head, embarrassed: he was not meant to see her like this. 'I'm sorry,' he said. 'If I woke you.'

But Irene did not look embarrassed, and she did not look, either, as though she had been woken from sleep. 'Come in, Mark,' she said, and led him to the sitting room, where an armchair was drawn up close to the television.

'I was just watching the end of the *Late Late*,' Irene said. 'Rubbish, as always, but I never want to miss it at the same time.' She seemed about to lower herself into the armchair, but she leaned instead against the door. 'Will you have something?' she said. 'Would you like a drink?'

Mark shook his head. 'I'm driving.'

Irene nodded, but still she did not sit down. 'So you're home for the weekend,' she said, and she smiled.

'I am.'

'Your father must be delighted. How is he? How's Aoife? Will you bring her up to see me?'

'I will, of course. She's gone to bed tonight. Otherwise . . .'

'Well,' Irene said evenly. 'I wouldn't expect to see the child at this hour.'

'No.'

A clock ticked loudly from the next room. The fire made its sounds of shifting and crackling. Mark felt as though he had taken a breath in his father's house and was exhaling it here. The photo over the television had been there the last time he was in the house too; it was nothing he had not seen before, but it was impossible to get it out of view. It pushed into every possible angle of his vision. It looked exactly like what it was: a photograph of a person who was dead now, a photograph chosen from an album and taken to a photographer's shop to be enlarged and enhanced and placed in a thick gold frame, and hung on a spot that had been cleared specially for it, right in the middle of the wall. The frame was too heavy: it made the whole thing look awkward. In the photo, Joanne seemed barely out of her teenage years, her features undefined, her smile determined but uncertain. Her eyes were Aoife's. He saw that now.

'Was there anything, Mark?' Irene said from the door.

Mark shook his head.

'Well, won't you please sit down anyway?' she said, and she gestured to the couch and watched him as he went to it. 'I wish you would take something to drink.'

She moved to her armchair and sat draping her dressing-gown more fully over her crossed legs. 'It's very nice of you to call around,' she said, and she looked at the television where the end credits of the programme were rolling. 'I wish that you'd call around more often. And I wish that you'd phone more often, a lot more often.' She glanced at him. 'I'd love it if you'd phone and tell me about Aoife. How she's doing.'

'She's doing great,' Mark said, as brightly as he could. 'She's great.'

'Yes.' Irene nodded, as though lost in thought. 'You've said that. And of course she's great. Of course she is. It's just I'd like to hear more about that. About what her being great entails.'

Mark was surprised by how sharp her tone had become, and how quickly. She was almost glaring at him now; he remembered what Joanne had said about her temper, about the swings in her mood. He tried to think of some way to respond, but nothing that occurred to him seemed wise. They sat in silence for a long moment that ended when Irene gave a shaky sigh and leaned over to dig with a poker at the fire.

'Look, Mark, I don't know what Joanne told you,' she said, when she sat back into her chair.

Mark swallowed. He shifted his legs uneasily. 'What Joanne told me about—'

Irene interrupted, frowning as though asking him not to pretend. 'About me, I mean. Obviously about me. I don't know what she said about me.'

'She didn't say anything,' Mark shook his head, but Irene held a hand up to stop him. 'I'm sorry,' he said, without knowing why.

'You don't have to be sorry,' Irene said, and her tone was now much softer, but still matter-of-fact. 'I'm the one who should be sorry. No matter what happened between us, I never loved her a tiny bit less, Mark. I only loved her more, the more difficult things became. You'll know what that's like when Aoife's that age. I hope you won't, but chances are you will. And if you have any sense, you'll tell your daughter how you feel about her. You won't sit around and let things

316

fall to pieces between the two of you without doing anything to mend it, without saying anything to put it right.'

'Joanne never talked badly of you,' Mark said. 'She never did.'

Irene smiled thinly. 'It makes me feel no better to think that she couldn't talk about these things,' she said. 'That she couldn't even talk about them with you.'

Mark said nothing. It was not true, what he had said to Irene. Joanne had told him about her mother. She had talked to him about her even on the first night they had met. Sometimes it had seemed that her mother was all that Joanne wanted to talk about, that she had needed to talk her mother out of her system, to give utterance to everything she knew about her, everything she did not understand about her. But Mark did not think it would be wise, or useful, now, to share this detail with Irene.

'I'd just love to know how she's getting along,' Irene said then.

Mark looked at her, startled. 'Who?' he said, and the words came out sounding almost hostile. 'I'm sorry,' he said, shaking his head. 'Who do you mean?'

Irene regarded him for a moment before answering. 'I mean Aoife, Mark,' she said slowly, putting a hand to her collarbone. 'I'm just saying again that I'd love to see more of Aoife. To hear more about her. You'd be surprised the small little things that would be of interest to me. That would mean the world to me.'

Mark felt embarrassed, and he felt guilty. He knew that Irene had spotted his confusion. He knew that she had seen him thinking for an astounded moment that it was Joanne she wanted to know about, not Aoife. She had seen him thinking her crazy, thinking her unhinged. She had seen it, and she had absorbed it, and she had corrected it, and he was the one who had come out of it looking crazy. He was the one who must seem unhinged.

'She's walking a couple of months now,' he said eagerly. 'Aoife. And she's got a good few words. The thing she's most interested in walking on is the stairs. And the footpath alongside the house in Stoneybatter. The narrowest bloody footpath in Dublin.'

With an effort, he laughed, and Irene laughed too. 'Hands full,' she said, and smiled at him.

Say it, Mark said to himself then. Get around to the reason you came here. Ask for him. Ask where he is. But then Irene took a deep breath, and he knew that she was going to say something it would be unkind to interrupt. He knew that she was going to come out with something that was important to her.

'This thing is supposed to have – what do you call it? – peaked, by now,' she said, stretching a hand out towards the fire. 'I don't find that. Do you?'

Mark stared at her. What was she talking about? Was she talking about the fire? He looked to it. Flames puttered and curled. 'I'm not sure,' he said to Irene. 'I'm not sure what you mean.'

'Oh,' said Irene, shaking her head as though she were airing a foolish indulgence, something that scarcely deserved to be heard. 'This. Grief, I mean. They say it hits some sort of height around the sixth month and grows more manageable after that. Evens out, you know. A plateau. I suppose I did find it to be something like that after my husband died. But it hasn't happened for me this time, not yet.' She paused. 'I don't know,' she said, very quietly.

If she cried, he would not know what to do with her, Mark thought in a panic, but she showed no sign of breaking down. She was smiling into the fire, that same thin smile.

'I've been doing a lot of reading about the whole thing, you see,' she said. 'There are a lot of books about it. I imagined that maybe you might be reading about it too.'

Mark shook his head. 'No,' he said. He knew he should say more than this, but he did not know where to begin.

'I don't know why I thought that,' Irene said. 'With your studies, I suppose. I don't know.'

'It's different for everyone, I think,' said Mark. He hoped that this statement might somehow bring the matter to a close.

'One book said that it's like magic in a way,' said Irene, and her eyes had the same brightness that had been in his father's an hour earlier. 'Grief, I mean,' she said, leaning towards him. 'That there's somehow something magical about what you go through.'

'They say all sorts of things,' said Mark, weakly. 'I suppose it's different for everyone,' he tried again. He could not believe this was happening; that he was getting some sort of primer on self-help from Joanne's mother. What had happened with his father in the hayshed, in the kitchen, earlier seemed almost reasonable compared with this. He wondered if it would be wrong to ask for a glass of water. He felt clammy. He wondered if it would be wrong to say that, after all, he wanted a drink. But Irene would only see that as an invitation to go deeper into her theories. Even as it was, he could see, she was warming to her theme.

'Not magic in a good way, of course,' she said, folding her hands in her lap. 'More that you're under a spell. Hypnotized, or ... What would you call it?' She searched for the word. 'Hexed. That you believe, really believe, that the person is going to come back some day. Any day. That all of this will end, and that you'll have them back again.' She looked at him. Her gaze was perfectly still. 'This has happened to me,

Mark. I catch myself thinking like this. I realize how foolish it is, but I still think it. And I still believe it. That Joanne might walk in that door. I mean, for Christ's sake.' She shook her head. 'Even as it was, Joanne hardly ever came in that door.'

Mark inhaled. Words seemed to slide behind walls and into formations, wrong formations, far away from him. He felt the heat of the fire furious against one cheek, against one whole side of his head, and he tried to lean away from it, but there was only so far he could lean. Worse still was that he found himself unwilling – unable – to look towards the door.

'Don't you ever think that, Mark?' Irene said, and she leaned forward suddenly and reached a hand out to him. 'Don't you find yourself thinking that she's going to come home?'

Mark stared at her hand. Something about it was familiar; something about it was wrong. It took him a moment, and then he saw it. The ring on her fourth finger. It was the ring he had given Joanne for Christmas, the first year. The silver ring, with the green stone; he had bought it from an antiques stall upstairs in the Westbury Mall. Joanne's fingers had been swollen, from the pregnancy; she had not been able to wear it for a while, had not tried to wear it until after Aoife was born. Then she had worn it often; not every day, but often. She had been wearing it that day in the car. It must have been on her hand when she had been brought into the hospital; it must have been in her things afterwards. Her things, which had gone to her mother. Not to him. They had not been married. That was not how it was done.

'Mark,' Irene said, and stretched her hand closer to him. He took it. He did not squeeze it; he held it briefly with one hand, patted it with the other. Then he let it go. He stood. She looked at him in surprise, her eyes moist.

'Is Frankie around?' he said quickly.

Irene frowned. She sat back; she folded her hands in her lap again. 'Frankie?' she said, as though he had asked after someone she did not know.

'I thought he might be in.'

Irene shook her head slowly, as if in sympathy at such a misguided notion. 'No, Mark. Frankie has his own house now. I thought you knew that.'

'No,' Mark said. 'I didn't know that.'

'I thought your father might have told you.'

'No,' Mark said again.

'Well, Frankie built a house for himself on the farm over your lane,' Irene went on. 'Was he not building that when—' She paused. 'He must have been. I suppose you wouldn't have noticed. I suppose you had enough on your mind.'

'The farm over the lane?' Mark said. 'Tommy Burke's old farm?'

'Yes,' Irene said, with a sigh. 'Tommy's old troublemaker. Frankie and his girlfriend have a new house on it now. They finished it over the summer. They've been living in it since September.'

'And he's farming it?'

'Oh, yes, somehow,' said Irene. 'He's stocking it himself. I don't ask too many questions. And his girlfriend is pregnant. I don't ask too many questions about that, either.'

'You'll have another grandchild,' was all Mark could think of saying.

'Another granddaughter, apparently,' Irene said. 'I told Frankie he should name her whatever he wants. He just told me to be quiet, that he *was* going to call her what he wanted to call her. I said, I just hope that's what Michelle wants to call her, too.' She smiled. 'I used to despair of Frankie, you know. But I suppose he's turning out all right. Eventually.'

The late news came on the television. The newsreader frowned and tilted her chin. There was a moment's footage of some disaster, some brand-new nightmare a whole world away. Veiled women beseeched the camera with their hands, with their eyes. Beautiful children stared. The newsreader returned. Irene picked up the remote and switched the screen to black.

'It's terrible, what's happening out there.' She shook her head. 'Wherever it is.'

'I should go,' Mark said, and he gestured towards the door. 'It's late.'

Irene stood, smoothing her dressing-gown. 'Well, it was really lovely to see you. It was really lovely of you to call around.'

'I just wanted to say hello.'

Irene looked at him for a moment. She did not smile. 'You wanted something other than that, I think, Mark,' she said. 'But it was good to see you.'

She held her arms out to him. He went to her. She smelt of smoke from the fire and of something perfumed.

'You go home and look after Aoife, now,' she said hoarsely, into his ear. She rubbed the back of his shirt as vigorously as though she were washing it on a board. She gripped him by the shoulders and held him away from her. 'None of this other rubbish matters, Mark,' she said, and there were tears in her eyes. 'Do you hear me?'

'I hear you,' Mark said, and she nodded as though he had said something very serious and very true.

'Now go home to my granddaughter,' she said, and she showed him to the door.

*

When he left Irene he drove the back way over the lane to Tommy Burke's old farm. He parked a good distance from it. It was a night of a full moon and a hard frost. The shape of his breath moved ahead of him on the air. He concentrated on the sound of his footsteps until he saw the light of the new house ahead.

It was a dormer, built close to the lane, the upstairs windows tucked like nesting birds into the roof. A single car was parked outside; Frankie's van was not there. One light was on upstairs and two downstairs. He could see the downstairs curtains were not drawn, and as he drew closer, he could see into the room; the side of a blue leather couch, a framed print – a Rothko – a large television screen. The woman was stretched out on the couch, her bare feet perched on its arm; her toenails were painted; her long fair hair was falling to the side. She was covered with a blanket. She put one hand to it, suddenly, and stroked it. She reached the other hand out towards a low table, towards a mug.

Mark walked around the darkened side of the house to the farmyard. Where Tommy Burke's cramped outhouses had been stood two new sheds, their roofs sharply angled, their sides open to the yard. Round bales were stacked in the higher shed. Mark knew they were the bales he had made the previous summer, the bales he and his father had made. He looked at them and thought of the afternoon with the panicked girl from over the road, the fright about Aoife, missing from her cot, his father returning from Keogh's, carrying her, proud as though he had won her in a game of cards.

*

Silence was what Tom was used to; he barely noticed that it had fallen on the house again. When the child cried out from upstairs, he looked to the radio, startled, before he realized what the noise was. He stared for a moment into the dark square of the window, seeing first the shape of the hayshed outside, then the reflection of his own stare, his chin leaning hard on his hand. He waited, and when she did not quieten, he climbed the stairs.

A small lamp was lit on the dresser and a bag was half unpacked on the bed. The room smelt of the electric heater and of something sour. The child was on her side in the cot, her face turned to the wall, the blanket tangled around her legs. Though she seemed to sense that someone had walked into the room, she did not look up. She kept wailing into the wall.

'All right,' Tom said, and something stilled in her, but then the crying started up harder and louder than before, and by the time he lifted her, sticky and damp, she was screaming, and leaning away from him so that it was hard to get a hold of her.

'You're all right,' he said to her, but she continued to scream.

'Your daddy'll be back,' he said to her, and at that moment she lifted a hand and brought it down – the sharp little fingers and the tiny edges of the nails – on his face.

'No,' he said, and she threw her weight backwards so suddenly that he came close to dropping her.

'Don't be bold,' he said to her, in a warning tone, and she howled as though he had dipped her low into a flame.

He put her into the cot. She sat, and then she stood, and then she lay down and curled herself into a ball, and all the time she screamed, and all the time she looked up at him with a twist of pure anger on her face. The dripping tears looked almost comically huge. The snot ran into her mouth, and when he tried to reach towards it with the edge of the blanket, the roar of her outrage was so loud and so over-powering that he could not help it.

'Jesus tonight,' he said, and the laughter took him so fully that he almost collapsed.

*

A tractor and a few pieces of machinery stood in the yard. They were not new: Frankie must have brought them from Caldragh. Frozen, clouded with white, the tractor's wind-screen looked as though it was not one pane of glass but a thousand tiny chips, held together for one last moment within the square of the frame.

He walked to the larger shed. He could hear the cattle inside. The sound they made was simply the sound of their being there, sleeping up against each other, resting on their knees and their stomachs in the straw, chewing on whatever they still had to chew on, breathing on each other and on the night.

Inside the shed it was much darker; the moonlight did not reach in here. But Mark's eyes soon grew accustomed, and he could see how Frankie had laid the place out. The stalls were built on a step up from the slatted ground, so that the animals could sleep on the warmer ground, away from where they pissed and shat. The gates were neat and properly latched. The animals had room to rise and walk around one another, as some of them, noticing him, now started to do. Behind him, he heard a patter, a low call. He turned. The calf was young, maybe a month old. It was loose. It came confidently to him, and it looked up at him with eyes that were bright in the half-light. It was a Friesian, white splashed on its forehead and across its back.

'Where did you come from?' Mark said.

The calf gave a warbling grunt and butted his hand with its small, hard head.

'Take it easy,' Mark said, kneading its crown, his eyes searching the darkness behind for its mother.

*

Or he had thought he was laughing. Or he had meant, at least, to laugh. It was only when the child stopped her own crying and changed the way she was looking at him – changed from a screaming fury to a curiosity that caused her to pull herself up on the cot bars and stare – that he realized that he was not laughing; he was crying, and he was crying hard. He was sobbing, and he was shaking, and he was getting snot on himself, and he was covering his face with his hands, and he was trying to get a hold of himself, but it was something outside himself that had the hold on things; it was something outside his power that was pushing up from his gut and his heart and his lungs. He tried to think of what was causing it, and all he could think of were the last words he had said, and then in the same moment he understood it, because they had never been his words. They had been Maura's. They had been Maura's way of letting out anger, or frustration, or sometimes a loud, long laugh at the ridiculousness of the day or the night or the world. *Jesus tonight. Jesus tonight. Jesus tonight.* She had said it to herself. She had said it to Tom or the children. She had said it to the empty air. She had said it while she was cursing whatever it was she was cursing, but at the same time she was always fixing or settling or sorting out the same thing: she was dressing a child, or closing a door, or knowing what to do with a form, or turning to Tom and making him feel less angry or less worried or less frightened about whatever it was he had on his mind. She had said it, and he had never heard anyone else saying it, and she had said it in a tone and a voice that were only her own. And, for a moment, that voice had been with him in the room.

The child let him lift her out of the cot when he calmed himself. He took her downstairs. Mark had left new food in the fridge.

'Otherwise you'd be eating rashers and sausages,' he said to the child, but when he looked more closely, nothing seemed like the kind of thing you would give to a child who had woken up crying at midnight: grapes, and a few pots of yoghurt, and a pack full of thick strips of cheese, and two cartons of juice. Surely something warm was better for her, he thought, and so he closed the fridge and opened the cupboard. He opened a can of beans, and he put her down to play on the floor. While she threw her arms around the dog's neck and tried to get up on its back, he warmed the beans in a saucepan, and all the time he talked to the dog in a friendly tone, sympathizing with her, praising her, in the hope that she would not get impatient and snap at the child.

'That's the girl, now,' he said, and the child looked up as though he had been talking to her.

He fed her with a teaspoon. She frowned, at first, at the taste of the beans, but soon she wanted him to feed her more quickly, to feed her the whole bowl, and she swung her legs and bounced on his lap as though to hurry him along.

'That's nice,' he said to her, and she blinked at him. 'Isn't that nice?'

She took a bean from the bowl and offered it, on the palm of her hand, to the dog. The dog tipped the bean with its nose and then took it on its tongue. It looked at her, ready for more, but she offered the next bean to Tom, balancing it between her fingertips and putting it to his lips.

When he took it from her she laughed at him and pointed to the dog.

'The doggie gets her own food,' Tom said, and offered the child another teaspoon of beans, but she shook her head and once again pointed to the dog.

'All right, whatever you say,' Tom said, and he rose with her in his arms and went back to the same cupboard to take down the can of food for the dog. He sat the child on the counter; she reached a hand to the brown mixture he spooned on to a side plate. He lifted it up out of her reach. As he gave the plate to the dog, the child shouted at him; she gave him a name he could not make out.

'Come on,' he said, and he took her up again and brought her to the couch. She would not sit with him, but stood beside him, bouncing unsteadily on the cushions, gripping the couch like a drunk holding on to a wall.

*

The calf called out again. From behind Mark, one of the other cattle answered it, or echoed it; several of them had gathered now at the feeding rails, nosing through the scattered hay and tearing clumps away with their teeth. But some were not eating: they were just standing, staring at him, waiting to see what he would do.

Now he could make out the section in the opposite corner of the shed where the calf had come from. It was a small, gated-off rectangle away from the slatted ground. There were other animals in there, he saw, as he moved closer; two cows and another, still smaller calf. He wondered at the calves being born so late in the year, so deep into the winter; he was surprised at Frankie's carelessness – until he realized it could not have been Frankie's carelessness. Those cows would have been heavy with calf when Frankie brought them here.

He looked down at the calf. Though it was too young yet to fodder, it was sniffing at the open end of the trough, looking up at the older animals as though to taunt them. They responded with indignant noises as it nudged through the rustling whorls of hay.

'All right,' Mark said, and reached for the calf's tail, twisting it gently, so that the animal jolted for a moment but then allowed itself to be guided away from the trough.

'That's you done now,' he said, and he moved it slowly back towards its pen. A long, demanding bawl sounded from one of the cows; she was up against the gate, pacing now within the small enclosure, but she could not get out.

Even standing right up against the pen, Mark could not see the gap through which the calf had escaped. It could only have slipped through the lower gate rungs, or slid out between the gate and the wall, but that was impossible; both spaces were too tight. He unlatched the gate quickly and hurried the calf back into the pen, still holding the tail, tapping the toe of his boot gently to the back shins. When he latched the gate again every animal in the place seemed to call out at once, and from somewhere he heard a dog. The calf, ignoring the attempts of its mother to nose it sharply backwards, stuck its head through the bars of the gate and watched him as he moved away. The eyes shone. Mark could not help himself: he raised a hand slowly in some sort of farewell. He felt intensely foolish and intensely calm.

At the back door, a woman with a pregnant belly was shushing the dog. Mark kept to the shadows of the house and walked back along the crisp white lane to the car.

He had been driving only for a couple of seconds when he met headlights coming around the bend. They dimmed. From the number-plate, and from the startled face in the glare of his own lights just before he dimmed them, he saw that the other driver was Frankie. As they passed each other slowly, both squeezed tight to the ditch on the narrow lane, he watched Frankie's face turn from surprise, through confusion, to suspicion. Mark raised his hand from the wheel and gave him the wave of one driver to another; a quick, light-handed salute. They were past each other before Frankie's hand could come any distance from his wheel. In the next instant, in his rear-view mirror, Mark watched the tail-lights of the van brighten and dim as Frankie stalled, as he tried to decide whether there was something he needed to do.

'Go home,' Mark said quietly, into the mirror, and after a moment, the tail-lights flickered again and the van moved away. Mark waited until the glow of it had gone from his mirror and been replaced by the dark. He drove on.

*

'What will I do with you?' he said to her, and he looked at the clock; when he switched the television on she took the remote out of his hand and pushed the buttons so that only static appeared on the screen. She pointed to it and shouted, but she would not give him back the remote. He got up and turned the set off at the switch. She pressed the buttons of the remote again for a while, but nothing could happen.

He looked around the room for something to entertain her. He could see nothing. Photographs he did not want to look at and newspapers he had not read. Ornaments that she could break and cut herself on. The dog. 'Look at the doggie,' he said, and she turned.

'What's the doggie's name?' he said, and she gave the dog a name of her own.

'No, the dog's name is Scruff,' he said, and she ignored him.

Then the dog wanted to go out, so he opened the door

for her. When he closed it again and turned back to the couch the child was regarding him with disapproval. 'Had to do her business,' he said, but the child just stared. 'Has your daddy no toys for you?' he said, and at the mention of her father she looked towards the door.

A bag of Mark's was leaning against the couch; it was like his old schoolbag, a muddy coloured canvas square buckled up with two straps. Maybe it was his old schoolbag, Tom thought, trying to remember. But there had been biro scrawls all over that; he could remember asking Mark what the hell he had needed with them, why he would write on his bag and let others do the same. There was nothing on this bag, no names or drawings or ink stains or cigarette holes.

'Open!' the child said, and he did as he was told.

'Just books,' he said to the child, an apology, but she tried to reach past him to pull out the books.

'Not yours,' he said to her, taking one of them from the bag; it was thick and heavy, hundreds of pages in it, the covers bound in thick plastic.

The child shouted her word.

'These are your daddy's books, not yours,' Tom said, taking out another one, and another; there was nothing in the bag that he could read, or even show, to the child.

Whatever the child was saying, she said it again, and this time there was the beginning of a whine in her voice, so he took a book and let the pages open where they fell. The words seemed to run into each other and the names were all strange, and whoever was telling the story was going about it a very long way. Along the sides of the page, Mark had written things in pencil. They made no sense to Tom. He chose a passage of the story, and he read it aloud. It was something about a wake, something about a pile of coats, something about not being able to hear. The child seemed to like it, or she liked the sound of the words; she watched his face as he read the sentences, as he did the different voices and spoke out the parts in between.

'This is awful rubbish this fellow is telling us,' he said to her, after a few minutes, but she put her hands to the book.

'Look, someone here is saying hello to you,' he said, seeing the word in pencil on the edge of the page. It seemed a strange word to be there, but no stranger than any of the others. 'Hello,' he said to the child, in a sing-song voice, and she frowned at him and shook her head.

'Open,' she said, and she grabbed at the book.

'Hold on, hold on,' he said, laughing, and she looked at him for a moment and moved her fingers to his hand. Her skin was soft and damp. She tugged at him.

'Open,' she said.

'Keep going?' he said, and she nodded and shouted a word he did not know.

'Right you are,' he said, and read on until the headlights of the car came up the avenue and spilled across the wall.

Epilogue

The phone conversation between Mark and Frankie the next morning was stilted at first. Frankie, Mark knew, was suspicious of him, and expecting that Mark would be equally suspicious in return. No mention was made of the way they had met on the lane to Tommy's old place the night before. No mention was needed.

Mark spoke calmly and explained what he was calling to ask, and when Frankie began to understand that he was not looking for an argument, not coming with an accusation, he began to talk, and he told Mark almost everything he needed to know. Things became clearer. This did not make them easier to take. It had not been easy to hear about the state some of the animals had been in when his father had put them up for sale. He had never known his father not to spot a lame cow, not to have her treated; whenever there had been fluke in the herd, the herd had been dosed. But this time had been different. The animals Frankie had paid for had not been the animals Mark had imagined. The price Frankie had given for them had not, after all, been so low or so unreasonable.

'They weren't a herd of fat tics, Mark,' he said, and Mark could hear that he would have preferred not to be going back over this ground. 'There was a couple of them only in middlin' shape.'

'They were never like that before,' Mark said, and immediately at the other end of the line Frankie murmured in assent.

'I know that, sure,' Frankie said. 'Everyone knows that.'

The tractors were something else Mark was glad of the chance to talk about. Frankie had seen them, and he agreed that they needed to be put up for sale. Their value, he said, would dwindle by thousands for every week that Tom held on to them.

'They'll be an absolute cunt to get rid of, the way things are gone,' he said, gloomily, 'but if you put a price on them that's any way reasonable, there'll be some fucker from Meath or Kildare that'll take them off your hands.'

Frankie told him other things as well. That for Tom to start again, to start small with a couple of animals, was the right idea; that there was a mart coming up in Edgeworthstown where he could buy a couple of heifers and bullocks to be going on with. He gave Mark an idea of much Tom should be willing to spend. He talked to him of the deadlines Tom needed to meet with his grant applications for the coming year. There was farm help Tom could get, too, Frankie said; someone who would come around a couple of times a week and help him to keep the place going.

'Just for when you can't be down yourself, like,' Frankie said. 'I can drop in on him the odd time, but it wouldn't be the same.'

'It'd be a big help,' Mark said, and asked when his girlfriend was having the baby. January, Frankie said.

'I don't know how the hell we're going to work out how to rear it,' he said. 'Michelle is in nearly more of a panic about it than I am. And that's saying something.' He laughed through a long intake of breath.

'You'll be grand,' said Mark.

'Jesus, I hope so. I suppose you'd know.' He was quiet for a minute then; worrying, maybe, that he had said the wrong thing.

'Let me know when she arrives,' Mark said.

'Will do,' Frankie said, sounding relieved.

Frankie was right; the tractors were hard to sell. Mark photographed them that same day and, when he returned to Dublin, he uploaded the pictures and the details to the websites Frankie had recommended, but it was almost a month after Christmas before an offer came through. A contractor from Meath called Mark's mobile and asked about both tractors. He said he had been looking at similar models new and this seemed too good to be true. It wasn't, Mark said, and gave him the directions so that he could go down to Dorvaragh and see them.

'Meath?' his father said, when Mark phoned him later to let him know that the contractor would be calling around. 'Whereabouts in Meath?'

'Near Slane,' Mark explained, though he knew his father did not know one town in Meath from another. 'Near Newgrange, actually.' It was early afternoon, and he was in the sitting room in Stoneybatter with Aoife. Sunlight was spilling through the blinds. She was on the floor, drawing with crayons in a notebook she had taken from him and declared her own. The crayons were making more contact with the carpet than with the paper. She sat back to survey what she had done and made a small noise that could have signalled anything from delight to disappointment. She turned to a fresh page.

'Frigg Newgrange,' his father said, through a mouthful of something.

'Are you eating?' Mark said, glancing at his watch.

'I am,' his father said. 'Though the price you brought it all down to would nearly put me off my food. He has enough with the money he'll be saving for himself on those tractors to build his own Newgrange if he wants.'

'There's an offer. That's all that matters. We need to get them sold.'

His father grunted. 'I suppose the fucker wants us to bring them up to him to see them and all?'

'No,' Mark said. 'He's driving down with his son to take a look at them on Saturday. Or his brother, or something. Anyway, he wants to know if that suits you. Saturday. Will you be there?'

'I suppose,' his father said. When he was silent for a long moment afterwards, Mark asked him what the matter was.

'Ah, nothing,' his father muttered.

'It's not nothing,' Mark said, leaning over to Aoife and guiding her to take a blue crayon back out of one nostril. 'Something's wrong with you. Say it out.'

'Ah,' his father said, and down the line Mark could imagine the heavy shrug. 'I suppose I wouldn't have minded getting a look at it all the same.'

'At what?'

'Ah, it's all right.'

'No, it's not all right,' Mark said, taking the crayon from Aoife once again. 'Not your nose,' he said, in a scolding tone. She gave him a deadpan glance.

'What?'

'I'm talking to Aoife. And it's not all right. Say it out, you, if you have something to say. What is it you want a look at? His farm, is that it?' He cringed inwardly at the vision of his father going up to Meath for a gawk; the questions he would have for the other farmer, the jealousies he would incubate, the new set of insecurities and aspirations he would come

336

away with. One look at a farm spread across the rich smooth-ness of Meath land and his father would take the tractors straight back off the market; he would hang on to them until they collapsed in a heap of rust and plastic sheeting if it meant having some trace of the trappings of a successful farm. His father had started referring to his cattle as 'stock' after seeing a couple of episodes of *Dallas* in the 1980s. A visit to a stud farm in Meath could only wreak worse havoc still.

'Ah, no, not the farm,' his father interrupted Mark's thoughts. 'Just that place, whatever you call it, that's all.'

'Whatever you call it?'

'The place where the sun goes into it.'

Mark laughed. 'You want to go to Newgrange?'

'I wouldn't mind,' his father said, in his most reasonable tone. 'I saw it on the television there before Christmas.'

'A minute ago you were saying it wasn't worth a fuck.'

'Ah, now,' his father protested. 'I didn't say that.'

'Near enough,' Mark said, and he laughed.

'Well, anyway,' his father said. 'Sure it's only meant to be ould rubbish they do in it anyway.'

'What do you mean, rubbish?' Mark said, looking again at Aoife. She was pushing scrawls of colour frantically on to a page that seemed certain to tear under the force. He thought for a moment about stopping her, but then that was what crayons were for. The carpet could be cleaned. She sensed his attention and looked up, showing him then the page she had made. It looked exhausted. Every inch of it was covered with her jagged scrapes.

'Very good.' He nodded to her, and she smiled and took the notebook back down to the floor.

'What are you saying to me?' his father said, with a snap of suspicion.

'Aoife,' Mark said, sitting back into the couch.

'Oh, Aoife,' his father said. 'What's she doing today?'

'She's drawing,' Mark said. 'Or she's making a mess of the floor. Depends on how you look at it.'

'That's how she learns,' his father said.

Mark turned and found himself blinking against the sunlight. 'I suppose.'

He looked out to the back yard, where the feral cats basked. They looked utterly at home, though if you knocked on the window or opened the back door they would scatter as though you had released a slavering dog. The morning's wash, on the clothes-line, looked shrunken, but it was still wet. The garden furniture, there now for more years than Mark knew, was faded and stained; it would need to be painted up when the summer came. He glanced back to Aoife, who was standing now and pulling at the undergrad essays he had left on the armchair; twenty separate ramblings on *Don Quixote*, to be graded and commented on by that evening. He lifted the pile out of her reach.

'Are you there at all?' his father said.

'I'm here,' said Mark, putting the essays on the windowsill. 'So you want to go to Newgrange, you're telling me?'

'Ah, I don't know,' his father said, but there was a silence after the words, and Mark knew how he was expected to fill it.

'You do know.'

'Ah, I suppose,' his father said. 'Sure, it'd be something different.'

'It would be interesting,' Mark said slowly.

'Would you be interested?' his father said.

Mark looked out at the cats again. One had climbed up on to the garden table, stretching now in an attitude of somnolent bliss. He put his knuckles to the glass, but dropped them without rapping. 'I wouldn't mind seeing it again,' he said.

'You were in it?'

'Yeah. On a school tour. Years ago.'

'Ah, sure, it might just be a load of ould shite.'

'Well,' Mark said, shrugging, 'you decide. I can come down some weekend and we can drive up in my car if you'd like.'

'Ah, you wouldn't have time.'

'I could make time,' Mark said evenly.

'Would we not do it when we were bringing the tractors up to your man?'

'That'd be this weekend,' Mark said. 'I can't be away from here this weekend. Besides, that'd be too much messing. Let him put in the work to see the tractors if he wants them. We can take my car up whenever suits us.'

'I suppose that's better, all right,' said his father. 'Whenever suits yourselves.'

'Right,' Mark said, skimming through the first paragraph of the essay on top of the pile. It was appalling. He leafed through some of the others. Worse. He had a long night ahead with a red pen.

'Would we go up for the morning when the sun comes in?' his father said then.

Mark laughed. 'You must be joking. Do you know how hard it is to get near the place that morning?'

'No.'

'You have to be on a list.'

'Ah, fuck them,' his father said, sounding disgusted.

'Anyway, that was last month. And it'd be far too early for Aoife.'

'You're bringing Aoife?'

'What else am I going to do with her?'

'Yeah,' his father said. All of the enthusiasm had fallen

out of his tone. 'Ah, sure, if the sunrise is over we may as well leave it. Sure there's no point in going to see it if you can't see what goes on with the sun. Sure that's the whole point of it.' He clicked his tongue. 'Ah, leave it to hell,' he said.

Mark sighed. 'You don't have to see the sunrise. They do a simulation of it for you.'

'They do what with it?'

'They imitate the sunrise. The light. When you're inside the passage, they switch off the lights and they shine in another light to show you what it's like on the solstice. It's exactly the same.'

'Ah, it's not the same,' his father said crossly.

'It's as near as. It's as good as you're going to get.'

'Ah, sure, if it's not the real thing, what's the point?'

Mark sat down on the floor beside Aoife. With a pencil, she was swirling dark trails through the clouds of yellow and purple she had shaded all over the page. She was talking to herself; she was singing. 'Good, Daddy,' she said, when she saw him looking at her, and she gave him the smile she had started using, lately, for the camera: a slightly unnerving squint of dimples and clenched teeth. 'Good, Daddy!' she shouted again, and threw the pencil in the direction of his head.

'Good girl,' he said to her, knowing that this, certainly, was not the right thing to say, but not knowing how else to respond. She laughed at him, a spit-mouthed splutter. He gave her back the pencil, which was probably not the right thing to do either. 'Don't stick that in your eye,' he said.

'Or what do you think?' his father was saying.

'I think,' Mark said, 'that you're never going to get to see the real thing anyway. Hardly any of us are. And if you want to see what it looks like, then this is your best chance.'

'So you think we should do it?'

Mark said nothing.

'Ah, I suppose it'll be something to do,' his father said.

'That's settled then,' Mark said. He needed to get off the phone: it was close to Aoife's nap-time. As though she had read his mind, she shook her head vigorously and stood, scattering her drawing materials to the floor. Mark told his father he would talk to him later, but already his father was saying something else.

'What?' Mark said.

'Do they always work?'

'Do what always work?'

'The lights,' his father said. 'The way they do the lights in the place of the sunrise. Do they always work? Do they always come on?'

'Yes, they always work,' Mark said, watching, with an eye-roll that nobody would see, as Aoife started to waddle her way to the sitting-room door. 'They always come on.'

'That's good enough, so,' his father said.

Aoife rounded the door. Mark let her go. He would follow.

Acknowledgements

I am grateful to Colm Tóibín; to my agent, Peter Straus; to my editors, Nan Graham at Scribner in New York and Paul Baggaley at Picador in London; to Paul Whitlatch, Kate Harvey, Kris Doyle and Jenny Hewson; to John O'Halloran, Amanda Glancy, Jane Hughes, Philip Coleman and Ciarán MacGonigal, and to those who were my teachers and classmates at the Writing Division in Columbia University's School of the Arts, where much of this novel was written. Sections were also written at the Tyrone Guthrie Centre at Annaghmakerrig in Co. Monaghan, Ireland; thanks to Sheila Pratschke and Pat Donlon for their hospitality there.

I wish to gratefully acknowledge the support of the Arts Council of Ireland and the Bank of Ireland Millennium Trust.

I found the following works on Maria Edgeworth useful: Marilyn Butler's *Maria Edgeworth: A Literary Biography* (1972), *Maria Edgeworth and Romance* by Sharon Murphy (2004); *Maria Edgeworth: Women, Enlightenment and Nation* by Clíona Ó Gallchoir (2005), and the articles 'Autobiographical Interpolation in Maria Edgeworth's *Harrington*' by Emily Hodgson Anderson (2009) and 'Maria Edgeworth and the Romance of Real Life' by Michael Gamer (2001). Anthony Steinbock's *Home and Beyond: Generative Phenomenology Beyond Husserl* (1995) is the inspiration for Clive Robinson's fictitious book.

Thanks most of all to my parents, Oliver and Angela McKeon, to my siblings, and to the Woods family, including my late father-in-law, Shane. This novel is dedicated, with love and thanks, to my husband.